Succeeding Love

C. HAZLEWOOD

To my own superhero husband.

CHAPTER ONE

The Divorce

"I'm in love with someone else," Nick said. "I'm sorry."

It didn't surprise me. I have been suspicious for months now. I'm just surprised he would do this today, of all days.

There's no reason for me to be surprised. He probably doesn't even realize what today is. If he doesn't love me anymore, why blame him for not remembering? When has he ever remembered a birthday without my reminder? I never planned on reminding him that today was my birthday, just out of spite for the emptiness I've felt from his neglect of this marriage for the past few months. If I had, it would have only delayed this inevitable conversation.

"Who is she?" I asked calmly, trying my hardest to swallow down my pain and not get emotional. It would do no good.

Nick's eyes narrowed almost accusingly. I don't know why. I'm not fighting him. I will not push back. I just want to know who this woman is.

"If you're leaving me to be with someone else, I deserve to know who it is that will be around my children." My heart paused. What if he is cutting the kids out of his life, too? What if this is him trying to start with a clean slate? As our kids progressed to teenagers, and he started working more, he hadn't exactly maintained a close relationship with them like when they were little, but they would still be devastated.

"You would let her around the kids?"

I swallowed deeply. "They still need their dad," was all I could say past the giant lump lodged in my throat. Letting his affair partner around my kids isn't my concern. It's his. I just pray he won't shrink on his duty to them.

Nick's features softened, a regretful look coming over his face. "They know her already," he mumbled. "Arlene, my case partner."

Arlene. That explains the awkward tension at the last Christmas party we hosted for Nick's entire firm. I thought the tension coming from her when she examined the pictures on our walls, and the wedding photo above our fireplace was because she had gone through a divorce just last year. That was the excuse Nick had told me, anyway.

She was nice, though. We've spent some time with her over the past year, as she assisted Nick in a big case. She had even brought gifts for me and the kids without obligation. I caught her laughing with my daughter over a board game once that night, too. I'm sure she won't be mean to Jessie and Preston.

"Alright," I whispered, trying to focus on the good in this, that my kids won't lose their father, even if I felt like my heart was being squeezed in my chest.

"Is that all you want to know?" He asked gruffly.

I bit my lip, not sure what to do or say now. The panic in me triggered the tears, and seconds later I was choking on a sob. His face turned to guilt, and he clenched his hands at his side. He didn't touch or try to comfort me. "I'm sorry," was all that he could say. "I'm so sorry."

Kevin, my two-year-old lab, ironically, a birthday present from Nick two years ago, nudged his way between my legs, licking my hands pressed to my face until I let them drop. He licked away the tears, nudging me with his enormous head until I nuzzled into him, wrapping my arms around his large body for support.

I wiped the backs of my hands across my face, trying to muster all my control and strength to get through this moment.

After a deep breath, I demanded softly, but firmly, "I want the house." I took one more shaking breath, looking all around. "This is the only home our kids have ever known."

I'm sure the affair couldn't have happened here. I work from home, and this is where our kids sleep. He may be a cheater, but he wouldn't have crossed that line, if only because the risk of getting caught was too great. Nick didn't take unnecessary risks.

"I will sign over the house and car to you." I'll keep Preston's car in my name and pay for the insurance. You and the kids will still have my full health coverage, too."

"How generous of you," I scoffed lightly, taking a tissue to my mess of a face. "You do not need to cover me. I can take it out through my employer."

"Fay," he sighed in annoyance. "Just accept the help."

"I need nothing from you," I smiled sadly. "It's fine, Nick. Really. I can support myself. Just, please don't neglect our kids after you move out."

He went silent, just staring at me as I anxiously pet my dog, playing with Kevin's cold ears.

"I won't, Fay. I promise. I love my kids."

"And they love you," I said roughly, forcing a smile. We stared at one another awkwardly for some time. I didn't know what to do next, and Nick looked like he still had more to say, but just couldn't say it.

After a few minutes, I asked, "Do you need help packing?"

He pressed his lips together, then slightly shook his head. "No. I have what I need for now. Movers will be here this weekend."

How thorough. He's been planning this.

"Well, the kids will be home soon. Do you want to stay to tell them, or would you like for me to explain?"

"I'll tell them," he said levelly, watching me with a wary expression as I got to my feet.

I nodded, the forced smile frozen in place. If I drop it, I'll break down again, which I'm not willing to do. Not yet.

"If you'll excuse me. I'm just.... Just going to collect myself before they get here."

I proceeded without waiting for his reply. Rushing to the bedroom we have shared for the past thirteen years, I found myself in a hurry, ever since Nick landed his current job at the firm. I don't know how I would sleep in here now. This room held all the most intimate memories of me and him.

I went into the bathroom, Kevin following me behind, then shut the door before falling to the floor. I hugged my arms around Kevin's neck, bawling into his fur. With Kevin, I let myself come undone.

***

"Are you serious right now?" Preston asked, his face red like he was ready to fight. "How could you do this to mom?!"

"You're leaving us?" Jessie asked through tears with a shaking voice, hugging a pillow to her chest. I wanted to go to her, to comfort her, but Nick should be the one to do it. I mentally urged him to be the one to step up. She fears being abandoned, and stepping in when it's his place to reassure her he's not would make him look worse to them.

"No, sweetie." Nick leaned forward on the ottoman where he was sitting, wrapping his arms around our daughter's shoulders. "I'll still see you just as much as I do now."

"But you won't be here with us," she wailed, clinging to his shirt.

"No, but I won't be far. You can come stay with me when you want to."

"You and your whore," Preston scoffed.

"Preston," I scolded, giving him a disapproving look. "Be respectful"

"She's sleeping with a married man! If that's not a whore, then what is?!"

"Come on, Pres." The tightness in Nick's eyes was the look he got when he was holding back his anger. And these two were already on thin ice. I didn't want their fragile relationship to shatter.

"None of this is Arlene's fault," I said, trying to be the voice of reason. It really wasn't Arlene I should blame for the affair. I'm not married to her. What's done can't be taken back, so there is no use in blaming anyone right now.

"You're right," Preston nodded, then glared at his father. "It's yours."

Nick opened his mouth, but I beat him to it before he could say something he would regret.

"It's not your father's fault, either. It's no one's fault. We just..... we just fell out of love. It happens," I smiled sadly. "It's a testament to why you don't marry young. People change so much just from the time they graduated high school to the time they turn thirty. Your father and I naively married my first year in college, so we were bound to grow apart. Wouldn't you rather we be happy than stay together and be miserable?"

Preston's eyes turned red, filling with moisture as he looked to the ceiling. "Mom, you always make excuses for dad. I'm tired of it. You can't excuse cheating."

My sweet son. Preston was truly my first love, and it breaks my heart to see his pain. Being nineteen when I had him, that being the real reason I married so young, I didn't know what love truly was until I saw Preston's little face after the nurses laid him on my chest.

"I'm sorry, Preston," was all Nick said, still with that sour look on his face.

"Whatever," Preston stood up from the couch, walking off towards the stairs. "Happy birthday, mom," he yelled out before heading up.

Nick's eyes went wide as he slowly turned his head to stare at me. He really forgot. I knew it.

"Mama," Jessie slid away from her father, then came to sit practically in my lap, holding me tightly as sobs overtook her. She cried harder than before, and I knew she wouldn't stop soon.

Nick's face as he stared at us was pure agony. He chose this, so I couldn't find it in me to feel sorry for him. Not when my kids were hurting so much.

"They'll come to terms with it in time," I said to Nick, running my fingers soothingly through my daughter's hair. "You can head out and I'll have them call you when they're ready."

Nick opened his mouth, then closed it again. He did this several more times, like he wanted to say something but couldn't.

Eventually, he just nodded, then grabbed his jacket, briefcase and suitcase, and left our home for the last time while I could still call it our home. It will be mine starting tomorrow.

"I'm sorry, mama!" Jessie cried. "I'm sorry!"

"Hey. Stop that," I said shakily, feeling the damn behind my eyes about to break free. "It's not your fault. It just happened, and no one is to blame."

"No," she hiccuped. "Not that. I've been texting her. Arlene. She was so nice, and I.... I was nice back."

"Oh, baby," I brushed away the tears under her eyes with my thumbs. "That's great! See. This won't be so bad."

It hurt me badly to know that even before today that woman was taking it upon herself to connect with my daughter, but showing that to Jessie will just make her feel more guilty.

"But Preston is right," Jessie sniffled. "She took daddy from us."

"She didn't take daddy. Daddy left, and it's not fair to blame Arlene for daddy's choices. I want your daddy to be happy, and I know you do too, so don't feel guilty about liking the woman making him happy now."

"But you made daddy happy."

My chest was sore from the emptiness I felt, thinking about all the effort I put in to keep Nick happy all these years. It made me feel hollow and used.

"Neither Daddy nor I were happy together, sweetie. Now, we can be happy apart."

***

Nick

I stood outside and listened to my wife through the open window near the front door.

Fay always opened all the windows in the house every morning in the spring, wanting fresh crisp air flowing through the house. She would never remember to close them before bed, and I would lightly scold her as I went around the house to do it.

She always had on this sweet, cheesy smile, saying things like, "that's what I have you for," or, "you close them better than I do."

She was always the sweetest, kindest person to be around, which was why I fell for her. Listening to her selflessly tell our daughter that it was okay to like Arlene reminded me again how kind Fay could actually be.

She's making this far easier for me than I deserve. She didn't even mention it was her birthday or blame me for anything.

I feel like shit. I thought I would feel relieved, but I feel the opposite. She didn't even fight it. She accepted everything except my offer to support her. Even after she came back down from our room, before Preston and Jessie got home from school, I tried to convince her to accept the health coverage and discuss alimony, but she would not entertain the notion. She kept saying she wanted nothing from me, besides for me to maintain my relationship with the kids.

She's selfless to a fault.

Regret was eating away at me, making it hard for me to take these irrevocable steps away from my married life to drive away into the exciting unknown.

I was so sure about this. I'd been going over everything for weeks. Arlene wasn't pressuring me for more than the affair, but it no longer felt good to hold Arlene during the day, then sleep beside my wife at night. I couldn't continue having both without risking my career and reputation, so I chose the one I thought I couldn't live without.

Now I'm not sure.

I was so bored with my mundane life, and Arlene was exciting. We have worked together for years, but it wasn't until she got divorced that she started showing the free side of her I fell for. She smiled more. Laughed more. She was ruthless in court and didn't take shit from anyone anymore.

I wanted that. The more I envied her new sense of freedom, the more I craved a new life like hers.

We won our first case together last year, and in the thrill and celebration, we started our affair. It was casual at first, just hooking up after work a few times a month, but then after the Christmas party Fay and I hosted at our house, Arlene asked me to go on actual dates, too. Not just meet ups in motels. Our relationship gained depth, and the closer I got to Arlene, the further I pulled away from my wife.

I forgot how thrilling dating could be, and she showed a level of dependency I craved. In bed, she was wild, with a wild heart, and she could be demanding and vicious when necessary. She was tall and slim, working out daily. She had purpose and drive.

She was the complete opposite of Fay in every way.

I knew I had to choose. I went over this so many times and knew I was doing what I needed to do to achieve that level of freedom and happiness I craved for so long.

So, why do I feel like I just made the biggest mistake of my life?

CHAPTER TWO

New Neighbor

Feighlynn

One year later....

"Hey, mom," Preston came into the kitchen behind me, swinging his keys around his finger. Kevin was leaping excitedly around him.

"Hey, sweetie. Where's your sister?"

Preston grimaced. "Dad came to get her."

"Again?" I turned off the water, wiping my hands dry on a tea towel after doing the dishes from dinner prep. "He's gotten her three times this week."

"I know," Preston said, not looking happy. "He said he'll bring her home after shopping for something like that."

"Shopping? Did you not get an invite?"

He shrugged.

I gave him a half-hearted look of disapproval. "You can't snub your dad forever. He is trying."

"Trying to be a pain in the ass," Preston muttered.

"Hey!"

"Butt. I said butt," he smiled teasingly.

"Uh, huh? Sure you did."

I grabbed the leash for Kevin. Jessie usually took him on his afternoon walk with me, but over the past few weeks, I'm doing these walks alone more than with her. Nick has been picking her up from school a lot. It's never been for long. They get ice cream, or he'll offer to take her to her dance lessons, or small shopping trips. He insisted on weekends in the divorce, which was completed six months ago, but has been spending the weekend here more. He kept talking me into letting him stay in the guest bedroom Friday and Saturday nights.

He says it's to get out of the city since his and Arlene's place isn't comfortable for the kids, but I think he and Arlene are having trouble. That's none of my business, so I haven't asked. To avoid misunderstandings so I don't get dragged into their problems, on the few weekends he's stayed here, I've gone to my sister's, that way he and the kids can have the house comfortably all weekend without my presence making things awkward for anyone.

He's tried to tell me to stay, that he didn't want to put me out, telling me it was my house, but I took it as an opportunity for him and Preston to repair their fragile relationship while I caught up with my sister, helping her with her young ones to give her a break. If I'm there, Preston gets defensive for me and is always looking for a fight. When I'm gone, he tolerates his father more. Since Preston refuses completely to go to his dad's apartment now that he is sixteen and fully licensed to drive on his own, trapping him at home with his dad is the only way to get him to talk to Nick.

Kevin and I do our lap around the neighborhood, waving at the neighbors in their driveways and the ones driving by. It's another beautiful day. You always have to focus on the beauty of each day.

"Hey, Feighlynn! My elderly neighbor, Velma Trude, flagged me down as I walked past.

There was a small Uhaul in her driveway. I looked at it curiously. "Hey, Mrs. Velma. Are you going somewhere?"

"Oh, goodness no," she waved her hands dismissively towards the truck. "No, no, no. I plan on closing my eyes for the last time in this house. That's not for me, but for my son."

"Your son!?" I could sense her excitement.

"Oh, yes. Kevin just moved back to the US from Germany. He's retired from the military and is going to stay here while he, oh, what's that word? Transitions? I forgot how he said it, but he's living with me now! He had to spend the last six months at some fort in the east, but now he's here!" She said excitedly.

I pressed my lips together, amused at her son's name. I knew she had a son in the army, but never knew his first name. She just calls him her son the few times he has come up. The old picture of him from when he first enlisted she keeps on her mantle just has 'TRUDE' written on his name tag, and I never thought to ask.

Velma was getting a little confused more days than not now, and I've tried stopping in to check on her every time I go to get the mail, but she never mentioned her son moving in.

"I'm so excited for you!" I said, matching her excitement. "I can't wait to meet him."

"Oh, you can meet him now. Kevin!"

My Kevin whined and perked up, shifting back and forth between his feet in response. "I think something is wrong with your dog, dear," Velma watched him.

"Maybe," I pressed my lips together to hold in my laugh.

Heavy footsteps echoed from upstairs, and seconds later a big, militant looking man, with faded brown hair and the beginnings of a bread appeared from behind Velma.

He was tall. Really tall. He had to be over six feet. He entirely filled up the doorway. I'm a short five foot three inches, and I felt like I was going to snap my neck looking up at him.

"There you are. This is Feighlynn Micheals, our neighbor across the street. Feighlynn, meet Kevin."

My Kevin howled obediently, like he was introducing himself, too. I could help but to laugh, covering my mouth with the back of one hand. Human Kevin was staring at us curiously, his green eyes surprisingly beautiful on his roughly handsome face.

"I'm sorry. His name is Kevin too. He says hi."

Velma looked offended, but human Kevin actually laughed. He squatted down, leveled with my dog, and let Kevin sniff him a few times before scratching between his ears. My Kevin pushed his excited face against his chest, eager for the attention. I was about to pull him back, but human Kevin laughed and hugged him in return.

"It's a good name. I don't mind sharing."

I smiled warmly, glad he didn't take any offense.

"Well, I guess it is. Since your husband, I mean, ex-husband, no good scoundrel he is, moved out, you could use a powerful guardian watching over your place."

My smile faltered. I know she didn't mean any harm, and was just coming to terms with her army-strong son's name being my dog's name too, but it still hurt to hear her air out my business so easily.

"Kevin is a good dog," I said, like I was agreeing with her. "I'm grateful to have him."

Human Kevin watched me from the ground, still petting between my dog's ears. He was shorter than me when squatting like he was, and he was very close to me right now since he was close to my Kevin. I gave him a nervous smile.

"It's good to meet you, human Kevin, and welcome to the street. If you both would excuse me, I'm going to get Kevin inside and finish up making dinner."

"Oh, yes. Your birthday dinner, huh?"

I cringed. I had asked Preston and Jessie both to just disregard my birthday this year. It's not really a day to celebrate for me any longer.

"Just family dinner. Birthdays aren't much to celebrate when you reach 35. I'll talk to you later, Mrs. Velma." I waved to her and her son, hurrying across the street before Velma could reveal any other embarrassing facts about me. I know I shouldn't let it get to me, but it still hurts from time to time. It still fills me with shame when someone pities me like that.

I went into my garage, closing the overhead door before unstrapping Kevin, then I took a minute to collect myself. Preston can usually sense when I'm upset, and I don't want to give him another reason to fight with his dad. I knelt down, hugging Kevin to my chest. He licked and nudged his head against mine, making me smile and chasing my stormy emotions away.

"Okay, boy. Who's a good boy?" I laughed when he nudged me hard enough to make me fall back on my butt. As he licked my face, I caught a whiff of something other than dog breath. It was cologne. Did Preston get himself new cologne? It smelled nothing like his usual go-to citrusy scents. It was deep and woodsy.

"Kevin," I said, as I realized where it could have come from. Human Kevin rubbed against my Kevin. It must have come from him.

It smells nice.

"Mom?" Preston was standing in the open door, watching me through the bug screen. "Are you sniffing the dog?"

My face heated with embarrassment. "No. I was just loving on him."

"You totally just sniffed the dog."

"So what if I did? He sniffs me all day long," I huffed, getting to my feet.

"Weirdo," Preston smirked, coming out to the garage and heading to the extra fridge to grab a coke. "You left your phone here. Jessie called while you were out sniffing the dog."

"I was walking the dog," I lifted my chin. "What did she need?"

Preston popped the top of his drink, looking uncomfortable for a second. "She asked if dad could have dinner with us. I said no, but she was insistent. I told her you'd call when you got back."

"Hmm," I went into the kitchen, the dog and my son following behind me like two watchful guardians. I didn't really want to entertain my ex husband tonight, but I don't want to put Jessie in an awkward situation or make Preston get up in arms for something so harmless.

Instead of calling Jessie back first, I texted Nick, not wanting my daughter to be the middleman.

> Me:| hey, Pres just told me that Jessie called about dinner. I made lasagna and know you don't like it. I'm also planning on doing more work after eating. Why don't you just take Jessie out for dinner instead?

> Ex:| I love lasagna.

Me:| No you don't.

Ex:| says who?

Me:| you, every time I made it.

Ex:| I kind of miss it now.

I sighed, not wanting to argue further. I know he hates lasagna. He would complain every time I made anything with tomato sauce in the past.

Seconds later, he texted me again.

Ex:| Jessie mentioned wanting all of us to eat dinner as a family again like we used to. I just want to make her happy. I haven't been able to hold a conversation with Preston lately, either. Please.

I couldn't say no to that.

Me:| okay. Dinner should be done by 6.

***

Kevin

I watched the pretty young neighbor woman walk back to her house and into the garage; her smile turning more and more sad with every step. She was far too small to be carrying so much weight on those slim shoulders of hers. It made a man want to reach out and comfort her, but in the brief conversation we had, I don't think the woman is the kind to cry on the shoulder of a stranger.

I've been through divorce. It was a long ass time ago, but I can still remember the sting of every reminder that you failed at the one thing you're supposed to fight for harder than anything else. I've been there and understood her pain. All of it. The darkest time in my life was coming home from a sixteen month-long tour to another man moved into my house, sleeping in my bed next to my wife. That was twelve years ago, but the memory still drives a stake through my heart when I least expect it.

"Mom, it might not be best to bring up other people's relationship troubles like that. You could hurt them."

Mom looked puzzled for a second. "Relationship troubles? Are you having relationship troubles again? Is it Mindy?"

There it is. The dull stabbing pain at the mention of that woman's name. Mom's mind seems to be stuck in the past more than it's not lately and she sometimes thinks I'm still in my marriage.

"No, mom. Your neighbor. The one with the dog named Kevin," I smiled at the dog's name. That woman seemed so apologetic about naming her dog the same name as me, but I really didn't mind. It was flattering.

Mom still looked confused.

"I think her name is Feighlynn."

"Oh! Have you met Feighlynn?! Sweet woman. Her and her kids are so helpful to me. It's too bad that the scoundrel of a husband left her for another woman. A colleague, no less." My mom sighed, shaking her head while staring at that woman's house. "Bless her heart. Left her on her birthday too. It was the talk of the neighborhood, seeing him leaving their house with a suitcase and that guilty look on his face. I would have just died."

"Mom, that's what I'm talking about," I groaned, rubbing my hand up and down my face, then cringing when it smelled like a dog. A dog named Kevin. Kevin needs a bath.

"Talking about what, dear?" mom strained herself, bending down over the flower bed to pick out a few yellow leaves at the bottom.

"Nothing, mom. I'm going to finish unpacking."

Her mind must be taking a turn again. She was fine most of the day, but I think the stress of me moving in is getting to her.

When I got a call from her months ago when she was having a moment of clarity, she told me she might have to move soon because she was getting too forgetful to live on her own. She had mortgaged her home a few years ago to do some major repairs, and had been for-getting to make the payments. Her house was going into foreclosure, and she didn't know what to do.

Since I was already leaving the Army and trying to figure out my next steps, I bought the house from her and started preparing to move after I left the military. It took several months to sort out all her banking shit, and to get to where I could purchase the house, but it's now officially in my name, and I can stay here and take care of my mom until I figure out what to do next.

By the time I finished unpacking the sparse belongings I brought, it was already getting dark outside. I got my old childhood room as livable as I could for now. I just needed to buy a better, bigger bed in the next few days. Right now, I needed to lock up the uhaul for the night. I'll unload all my army shit into the attack tomorrow before taking it to be dropped off.

"Oh, Kevin! Just the person I want to see," mom sang out, clapping her hands when I finished with the truck and walked into the kitchen.

She had a pretty bouquet made from her greenhouse flowers arranged in a vase with a ribbon around the curve of the glass. The ribbon had a 'HAPPY BIRTHDAY' pattern. "It's my neighbor's birthday today, and I always give her a little something just to say thanks for all the help she gives me. Would you mind running this over for me? I would hate to trip in the dark and ruin her gift."

She may be forgetful, but the flickers of the sweet woman that raised me still shine through often, which is why I could never put her in a home or leave her on her own during the last years of her life.

I wrapped my arms around her shoulders, giving her a gentle squeeze. "Sure, mom. I'll take it for you."

CHAPTER THREE

The Dinner

Feighlynn

"**P**erfect!" I smiled as I pulled the lasagna out of the oven. "Absolutely perfect."

"Who are you talking to?" Preston asked, watching me from the breakfast bar. He's on his laptop with headphones in. I didn't know he could hear me talking to myself.

"You," I said, lifting my chin stubbornly.

"Sounded like you were talking to the food," he smirked.

"Was not."

"Was too. You were using your Kevin voice. Praising the noodles for being perfect."

"Well, look at it." I angled the pan so that he could see. "It looks perfect, does it not?"

He laughed at me, nodding along. "Yeah, sure. Perfect pasta."

"I know!" I placed it down merrily, removing my oven mitts with pride.

"No one gets excited about cooking like you do."

"I only get excited when the food looks this good."

Preston watched me as I meticulously checked every corner of the piping hot lasagna to ensure it was cooked to perfection on the way through. I couldn't stop myself from doing a little happy dance at the bubbling cheese. I had already made the garlic bread and salad. I just had to pull the salad out of the fridge and the bread out of the warming drawer to serve.

My excitement died a bit, checking my watch. Jessie should be here with her father any minute.

If he's eating here, I wonder where Arlene is having dinner. Should I offer to let her come over too?

No. It's none of my business. I don't have to go that far for my ex-husband and his new partner. That would just upset Preston, too.

Just then, the doorbell rang. Preston heard it, judging by the sudden frown on his face, but he made no move to answer it.

I sighed loudly. "Be nice," I whispered after lifting one side of his headphones from his head. "He's still your dad."

Preston rolled his eyes, but muttered, "Yep. Got it." He's a good kid. He'll keep his comments to himself, if only for my sake and for the sake of his sister.

After another deep sigh, I put on a smile and opened the front door. But instead of seeing Nick with Jessie, Kevin was standing there. Human Kevin, with a large flower bouquet in his hands.

"Human Kevin?" I said, not meaning to say the 'human' part out loud.

"Human Feighlynn," he chuckled. "Mom wanted me to bring this to you. Happy Birthday."

"Oh, wow. Tell her thank you for me," I hurried to take the heavy-looking vase from his hands. My hand accidentally brushed against his, shocking me, almost causing me to drop the arrangement on the tiled surface.

"I got it," he said, easily catching it. "Where do you want it?"

"Oh, um," I frantically looked around for somewhere to set it. "How about here?" I motioned to the entry table, moving a pile of mail out of the way.

He set it on the center of the table, turning it to display the ribbon in the middle. "Looks good," he said, stepping back to admire his work.

"Your mom grows the prettiest flowers." I smiled at the arrangement. "She's the sweetest."

"She has her moments." He crossed his arms nervously, oblivious that it was making his chest flex and strain against his shirt. Are all military men built like him? "She, uh, shouldn't have said those things about your personal life, though. I'm sorry about that."

"Oh, don't worry about that," I waved away his concern. "She wasn't trying to be malicious."

"No, but I know how much those kinds of words can sting."

I smiled gratefully. "Thank you, human Kevin," I patted his arm, taking a split second to appreciate the firmness. I looked up quickly, then a ferocious blush painted over my skin. By his small smirk, I could tell I'd been caught ogling his muscles. I dropped my hand quickly, holding both of them behind my back and feeling so embarrassed. I know I've been feeling lonely lately, but it's completely inappropriate to fawn over my neighbor's muscles.

"Smells good in here," human Kevin said, taking mercy on me and changing the subject, cutting through the awkward tension. "Spaghetti?"

"Lasagna," I corrected.

"Ah, lasagna," he smiled. "I love Italian food. Smells amazing."

"Have you eaten already? Would you like to stay for- "

KNOCK KNOCK

Two quick knocks on the door, followed by the front door swinging open, interrupted my invitation to human Kevin.

"Mom!" Jessie sang out, then startled back when she saw me standing in the foyer already. She looked nervously at Kevin, then back at me. "Um, hi," she whispered, acting shy.

"Hey, sweetie!" I pulled her in for a hug. "How was shopping with your dad?"

"Exhausting, but fun," Nick said as he struggled through the door, several shopping bags in his hands. He stopped short when he noticed Kevin, too. Kevin was quite taller than Nick. It was almost comical seeing Nick look up to study Kevin's face. "Uh, hello. Who's this?"

"This is Kevin. Our new neighbor," I smiled warmly at Kevin, who was now stuck in an awkward situation because of my daughter's shy demeanor and Nick's hard stare. "This is my daughter, Jessie, and her father, Nick."

"Hello," Kevin waved awkwardly. "I'll, uh, get out of your hair for now. Enjoy the flowers, Feighlynn, and happy birthday."

"Thanks for bringing them over, Kevin. I'll see you later."

Nick's eyes stayed glued on my new neighbor the entire time he was walking out the door and shutting it behind him.

"Uh, Jess, why don't you go take your things up to your room," I said, helping her out of her backpack so that she could shrug out of her coat. I hung her coat up while Jessie took her backpack and only two of the bags her dad was holding up to her room with her. Nick set the rest down against the wall, then shifted back and forth on his feet, just watching me as I hung up the coat in the closet. I then made sure my new flowers had water, trying to ignore his observant stare. The flowers were really gorgeous. I'll have to send some cookies, or maybe even a whole pan of lasagna, over to Velma and her son later to show my thanks.

"So," Nick spoke, still looking awkward. "New neighbor?"

"Yeah, he just moved in today."

"And he already knows it's your birthday, and he's bringing you flowers?"

I could be vindictive and let Nick assume whatever it is he's assuming right now, but that wouldn't be fair to Kevin. "He just brought them over as a favor to Velma Trude. You know how careful she has to be now that she's having all that trouble with her memory."

"Oh," Nick frowned, eyeing the flowers suspiciously. "Yeah. I guess. So, what did you mean by 'I'll see you later'?"

I shrugged, walking towards the kitchen. "I'll be seeing him later, I guess? We are neighbors. Speaking of, did you get the booster club email from Kently Ferguson from next door? Her son's band still needs sponsors and your firm has done it in the past."

I hurried to change the subject, not wanting to wallow in awkward tension when entering the same room where our son was sitting. I understand Nick's curiosity, because I'm becoming pretty curious about human Kevin too, but Preston will use Nick's questioning to start a fight in my defense. Plus, Nick really isn't in the position to ask me anymore about neighbors and such. I'm sure he and Arlene have neighbors they can discuss if they choose to.

Preston stayed pretty quiet throughout dinner, but he didn't pick a fight, which I took as a good sign. He nodded or shook his head when someone asked him a question, and snuck food to Kevin under the table when he thought I was not looking. Nick would always get upset when any of us fed the dog at the table, and I suspect Preston was only doing it to make his dad mad, but Nick never said a thing.

Jessie talked non-stop about her father taking her to the mall and all the stores they went into. She was a daddy's girl when she was little, and has regressed back into that mindset ever since we announced our divorce. I appreciate Nick always going above and beyond for her, paying more attention to her than ever before. It made what could have been a messy divorce so much simpler, because I felt I could trust him with my daughter's fragile emotions. When he insisted on all weekends, and going 50/50 during summers and holidays, I didn't fight him. I think that shocked him, but I would rather our kids have a dad that wants to be there more than have to suffer years of custody battles, especially since they are already in their teenage years, anyway. It would make co-parenting so much harder.

I can't change what happened between Nick and myself, but I can control how I react in the future, and my reactions should be positive for my kids. That's where my head has been throughout this.

"So," Nick wiped his mouth, clearing his throat after finishing his tiny sliver of lasagna, which I knew he still hated, and all of his salad and garlic bread. "I told Jessie earlier, but hadn't told either of you yet. I just closed on a condo downtown. I'm moving into it next week, but get the keys tomorrow."

"Congratulations," I said with a smile, though I was wondering why he would suddenly purchase a condo when he was already living in one with Arlene.

"By yourself?" Preston asked his first question of the night.

"Uh, well, no. Not really. I'll have a room for you and your sister, and a spare room I plan on turning into an office."

"Tell them the best part," Jessie said eagerly.

"What's the best part?" I felt a little more energized seeing her enthusiasm.

Jessie and her dad exchanged a look, both of them barely containing their grins.

"It's in the high-rise close to the library. The building that is right next to the garage we would park in when we went to watch the Christmas parade. Skyland Heights," Nick said proudly.

"The one overlooking the river by that pizza spot we like?" Preston sounded impressed.

"That's the one," Nick grinned.

I knew exactly what building he was talking about. I felt like a knife had just been stabbed through my heart. That was the building we had talked about buying a condo in for forever so that we would have a place to stay in the city after the kids grew up, and I didn't need to be at home as much. It was a dream we talked about all the time, every time we went to the city, and even late nights in bed. It was a five-year goal we had, and we even talked about it the last Christmas that we were together.

He crushed that five-year goal along with all my other lifelong hopes and dreams when he told me he was leaving me, but I guess it didn't have to be crushed for both of us.

"I'm happy for you," I said softly, piling up my dishes to take to the sink. "I think you and Arlene will be thrilled there. It's a beautiful building."

I pushed myself up from the table, fighting to keep my smile in place. If I just smile, I can get through this. I can bottle this up to unpack later tonight when I'm all by myself.

I took a few deep breaths at the kitchen sink where no one could see me, and I regained my composure. It was stupid to get hurt by something as silly as real estate. Good for Nick for sticking with a dream. I thought it was ours, but that doesn't mean he can't keep that dream alive by himself, or even with Arlene. It has nothing to do with me.

I had thrown a store-bought chocolate pie to thaw out in the fridge since our simple dinner turned into entertaining a guest, too. I went to get it out but saw a cheesecake sitting on top of it. An entire cheesecake from Cheesecake Factory. I opened the top of the box and caught the delicious scent of lemons and tangy cream. It was lemon meringue cheesecake. My favorite.

"Jessie said you asked to skip your birthday this year, but I wanted you to at least have a cake," Nick said from behind me. I didn't even notice he had walked into the kitchen.

"Thank you," I mumbled softly. I didn't know how to feel about him giving me a cheesecake today of all days.

He came right behind me, so close that I felt the heat from his body coming off of him in waves. I moved to give him some room as he leaned into the fridge and gingerly lifted the cake, carrying it over to the counter.

"Do you want me to cut you the first piece?" he asked, looking hopeful.

"Um, sure."

He grinned excitedly, but then a confused look came upon his face. He looked around the kitchen, spinning in a half circle until his eyes landed on the wooden block that holds all of my knives.

I stopped him before he could ruin the cake with my large butcher knife. "Here. Let me get the cake knife instead."

I cut up pieces for everyone except Jessie, who wasn't a fan of lemons and would rather have that chocolate pie. Nick stood back awkwardly, and I could tell he wanted to help, but showing him the right way to cut the cake would be more work than me just doing it. I just asked him to carry the slices to the kids instead.

The cheesecake was delicious, and there was plenty left over. I tried to wrap up half of it for Nick to take back home, along with some lasagna for Arlene, but he refused. He muttered something about her eating out with friends tonight.

"So, about the condo," he said, leaning against the counter and watching me clear the dishes after everyone was done.

"I'm thrilled for you," I smiled at him. "You've always liked that building."

"So have you," he said with a serious expression. "That's why I was thinking, do you want to come with me tomorrow when I go to get the keys?"

I froze for a second, hoping I heard him wrong.

"You could come and see the inside of the place before any furniture goes in. There's a huge gym, an indoor pool, a rooftop garden, and the condo is on the top floor, so you can see the entire city from up there."

He's seriously asking me to go see his new home he will share with Arlene? A condo which used to be our dream? He hasn't always been this insensitive, has he?

"I really rather not, Nick. I'm happy for you, but I'm sorry. Going there and being happy for you are two different things."

"But you've wanted one of those condos since Jessie was in diapers. I thought-"

"You thought I would want to go with you, my ex-husband, to see it under the harsh reality of you buying it with your partner after we divorced? No, Nick. I do not want to go see it. I'm disappointed you would ask me that."

"I didn't buy it to live with Arlene, Fay," he took a step towards me. "I.... I bought it because I needed an actual home for the kids. Somewhere that is theirs. They don't have that at her place."

That's true. Jessie sleeps in the guest room when she goes over, and the few times Nick has gotten Preston to stay, he's slept on the pullout couch in Arlene's office. He really needed a place where the kids could have their own space.

"Arlene won't be living there at all. We decided we both needed our space. She won't even have a key."

"That seems extreme. Why wouldn't she have a key?"

He shrugged. "What's the point of getting my own space if I give her a key?"

It sounds like their relationship is regressing, but that is none of my business. I'm sure Nick doesn't want relationship advice from his ex-wife, and I don't want to offer any, so I'm choosing not to ask any more questions.

"Would you like me to make a to-go container for you?" I asked again as I moved across the kitchen to the pan of lasagna. I began dividing the remains into sections for tupperware.

"No, thanks," he eyed the tomato sauce warily.

I smirked to myself. I knew he still didn't like lasagna. Too bad, because there was a lot of it left over, and tomorrow was Friday. Both kids will be with him for the weekend, so the leftovers I can't eat will go to waste. I could freeze some....

Or maybe they don't have to go to waste after all....

"Kevin," I murmured under my breath, thinking out loud.

"Huh?" Nick furrowed his eyebrows.

"Oh, I was just thinking about taking Kevin for a walk," I said, embarrassed that I was talking to myself, thinking out loud again.

"I can come with you," Nick offered.

"Seriously?" I sent him a dubious look. He has never taken my dog for a walk, or gone for a walk at all in this neighborhood since the kids were toddlers.

"Why not?" He had a hopeful glint in his eye that made me feel uneasy.

"I like my walks alone with Kevin. It gives me time to breathe and think. And you are supposed to be spending time with the kids. Preston is probably in the den watching baseball if you want to join him."

Nick grunted, then stood quietly, watching me as I divided up the lasagna, putting half of the leftovers in a large Rubbermaid container to take across the street, and the rest into smaller containers to freeze. I was dumping the remaining garlic bread into a ziplock bag when Nick spoke again.

"I'd really like it if you could come with me tomorrow, Fay."

My mind was thinking of Kevins, both canine and human, and was wondering if it would be appropriate to pack a slice of the cheesecake too, given that it was technically a birthday gift. It took me a minute to register that Nick was talking about the condo again.

"I can't, Nick. I'm sorry."

"It would only take a few hours in the morning. We could stop at the fondue place you like for lunch and-"

"Nick," I stopped him, not wanting to hear any more. "I can't. I won't. I'm really sorry, but that's just..... It's too much." I stared back at him, imploring him to understand.

"But it was our dream," he whispered, reaching out to take my hand.

I pulled my hand away as quickly as he took it. "All those dreams died the moment you told me you didn't love me anymore."

Chapter Four

Leftovers

N ick went to watch the game with Preston like I suggested, giving me space to pack the rest of the dinner I planned to take over to human Kevin and his mother.

Kevin was pacing by the garage door, knowing the routine. I had a grocery tote with the lasagna at the bottom, garlic bread on top of that, and then a thermal bag with half of the chocolate pie in a plastic container and the rest of the salad in another. It was a full meal, enough to feed three or four people.

After checking in on Nick and the kids, seeing that they were alright, I took Kevin and the bag and headed out, going straight towards the Trude's home. The lights were on, which I was grateful for. The sprinklers came on at night, making her walkway slippery in some spots. She had tripped on those slick spots in the past, and I'd lost my footing a time or two. Maybe her son could do something about those spots now that he was living with her.

I rang the doorbell, expecting Velma to answer, but I was face to face with human Kevin once again.

Having to turn my face up so suddenly to greet him, "Wow, you're tall," slipped out of my mouth before I could stop myself.

He laughed wholeheartedly, his smile making his tough demeanor seem so much more gentle. "Wow, you're short," he answered, patting my head.

"Am not," I muttered. "I'm average."

"If you say so. What can I do for you, average Feighlynn?"

I lifted the bag I had carried over in front of me like an offering. "I come bearing gifts! Well, leftovers. We had a lot left, and I thought maybe you would want to try some."

"Yes, thank you!" He took the bag from my hands, taking a deep inhale from inside of it. His eyes rolled back in satisfaction, which made something tingle in my chest. "I was just about to microwave two cans of Spaghettios and pretend they were lasagna."

"That sounds horrible," I giggled.

"A man's got to do what a man's got to do."

"Well, I hope this eases that burden a little. If you ever find yourself in a Spaghettio crisis again, feel free to stop by. We always have enough to share."

"If this lasagna is half as good as it smells, I'll have to take you up on that."

I smiled, blushing slightly from the praise. Cooking was just another task on my daily list of things to do. It always has been. I haven't received genuine praise about anything related to my cooking in a long time.

Human Kevin stood awkwardly for a second, and I was about to bid him goodnight and finish my walk, but then he asked, "Would you like to come in?"

"That's okay," I grinned gratefully. "Your mom isn't too fond of dogs, and Kevin still needs to go for his walk." I pressed my lips together, seeing the playful grin spreading on his face. "Doggy Kevin. Sorry."

"Don't apologize," he chuckled. He crouched down to pet my Kevin just like he did earlier today. "This Kevin is a good boy. Aren't you? Aren't you, boy?"

"Aw, are you baby talking to my dog?"

It was his turn to get all flushed in the face. "Maybe." The muscled military man looked shy and pouty. "I like dogs." He then reverted to the baby talk. "Especially dogs with cool names like Kevin."

Kevin licked at human Kevin's face excitedly. Human Kevin leaned into it, rubbing his neck with matching enthusiasm.

"Kevin is a cool name, but having two of you around might get confusing. I'm going to stick my head outside and yell for Kevin one day and you might come running over."

"That would be a problem," human Kevin chuckled. "You could just call me Trude. I'm used to it after twenty-two years in the Army."

"But then, what if your mom comes running?" I giggled.

"Do you plan on sticking your head out the door and yelling Trude very often?" he smirked.

I shrugged. "I have leftovers often."

"Hmm, you're right. That may not work then. How about this," he rubbed his hand on his chin, "What about a nickname?"

"I could just call you the human," I said jokingly.

"Nah. You'd have all the neighbors running for my leftovers, then. How about just Kev? Or Vin?"

"I like Vin," I smiled. "You have a Vin sort of vibe."

"Like a certain actor that stars in a never-ending series of movies about fast cars?"

"I was thinking of *Riddick*, but sure," I shrugged.

"Oh, that's a good movie. I forgot about *Riddick*. I'll have to see if I can find it to stream later while I'm eating my leftovers."

"You can borrow it if you like. I have the Blu-ray."

He laughed softly. "Thanks, but I don't even think mom has a Blu-ray player."

"We don't either. My son's old Playstation is in the den, which is what I use."

"I don't even have a Playstation," he chuckled dryly. "At forty, video games aren't really my thing anymore."

I wondered what his *thing* to do for fun could be, but I don't want to be intrusive by asking. I was thinking about inviting him over to watch it, but it seemed a little inappropriate to ask that of my new neighbor. Thinking about it in my head, it sounded like a cheesy line from a chick flick when a girl is trying to get a guy up to her apartment. I don't want Kevin, or Vin, to get the wrong impression of me, or have his mother getting the wrong idea.

Just then, a stray cat leaped down from a tree in the Trude's front yard and went darting down the street. It caught Kevin's attention, and he bolted after it in a flash, too fast for me to tighten my grip on his leash. He broke away and sprinted after the stray.

"Kevin!" I yelled, but it was too late. "Well, shoot," I muttered, then went chasing after him. I'm not athletic, so running wasn't my forte. After about fifty feet, my lungs were already burning, and I knew I would not catch up with my dog. I hunched over, trying to catch my breath, debating if I wanted to get in my car and chase him, or just wait right there until he came back.

Before I could decide, human Kevin sprinted past me, surprising me and making me falter back. He was fast. Much more athletic and faster than me. Luckily, the cat stopped to climb a tree at the end of the street, and Kevin stayed at the base, jumping up to find some foothold on the bark. Human Kevin quickly approached him seconds later, grabbing the leash while my Kevin continued to frantically chase after the cat.

"Thank goodness." I placed my hand over my heart. Last time Kevin ran off like that, it took both me and Preston circling the block for half an hour to get him back home. He's an obedient dog, but likes to chase.

Walking to meet the two Kevins halfway, I laughed, replaying what had just happened over in my head.

"What's so funny?" Vin asked as I got closer.

"You," I bit my lip, trying to hold in my laughter, but it was no use. "You're funny."

"Uh, I just saved your dog's life," he said defensively. "That cat was about to claw his face off."

"You're our hero," I giggled. "Just like *Riddick.*"

He threw his head back and laughed. "That was a fast and furious moment."

"How so?" There were no cars, so I was curious.

"Um, I was running fast, and that cat was furious."

"Of course," I bit back my grin.

"I almost died."

"You're right," I nodded seriously. "It was a close call."

"As long as you know," he grinned crookedly, handing me the leash.

I took Kevin back, then started lightly scolding him for chasing the cat. "Bad, Kevin. We don't chase cats."

"Aw, he's still a good Kevin. He was protecting the street from the devil cat."

"Devil cat?" I lifted a brow.

"All cats are demons. Didn't you know that?"

"No, they're not," I laughed. "They're fluffy and cute."

"And selfish and total assholes. They take pleasure in knocking shit over and tripping unsuspecting humans."

"I take it you don't like cats?"

"Nope," he gagged. "Hate them. I'm definitely a dog man."

"I think you need a kitten as a housewarming gift," I teased him.

"I think the neighborhood will get another stray if you do."

"Aw, would you really throw a kitten out into this cold, cruel world all alone?"

"You're right," he nodded seriously. "I'll re-gift it back to you."

"Well, that's better, I guess," I laughed wholeheartedly. I don't think I have laughed or smiled this much without forcing myself to in years. "You know, you're really easy to talk to, *Vin*, my action hero." I looked up at his face and caught the pink hue on his thick neck and cheeks highlighted under the streetlights. It stood out from the tattoo on his nape.

"Well, thanks. You're tolerable too, I guess."

"Aw, aren't you a sweetie?" I giggled.

We were almost back at our houses when Nick's car came to life in my driveway. We stood still and watched as he backed up and sped away. I guess it is getting pretty late, and Preston isn't one to make his dad feel welcome.

"Was that your, um, your ex-husband?"

I smiled tightly and nodded. "It's getting late. He probably needed to get back to his girlfriend. He just wanted to hang out with the kids for the evening."

"Must be awkward for you," Vin commented.

I shrugged. "It's not too bad. I don't want my kids to have a poor relationship with their father. I would rather feel awkward than have them feel abandoned."

Vin stared down at me, contemplating for a moment. "Don't take this the wrong way, but I thought you were way too young to have a daughter that old."

I smirked with a glint in my eye. "I have another child, too. He's older. Sixteen."

"Sixteen?! You can't be over twenty-eight."

"Aw, you just became my new best friend. No, I'm thirty-five. We had Preston when I was young, then three years later, right after I graduated from college, we had Jessie."

"So young," he whispered.

"Yeah. I'm using myself as an example to my kids of why you don't marry young. People change too much," I sighed. "But I got my babies, so I have no complaints. They're pretty outstanding."

"They must take after their mother." He continued to stare at me, and I felt self-conscious under his gaze. It wasn't a passive stare, or merely observing. It was a look that I felt against my skin, and made me feel that tingling feeling inside once again, just like I felt when his face lit up seeing I brought him food. He's a little disarming, which makes me feel vulnerable.

Man, he could probably hear my heart pounding in my chest. I can hear it pulsing behind my ears. "I, uh, should go in," I murmured. "School day tomorrow."

He slipped his hands in his front pockets, smiling gently. "Alright. Thanks for the food, Lynn."

"Lynn?"

He smirked. "You gave me a nickname. I think you need one too."

"So, Lynn?"

"Do you not like it?"

I shrugged. The only nickname I ever had was Fay, but that is tainted by memories of Nick calling me only Fay for the past seventeen years. "Vin and Lynn," I said out loud, then giggled. "They rhyme."

"Makes it even better," he chuckled, then started walking towards his house. "Thanks again for the lasagna, Lynn. I'm going to eat it all right now."

"Save some for your mom!"

"Nope!" He shook his head. "Snooze you loose."

I was laughing and smiling at myself, all the way inside, until I got to my room to get ready for the evening. Vin and Lynn. I like my new neighbor. I think I like him a lot.

I was just about to slip out of my jeans when I glanced over at the bed. Dozens of wrapped packages were on top of the bedspread.

"What the heck?" I muttered, buttoning my pants again before walking towards the pile.

"I told him to take those with him," Preston appeared at my door as I was examining one of the wrapped boxes. "After he went around the entire house to check the windows like a freak, he put them there anyway. Want me to throw them in the trash. Tomorrow is trash day."

That's what all those other bags were for. I thought Jessie was just being lazy.

"No, that's alright. Do you know what he did with the bags that they came in?"

"Trash," Preston murmured. "I can put them with the bags if you want."

"And leave them in the trash?" I chuckled. "No, baby. It's fine. I'll give them back to your dad tomorrow." I grabbed a large tote bag from under my bed and stuffed the wrapped presents into it. Preston helped, and soon my bed was clear.

"I think dad's trying to get you back," Preston said warily.

"No. He's with Arlene, and your dad doesn't change his mind when he's made it up. You know that."

"Then what's with the cheesecake, gifts and that bullshit about the condo?"

I overlooked the curse word slip, because I could tell Preston was about to get heated.

"He's just trying to remain friends. We still have to co-parent Preston. Would you rather your father was mean to me?"

"I would rather he just left you alone."

I sighed, sitting on the edge of my bed. Preston plopped down beside me, and I rested my head on his shoulder. "Your dad isn't a bad man. He made some choices for himself, but he is still your dad, and you only have one."

Preston pursed his lips, and I could tell he was coming up with some smart-mouth rebuttal. It made me grin.

"You could start dating again. Get me a step-dad."

"Please," I rolled my eyes. "I have you and Jessie, and then there's Kevin. That's all I need."

***

Nick

"Where have you been?" Arlene asked the moment I walked into the apartment. I didn't even set my keys down, and she already had that look on her face, ready for an argument.

"Please don't start with this again. I'm not in the mood. Where do you think I was?" I muttered, sitting on a chair by the front door to untie my shoes. I hate taking off my shoes anywhere but the bedroom, but Arlene has a thing about shoes on her floors and rugs. Arlene has a thing about a lot of things. Everything. Things that I don't have issues with, and never thought of being a criminal offense before. Arlene will put me on trial and run me through the coals for committing any of them.

Arlene narrowed her eyes on me. "It's not Friday."

"Does it have to be Friday for me to want to see my children?"

She strummed her fingers against her crossed arm, tapping her slippered toe. "Your visits have been excessive lately."

Not this fight again.

"It's not excessive. You don't have kids, so you don't understand."

Her face crumbled, and I instantly regretted those words. Her inability to have children broke her marriage. I didn't want more kids, so that never bothered me, but it still hurt Arlene.

Before I could apologize, she snapped, "I'd like my space tonight," then started walking towards the bedroom.

I sat there, wondering for a second if I should go after her, but what's the point?

Grabbing my shoes, I headed for the guest room, reaching for the bottle of Johnnie Walker on the way. It's the only way I can get to sleep anymore.

I stripped to my shorts, then sat on the bed, using the glass rinsing cup from the bathroom, the one Arlene leaves for Jessie every weekend, to pour my first shot. Jessie hasn't used this bathroom, or even been in this apartment in over a month now. She likely won't be here tomorrow, either. By next week, Jessie won't ever have to spend a second in this apartment again, and neither will I. I still don't know how to handle things with Arlene since we work together, but I know I can't stand living with her another second. She doesn't seem very fond of living with me anymore, either.

I downed my first glass of whiskey, then poured my second before I began flipping through the channels to find something to get my mind off the failure of tonight.

"All those dreams died the moment you told me you didn't love me anymore." I felt those words like a blade. I was so stupid. So disillusioned back then. I thought I was leaving my mundane, boring life for excitement and freedom. I thought I was elevating myself to reach for higher goals. I have never been so wrong.

When I met Fay when I was completely broke and halfway through law school, she was like the sun, lighting up campus everywhere she went. I thought she was the type of woman all men would envy me for being with. I hurried to marry her, infatuated with her vibrant personality and her adorable charms. She was lovely in every way, but she was always safe and controlled. She was happy with her simple life. After seeing the change in Arlene, and after we started our affair, I thought maybe I was too fast to marry and should have waited for someone that was more aligned to the station I wanted to reach for.

I was wrong. I was too quick to leave her. It wasn't even two weeks before I regretted everything, but by then it was too late.

Arlene had already begun to show affection openly at work, so those that weren't previously aware of the affair suddenly knew. I didn't want to be that flake of a man who crumbled under judgment and pressure, which is what I deduced that my regretful mindset was coming from. I tried to sum the regret up to just mourning my old life, but I was just fooling myself.

Then the divorce started. Fay's attorney submitted the separation documents while I spent two weeks staring at mine on my desk, debating if it was nerves or something else preventing me from filing. Fay wanted nothing from me. Not even child support or alimony. She was true to her word, only wanting the house.

She was calm and steadfast through the entire ordeal while I was a disaster. I tried to keep it together on the outside, but I would lash out at mediation hearings, and always had a reason to push court dates back again and again. I used my connections to get a rise out of Fay, wanting her to show a hateful or resentful side just once, but no matter how many times I motioned for continuance, or what allegations I threw Feighlynn's way, she remained her sweet, positive self. She didn't fight me about anything she deemed reasonable, like the custody agreement.

In the end, even the judge that completed our divorce was smitten with Fay's sunshine personality, and I realized through it all what I was scared to admit before.

I was wrong. I was so wrong to leave her, and I was miserable. I was seeking excitement and freedom to rise to a higher position, but I'm living in a prison of my own regrets.

I can't keep living like this. Every night, I cannot drink myself to oblivion to drown my guilt and regret. I can't keep making excuses to stay at the home I once shared with my wife, just so I could sneak into the room we used to share and cry into her sweet-smelling pillow while she avoids me by staying with her sister.

I want my wife back. I want to hold her small but curvy body while going to sleep, burying my face in her soft hair. I want to listen to her adorable ramblings as she talks to herself throughout the day. I want to hear her laugh again. Lord, it's been so damn long since I heard Fay laugh.

She was laughing with *him*. Her new neighbor. I never felt jealousy like that. Men have flirted with my wife in the past, but that was when I knew she would never sway from me. Seeing her walking her dog with that thug, his arms covered in tattoos, I wanted to step in and tell her to go home and demand he never speak to my wife again.

But she's not my wife. Not anymore.

She said the dreams we used to share died, but I refuse to accept that. If I'm this regretful, she has to be feeling some regret, too. She has to. After fifteen years of marriage, she couldn't have rid herself of all the affection for me. Not when I can't forget any of the reasons. I fell for her so hard and so fast sixteen years ago. Such a short amount of time in confusion on my part can't erase what we once built.

Maybe the redemption gifts I left on her bed to make up for last year's disaster and more for this year will be enough to start a conversation at least. Maybe I should text her now and see if she has noticed them yet.

The image of her laughing with that neighbor man flashed in my head, stopping me from texting when I lifted my phone. Maybe I should call her instead, just to make sure she made it home okay.

I was unlocking my phone, scrolling through my contacts, when an incoming text pinged and my phone vibrated in my hand. I excitedly went to my messages, hopeful it would be praise for my thoughtfulness. Fay was always so grateful for any little gift I gave her. Whether it be drugstore flowers when we first dated, to that expensive mutt I bought her some years ago. She was the most cheerful and grateful person I knew.

My face fell when I opened the text. It wasn't from Fay, but from Preston.

> Pres:| I told you not to leave the gifts. I'll bring them tomorrow when I bring Jess to your place. Mom doesn't want them, and she doesn't need you over here guilt-tripping her

about not wanting them. You're not staying over here this weekend, either.

She didn't want them? Did she not open them? I spent hours combing through Dillards and Neiman Marcus with a sales associate, picking out the best of everything they offered. I even got the quirkier designs, knowing she preferred unique to regular designer stuff. Arlene only wants the top brand's top products, while Fay adores the thought and meaning behind everything. Damn it, I was so idiotic. So moronic.

Me:| Did she even open them?

Pres:| No, and she's not going to.

I shot back my glass of whiskey, the liquid burning through my chest. She didn't even open them.

"All those dreams died the moment you told me you didn't love me anymore."

No. I refused to believe that. She still had to hold some feelings for me. She had to. I didn't know if I could live with myself if I believed otherwise.

Me:| Okay. I'll see you tomorrow, son.

There has to be something I can do. Once I'm in my own place, the place we always wanted to share in our dreams, I can really start trying to win her back. There has to be a way.

***

Arlene

He didn't come after me. I'm too stunned, or I might cry right now.

After leaving the bastard at the door, I went and sat at the end of my bed rim-rod straight, protruding my chest and letting the slit of my robe fall open to expose the full length of my leg. I was ready for a petty fight, ready to vent out some of my anger, then get the rest of it out with a fury fuck. The best kind of fuck. I had my arms crossed, tapping my foot, but he never came.

Just seconds later, I heard a door close. He went straight to the guest room. He didn't even waver. He went straight there. Not before grabbing the bottle of whiskey from the bar cart. I guess sex is off the table for the night.

What is wrong with him? As of late, he isn't present in this relationship. Not like he was before.

And that kid comment. It stung like hell, but I expected him to feel remorse finally and come after me to apologize at least.

Does he just not care anymore?

No way. There is absolutely no way. He left his wife for me. I never thought he would, but he easily abandoned the woman and moved right in with me.

But he has been acting off. Sex was what started all this. Raw, carnal, desire-driven sex. It's been two weeks, at least since we last had any intimacy, and it hasn't been carnal for a long time.

Is he getting bored with me already?

I paced back and forth in the bedroom, worrying myself to death.

He said he was with his kids, right? Would it be inappropriate to text Jessie and just confirm?

Going back and forth in my head, I finally decided to just send her a basic 'how was your day' message. Opening my phone, I smiled at the background image. A picture of Nick, Jessie and me at the amusement park. Nick wouldn't ride anything, giving Jessie and me plenty of time to bond. I love this girl. She's so sweet and kind hearted. Going through my messages with her confirms that. She texts me at the most thoughtful times. If I have a court hearing or an important meeting she knows about, she always checks in to see how things went. Nick hasn't brought his kids over for a few weeks now, and I'm really missing Jessie.

> Me:| Hey girlie! How was your day?

It took maybe ten seconds for a reply.

> Jess:| Hey Arlene! My day was great. Just school and hanging out with dad after. How was yours? I've missed you!

My heart swelled and a smile spread across my face. She is so adorable and sweet.

> Me:| I'm glad to hear that! I miss you too. I'm hoping to get some girl time this weekend.

I sent a heart and smile emoji, then a GIF of a cutesy 'I miss you' icon. She was the one that showed me the GIFs on my phone. I try to always include one now.

> Jess:| For sure. Pres is dropping me off after school. I'll see you then!

> Me:| Okay, girlie. I've got to plan. We're going to have a blast.

So Nick really was with his kids. That's a relief, but not as much as knowing Jessie is coming over tomorrow.

I'm probably reading too much into Nick's recent behavior. At least, I hope I am.

Chapter Five

It's A Date

Vin

"One. Two. Three...." I'm sitting in my late father's rocking chair, which was angled to look out the front window, counting the dust particles in the air. The morning sun was shining brightly through the slits in the blinds, making them easy to see. "Seventeen. Eighteen. Nineteen. Twenty."

I leaned forward, pushing two fingers between the blind slits, opening the crack wide enough to see across the street.

Nope. No sign of her yet. She leaves her garage open when she walks her dog, and it was still as closed as it's been the first three dozen times I've looked out while sipping my energy drink.

I went back to counting, starting back at one again. My ears perked when I heard the sounds of what I thought was a garage when I'm at number twelve, and I hurried to look outside again. "Bummer," I muttered, seeing it was the neighbor beside her, and not her house. I was about to sit back and start counting again, but then I noticed Lynn's neighbor, some woman in a shower cap and fluffy robe, pulled her trash cans out to the curb.

Shit, it's trash day. All the houses have their trash cans out. Mom said she wasn't sure what day trash came on anymore, so I didn't know. Surprisingly, her trash wasn't too full, not like she had forgotten to take it out at all in the past weeks, so I wasn't in a rush to figure it out. I was going to go into the city later to get utilities switched to my name and find out the schedule then, but I guess I can put the trash out now.

I checked one last time out the blinds, seeing if my giggling, happy neighbor that cooks killer lasagna might have come out yet, but the garage was still closed. Bummer, because taking out the trash would have been the perfect opportunity to see her again.

Damn, I'm acting like a freaking stalker now. I can't help it. I had fucking dreams of her laughing and giggling last night. I thought I was going crazy. When I sat down in that chair fifteen minutes ago, I told myself I was just waiting to see her so I could return the food containers and bag to her, but then I had to face the fact that I was just eager to see *her* again.

I dropped the bag with her stuff on the kitchen counter, then slipped on some shoes as mom was coming down the back stairs into the kitchen. She's taking them slower than I would like. Maybe I should get a lift installed for her soon.

"Morning, mom," I kissed her cheek as I went around her to the garage door.

"Oh, you're up early. How did you sleep?"

I cringed, our neighbor across the street's face coming into my head. "Great," I muttered.

"That's good, dear," she said, moving to the cabinet with her tea.

I slugged back the rest of my energy drink as I pressed the garage door opener, and when I looked back down, there were legs on the other side of my garage. Distressed jeans and sneakers. As the door opened more and more, it uncovered a teenage boy. He had both the trash and the recycling carts and was dragging them out to the curb.

"Hey, kid," I yelled, but he must have not heard me. The white ear buds poking out from the sides of his head are probably to blame. I followed behind him, then scared the snot out of the boy when he turned around. He dropped the wheeled carts in the process. The black garbage one skidded to a stop, but the blue recycling fell over, cardboard boxes tumbling out.

"Jeez," he gasped, "You scared the crap out of me." He pulled out his ear buds and slipped them in his pocket before bending over to clean up the mess.

"Sorry," I chuckled, going to help him. "I yelled out to you, but guess you didn't hear me."

"Headphones," he muttered.

"Ah," I nodded. Teenagers and their headphones these days. He doesn't look like a bratty kid like most teenagers, though. And he was even taking out our trash for us.

He eyed me warily for a second, then looked back at my house, seeing my mom in the kitchen window. "Are you visiting Mrs. Trude or something?" He kept looking at the window at my mom until she looked up and saw him. When she smiled and waved, he returned it with a more relaxed expression. He was obviously worried about the stranger in my mom's house. I liked this kid more and more.

"I just moved in." I held out my hand to shake him. "Name's Kevin. I'm her son."

"Kevin?" He snorted and smirked, but returned the handshake firmly. I was taken back for a second. Was my name that funny? "Sorry. That's my dog's name. I'm Preston. I live across the street."

That explains the humor. This must be Feighlynn's other kid. I guess she didn't mention me to him yesterday.

"Hi, Preston," I said, tossing my empty can into the recycling. "Um, thanks for taking the trash out for us."

"Yeah, no problem. Mrs. Trude forgets, so we try to get it for her every week. Don't scare my mom if she brings it in later for you. She usually gets to them before I get home from school."

"I won't," I grinned. This is a good kid. Feighlynn did well.

"Well, it was nice meeting you human Kevin. I got to get my sister and me to school." He waved and hurried across the street as I stood there in stunned amusement.

Human Kevin. Yep. The kid was definitely Feighlynn's.

I watched the kid go into his front door before I adjusted the trash cans a bit. They were in the driveway halfway and I was getting my car delivered today. Plus, I had to get the uhaul back this morning. I needed all the driveway space.

Right when I was about to walk back inside, I heard a garage open, and sure enough, it was theirs.

"Did you grab your lunches?!" Feighlynn called out to the mustang backing out of the third car spot.

Preston stuck his head out of the window. "Jessie got them. Thanks mom."

"Have a good day! Make good choices," she waved excitedly, her dog on his leash in her other hand. "I love you!"

She had to be the happiest person I have ever met. I was stunned, just standing there and watching her until her son drove by and waved again at me before rolling up his window.

"My action hero!" Feighlynn said when she saw me. I felt like puffing out my chest and flexing my arms when she called me that.

"Hey, Lynn," I smirked instead.

"Morning, *Vin*," she giggled. It was just like in my dreams. Maybe even better. "Pres said he met you this morning."

"He did," I grinned, remembering him calling me human Kevin.

"He asked me if we should make sure you're really Velma's son and not some friendly robber." She bit her bottom lip, her eyes shining with humor.

"At least he called me friendly," I huffed, acting offended, but I'm actually just impressed.

"Yeah," she giggled. "You went from hero to robber overnight."

"I think that's a different Vin Diesel movie," I chuckled.

"We should make a list and start checking them off."

That gave me an idea. I don't know if it's a good one, but I wanted to take the chance. I looked down at her dog, nervously petting his ears. "We could, um, have a movie night some time then?"

She fluttered her eyes in the cutest way, brushing her hair behind her ear while she looked down shyly. Man, she's pretty. "You really want to watch that Riddick movie, huh?"

"That, and I could handle your leftovers for you," I chuckled nervously. "I mean, I scarfed that lasagna down. It was amazing."

"It was pretty amazing, huh?" she giggled.

Damn, she was cute. Her ex-husband must have been a moron.

"I, uh, I don't have the kids on weekends, so I wasn't planning on cooking tonight."

"Even better," I said. "I could take you out? Maybe see an actual movie?"

"Are you saying Riddick isn't an actual movie?" she grinned adorably. "It happens to be one of my favorites."

I shook my head and burst into laughter. "Well, what I meant was a movie playing in theaters. I'm sure there's something out there like it."

She bit her lip, looking up at me. I could see she was thinking it through, and I'm sure she's uncomfortable being put on the spot like this.

"Tell you what. Think about it for a second. I'm going to run in and get your containers for you and your bag."

"You really ate it all?" Her large brown eyes went even wider.

"Every bit of it." I rubbed my belly and smiled. "I'll be right back."

I jogged up to the house, passing through the garage to grab the bag quickly from the kitchen. Mom was in the backyard looking at her flowers with her cup of tea and toast for breakfast. After making sure she was okay, I hurried back out to where Feighlynn was still waiting at the end of my driveway.

"Here you go," I handed it to her, but her fumbling with the leash to grab it had me pulling it back towards me. "Uh, I can just place this on your porch or in your garage for you until you get back."

She smiled, biting that bottom lip and shaking her head. "I have a better idea. How about just bringing it to me tonight? Say, around six?"

My heart was thundering in my chest, and a relieved, rejoicing smile split across my face, making my cheeks hurt, but I didn't care.

"At six? Sounds great."

"It's a date," she giggled, then hurriedly started walking with Kevin in tow.

***

Nick

"What do you think?" Arlene asked me, shaking my knee.

"Huh?" I snapped out of my thoughts, glancing at her before focusing back on the road. She's been awfully chatty since we left this morning, which I didn't expect after what happened last night.

"Nicholas, are you serious? Were you really not listening to a single word I said?"

"Sorry," I muttered. "I was thinking of my case."

That was a lie. I have been fighting a headache from drinking too much last night, then thinking about my wife and the new condo.

Arlene scoffed like she didn't believe me, but continued talking anyway. "I was saying, why don't we take Jessie to that new dive bar down the street for dinner tonight? I hear the tartar is astounding."

"A dive bar, Arlene? Really? Jess is only thirteen."

She huffed in exasperation, "It has a restaurant side, too."

"No," I shook my head. "I'm taking her and her brother somewhere tonight. Even if I wasn't, we wouldn't be taking her to a bar."

"It's a restaurant," she snapped, crossing her arms over her chest. "I haven't seen her in weeks, Nicholas."

It's really beginning to grate on my nerves when she calls me that. Nicholas. Fay always only called me Nick, and Nicholas was only what I went by at work. Arlene called me Nick most of the time, unless she was upset with me. She's frequently upset with me now, so Nicholas is all I ever hear anymore.

"She's not your child, Arlene. She's mine, and my other child won't come over anymore. If I want to spend time with him, it has to be away from your place." I should probably mention the condo I bought soon, but I still haven't figured out how to tell her without her causing a scene. We will still have to work together, and cutting her off cold turkey would not go well.

Her face fell just like it did last night, and I almost felt bad, but I stand by my statement. Preston hates Arlene, and if I want to spend time with my son, it has to be on his terms. His terms don't include her.

"I have done nothing but be nice to your son. It isn't my fault he does not wish to have a relationship with me."

"No, but you are the woman that broke my marriage. I don't expect Preston to like you."

"That's not fair," she seethed. Lord, I shouldn't have said that out loud. This is going to turn into a massive fight. "You said you wanted more."

Arlene's growing dependence on me pushed me to say it, even though I may have not wanted to. I was confused and made a mistake. I will not tell her that right now, though. I need to get my belongings from her place in the next few days and into the condo, then I'll tell her I made a mistake.

"I'm not trying to fight, Arlene," I said, pulling into a parking spot inside the parking garage. "I'm just telling you, my kids, and I won't be at your place this weekend."

The second the car was in park, she threw open the door in a huff and slammed it shut behind her.

I was not in the mood for this today. It's adding to my headache. I'm still reeling over the condo and Fay's blunt refusal to even go see it. Maybe after getting the keys, I can stop in on her and just be blunt with her, too. I can just tell her I know I was wrong. It would be after I got the kids. I need to send Preston the address for the hotel I booked near the condo. Maybe after the kids settle in for the night, I can stop by the house and have an actual heart to heart with my wife. I can lay it all on the table.

Walking into the building, I saw two partners of the firm, Stevens and Leroy, waiting at the elevator.

"Ah, Nicholas!" Stevens gave me a friendly tap on the shoulder. "You look rather shipper today."

"Arlene Settles had a look that could kill on her face just seconds ago before taking the stairs. I thought maybe you two had had a fight," Leroy said.

"Nope," I forced a smile. "Just excited to get my kids tonight."

"Right, you got the kids on the weekends," Stevens chuckled. "No wonder your girlfriend is in a mood. Kids are a handful. You should have done every other weekend like I did with my ex-wife."

"Speaking of which," Leroy reached into his pocket for his phone. "My wife was asking me to get your ex-wife's number."

"My wife?" I said. "Do you mind me asking what for?"

"Well, I'm not entirely sure. She rambles, you see, but it sounded like she wanted it to give to her younger brother."

"Her brother? Why would she do that?"

"Don't get all grouchy, Nick. This could be beneficial to you. You wouldn't have to pay those hefty alimony checks anymore."

"I don't pay alimony, Stevens. I don't pay her anything."

"Oh, good. You had a prenup. Smart man," Leroy wagged his finger proudly at me.

I didn't have a prenup either. I just have a saint of a wife that wanted nothing from me.

"Anyway. I guess my wife's brother met your ex at her baby shower a year and a half ago. He is recently single too, and Mary thought they might hit it off."

Rage was bubbling inside of me, but these men were above me in the firm. I could lose my job if I lashed out right now.

"Do you mind if I discuss this with her first? She may not feel comfortable with me handing out her phone number."

"Sure, go ahead," Leroy said. "I'm telling you, though, the sooner she moves on to a new relationship, the better things are going to get for you."

"We know from experience," Stevens chuckled.

"Sure," I smiled tightly, watching the numbers move up on the elevator wall. "I'll, uh, give it some thought."

I have no intentions of giving anyone her number, or seeing her move on. The fire is lit inside of me now. I'm going to go talk to her tonight.

CHAPTER SIX

Action Hero Vin

Feighlynn

"You didn't!" Kaitlin, my sister, gushed on the phone. "You said yes to a date!?"

"I don't even know for sure if it's a date," I sighed.

"You told him it was!"

"Well, yeah, but I didn't stick around to see if he agreed. He could just want a friend."

"Who asks a friend to dinner and a movie?" Kaitlin scoffed.

"Um, I go to dinner and movies with you! Are we dating?"

"That's different and you know it! This is totally a date."

"Maybe," I bit my lip. I can't believe I just ran off with Kevin like a coward after saying that. Preston's little suggestion from last night polluted my head. I can't believe I said yes at all. I can't believe he asked me. I'm a newly divorced single mom of two teenagers. Not really the pick of the litter, and human Kevin is the type of man who'd get the top pick.

Still, I'm excited, and despite his reasons for asking me to dinner and a movie, whether it be as friends or a date, I plan on enjoying myself.

"I'm coming over," Kaitlin declared.

"Right now? For what?!"

"To make sure you shave your legs and kitty cat."

I giggled to myself. "Vin doesn't like kitty cats."

"I bet he'd like to pet yours."

"Friends don't pet each other's kitty cats."

"Oh, so our action hero has a kitty cat?" Kaitlin teased.

"Stop. You know what I mean."

She laughed into the phone. "I know you want to tug on his snake."

"Jeez. Stop with the animals."

"Okay. I'll stop. I gotta get ready to head over there, anyway." She pulled the phone away and yelled at her husband to watch the kids. I sighed, shaking my head. There was no stopping her.

"Kate, I need to get some work done."

"I know you do. To your vag. Gotta get it ready for your date. Don't worry. I just got a waxing kit that will make your kitty look like a naked mole rat in no time."

"Gross!"

"I agree. I can't wait to try it out on you to see if it works or not. You can be my guinea pig."

Gosh, has she never waxed herself before? Or anyone else? "You're not touching my-"

"See you in fifteen!" She cut me off and hung up before I could tell her she wasn't touching my cat with her wax.

"Darn it," I muttered to myself. I plopped down in the middle of the floor in my office, opening my arms for Kevin to snuggle into me. "Aunt Kate is coming over, boy. Wanna see Aunt Kate? Do you?! Do you?!"

I hyped my dog up to get myself energized for the visit to come. Kevin loves when we spend the weekend with my sister, so he started doing laps around the bedroom upon hearing her name. He was ready. I guess I should get ready too.

I heated the lasagna I had left, and it was ready by the time Kate let herself into the house.

"Smells good!" She sang out, dropping her bag on the breakfast bar. "Hey, does our action hero have tattoos, a giant physique, and drive an old muscle car?""

For a second, I felt puzzled. I didn't mention tattoos to Kate and I'm not sure what kind of car Vin has. I just saw the uhaul in the driveway. "Why?"

"There's some hot guy across the street getting some old muscle car delivered right now. I waved when I pulled in."

"Huh?" I rushed to the front window in the living room, looking out through the curtains. There he was, standing at the end of his driveway, talking to a tow truck driver with a smile on his face and his tattoos on full display in his tight-fitted tank top. "Wow," I whispered.

Kate giggled. "Want me to wax your kitty cat now?"

"Maybe," I whispered distractedly. "Wait. No! He's not seeing my kitty cat!"

"Can I show him mine?"

"You're married!"

"Yeah," Kate sighed, like she was disappointed, even though I know she loves her husband. "Guess you'll have to show him yours for me."

"You're ridiculous." I poked her between the eyes, making her playfully snap her teeth at me. "Go eat. It's lasagna."

"Yummy! Are you going to stay over here and fill up on looking at him?" She opened the curtain wider, waving her fingers flirtatiously.

"Go!" I pushed her back, looking over my shoulder to see Vin was staring at us with an amused look on his face. "Jeez, Kate!"

"He looks yummy too," she said, leaning closer to wave at him again.

When I finally got her to back up, retreating to the kitchen while laughing her annoying butt off, I looked back to see Vin still standing there, the tow truck guy beside him now watching my house too.

He really is yummy looking. His car is exactly like something an action hero would drive too. I don't know cars, so I do not know what it is, but I'm sure it is something impressive.

I waved shyly, then hurried to close the curtains. His laughter was clear in his body movements. Gosh, my sister is so embarrassing.

"You're annoying!" I huffed at her as I walked into the kitchen.

"I do my best," she said, savoring a bite of her food. "Hey, do you have more of this?"

"Not for you!"

"Fine," she smirked, sliding my plate closer. "I'll just steal yours."

I rolled my eyes and laughed, knowing there was no point in arguing with my bossy, stubborn sister.

"Did you shower yet?"

I shrugged. "I did this morning."

"Not good enough. Go shower again, shave and exfoliate. I'm not waxing a stinky kitty."

"You're not waxing me at all!"

"Oh, yes, I am." Her eyes twinkled wickedly. "By the time I'm done with you, you're going to be the hottest woman in this town, hairless kitty and all."

***

Vin

"You look nice," mom praised my appearance as I came down the stairs.

I had on the nicest jeans I own, a white fitted shirt, and my boots. I felt like a tool bag, dressing like most privates did on a Friday night before hitting the strip clubs. I hadn't been on a date in so long; I agonized over what to wear until this was what I settled on.

"Do you really think so?"

"Sure!" Mom said enthusiastically, her knitting needles clinking away in her hands. "Where are you going this evening?"

"Just out to dinner," I kissed her head before checking my appearance once more in the hall mirror one last time.

"You and Mindy have fun, sweetie."

I cringed at my ex-wife's name. Far too often, Mom forgets I divorced my ex-wife more than a decade ago.

Instead of correcting her this time, I just grabbed my keys and headed out, wishing her a good night as I closed the door.

My 1970 Dodge charger sitting in the driveway lifted my mood as I walked past. I worried when it was delivered that it may have scratches or damage, but it was perfect. No dents or anything.

Feighlynn and the visitor she had today were funny, watching me in her window as I was finishing signing the papers for it. The woman with her seemed as friendly as Feighlynn when she pulled up. She waved excitedly and stared as she walked to her door. Feighlynn seemed completely embarrassed. It was cute. So fucking cute.

It was just about six. I fidgeted with my shirt, looking down to check my pants and boots one last time as I crossed the street. I looked as good as I could; I guess. The young guys must dress like this for a reason, right? She called this a date before I could and then sped off with her dog. I'm not exactly sure what she was expecting, but I think I pulled myself together enough.

When I knocked on the front door, I laughed softly to myself, hearing Kevin go crazy on the other side. Seconds later, his face poked through the curtains, just like his owner did earlier.

"Oh, hush!" I heard Feighlynn yell, making my smile stretch further on my face. "It's your friend. We don't bark at our friends."

Damn, she's cute. I couldn't see her yet, but I could imagine her face.

My imagination didn't prepare me for when she opened that door.

My lord, she was gorgeous. Looking at her, I never felt more like a schmuck. I tried to dress like a brat and she looked like a tiny goddess. Her hair was framing her small, heart-shaped face in gigantic waves. Her eyes were smoky but not overdone. She had just enough makeup on to make her eyes pop. And her dress. I knew Feighlynn wearing this dress would be what haunted my dreams tonight. The red fabric bunched and clung to her small, curvy fame. My hands flexed with the urge to touch her hips where it clung to her the most.

"Hello, action hero Vin," she giggled, opening the door wide while holding back Kevin by the collar.

"Damn," I slipped and said. She cocked her head to the side in confusion. "Sorry." I ran a hand over my chin. "You, uh, you look fantastic."

She smiled warmly. "Thank you. My sister helped. You look pretty good yourself."

I adjusted the sleeves of my shirt, nervous about my clothes again until I caught her eyes lingering on my biceps. She bit her lip in that way women do when they like what they see, and my confidence suddenly returned.

"Ready to go?" I asked, holding out my elbow as she pushed back her dog to lock the door.

"Ready," she grinned, linking her hand behind my elbow. My heart pounded, feeling her direct touch. Her perfume wafted up to me, making my mouth water. She smelled as sweet as she acted.

I'm way too old to be getting all flushed and fluttery because of a first date, but here I am, nervous like a kid. Damn, I hope I don't sweat through my shirt.

After opening her door for her, she giggled in that sweet way while checking out my car. "You really are an action hero. You have the car for it."

"You like it? I restored it myself."

"It looks really fast."

I shrugged. "It should be."

She ran her hand over the smooth dashboard, an awestruck look in her eyes. "The inside looks new!"

Pride filled my chest. I worked hard on this car, and it's nice hearing praise for it.

She leaned back to look in the backseat, lifting her butt slightly in the air. Her dress rode up just enough where I could see the tops of the back of her thighs. My face grew hot, and I had to look away and shut the door so as not to embarrass myself. Her skin looked so smooth and soft. I had to take my time walking around the car to make sure my face, and my pants, weren't displaying my inner thoughts.

"So, where are we going?" She asked as I got in.

"I was thinking Luigi's?" I looked up restaurants all day, and that one looked the most promising, with excellent reviews, a patio view of the river, and it was close to the theaters and bars, so we had a lot of options for what to do afterward.

"Oh, I love Luigi's! My sister and I go there on girl's nights sometimes."

I mentally high-five myself for putting in the work to find a good Italian restaurant. Judging by her lasagna, I thought she would like that.

The car ride was fun with Feighlynn. She liked to touch everything in the car, which I found cute, just like most things she did. She turned on the radio and set the stations for me. That started a heated discussion on country music versus soft rock. Surprisingly, she preferred rock to country. I grew up on Alan Jackson, George Strait and Reba, so I prefer the older country stuff. She was so fucking adorable singing along off-key with Journey and the Eagles, so I conceded to her by the time we pulled into the restaurant.

Damn, I felt like a king walking into the restaurant with Feighlynn on my arm. Ushering her through the door was my first excuse to touch her, resting my hand on her lower back. When I saw her cheeks color over with a rosy pink hue, her eyes shyly averting to the ground as she bit that bottom lip, I knew she didn't mind. I kept my hand proudly on her lower back until the hostess showed us to our table out on the patio.

The view was as good as the reviews said it would be. You could see the city glittering on the other side of the river, and even though it was getting dark, there were still people lingering in the park on the other side. Music and children's squeals traveled over to us, making Feighlynn laugh softly. She looked enamored with the sights. I was feeling pretty enamored by my view too.

"Can I start you off with drinks?" the server asked. "Our cocktail list is at the back of the menu."

"Hmm, can I just get the house white for now? And water?" Feighlynn asked.

"Sure," the server smiled. "And you, sir?"

"Shiner and a water too."

"Great. I'll bring those right out while you look over the menus."

Feighlynn's infectious grin made my heart race as we talked about the park. She said that her kids used to love going there when they were little, and it brought back a lot of wonderful memories for her.

"Your son seems like a good kid," I told her. "I was surprised to see a teen boy taking out my mom's trash this morning," I said.

"He is a good boy." She had this fond, loving look in her eyes. "He's a nurturer. Always has been. I always tell him he was my first love."

"Wouldn't that have been his father?" I asked, kicking myself for asking it afterward. I'm as bad as my mom with putting my foot in my mouth.

Of course, Feighlynn didn't act offended or down. "Not really," she shrugged, taking a long sip from her wine glass. "I mean, sure, I loved Nick, but that came after having Preston, and it stemmed from him being my baby's father. The only reason I married so young was because of Preston. Nick was always a little more stiff than me, so I wasn't sure it would work out." She sighed, leaning back in her chair while gazing at the children playing in the lit city park. "It didn't in the end."

Nick must be a complete idiot. I'm not completely sure about the circumstances of their divorce. Just the small amounts of information Feighlynn has told me, and the gossip from my mom, but it sounded like he was the one that fucked up. I'm just surprised that Feighlynn has remained as positive as she has. I was a fucking mess for years after my divorce.

"My marriage didn't either," I said, opening up too. She was talking about her divorce because of my stupid question, so I felt the need to be vulnerable as well. "It was thirteen years ago, and we didn't have kids, but it still fucked me up for some time." I reached across the table and brushed my fingers over hers. "I'm impressed that you can stay so positive."

She smiled warmly. "I just wanted my kids to remain happy. Plus, it helped that we both checked out months before he told me about..... Well," she bit her lip nervously. "We drifted apart for some time before, so that made it easier to accept. I didn't want to waste energy on getting angry or being hateful. Maybe if I didn't have the kids, but it would have done them no good. He is still their father."

"Is he a good father?"

At that, her smile grew. "Yes. Seeing him be their father made me fall for him. He's remained a good father through everything, so I can still respect him for that."

I never thought about having kids before, but seeing the way Feighlynn's face lights up as she went into more stories of her kids, it had me craving something I never considered before. Even the way her ex fit into the stories had me amazed. She spoke of him not like a resentful ex, but like a partner in parenting that she held respect for, just as she said.

"Your kids are with your ex tonight?" I asked between forks full of pasta.

"Yep. He still gets them every weekend."

"Every weekend, huh?" I smiled crookedly. "That leaves your weekends mostly open?"

"Maybe," she said shyly, twirling linguine in her spoon.

"What about next weekend?" I sat back in my chair with a smirk. She is so adorable when gets shy.

"I might be free next weekend," she said teasingly. "But I think since you planned tonight, I should be the one to plan our next, um, outing."

"Outing?" I lifted a brow. "What happened to calling this a date?"

She shrugged. "Is it a date?"

I reached across the table to rub her elbow resting on the table's edge. "I was hoping it was." I rubbed my thumb over her smooth skin, trying to not look like a freak as I inhaled deeply her vanilla-scented perfume.

"Good," she mumbled, looking at me through her lashes. "I was hoping it was one, too."

Now that we had the understanding that this was definitely a date, Feighlynn was more shy than she was before. She looked so vulnerable that I leaned in and touched her in the subtlest ways. She was the type of woman a man wanted to protect and defend. The urge to shield her against any awkward tension grew inside of me.

When we pulled into the drive-in theater, her face lit up like the fourth of July.

"I haven't been here in ages!" She said, looking around at all the old-fashioned food stalls.

"Me neither. It surprised me it was still around.

Last time I was here was when my dad was alive. I had to have been fourteen when he brought me to see the Terminator with my mom. This place had a lot of excellent memories for me.

I parked beside a speaker stall towards the back, then we got out to get popcorn and drinks. Feighlynn insisted on paying for the popcorn and drinks since I paid for dinner. I tried to refuse, but she scanned her card before I could get my wallet out. The way she victoriously stuck her tongue out at me afterward made me laugh. Then she hummed as she sampled the popcorn on the way back to my car. She was so fucking cute. I wanted to just squeeze her, to hear her squeal.

When the movie started, she rested her head on my shoulder with my arms slung behind her head. I couldn't even tell you what the movie was about. I was too busy enjoying having her so close to me.

Is it weird that I'm already this infatuated with my neighbor? I was truly disappointed when the movie ended and she lifted her head off me. A dead arm and stiffness were so worth it.

"Do you, uh, want to go get some coffee, or maybe ice cream?" I asked, wanting the date to go on.

She gave me another shy look, then said, "I have coffee and ice cream at my house."

My heart hammered. She was inviting me over, and I would not turn her down.

"Sounds fantastic," I said, my voice cracking a bit. I coughed, feeling embarrassed, especially when she giggled. "Sounds good," I said in a much deeper tone, making her laugh harder. It was infectious. I began laughing with her, all embarrassment fading away just because of her laugh.

I was still riding high from our date and the prospect of it not being over as I drove all the way back to our neighborhood. I wanted to hold her hand so badly, but had to shift gears so I couldn't. She kept teasing me about my car being all show, so I revved the engine several times, the last time being when we turned onto our street.

We both laughed when a neighbor's car alarm started going off, but our laughter died when she saw a car sitting in her driveway.

"What's Nick doing here?" She pulled out her phone to see if she had any missed messages or calls. There weren't any from him, but a string of texts from someone named 'Kate' was at the top, the first asking 'Did he pet the kitty yet?'.

I pressed my lips together, looking back up towards her driveway, pretending I didn't see it.

"Everything okay?" I asked.

"I don't know," she mumbled, looking concerned.

I parked in my driveway, then went around to open her door while she was still looking at her messages. Her ex got out of his Cadillac and stood stiffly beside it. He was sizing me up as I gripped Feighlynn's hand and helped her out of the car. He straightened up a bit when she put away her phone and looked up at him.

"Are the kids okay?" was the first question out of her mouth. After hearing her talk about her kids most of the night, I knew that was what she was checking on her phone. She was checking on them.

"They're fine," her ex said gruffly. I didn't let go of her hand as we walked towards her house, and he made a point of staring. "Where were you?"

She looked at him in confusion. "What do you mean?"

He looked down at our joint hands pointedly, then repeated, "I mean, where were you, Fay?"

"She was out with me," I answered for her, feeling her tensing up beside me. "We met yesterday," I said, holding out my free hand, refusing to let go of my grip on Feighlynn. "I'm Vin, the action hero."

CHAPTER SEVEN

Delivery

Feighlynn

"I'm Vin, the action hero."

I could barely stop myself from bursting into laughter from the serious tone he just said that in. He used the phrase I had been teasing him with as an official title. The fact that he used it with my serious ex-husband made the situation even funnier.

Nick was looking at him like he was crazy, making no movements to shake his hand.

"Vin saved Kevin from a killer cat and me from a heart attack yesterday," I explained, passing Vin a grateful smile. Vin dropped his hand and returned my gratitude with a proud smirk. "That's why he's my action hero. We just got back from dinner and a movie. What are you doing here, though?" I waved my phone at him with the hand not gripped in Vin's. "The kids didn't text me."

Nick's expression remained hard, glaring like I did something wrong. I do not know what he could be upset with, though.

"I'm not here because of the kids," Nick said gruffly. "I'm here to speak with you."

"With me? You left the kids alone to speak with me?"

"They're both at the hotel, perfectly fine," he snapped.

I tilted my head in confusion. "Okay. So, why do you need to talk to me this late on a Friday night if it's not about the kids?"

His eyes shifted to Vin, looking uncomfortable, before glaring back at me. "Can we talk in private?"

I grimaced. He was being needlessly difficult.

"Want me to wait for you inside?" Vin asked me. "I can let Kevin out while you two talk out here?"

A thankful smile lifted my lips. "That would be great. Thank you."

"Actually, I think you can head on home and my wife and I can speak inside," Nick said as Vin took my keys from my hand.

At the term "wife" my heart froze and an icy chill ran through me. What was Nick doing? My night with Vin had been so satisfying, and so amazing, but Nick was taking all of that away with whatever this display was. It was my first date since our divorce, and the excitement I had felt all night was turning into dread at how Vin would interpret this interaction.

Vin was looking at me, waiting for my say on what to do. He's so nice and kind, and too good of a man to say if I'm making him uncomfortable. The right thing to do would be to thank him for the date, and send him home before Nick's hostility can affect him any more than it already has. Vin is a total catch, and doesn't need this sort of baggage in his dating life. Especially on a first date.

"I'm sorry, Vin," I whispered softly. I tried to smile, but it just felt like I was pressing my lips together. I couldn't force the corners of my lips to turn up. "I had a wonderful time with you tonight, and don't want to ruin it by making you more uncomfortable. It's getting late and I'm sure you're tired."

Vin stared into my eyes, his green irises boring into me. I tried to keep the painful smile in place, feeling mortified and embarrassed, but trying not to let it show too much. Even if we didn't go on another date after this painful encounter with my ex, I still wanted to be on friendly terms as neighbors. I hope he didn't think too badly of me for this later.

"Okay, Lynn."

A heavy breath escaped me when he used that little nickname, something between a laugh and a huff. It made me feel even worse about my ex showing up to ruin our date.

"I'll see you later, I guess."

My smile tightened, my brows pulling down at the corners as sadness weighed in on me. "Okay," I said.

He squeezed my hand one more time before letting it go and heading back to his house. When I was sure he was out of earshot, I turned to Nick, anger like I had never felt before gripping me.

"What the hell was that?" I asked in an icy voice.

Nick's eyes went wide for a minute, like my coldness surprised him. "Fay, I just...." He looked at the house, and then back at me. "Can we talk inside?"

"No. We can't. What the hell are you doing here, Nick?"

"I came to talk to you! I'm sorry to interrupt your evening, but this is important. I didn't want to wait another second to-"

"Excuse me," Vin's deep voice cut in, his hand suddenly gripping my elbow and pulling me back. I looked up at him in surprise. I thought he had gone back home. "I forgot this," he husked, bending over me and swiftly pressing his lips to mine. It took me by complete shock. His hands cradled my face. His hot fingertips seeped their warmth into my skin, and a second later, I was kissing him back.

No one had ever kissed me like this before. It was just a kiss, but it felt so much deeper somehow. I felt it burning all over my face, and my knees were getting weaker by the second. He overwhelmed my senses, leaving me faint and breathless. All the icy fury I just felt was being melted away.

"Wow," I gasped as he pulled back. His crooked smile shone in the dim streetlight. I could take my eyes away from his lips.

"Your neck okay?" he husked, rubbing the back of it. I held my head in a tilted position for him. His height and mine must look comical right now. "I'll have to get you a step stool for next time."

Next time? My already hot face grew even warmer at the implications. I bit my tingling bottom lip. It tasted like him, like popcorn and soda.

"Goodnight, Lynn," he whispered roughly, kissing my lips one more time.

"Night, Vin," I breathed out.

His eyes sparkled, mesmerizing me for a moment. Then they grew hard as he looked back at Nick. "Have a safe drive back to the kids, *Mr. Ex*. I'm sure I'll see you again soon, too."

Wow, wow, wow.

I pressed my hand to my chest, still feeling breathless as I watched him walk across the street with much more pep in his boots. His broad shoulders leaned as he walked, showing his confidence. I don't think I have ever felt more attracted to a man in my life.

My action hero.

Nick left soon after that. I was still a bit dazed, and he just mumbled something about the returned presents. He said he'd bring them back later, then got in his car and left before I could fully refuse.

Oh well. Whatever he was here for, it must not have been too important. He was probably just shocked seeing me on a date for the first time since the divorce. I know it was like a knife to the gut the first time I saw Arlene hanging off him after he left me, so I imagine he felt something similar. Even if he moved on, we were still married for fifteen, almost sixteen years. It's still a bitter feeling.

I felt anything but bitter for the rest of the night. As I laid in bed, staring at the ceiling, I was smiling and giggling to myself, replaying the kiss repeatedly in my head. Kevin kept whining every time I squealed, laying his head over my legs to tell me to quiet my excitement and go to bed. I was disturbing his sleep. I couldn't help myself. I had never had a first date like that.

Honestly, I had very few first dates in my life, so that's probably not saying much to most people. After Nick and the two boys I dated in high school, my bar might be really, really low. Something tells me it wasn't just me, though. It had to be Vin. Everything from the moment he picked me up, to the dinner and deep conversations, to cuddling against his firm body as we watched an action movie I now couldn't even remember. Then that kiss......

Everything about the date was amazing. Even when I thought my ex ruined the night, Vin blew me out of the water when he came back.

***

Nick

"Where did you go?" Preston asked the moment I walked back into the hotel room.

I almost jumped out of my skin. It was almost one in the morning. I thought he and his sister would be asleep. Jessie was nodding off before I left in the bedroom where they were watching TV. I thought Preston wouldn't be too far from sleep, either.

"The bar," I muttered, walking to the ice bucket to retrieve a glass as I kicked off my shoes. I went to the bar for a few drinks after getting back to the hotel. I wasn't ready to face my son after everything that transpired tonight. I need water to sober up.

"You went to the bar? For four hours?"

"What are you still doing awake?" I deflected his question before taking a long gulp of tap water.

He watched me with the same distrust and wariness I've received from him since the day he learned of my affair. I deserve no less, but it still hurts. Preston and I were as close as a father and son could be when he was little. Now he tolerates me at best.

"Mom texted me," he said as I filled my glass again at the sink. "She asked me if we were alright. Do you know why she would do that?"

By his tone, I'm sure he knows the answer already, and I'm tired of pretenses. I don't have the strength right now to pretend.

"I went to go see her," I told him honestly, dropping my heavy, tired body on the chair beside him where he was sitting on the couch.

"You went to go see mom?! Why?!"

"Because I miss her, Preston." I dragged my hand down my face. "I miss my wife."

That hasn't changed. Even after witnessing her getting home from a date, and after seeing her thug-looking date kiss her breathless, I still miss her. It feels like there is a hole inside my chest that just gets bigger and bigger by the day.

"Ex-wife," Preston muttered.

I closed my eyes, remembering the way her date called me "Mr. Ex".

"I don't want to think of her that way." My voice was hoarse, thick with emotion.

"Well, that's too fucking bad."

"Preston!" My eyes snapped open.

"Dad! You don't get to be that shitty, so cut the crap. What? Is your whore not enough for you now? You want to string mom along again until the next one comes along?"

"It's not like that. It's not like that at all."

"Then what's it like, dad?!"

"I MISS HER!" I shouted, the emotions heating and stirring behind my burning eyes breaking free. "I messed up, and I miss my wife! If I could go back and change everything, I would. That's all I want now. More than anything."

Preston shook his head at me, his jaw growing more tense. "Do you know what I want more than anything? For my mom to be happy."

A guilty sob broke through me. "I want that too."

"I don't think you do. Even before you left and said you were cheating, you weren't making mom happy."

"We were happy," I argued desperately.

"No, she wasn't," Preston glowered. "You know deep down she wasn't, and neither were you or you never would have done it. You wouldn't have cheated on my mom."

"I was just confused, Pres," I begged him to understand.

"You don't cheat from confusion. You *left her*. You cheated on her repeatedly and left my mom for the other woman. Are you really trying to get my sympathy now that you regret it all?"

I shook my head, knowing I didn't deserve his sympathy, forgiveness, or anything else. "I miss my family," I said brokenly. "I know I don't deserve her anymore, but I still miss your mom. That will never change."

"I doubt that," Preston scoffed, pushing himself off the couch. "Don't hurt my mom more than you have." He walked to the bedroom and closed the door behind him.

I sat there crying into my hands for I don't know how long, feeling the weight of my sins pressing in. "I'm so sorry, son," I heaved. "I'm sorry I hurt you, too."

***

Feighlynn

"So, I waxed your kitty cat for nothing?" Kate sat across the island, sipping on coffee, watching me as I scrubbed out the fridge to get ready for a grocery trip.

"You waxed my kitty cat because you're persistently annoying." I gave her a pointed look, and she stuck her tongue out at me.

"Stupid Nick. He's the really hairy kitty cat, if you know what I mean. What did he stop over for, anyway?"

I shrugged. "Your guess is as good as mine. He said something about those presents Preston returned to him, but then just left."

"Mm hmm," Kate laughed. "Sounds like our action hero scared him off. Good for him."

I bit my lip, remembering that kiss. Good for me and him. Really good.

"So, have we heard from our action hero today?"

"No," I murmured.

"And why not?"

I shrugged. "We never really exchanged contact info or made plans again."

"You're acting like you're not already neighbors, weirdo. Just go across the street and ask to borrow a cup of sugar and see if he'd like to pet your naked mole rat while he's at it."

"Kate!"

"What?" She took a long sip of her coffee. "Want me to ask him for you?"

"Do I want you to ask him to pet my naked mole rat?" I giggled.

"Yes. Yes you do," she answered like I was asking her the question and not pointing out how ridiculous she sounded. "I kind of want to meet him face to face, anyway."

Right then, my doorbell rang and Kevin went nuts. He barked at the window, and Kate looked at me with that gleam in her eyes. She hopped up and ran for the front door before me, looking excitedly through the peephole. Her excitement grew, and she threw open the door when I reached her.

"Flowers!" She bent down and lifted the vase full of roses from my porch. I was busy staring at the handsome man getting into the driver's seat of his action hero car. "To Lynn, I had a great time with you last night. I believe the next date is yours to plan, so give me a text when you can with the details. I'm looking forward to hearing from you soon. Your action hero," Kate read the card in the petals as I waved to Vin, who was driving off down the street. I swear I could see him blushing, which made him even more attractive. "Oh my gosh, Fay! Or should I say, *Lynn*," she laughed. "This is the sweetest! I'm going to text him for you right now!"

"Don't you dare." I snatched the card from her hands, cradling it to my chest. "Get your own flowers."

"I should," she sighed. "I'm texting my husband instead."

I carried the flowers and card back to the kitchen, reading the card repeatedly with a big smile on my face as Kate called her husband and picked a fight about wanting flowers. This really was the sweetest gesture ever, and I wanted to plan so I could text him soon.

CHAPTER EIGHT

Tattooed Hoodlum

Vin

"You just dropped the flowers on her porch and drove off?" Al Milton, my childhood friend, laughed at me. "Scared she would call the cops on you for assaulting her the night before?"

"I didn't assault her," I muttered, knocking back my beer. "I just kissed her."

"Oh, my bad," Milton snorted. "Kissing her in front of her ex-husband to make him jealous could never be construed as assault. Especially when she tells you to go home."

I glowered at my friend. "I'm not telling you shit anymore." I'm embarrassed enough thinking about that night. Not that I regret a damn thing. She loved it. I could tell by her reaction, and I've been thinking about that kiss endlessly ever since.

"Ah, come on," he chuckled, signaling to the bartender to bring us more beers. "I'm just playing. You know I got to tease you a bit. I'm jealous you went on a date with your milf neighbor before seeing me after moving back home."

"You told me you were busy when I asked you to help me move!"

"Oh. Yeah," he smirked. "I was busy."

"Bull shit," I scoffed.

"Hey, some of us still work for a living. Not all of us become lifers with a nice early retirement like you. Must be nice."

"It is pretty nice," I grinned. Because of retirement and military disability from my deployments, I never have to work again if I don't want to. I'm set for life. The army uses and abuses you, but they pay for it afterward too. Milton joined and went to basic with me right out of high school, but he just stayed in for four years, then used his GI Bill for school back in the civilian world while I reenlisted.

"Well, when you're bored again, I spoke to my boss like I said I would. He wants to meet with you if you're still interested in the security manager position at the district courthouse. The current manager is retiring in a few months, so they'll start putting out employment ads soon."

"At the courthouse? I thought it was for city hall?"

"Both, but the manager works out of the courthouse building."

"Maybe," I pondered, taking another drink. Going from Military Police to a civilian job, I thought I would look at joining the regular police force, but I'm still not sure what I want to do yet.

"So, tell me about this neighbor you assaulted. Has she texted you yet?"

I grinned, despite myself thinking about Feighlynn. After I dropped the flowers off two days ago, it wasn't even ten minutes later that she sent me a text saying thank you for the roses. I was standing at the gas pump, pumping gas while smiling like a freak, reading the sweet message she sent me.

"We've been texting," I shrugged, trying to play it cool.

We've been texting quite a bit, and I even called her last night, asking if she wanted to slip out and go for a walk with me and her dog. We walked for so long that I had to walk her back to her door. It got too dark, and she was squeamish about stepping on a frog on a way back inside. She's so fucking adorable.

"Guess she's not one of those women that thinks you have to wait days before texting a man back."

"No," I laughed. "She's definitely not."

"She sounds great, man. I'm happy to see you taking an interest in a woman again. I thought your ex had fucked you up for life. What's your milf's name?"

I grimaced a little at the mention of my ex, and the term Milton keeps using for Feighlynn. Not that he's wrong, but he decided on the term when I told him what she looked like. I didn't. "Lynn."

"Lynn? A bit old-fashioned."

"Well, it's Feighlynn, but I've been calling her Lynn since we met, since she shortened my name to Vin."

"Vin and not Kev?" Milton raised an eyebrow.

I shrugged, feeling a bit smug. "She has a thing for Vin Diesel."

"Ah, I get it," he chuckled around a drink from his beer. "You give off that vibe. She must have a thing for hunks like you then."

I shrugged, not really sure. Her ex looked nothing like me. The man looked like a well-kept city boy with stiff hair and expensive suits. He didn't even have stubble late at night. I've been worried that I was nothing like her type, but the more I learn about her, the more I can see she never had the chance to have a type. She got married way too young.

"Your mom like her?" Milton asked.

"Mom loves her. She and her kids had been looking after mom for a while before I moved back." From what I can see, everyone on our street loves her. When we went for a walk last night, at least ten neighbors had her stopping to talk to them, and she was as personable as could be. I would just watch her, becoming more and more captivated by her happy spell of positivity and kindness.

Damn, I really like her. I like her more than I thought possible, having not known her for even a week.

"Good. That goofy smile looks good on you, man. For real."

"Thanks." I ran a hand down my face, feeling self-conscious suddenly.

"Feighlynn, huh? That name sounds familiar. Does she work for the city manager's office or anywhere at city hall?"

"No. She works for a graphic design firm from home."

"Hmm, I wonder why that name sounds so familiar then. It's not a very common name."

I shrugged. "No clue, man. Maybe I said it before and you just didn't remember."

"Maybe," he shrugged before checking his phone. "Ah, I have to get back. We have a meeting with a couple of attorneys over a land acquisition case."

"Is it okay that you go out for a drink on your lunch break like this?"

Milton waved off my concern. "It's fine. It's a done deal. Just signing and putting the city's seal over the final documents. Two beers with my burger is a regular Monday lunch for me."

He walked here, so I paid the tab, then walked him out, so he could go on his way. I just ran into him when I got the final utilities in my name at city hall. It was good to catch up in person.

As I was walking back to my car, my phone buzzed in my pocket. I smiled like crazy the second I saw her name on the screen.

Lynn|: I have an idea

Me|: What kind of idea?

Lynn|: For our date!

I chuckled out loud, imagining her upbeat voice as I read that.

Me|: Let me hear it

Lynn|: I would rather it be a surprise!

She's so cute. She wanted it to be a surprise, but she still had to tell me she had an idea.

Me|: I can't wait!

Lynn|: Me neither. Lol. Be at my house on Friday at 6:30 with your swimsuit.

With my swimsuit? Does that mean she's going to be in a swimsuit? Oh, damn, I really can't wait.

***

Nick

"That's the last one," I said to Albert Milton, the assistant city manager. "My client will look over these and let you know by Friday, but we should be good to go."

"That's great to hear. My boss has been on our asses for the past year for this plot of land." He sat back and sighed in relief. "Now we can celebrate. Why don't you join our office for a drink tonight?"

"Not tonight. Thanks though. I'm going with my daughter to pick out furniture for her room in my new condo."

"Oh, you got it!" Albert Milton sat straighter in his chair. "What did the ex think? Was she touched?"

I sighed heavily, moving the documents back into my briefcase. "Not exactly."

"I'm sorry to hear that," he murmured.

"Yeah, me too." I stood up from my chair, feeling exhausted already. "I'll be in touch about the contract."

"Sure, sure. Have fun with your daughter, Nicholas. I hope things turn around with the ex-wife soon."

I nodded, exiting the meeting room. Damn, I'm glad Arlene didn't come with me to this meeting. She was supposed to, but another client for a different case came into the office before I left. She had to stay and manage that.

I still haven't told her I was moving out. I haven't told her much of anything. Things have been pretty icy between us. This morning in the office was the first time I had seen her since I left Friday night to spend the weekend with my kids. She didn't even look at me. She walked by my office multiple times, huffing loudly, wearing one of her shorter skirts and leaving her jacket behind. She was waiting for me to break the ice first, but I wasn't ready for that headache just yet.

If she had been with me when Albert Milton asked about the condo and Feighlynn, she would have lost it on me already.

She knows something is up. She had to. She is a clever woman who does not easily give up. This is going to hurt her pride and make it awkward for some time at the office.

Honestly, I'm not sure if I should say anything until I know I can get Feighlynn back. I have to tell her I'm moving, but I'm thinking I need to keep the reasons to myself and let us fizzle out naturally. Arlene will get bored with me eventually if things stay as they are. She might take the leap and dump me before I have to reveal all my regrets.

I opened my trunk and tossed my suitcase inside, trying not to look at the bags of gifts Preston returned to me. I never got the nerve to see Fay again to give them back. The disappointment I felt from my son was enough to keep me at bay for the weekend. I'm surprised Preston didn't return home after Friday night, but he stayed. The entire weekend. I was happy to have time with my son, but I knew he just stayed to monitor me. I can't blame him. He's just looking out for his mother, and after what I did to her, he doesn't trust me or understand my regret.

It kills me. It really does. I lost my wife and my son by asking for a divorce. When I asked him to come with me and Jessie to pick out furniture for his room at my new place, he muttered to just get him whatever and said he was going home.

I groaned out loud when I pulled into the parking garage at work. Arlene was standing near the elevators, obviously waiting for me. She had her back rim-rod straight and that sour look on her face. The second my car was in park, she started walking in her over-priced heels towards me.

I steeled myself, readying for the inevitable confrontation.

"How was the meeting?" she asked coldly as I closed my driver's side door.

"It went well. They signed the new terms with a few added clauses. I'll send them to the client now, and I expect positive feedback."

She nodded, like she expected that. I could tell she wasn't here out of concern for the meeting.

I popped my truck, reaching for my briefcase, then nearly jumped out of my skin when I heard her gasp loudly.

"Nick?!"

I looked around frantically. "What? What happened?"

"Is this your way of an apology?!"

I followed her line of sight, then my stomach dropped. She was staring at the bags of presents meant for Feighlynn. She reached for the light brown designer purse gift box, but I pushed it away before she could touch it.

"Sorry, but no. These are for.... For someone else."

Her eyes went wide, and her mouth gaped slightly. "Who?!"

'None of your fucking business' wasn't an appropriate response, given the circumstances, but it was on the tip of my tongue.

"Preston left them in my trunk. They are for his mother." It was close enough to the truth without being too incriminating for me.

"For your ex-wife?!" Arlene was still looking at me with disbelief. "You have presents for your ex-wife in your trunk?"

I narrowed my eyes at the irritating woman, slamming my trunk closed. "I have gifts for the mother of my children, yes. They're for her birthday."

"Don't you think that is inappropriate?"

"How so?" I challenged.

"She's your ex! Wouldn't that cross boundaries that don't need to be crossed?"

My anger was rising. It's really none of her business, and she has some nerve in trying to shame me for having gifts for my wife in my trunk.

"I'm not arguing with you about something that is none of your business. I told you the reason, and if you don't like it, that's your own problem."

She tapped her foot angrily as we waited for the elevator. The tension was so thick, but I would not be the one to break it.

We were in the elevator and almost up when she broke first. "Don't you think you're being disrespectful to me by keeping presents for your ex-wife in your car? Did that ever cross your mind?"

"No," I snapped. "That woman is the mother of my children and the one who *I* cheated on with *you*. "No," I snapped. "I think all the disrespect has been shown to her, and if I want to keep gifts in my car for the woman that gave me everything and I threw away like trash, I don't expect the reason for my disrespect to have a damn opinion on the issue."

I left her gaping in the elevator as I walked out, heading past the receptionist to my office. I'm tired, irritable from sleepless nights and not being able to drink heavily around my kids, and from the fear of my wife moving on with that tattooed hoodlum that just moved in across the street from her. Listening to my fucking mistress bitch about gifts I got my wife is not tolerable in my current state.

I may have to move out of Arlene's place sooner than I expected. I can't keep up this disillusion any longer.

***

Arlene

"That woman is the mother of my children and the one who *I* cheated on with *you*. I believe I have shown all the disrespect to her, and if I want to keep gifts in my car for the woman who gave me everything and whom I threw away like trash, I don't expect the reason for my disrespect to have a damn opinion on the issue."

The chill in the air was sucked into my lungs when he snapped at me. My blood ran cold. He said so much with that one statement. The woman that gave him everything was the one those gifts were for, and it's not me. He just told me I was the reason he lost her, too.

I can't cry. Not at work. I just stared in shock as Nick walked out of the elevator and towards his office. The receptionist stared after him, then looked at me curiously. I quickly got control of my face when she turned away from me, unable to meet my eyes. I don't know what my expression looked like, but it surely must be horrendous for her to look so nervous.

I stomped towards my office, ignoring Nick's as I strode past. Not that he would have noticed, anyway. I walked by him a dozen times today, and he never looked up at me once.

That bag alone would have had to be at least a few thousand dollars. Nick had several bags from stores just as expensive, too. His son doesn't have the money to buy Feighlynn gifts that are expensive. That means it was Nick who bought them. He couldn't even text me or call me the entire weekend, but he was out buying thousands of dollars' worth of presents for his ex-wife?

He has some fucking nerve. He's still living in my apartment. It's he who left her for me. I did not make him. He thinks I'm just going to accept this kind of treatment, allowing for him to still treat me like the other woman?

"Maybe I've been too passive," I murmured to myself as I sank down in my chair. I opened the top drawer of my desk, pulling out my old wedding band. I told myself after the disaster of my first marriage that I would never submit to a man again, and here I am, agonizing over a guy who hasn't done a damn thing for me in too damn long.

I think Nick needs an ultimatum. I will not be his weekday convenience as he goes off every weekend and continues to play house with his kids without me. I deserve respect, too.

CHAPTER NINE

Déjà Vu

Nick

"Daddy!" Jessie smiled excitedly as I pulled up to the curb of her school.

"Sorry I'm late," I cringed. Jessie was one of the last kids at parent pick up. I'm about thirty minutes late. I had a phone call with a client right before I left the office. One partner patched it over to me, so I couldn't ignore it, and it took me forever to reassure the client that their case was in the right hands.

"It's okay. My friend just left, so I was only by myself for a few minutes." My beautiful daughter was always so upbeat. I'm not sure if what she said is true, or if she is just trying to make me feel less guilty. She's like Fay in that way. She's too sweet for her own good sometimes.

"I'm still sorry, honey. Next time you can go home with your brother and I'll pick you up from there."

Jessie made a face. "It's okay, daddy. I don't mind the wait."

I studied her face for a few seconds. She looked guilty for some reason.

"What?" I stared in confusion.

She quirked her lips, making a face she learned from her mother when she's trying not to hurt someone's feelings. "Pres told us to call him when we finished shopping." That's all. He's going to come get me after his baseball practice."

"I was just going to drop you off, Jess. You don't have to call your brother."

"It's okay," she smiled stiffly. "Preston said-"

"Jessie," I stopped her. "Did Preston say something about me and your mom?"

She bit her lip, shrugging her shoulders. "It's nothing, daddy."

I sighed, feeling exhausted and more beat down than before. Preston is even getting his sister involved to keep me from Fay. I can't even blame him. I did this to myself.

"Okay, sweetie," I said, putting a smile on my face. "How does Starbucks sound first?"

I took Jessie to get her favorite lemonade drink and a pastry before we headed to the furniture store. She excitedly skipped around the displays, picking out a whitewashed canopy bed with matching furniture before helping me to pick out furniture for the rest of the condo. I liked the dark leather motorized couches and loveseats with charging ports and massage functions, but Jessie turned her nose up at them. She pointed out brighter colors, and I ended up getting what she preferred instead. Honestly, Fay had similar preferences to our daughter, and I was still hoping to share this condo with my wife.

The bedroom furniture for Preston's room was easy. I sent him a text of the first display I saw he might like, and he gave me a thumbs up emoji. It wasn't until I started picking out furniture for the master bedroom that I felt frantic. I took our old bedroom furniture during the divorce. Fay bought herself a new set and told me she was just going to give our old bed and dressers away. I had it taken to storage with the bulk of my belongings instead, and now I'm wondering if I should just use that instead of getting something new.

"What's the matter, daddy?" Jessie asked as I was running my finger over a paisley bedspread similar to the one Fay once had on our bed.

"Nothing, sweetheart. What do you think of this?"

She shrugged. "I like it, but Arlene doesn't like things that are girly or flowery. She might like the cheetah one instead. Or maybe just a dark color?"

I pressed my lips together, wondering for a few seconds if I should break it to Jessie that Arlene's opinion wouldn't matter.

Jessie skipped to a display of more masculine and dark printed bedding, shifting through the shelving until she found a deep forest snake skin pattern. "This one looks like her favorite dress."

"Oh, Jess," I shook my head. I know Arlene and Jessie are close, and I feel guilty for allowing that to happen, even though I've known for a while that Arlene and I wouldn't work out. I should tell her though, so she's not put in any awkward situations later. "Arlene won't be coming over to the new place."

"What do you mean?" She tilted her head to the side.

"It's just not working out, honey. I know you like her, but this move is going to be a new start for me. Away from Arlene."

"But," Jessie looked at the ground, her brain working to make sense of what I just said. "Did you two break up? Arlene still talks to me like you both are together."

I winced internally. "It's complicated. I'm planning on talking to her soon."

Jessie stared at me. Her eyes, which were so like her mother's, were swimming with some emotion that had me feeling on edge. "Is.... Is it because of mom?"

My eyes went wide for a second, and I hesitated. "What do you mean?"

She picked at the threading of a decorative pillow on the display in front of her. "Preston said something, and now I'm wondering if mom is why you don't want to be with Arlene."

"What did Preston say?"

She shrugged. "That you need to quit bugging mom."

That hurt. My son might be the biggest obstacle to getting my wife back, and he's an obstacle I'm not willing to fight. I want Fay back, but I love my son too much to keep driving the wedge deeper between us.

"It's an adult problem, Jess." I wrapped my arms around her shoulders. "Don't worry about any of that. Your mom and I can handle these issues ourselves."

"I know," Jessie sighed, hugging me back. She tilted up her face to smile sadly at me. "I want you and mom both to be happy. I thought you said Arlene would make you happy. I'm sad she couldn't."

I kissed her forehead, loving my sweet little girl. "I'm sorry too. I'm sorry I made such a huge mistake to begin with."

Jessie held my hand as we walked to the front of the store. I paid for all the purchases and arranged for them to be delivered at the end of the week. Jessie was quiet until we got out to the car. She just buckled in and looked out the window, seemingly deep in thought.

"What are you thinking about, sweetie?" I reached over and squeezed her hand.

She smiled and shrugged. "I'm just daydreaming, I guess."

"Are you daydreaming about what you want for dinner? I'm thinking burgers," I wiggled my eyebrows. Arlene hates food you eat with your hands, so burgers are a common meal when it's just me and Jessie.

"Sure," Jessie giggled, looking in a more upbeat mood.

After dinner, Jessie called her brother, but I insisted on taking her home. I told her I would just drop her off at the door and not go inside, so her brother wouldn't be upset. She agreed, but judging by the faces she made while looking at her phone for the few minutes after, I'm guessing Preston still didn't like that plan. I was going to have to talk to him soon.

"Thanks for dinner, daddy," Jessie said happily when I pulled up to the curb.

"No, thank you," I grinned. "You helped me a lot today."

"I know," she giggled. "Your apartment would have looked like a western spaceship if I didn't come."

"Hey. My taste isn't that bad."

"It kinda is," she laughed, making my father's heart happy. Her laughter died down, and she looked a little more serious as she leaned over and hugged me. "I love you, daddy, and I hope you can be happy with mom again soon."

With that, she grabbed her backpack and hurried to the door, waving at me with a glee-filled expression before going inside. I just sat there in stunned silence, my chest feeling like it was being squeezed tight.

I may not have my son's approval, but I think I just got my daughter's blessing.

As I pulled into the parking garage for Arlene's, my smile still hadn't faded from my face. I felt hope for the first time in a long time.

Arlene looked at me questioningly as I strode in through the front door. She was sitting in one of her leather wingbacks with a glass of red wine in her hands. She couldn't even temper my good mood.

Or so I thought.

I nodded at her perplexed expression, then walked back to the guest room to change out of my suit and ponder over what to do next. I felt like I was on a high. I wanted to use this energy for something productive before the inevitable gloom returned.

Arlene must have followed me back. She was looking at me with scrutiny while I hung up my jacket and undid my cuffs and tie.

"You seem to be in a good mood for once," Arlene said, leaning against the open doorway. She was watching my every movement with a sharp stare, probably still hung up on our tiff earlier this afternoon.

"I had an excellent dinner with my daughter," I offered blandly. My glee is already fading in her presence. She has that look like she wants to fight.

"I had takeout sushi and wine for dinner," she said snarkily, holding up her glass. "Thanks for asking."

"Don't start, Arlene," I huffed, throwing my tie down on the bed.

"No, you don't start. I'm tired of this, Nick. I'm tired of you treating me like I don't matter. I'm tired of you going off with your family during the day, a family you don't feel inclined to involve me with any longer, and then coming back to my place at night like some distant roommate."

I glared at her, heated with fury for so many reasons. "Are you telling me to quit spending time with my children?"

"What?!" She looked at me like I was the crazy one. "No! I'm saying that if we're partners, I want to be included. You used to include me. I don't know why you stopped, but I want to feel like I matter, too."

"I told you that Preston won't spend time with me here. I have no reason to make him either."

Hurt flashed in her eyes. "What about Jessie? Jessie and I were close."

I know they were. It was the only thing that had made me hesitate and caused me to doubt leaving sooner. But that was before my daughter told me she wanted me to be happy with her mom again.

"You're not her mom, Arlene. You keep trying to be, but you're not, and I'm not comfortable bringing her here with your misconceptions. It's not right."

Tears were spilling from her eyes now. She hurried to look away, dragging her acrylic nails across her face to drag the moisture away.

"I know I'm not her mother. I'm not trying to be. I just.... I just love that girl, too."

The guilt was creeping in, but I kept it from showing. "That changes nothing, Arlene."

Her eyes sharpened, staring at a single point at the ceiling while she willed away her tears. I could see the resentment building in her strict features from my words. She was once so vibrant, still youthful for someone so driven. Now, she looks older than I remember, worry lines looking like wrinkles in the soft light shadowing her face.

"Fine. If you don't care about me enough to include me in your daytime affairs, I shouldn't be at night."

My brows pulled down in confusion. "What are you saying?"

"I'm saying," she sniffed, wiping the last of her tears away, "if I'm not good enough to be included in your family, then you can't stay here any longer, Nick. I'm not just here for your convenience. Include me, or get out."

I closed my eyes, trying not to show my relief.

She said it first.

When I opened them, I felt a resolve settle in my chest. "Okay."

Her eyes widened. "Okay?"

"Okay," I said again, picking back up my tie from the bed. "I'll get out."

She sputtered, opening and closing her mouth several times like she didn't believe I had just agreed to leave so easily.

"I'll pack what I can for tonight and send for the rest." I moved past her, heading to the bedroom to get everything I could. Seconds later, she was in the room too, mouth gaping open and eyes wide.

I had most of my clothes in a suitcase and was pulling out a duffel bag when she found her voice.

"You're just going to leave? Really?"

"You told me to," I muttered, going through the drawers.

"It didn't have to be right now," she huffed. "You can, well, sleep on it or something."

"I'm not going to change, Arlene. You were right. I'm not being fair to you."

She looked at the ceiling as her eyes started to fill and glisten again. "Fine." With that, she left the room, going to sit in the living room to finish her wine as I finished gathering my belongings. I left my key on the kitchen counter on the way out. She didn't even look up at me. She just stared into the void blackness of the night over the city, her reflection clear in the plane window.

"I'm sorry," I murmured before walking out, closing the door behind me. As I got in the elevator and traveled down to the parking garage, a sense of déjà vu washed over me, but I was surprised at how easily I left the place I had lived for the past year.

Chapter Ten

Can't Wait

Feighlynn

"Y ou seem to be in a good mood, mama," Jessie said, coming down the stairs for breakfast.

"Am I?" I smiled to myself, arranging a couple of chicken breasts in a crock pot to slow cook.

"I could hear you singing *Don't Stop Believing* all the way from my bathroom."

"It's a catchy song," I said, then whistled the melody as it played through my head again. I was thinking about my date last weekend with Vin and the song was one we listened to. Now I can't get it out of my head, or keep the smile off my face.

Jessie grabbed her waffle I made for her from the counter, covering it in syrup before sitting at the bar to eat. I grinned at seeing the fresh roses from Velma's greenhouse on the counter beside her. Vin brought them over yesterday with a note saying how excited he was to see me tonight. I squeal with glee every time I read the note.

Jessie was watching me with curiosity as I seasoned the chicken before fastening on the lid. I am feeling hyperactive, but I don't know how to rein it in. I'm just so excited about tonight.

"I just love Fridays," I sighed. "Don't you?"

Jessie's little brows pulled down. "You never like Fridays, mom."

"Of course I do!" I twirled around and went to the fridge to pull out their lunches. "Why wouldn't I?"

"Because we're not here," she reminded me.

"Oh. Yeah," I smiled apologetically.

"What are you cooking for, anyway? Is Aunt Kate coming over tonight?"

"Hmm?" I busied myself with their lunches suddenly. I haven't told either of the kids about our new neighbor across the street yet. It felt premature for that. Preston might approve, but I didn't know how Jessie would react.

"The crock pot. Are you having a girl's night with Aunt Kate again?"

"Oh, that. Nope." I pressed my lips together and shook my head. "I'm just cooking my dinner tonight."

"Hmm," Jessie gave me an appraising glance, then looked at the flowers beside her. Before I knew it, she was pulling out the note stuck between the stems and reading the handwritten sprawl. I held my breath, nervous about her reaction, but then a slow smile spread across her pretty face. "Just cooking for yourself, huh?"

I shrugged, unable to confirm or deny. She read the note. There's no point in denying it, but I'm not ready to share who I'm seeing tonight with my sensitive little girl. She doesn't appear to disapprove though.

"What's going on?" Preston asked, coming into the kitchen. He has the added baggage of all his baseball gear. He moved up to varsity this week because of a senior's injury, and he has an away tournament this weekend. He's staying in a hotel with the team tonight, and I'll drive to watch him in the morning.

Jessie took the note and hurriedly hid it behind her back. "Nothing," she said, sounding all kinds of suspicious. I tried not to laugh. She's so cute.

Preston set his overflowing duffel bag and backpack on the ground, eyeing her.

"Here's your breakfast, sweetie," I said, kissing his cheek and handing him a plate of waffles and bacon with peanut butter on the side. He eats waffles like his dad does. Peanut butter and no syrup. "Are you nervous about this weekend?"

"Not really," he smiles slyly. "Are you nervous?"

"My little boy is spending the night with seniors." I pretended to pout. "Of course I am."

"I'm not that little anymore, mom," he laughed with a crooked smile. "Are you still coming in the morning?"

"Yes! I wouldn't miss it. I've got my giant print out of your face that I'm planning on waving around the whole time. I wouldn't miss it."

"Please don't," he groaned.

Jessie laughed at her brother's grim expression. I noticed she slid the note from the flowers under her bottom when Preston was distracted with me.

"I want to come," Jessie whined.

"Is your dad not going?" I looked at Preston. He had a guilty look on his face.

"I didn't tell him," Preston admitted.

"Pres," I looked at him disapprovingly.

"What?! He's busy moving this weekend. He won't have time to come."

"I'm sure he would make time," I argued.

"I'm sure I don't want him to," he grumbled.

I sighed, wondering if I should be the one to bring it up with Nick or not. I don't know if it will make things worse for their relationship if I do.

"Is Aunt Kate coming with you tomorrow?" Preston asked me, changing the subject.

"I'm not sure yet. I think she has plans already." Preston made a face, so I added, "Why?"

"It's a long way to drive, mom."

"I know," I nodded.

"You have to leave at five to make it there on time," Preston said, looking at me like I was missing something.

"I know. I'll listen to an audio book. Have some me time."

"Mom," he said levelly.

"What?!"

Jessie giggled at us. "You're not the best driver, mom. I think that's what Preston is trying to say."

"I am a perfectly safe driver!"

Preston scoffed. "Until that audio book of yours gets to a sad part. Or a hilarious part. You get distracted too easily, mom."

"Well, I'm not missing your game! Do you want me to fly down there instead?"

"No, but I don't want you driving by yourself."

I looked up at the ceiling and shook my head. In these ways, he is just like his father. Nick would get like Preston is now if I tried to do anything by myself that he considered dangerous. He used to get mad at me for silly stuff like keeping the windows open in the house all day while I was home alone.

"Mom, why don't you just ask someone else to go with you?" Jessie said, looking pointedly at the flowers. Preston was busy spooning peanut butter covered waffles in his mouth and missed it.

"Maybe," I bit my lip. Would it be weird for me to ask Vin to go with me?

"You should," Preston said with a mouth full of food. "I have to stay with the team anyway, so you should bring a friend and spend the night in the city or something tomorrow night." He smirked at me, "Someone who wouldn't mind doing all the driving."

"Watch it," I pointed a butter knife at him after cutting his turkey and cheese in half.

He held his hands up with a smirk, like he was surrendering.

I finish the kid's sandwiches for their lunches, then put them in the bag with the rest of their food before they finish eating. I kissed them both bye and went to follow them out like I always do before I walk Kevin.

As Preston was shoving his stuff in his trunk, and I was fastening Kevin's leash, Jessie leaned in to whisper to me, "I put your note back. I'm happy for you, mama."

My heart swells, and I'm truly touched. I didn't expect her to accept me dating again. She's so close to her dad that I feared she would reject the idea completely.

"Thank you, sweetie." I pulled her close and kissed her head, feeling like a weight was lifted off my shoulders.

She got in the car with Preston, and I waved them off as I walked down the driveway with Kevin. The curtains moved in a window across the street. Then a few seconds later, human Kevin was opening his garage, taking the trash to the curb as I slowly approached with a huge smile on my face.

"Oh, hey! Crazy running into you," he said with a sly grin. "What a coincidence."

"A coincidence, huh?" I giggled. Kevin jumped up for pets, and Vin was happy to give them. "What do you have planned today?"

"Well," he stretched his arms above his head, smoothly resting one around my shoulders, "I was thinking of going for a walk right now, then later I'm going to my sweet little neighbor's house in my swim trunks."

"In your swim trunks!" I feigned shock. "Whatever for?"

"Beats me," he smirked. "Apparently, it's a surprise."

"Maybe she's going to greet you with water guns at her door," I pressed my lips together, trying to hold back my laughter.

"My excitement level just rose," he laughed.

We walked our usual route, twice, laughing and joking together as we had been doing every morning and most evenings. I offered to go around the block a third time, but he had a meeting to get to this morning. I wanted to ask what the meeting was for, but held back. He seemed nervous about it, whatever it was, so I just wished him luck and told him I would see him tonight.

He squeezed my hand, then kissed my fingers before letting me and Kevin head back in. It made me think of his kiss a week ago, and my face grew hot as I hurried into the garage. I shut the overhead door before I self combusted right in front of where he stood in the street, watching me with that handsome half-smirk.

It's become a bit frustrating. Really frustrating. I've thought about that kiss much more than I probably should. Maybe tonight, just maybe, he will take mercy on me and kiss more than my hand again.

***

Vin

I watched my pretty little neighbor with her blushing cheeks and those swinging hips in her fitted leggings walk double time to her garage. I need to quit teasing her, but her reactions are so fucking cute.

Today was going to be so long. I knew it, because I was so looking forward to tonight.

I have that meeting to get to, though. I talked to Milton again and decided I wanted to at least talk to his boss about the security manager's position. I wasn't sure I wanted to go back to work, especially this soon, but when Milton told me the annual salary for the position, I couldn't help but think of what might be in store for the future, and how that salary could make it a lot brighter for me and whoever was in it.

To be honest, the more time I spent with Feighlynn, the more I wanted to do something that would give me more to offer her. I'm not at the age to waste my time casually dating, and I'm liking her more and more the more we interact. Everything about her drives me crazy in all the good ways. I crave her time, and it's unlike anything I have ever felt for anyone before.

I had a quick breakfast with my mom. She seemed to be having a good day so far today, and was cooking me bacon and eggs when I came inside.

I put on navy pants with a white shirt and brown dress shoes with a matching brown belt. Nothing too over the top, but professional enough. As I drove to the office, I just thought about Feighlynn, which had me in a smug and smiling mood when I got to city hall. If I could attract the attention of a woman like her, this meeting would be a walk in the park. That's the Feighlynn effect. She makes me feel like a real action hero. Her action hero.

When I asked the receptionist which floor the city manager's office was, she gave me a flirty grin, but it had nothing on Feighlynn's smile. It didn't affect me at all. I found that no woman could compare to my little neighbor. She was definitely one of a kind, with her positivity and all her happy little quirks.

Damn, I already miss her. Tonight can't come soon enough.

On the elevator ride up to the sixth floor, I pulled out my phone and sent her a text telling her I missed her smile already. About ten seconds later, I got a text back of a goofy picture with her and Kevin. She was sticking out her tongue with her eyes crossed, and had her fingers pried in her dog's mouth, forcing him to smile. Even being silly like that, she was beautiful. That's what I texted back. Just a one word response: beautiful. She sent me an emoji with a smiley face and a heart all around it. So fucking adorable.

I took a second to admire her dimpled chin and the way her hair hung over her shoulders. I bet her hair smells amazing. I'm going to see if I can get a whiff of it tonight. I just want to bury my face in it, and hold her tight enough to make her squeak. I bet she would let me. I am sure if I asked to hold her, even for a second, she would be all for it. Her cheeks would get all flushed, and she would avert her gaze in that shy way she does, but that eager little smile would still be on her perfect lips.

Shit, I can't wait for tonight. I wonder what she has planned for us, that I need to wear swim shorts. Should I *just* wear swim shorts, or should I bring them and change into them when needed? I should stop by the store on the way home and get a couple of water guns, too, just in case. I know she would get a kick out of it if I did. I'd buy many things to hear her laugh or see that smile on her face.

When I got to the right floor, I saw Milton almost right away. He was walking out of a room that was labeled as a conference room with a tall, well-dressed woman. She had on bright lipstick and painted fake nails to match. Milton looked a little uncomfortable with her, but if she noticed, it didn't show. She was grinning in that sly way some women do when they think they're desirable. She might be to some people, but Milton has tastes similar to mine. Some overly confident corporate woman would not impress him.

"My apologies again that my colleague couldn't be here. I'll pass along the revisions, and he can call you on Monday." She pressed towards him a bit. "Or maybe we could discuss all of it over lunch?"

Milton's face remained passive until he caught sight of me, and then he looked relieved. "Just have Nicholas call Monday. I'm sure we can do the final paperwork by email." He dismissed her and her face subtly fell. Not like she was disappointed, but just tired. It made me pity her a bit. "My next appointment is here. My secretary can show you the way out."

The woman looked at me appraisingly, her mask of confidence returning. "I know the way." She offered that sly smile to me, but I just nodded in return, my face remaining passive. "Thank you again, Mr. Milton."

"Yep," Milton let the professional facade drop, then sighed with relief when she got in the elevator to leave.

"Rough morning?" I raised an eyebrow at him.

"Tense," he groaned. "I've worked with that woman for months now on this deal, and today was the first time I saw her without her partner. No wonder he's tired of the chick. She's exhausting."

"Was she trying to jump your bones?" I laughed as he led me back into that same conference room.

"I don't know what the woman was trying to do. I wouldn't be surprised, though. She's got a reputation." He looked around like he was seeing if anyone was around to listen. "She goes after married men. A buddy of mine ended his happy marriage over her and is living in hell because of it." He shook his head sadly. "Poor chump."

"Sounds like he did it to himself," I scoffed.

Milton frowned. "Yeah. I know how you feel about cheaters, but I still feel bad for the guy. His ex was great."

I shrugged. "He shouldn't have cheated, then."

"Yeah, yeah. I know," he said dismissively. "Let me get my boss and we can start this meeting. I think you two will hit it off," Milton chuckled. "He's no nonsense like you."

CHAPTER ELEVEN

Drugs

Feighlynn

I t was almost time! I had the chicken enchiladas in the oven, keeping warm, freshly made salsa in a bowl ready to bring outside, along with a bag of tortilla chips from the Mexican restaurant I like. I was standing in my kitchen, wearing my bathing suit and a dress cover up while smashing avocados for guacamole when Kevin's barking started. I was startled, then bounced on my heels in excitement.

I could see my dog pacing at the window, going nuts like he does when someone is getting close to the house. I knew any second now, Vin would knock on my door. I squealed, having waited all day for this. I couldn't find water guns anywhere, but I found something just as good. I ran on my tiptoes when I heard the knock, grabbing the Nerf gun I found in Preston's old toy box where I left it on the counter.

I threw open the door excitedly, taking maybe half a second to appreciate Vin in his snug shirt and board shorts. When Vin saw the bright blue gun in my hands, that crooked smile lifted his face, and he let out a deep, throaty laugh as I shot him in the chest.

"Ah, you got me," he clutched his chest in laughter. Kevin got excited about my gimmick and tried to tackle Vin to the ground in a playful attempt to help me, and Vin went along with it, going down on one knee and letting Kevin attack his face with wet kisses.

"Not fair," I murmured. Seeing Kevin kiss Vin made me a little jealous, but it was still cute. Kevin kisses me all day, so in a way, it was like an indirect kiss.

Vin was still laughing as she stood back up and pushed Kevin fully in the house to close the door. "I don't feel so childish about bringing these," he said, lifting a shopping bag with two big water guns inside.

I burst into a fit of giggles. "Great minds think alike."

"That, and you warned me," he said, coming up next to me to give me a sideways hug, kissing the top of my head. "You're so adorable. You know that, right?"

My cheeks flamed at the compliment. "I got it from my mama," I said jokingly.

"I bet your daughter gets it from you," he said lightheartedly.

"She does!" I boasted, laughing as we walked further into the house. "Speaking of Jessie, she saw your flowers and card this morning."

"Uh, oh." Vin looked at the flowers on the breakfast bar with a guilty expression. "How did that go? I know you said you haven't talked to your kids about, um, *this* yet." He pointed between me and him.

This. I enjoyed thinking about us as a *this.* I enjoyed thinking about Vin all together.

I smirked, feeling pride in myself and my daughter for our exchange this morning. "She actually took it really well. She said she was happy for me."

"Good. I know you mentioned she was still really close to her dad. Divorce and parents dating again has to be hard on a kid."

"Yeah, that's why I was holding back from telling them. But Jessie likes Nick's girlfriend, so I guess I shouldn't be surprised."

"She sounds extra sweet," Vin leaned against the counter, "just like her mama."

"Adorable and sweet," I chuckled. "I must have good genes."

Vin gave me that look, the one that had me biting my lip as my face grew hot. He pushed himself off the counter, walking over to me. I craned my neck to stare up at his face, which suddenly grew serious.

"Can I get something out of the way?" he asked in a raspy whisper. "Something I've been wanting to do all week?"

"W-what?" I blinked as his face got closer to mine. His intentions were clear, his eyes lingering on my lips. I don't know what came over me. It might have been nerves or just my inability to keep my rabid thoughts to myself. "Oh, gosh, did I brush my teeth?" I whispered frantically.

Vin froze, and then just burst into laughter, buckling over and gripping the counter with one hand to support himself. His other hand was clutching his stomach.

My face flamed more than ever before. I covered it with my hands, mortified that I said that out loud. "I'm sorry!" My voice came out muffled through my fingers. "I didn't mean to say that out loud."

"Oh, man," Vin stood up and wiped a thick finger under his eye, wiping some moisture away. "You are so fucking cute."

"I'm an idiot," I groaned, peeking at him through my fingers. "I have no brain to mouth filter."

"That's not a bad thing," he smirked, taking my hands and pulling them away from my face. "I like your no-filter, stinky mouth."

"Does my breath really stink?" I groaned.

"I don't know. Let me check." He gingerly placed his lips on mine, and despite my best efforts to hold my breath, I ended up melting into the sweet feeling of the moment, whimpering softly. I don't know about my breath, but he tasted like mint. Sweet mint. Like the sweetest mint in the world.

"So sweet," I gasped when he released my lips, resting his head on mine. The filter was still missing inside me, it seems.

He smiled and said, "Thanks. You taste like chicken."

"Do I?!" I sampled a lot of the chicken as I was cutting it up. Darn it, I wish I had remembered to brush my teeth.

"I love chicken." His deep laughter fanned my mortification, until he leaned in and kissed me again, this time deeper than before. His tongue pushed between my lips, and I moaned, no longer caring what I tasted like, as his sweet mint flavor overpowered all my senses. I leaned into him, gripping his shirt with both hands. His large hand encompassed the back of my head, holding me to him, commanding more.

My knees were weak by the time he pulled away, his green eyes swimming with smug affection. His face, his scent, his body, and the way his large body was holding mine did nothing to help my inability to think or filter my words.

"Wow. Just like an action hero," I murmured.

He chuckled. "Your action hero."

I mewled, and he laughed even deeper. Those green eyes of his glinted, watching me intently. His hand on the small of my back rubbed rhythmic circles that tingled up my spine. My swim bottoms were getting uncomfortable under my dress. If he kept this up, I was going to have to change into a new swimsuit *before* we got in the pool.

"Speaking of action heroes," I mumbled, trying to avert my gaze so I could think straight again. It wasn't working out for me very well. "I, uh, set up our date in the backyard."

"The backyard?" He leaned up and looked out the kitchen window.

I bit my bottom lip, nodding. He couldn't see the pool or the projector screen I had set up beside it. I was thrilled to show him the plans I had been working on all week. "Help me carry out the food and I'll show you."

Vin laughed excitedly when the pool came into view. He set down the pan of enchiladas on the hot pads I had arranged in the center of the outdoor table and walked over to the projector. The first DVD box sitting beside it on the little table was none other than *Riddick*. I have the older movies from the series in a pile beneath it.

My in-ground pool had a kiddy pool floating around on top of the water. I had the outdoor pillows and a few blankets from the couch set off to the side, along with a pile of swim towels. The pool lights were glowing beneath the surface, and the waterfall was turned on, making the babbling sounds of water waft through the chilly night air. The pool was heated, and I even turned on the hot tub earlier today, so it was steaming, almost glowing with the fluorescent lights below.

"Of course it's *Riddick*," Vin said, lifting the first DVD box and waving it towards me. "This is awesome. Seriously."

"Thanks," I said giddily. "I saw it on a video and thought it looked fun."

When we finished bringing all the food out, I felt the cold in the air. My teeth were on the verge of chattering, so I went to turn on the gas heater.

"Righty tighty, lefty loosey," I muttered to myself, trying to remember the right way to turn on the gas. I'm usually not the one that does it. Nick never trusted me with gas or matches, or fire, and that rubbed off on Preston. Preston usually turns the outdoor heaters on for me now.

"Need some help?" Vin asked, squatting down next to me.

"I can get it," I grunted, turning it too hard in the wrong direction for the fourth time while trying to push the ignitor button at the same time. "Maybe. Why won't it light?"

"Hold down the gas valve after opening the tank." Vin leaned in to show me the correct button. I pressed the button, and Vin leaned over me to turn the tank valve the right way, and I smiled sheepishly. I pushed the ignitor button again, and when I released the other button that Vin showed me out of frustration, he reached out to hold my finger in place for a few more seconds. Finally, the heater came to life. "Keep holding it for thirty more seconds or it will kill the flame."

I did as he said, feeling accomplished for almost doing it on my own. No one else has ever shown me how to do it before.

"I did it!" I cheered, hopping on my feet.

Vin watched with amusement. "You did. Good job." He had that look in his eyes again. The one that makes me blush and want to squirm.

My dancing died down, and I averted my gaze shyly. Being praised by such a big man while he looks at me like that isn't helping my swimsuit bottoms situation.

After serving both of us a generous helping of enchiladas, I started the movie to play as we ate. However, neither one of us was very invested in watching it though. We talked as we ate, missing most of the first half of the movie.

"Damn, I want more," Vin said, rubbing his belly after his second helping. "What do you season your food with? Crack? I can't ever get enough."

"Yep. It's labeled "oregano" in my spice cabinet," I giggled.

"Wrong drug," Vin smirked.

"Oh," I shrugged. "I wouldn't know. I've never used them."

"Except in your food?"

"Well, yeah," I bit back a laugh.

Vin looked at me that way again, murmuring, "Adorable." I didn't know how being unfamiliar with drugs made me adorable, but I was growing addicted to that appraising stare of his.

I bashfully looked at the mounted white screen at the back of the pool, then back at him. "Before you get any more full on my drug-laced enchiladas, do you want to go for a swim?"

He looked at the pool and the makeshift raft floating around in it. There was still plenty of room to swim. He looked at me from the corner of his eyes, smirking, then asked, "Wanna have a water gun fight?"

"Uh, yes!" I squealed, squirming in my seat.

He chuckled. "Be right back. Gotta go get them."

On his way back inside, he pulled off his shirt, so he was only in his swim trunks, hanging low on his waist. My mouth dropped to the concrete ground. I knew he was fit, but didn't know to what extent.

"Wow," I accidentally whispered loudly as I got up to jump in the pool before he got back. My swim bottoms felt ruined, and I needed to get them back before he got back. Stupid Kate. If she hadn't waxed me down there, it might now be this sensitive.

I heard his deep laughter as he went inside and knew he heard me.

Well, he now knows I have no filter. He's not running for the hills yet.

I tugged off my dress, tossing it on a chair before I jumped in the warm water. Hopefully, this hides all the evidence of what he's done to me this evening.

CHAPTER TWELVE

She's Mine

Vin

"Oh, fuck me."

I looked back right before I turned out of view when I heard her little "wow" slip out again. She was pulling off her dress, revealing her bikini underneath. Now I'm leaning over her kitchen counter, trying to get in the headspace to not embarrass the crap out of myself when I go back out.

How the hell can a woman that has had two kids still look that hot? She is so tiny, but thick in all the right places. I wasn't expecting the curves she had.

I heard a little yelp, then her dog started barking. I rushed outside with the water guns in hand, thinking maybe she had hurt herself. Military training ingrained in me, I had one of the fucking water guns ready in my grip like I was running into a hostile territory. Instead of a crisis, I found Feighlynn in the pool, splashing Kevin and trying to get him to jump in.

"Come on, Kevin! Come on, boy!"

Seeing her expression brought a smile to my face. She's so adorable. Hot, especially in that swimsuit, but adorable in everything she does.

"You got in without me?" I held my hand over my bare chest, pretending to be offended.

Her eyes traveled down the front of me. I tensed my body, trying to flex without making it obvious. She made me feel ten feet tall when she looked at me like that, and she does it a lot.

"I was testing it out, making sure it was nice and warm."

"It looks warm." I crouched down by the steaming water. Kevin pushed against my side, still riled up. I rubbed between his wet ears.

"It is." Lynn gave me a coy smile. "Wanna get in?"

She didn't give me a chance to answer, grabbing my arm and pulling me forward. I landed in the water with a hard crash, going under for a second before emerging again with a gasp.

"Oops," she giggled, swimming away as I was pushing the water out of my face. "I got one Kevin in the water."

"Oh, you're going to get it now."

I couldn't wipe the smile off my face as I dove under and swam right for her legs as she squealed, trying in vain to run away. I caught her waist and lifted as I came up, then tossed her lightly a few feet away. She screamed and squealed, still looking beautiful when she came back up.

When I went for her again, she wrapped her legs around my waist to prevent me from tossing her again. We wrestled and splashed one another until she gleefully got free and swam for the side of the pool where I'd dropped the water guns.

"Dibs on the blue one!" She took the water gun and swam quickly to the other side of the floating kiddy pool to open it and fill it up.

"Orange is my favorite color," I chuckled, picking up the other water gun and doing the same. "I've got to warn you," I took a careful step around the kiddy pool as I filled the water reservoir, "I'm a highly trained killing machine and an excellent-"

"Take that!" She pushed the pool out of the way, hitting me right in the face with her stream of water. Before I could shoot her, she ducked under the water and swam away. I stood stunned for about half a second, then took off after her, catching one of her feet underwater as she swam furiously to get away.

She was so fucking cute. We took shot after shot at each other, like little kids, with no actual goal in mind. We were playing like I have never done before in my adult life. After some time, we were both winded, panting as she clung to my back, trying to force me under the water again. I went along with her one more time, pulling her over my shoulder at the last minute so she fell into the water too, then pulled her close as I brought us both back up.

"You win," I laughed, smiling as she wrapped her legs around my waist.

My hands were on her hips, and she was clinging to my neck. It only took us a few seconds of sputtering laughter to realize the position I had put us in. Her wet cheeks colored over with her familiar blush. Her eyes kept glancing at my chest as her fingers played with the buzzed hair on the back of my neck.

Taking a chance, I slid my hands to her lower back, barely grazing the top of her soft, full ass. She gasped so softly, but I felt it in my chest. There was this growing tension between us, and my control was on the cusp of snapping. I moved us back to the steps of the pool, sitting on the middle one so she was rattling my waist in the water.

Lynn averted her gaze to the side as the credits rolled on the white screen. The music was filtering through the speakers, adding to the mood of the moment. "We.... we didn't watch any of the movie," she told me softly.

"Next time," I husked, then leaned in, capturing her pouty lips. She still faintly tasted like chicken, but now she tasted like cool water, beer and just her sweet natural flavor. I loved it. She could taste like fucking bleu cheese and sauerkraut and I would still love the way she tastes.

She groaned in the sweetest way, leaning into me and holding my face to hers. This was the deepest kiss we have shared yet. The kind that seeps into your bones and you feel deep in your soul. I couldn't get enough of her. As her tongue moved with mine, I let out a hungry growl as all my rationale snapped. My hands squeezed her ass, which felt so perfect in my grip. All of her felt amazing, and the warm pool water with her wearing nothing but a bikini didn't help my control any.

I wanted her. All of her. I knew at that moment that Feighlynn was mine. Someone else may have been fool enough to let her go, but I never could. I could let no one else touch this perfect woman in my hands. I wanted to be the one she had water gun fights and movie nights with for the rest of our lives. I wanted to taste every flavor of all her cooking on her soft lips, and be the reason for every one of her adorable giggles.

Feighlynn was mine. Nothing was going to change that.

***

Nick

"Sign here, sir." The last of my belongings was being carried into my new condo, Jessie helping by directing the movers to the right room as I signed the delivery papers.

"Here's something extra for your help." I handed the lead a couple of folded hundreds. Using the service elevator looked like a pain in the ass, but the movers got everything up without breaking a thing.

"Thanks!" He held it up gratefully with a nod. "Enjoy your new home!"

My new home. I looked around the apartment, messy with boxes and disarrayed furniture. I thought this place would feel more like a home once I got all my belongings from storage moved in, but it still feels like something is missing. It doesn't really feel like a home just yet.

If I am being honest with myself, I haven't felt like I was home since the day I left Fay. I tried. I tried to fake it with Arlene as long as I could, but her apartment was too pristine and too cold to feel like an actual home.

A new condo filled with new furniture and packed boxes doesn't feel like home either. Maybe when I get everything unpacked and put in place, it will, but deep down, I know what's missing.

Fay.

Feighlynn warmed up any space just by being in it. She could turn any dark, dreary place in my life into something exciting and lovely.

Why didn't I see that before I left her? Why didn't I recognize how blessed I really was?

"We got a lot of work to do, daddy," Jessie said, putting her hands on her hips and looking around at the place.

"Yes, we do," I smiled fondly at my little girl. "First, wanna order some pizza?"

She squealed excitedly, and my heart panged, seeing so much of her mother in her. Fay would dance for the food she loved, too. She would dance and sing for just about anything that made her happy. I had seen little of that the last year of our marriage, and I know that was mostly my fault. I'm glad I can at least see those sides of the woman I still love in our daughter.

Jessie helped by making beds while I unloaded kitchen boxes to find cutlery and plates while we waited for the pizza. I didn't find plates, but I found an old box full of the plastic cups and cheap forks and spoons Fay and I used when we first got married. It brought back so many memories of the struggles we first faced in our marriage, being two broke college kids, that I felt a heat behind my eyes as I stared into the messy box.

When we first got married, it was the most stressful time of my schooling career. I was studying for the bar exam, and she was heavily pregnant with Preston. I was getting a stipend for student loans and working part-time too. Fay stubbornly said she was staying in school and also found part-time work at the child-care center until I finished my exams and started working full time. She always refused to be just a stay at home wife and mother, but changed her career path to one she could do from home.

She always improved my life, not letting her work interfere with keeping up with the house or the kids. I remember being in awe of her during our first years married. It became such a common occurrence for her to be the wonderful wife and mother that she was, that I stopped valuing her as much.

I was such a complete moron. That woman stuck with me when I could only offer her thrift store cups and silverware. Most women wouldn't do that. I can't think of a single other woman that would go through the struggles we went through together with a smile on their face and the same positive, bright personality that she always had.

Going through all these old boxes will be excruciatingly hard. All the memories that come with them are weighing on me like a ton of bricks. The guilt of my bad choices keeps hitting me in fresh waves.

Most of these boxes from storage were things Feighlynn boxed up to get rid of during the divorce. I took them when I took our old bedroom furniture and all the furniture from my office. She didn't want to keep anything with any memories of me. That realization is the heaviest weight of them all.

"Pizza's here!" Jessie skipped out of her bedroom when the doorman buzzed.

With a pizza box in hand, and a bag of drinks and cheesecake on my arm, I looked at the new dining room table in dismay. The new dining room table was cluttered with small moving boxes full of books that I needed to go through and organize.

"Let's just have a picnic, daddy!" Jessie called, pushing boxes out of the way to clear up a large space in the living room.

That's what we did. Jessie brightened up my mood with her little laughter and smiles as we sat on the floor and ate pizza right out of the box. She was telling me about her upcoming dance recital and about the upcoming trip to Disneyland with her team. Her mother was going to be the one to take her to that, but I'm wondering if she would mind if I tagged along. Originally, I was going to stay back to work, but I know I can get the time off if I ask. Preston might not like it, but I don't want to miss my daughter's parade appearance, or the chance to feel like a family again.

"Oh, and did mom ask you about tomorrow yet?"

I looked at my daughter in confusion until she continued on.

"About Preston's tournament in San Antonio! Mom said she was going to ask you to drive her."

"Me?!" I gaped. "Your mom wants me to drive her to San Antonio tomorrow?" This is the first I am hearing about any of this. Fay hasn't talked to me at all this week. Not about anything but the kids.

"Yeah. Did Preston say no? I know you two are fighting a lot, but even he said he didn't want Mom driving herself. You know how mom is. She'll see a squirrel and turn the car off the road while saying how cute it is."

I cringed, knowing full well what Jessie meant. It is not safe to keep Feighlynn, who has too much energy, cooped up in a car for so long. "Preston didn't tell me about any tournament," I said solemnly. "What's it for?"

"It's for seniors on the varsity team, but there was an injury, so they moved Pres up. He is going with the team today and mom was supposed to leave in the morning to watch."

"I have heard nothing about it," I mumbled. I didn't want to spoil her mood, but I was feeling left out and deeply saddened that my son didn't tell me about something so important himself. He just texted me he had something come up and was spending the weekend with his friends. Nothing else.

Jessie lifted one shoulder in a half shrug, getting another slice of pizza. "Maybe mom was planning on telling you tonight. She looked excited about it."

"Are you sure you're not mistaken?" I really have no recollection about anything this could pertain to. I didn't have plans to meet Fay tonight.

Unless.... No. She wouldn't have changed her mind about the condo, even though she knows I was moving into it today. I invited her, but she turned me down.

"No!" Jessie said with her mouth full. She swallowed and continued. "I even told mom I was happy for her. She didn't deny it. When I suggested you drive her tomorrow, she even smiled and said, maybe."

Hope bloomed in my chest. If Jessie asked her mother directly, then maybe there was still a chance for me. Fay isn't one to put on airs, and she sure as hell wouldn't lie to our daughter or mess with her feelings. She can get shy in matters such as these, and she hates asking for favors. Maybe.... Just maybe.....

"Preston was okay with me driving her?"

"I don't know if he was okay with it being you, but he agreed she should ask someone else to drive. He even told her to get a hotel room and stay for the night."

"Really?" I dropped the pizza back in the box, my mind reeling with this revelation. "Should.... Should I call her and ask *her*, since she mentioned nothing to me?"

"I would," Jessie giggled. "No, no!" She waved her hands around frantically. "You should go ask her in person! Didn't you want to see her tonight too?"

"I am always eager to see your mother," I said honestly.

"Then go!"

"Well, what about you? It's our first night in the new place."

She waved her hand at me. It was another gesture like her mother's that brought a smile to my face. "I can stay home by myself, dad. I got a pizza, cheesecake, and a room to set up. I'll be fine."

The building had security and a doorman. She's older than Preston was when we started letting him stay home alone. "You won't leave the apartment?"

"Nope! I'll be waiting right here for the good news when you get back."

I chuckled, reaching over to ruffle her hair before standing up. I needed to get cleaned up if I was going to see Fay. I'm wearing athletic shorts and an old college shirt for pete's sake.

My phone rang when I was getting on nicer slacks and a sweater. I pulled the knit fabric over my head quickly and checked the caller ID. It was Arlene, who I haven't heard from outside of the office since we broke up. I sent her to voicemail, then finished getting ready. I would not let that woman or anything else ruin this chance for me.

If there was any possibility that Feighlynn could be mine again, I was going to take it. Nothing could deter me.

"I'll be right back, sweetie. Please, stay in the apartment and call me if you get scared. I'll come right back."

"I'll be fine," Jessie said from the couch, finishing both cheesecakes. "Go!"

The whole drive to Feighlynn's house, I felt like I was having an out-of-body experience. I have dreamed and longed for a chance to make things right again with my wife, and there was this building anxiety in me at the chance of it coming true. Having a weekend away with her to watch our son play baseball, then having the night to ourselves to reconnect is more of an opportunity than I ever expected to have this fast. I thought it would be a long battle to get back in Fay's good graces. This felt like a miracle.

When I pulled up to her house, I was relieved to see that her neighbor across the street had his ancient, tacky car parked in his driveway. Part of me suspected she would spend her Friday night free of the kids with him again, but the lights were on in his living room, and so were the lights in Fay's house. Maybe it wasn't anything serious after all.

It still makes me want to empty my stomach to think about how a barbaric man kissed her last week. It's a haunting thought I try to dispel whenever it creeps in.

I knocked on the door, but got no response. Her loud dog didn't even bark behind it like he normally would. I looked in the window, concerned. Did she go somewhere and leave all the lights on? It wouldn't be the first time.

After pulling out my phone to call her, I suddenly heard her dog barking from the backyard. Listening carefully, I heard more sounds. Music and maybe even the trickling sounds of the pool's waterfall.

Is she going for a night swim?

Opening the gate to the backyard, I carefully made my way through the shrubbery to the patio by the back door. The music was growing louder, sounding like a soundtrack to some movie. My heartbeat quickened when I heard her dog bark again, followed by the joyous sound of her laughter.

Then, my heart stopped completely.

Following that laughter was a deep moan, and something like a growling grunt. Fay squealed and giggled again, then her whimpering moans followed.

No....

There was no way.

I looked around the tall bushes blocking the pool from view, and that's when I saw them. My wife straddled that thug covered in tattoos from across the street on the steps of the pool. He was nuzzling and kissing her neck, and she was holding him close, her eyes close softly with a smile on her face.

"You're going to leave a mark!" Fay squealed, but made no moves to stop him.

"Good," he said darkly.

"Not good! I have to see other parents tomorrow at Preston's game."

"Since I'm going with you, I don't see the problem."

My stomach just dropped.

Chapter Thirteen

Pissing Contest

Feighlynn

A few minutes earlier....

"Damn, I could kiss you all night," Vin groaned, running his lips from my chin, down my neck to the hollow of my throat. "I want to kiss you all night." He stared up at me, like he was asking for permission. Permission to continue kissing me, or permission for more, I wasn't sure, but I knew I wanted both.

I wanted both, especially the *more*, since Kate waxed my kitty last weekend, but I have tomorrow morning to worry about too.

"I should probably get some sleep tonight," I whispered. "I, uh, I have to go to a game for Preston tomorrow, and it's kinda a long drive."

"Oh?" Vin pulled away, putting on a mask of restraint, though his eyes kept wandering to my lips. "Yeah. Yeah," he looked like he was trying to clear his thoughts. "I, uh, should probably let you get to bed soon then, huh?"

"Well," I bit my lip nervously, still holding tight to his neck so he wouldn't make any moves to go. "What are you doing tomorrow?"

A slow grin lifted his kiss-swollen lips. "I have no plans. Why?"

"Then......," I looked down nervously, "do you, um, maybe want to go on a small road trip with me?"

His deep chuckles vibrated between us, and my breath caught in my throat from the look on his handsome face. He looked like I had just made all his dreams come true. "I would absolutely love to go on a road trip with you." He leaned in towards me, a playful glint in his green eyes. He made me squeal as he bit my shoulder and squeezed my side at the same time. It tickled, but felt so good.

"It's to San Antonio," I said, after laughing and squirming away. "We.... we might need to stay overnight."

"Even better," he growled, burying his face in my neck. "I thought you were about to send me home."

"No!" I giggled. "I'm just trying to bribe you for a free ride."

"Oh yeah," he laughed darkly, then tickled my sides again, making me buck and squirm wildly as I laughed. Then, his movements became more smooth and sensual. My center pressed firmly against him in a way that made me feel ticklish on the inside, too. "Fuck, you are so damn cute. So freaking adorable." He grabbed my face in his large hands. "I really like you, Feighlynn."

My face grew warm from his intense gaze. "I really like you too." A nervous laugh left me, and it moved my body just enough to build the friction between us. He moaned deeply as I gasped.

"And I fucking love when you laugh," he husked, before tickling my sides one more time. I bucked and squealed, but then his hands wandered to my butt and I let out a lusty moan instead.

I bit back my smile, glad that Vin didn't find it weird when I asked him what he was doing tomorrow and if he was up for a brief road trip. I was nervous about asking all night, and almost didn't, but then when he started kissing me and caressing my body, I just didn't want this date to end.

As his lips traveled over my neck, nibbling and sucking on my skin, I felt desired, like never had before. This was something carnal, and I don't know if I had ever felt this way with anyone. Not even with Nick.

Vin sucked harder on my neck, his tongue messaging my skin taunt in his mouth. He was sucking with a purpose. "You're going to leave a mark!"

"Good," he grunted.

"Not good," I laughed softly, enjoying the way his tongue and lips felt on my skin. My eyes closed, absorbing every sensation. "I have to see other parents tomorrow at Preston's game."

"Since I'm going with you, I don't see the problem." His deep, rough voice was like a blanket falling over me, wrapping me in this warm feeling.

Oh, whatever. I have makeup if I need to cover any marks in the morning. The only problem I could really think of was Preston, since he is a bit overprotective and this will be my first time revealing that I'm dating our new neighbor from across the street. The one he thought was robbing poor Miss Velma.

I am dating Vin, right? This feels too great, too deep to be something casual. It's not just casual for me, or a passing thing. I really like

Vin. I like everything about him. I have never, ever felt this way before, and I want to take steps towards a relationship.

Hopefully, he does too.

Suddenly, Kevin barked excitedly several yards away. It wasn't his playful bark, but his loud bark for when someone is at the door, or when he sees a cat.

I opened my eyes and looked up, then gasped when I saw what had my dog's attention. Kevin was barking and jumping up on the last person I wanted to see tonight. "Nick?!"

Vin turned quickly, holding my hips in place to keep me on top of him as he peered back at my ex-husband. "Are you fucking serious?" he muttered under his breath, and I suddenly felt so sorry once again.

Why the heck does Nick keep showing up at the worst of times? I haven't seen or heard much from him all week, but he just shows up when I'm on a date with Vin again?

"What are you doing here?"What are you doing here?" I asked, my voice sounding a lot more unfriendly than usual because of my irritation.

Nick's expression went hard for a second, glaring at Vin while muttering curses at my dog for jumping, but then his expression softened when he looked back at me. His eyes roamed my body and the lack of space between me and Vin. I saw so many emotions pass over his face in a few seconds. It was unnerving.

I suddenly felt uncomfortable with the position I was sitting in, feeling like he was judging me. Like he had the right to do so. I felt like someone had just caught me doing something wrong. I didn't want to move away from Vin at all, but I slid down off his lap so I could emerge my body back into the water. I didn't like being in a bathing suit straddling my date in front of my ex. Vin, to my surprise, moved with me, keeping a hand on my waist as we waded into the water. I guess he didn't want to let me go, either.

Nick's eyes narrowed at the action. "I'm sorry to interrupt, uh, whatever this is. Jessie sent me."

"Jessie's here with you?" I looked around behind him nervously, but it was just him standing in my backyard, waving his hands around while trying to ward off my dog, who was still jumping excitedly all over him.

"No, no. Damn it, dog, quit jumping!"

Vin sighed and swam to the edge of the pool, reluctantly letting me go. He whistled loudly. "Come on, Kevin. Come here, boy." Doggy Kevin turned to look at Vin with his tongue flopping out of his mouth, crouching down on his front legs before lunging his body towards Vin. Vin caught him with a laugh, petted his ears and held tight to his collar, rubbing his face against Kevin's snout. "Who's a good boy? You're such a good boy."

Vin had on a smirk, and when I looked back at Nick, I suspected it had to do with the muddy paw tracks all over the front of Nick's pants.

"Damn it," Nick cursed, looking down at his clothes in frustration.

I tried not to roll my eyes, or voice that this is Kevin's home and not his, so he shouldn't get mad at my dog. I smiled apologetically at Vin, thankful for his help to make this a little less chaotic by getting my dog, then walked out of the pool towards the towels. I wrapped one around my body, then went to hand another to Nick.

"Here." I pushed the towel out towards him, but he didn't move right away to get it. His eyes were on me. There was such a deep sadness in them, it caught me off guard for a second.

"Thank you," he said in a defeated tone, gently taking the towel from my hands.

"Yep," I murmured. After giving him a minute to wipe the mess away, I asked him again, "What are you doing here, Nick? Is Jessie okay?"

He sighed, and his shoulders fell. He looked down at the crumpled towel in his hands for a long time before looking back at me. "It's nothing. Really." His eyes looked tired, with faint bags underneath. He looked skinnier, too. I guess that is to be expected. He has been dating a woman who religiously works out, and I wouldn't be surprised if she motivated him to get in shape too.

"So, Jessie is fine?"

"Um, yeah. But, I just moved into the new place and can't find anything yet. Boxes everywhere. Could I get clothes for her for the weekend in case we can't find any?"

"Oh," I had forgotten while getting ready for this evening about Nick moving today. Jessie and I texted a little after she got out of school either. She just let me know her dad picked her up. She usually packs clothes on Fridays though. I understand the boxes, but what she left the house with this morning shouldn't be packed away. Oh, well. Maybe she just can't find her backpack in the mess. Moving can be chaotic. "Yeah, sure. I'll be right back."

I looked back at Vin, and he gave me one of his lazy smiles that makes my heart race. If Nick's presence still annoyed him, he was hiding it well. He was still holding onto Kevin and petting his neck to keep him still.

I sent up a silent prayer, hoping that leaving them alone for a few minutes would be alright as I walked away to get what he needed.

***

Vin

This asshole. Out of all the nights for this guy to show up, of course, it was tonight.

Annoyance, like a burning itch, spread over my skin when his eyes followed her every movement, lingering on her bare legs and the water dripping down her smooth skin. It hasn't even been ten minutes since I decided beyond any doubt that this woman was mine, but I don't know if my cheery little Lynn would be okay with me asserting that here.

When she was out of sight, gone into the house, he let out a heavy sigh and looked around at the setup for our date. His expression got more and more cross as he took everything in.

I couldn't help myself.

"She planned all of this." I let go of Kevin, who was much calmer now, and pulled my body up to get out of the pool. Lynn looked all cute stepping out of the pool the way she did, but cute wasn't what I was going for here.

The guy had a distasteful expression as he glanced at me. "Excuse me?"

"Lynn. She planned this whole get up. She teased me all week about it. It was fucking adorable. I was just as surprised as you when she brought me back here. Well," I huffed and smirked, "I'm sure the surprise was a little different."

He wasn't even trying to hide his hostility. Seeing the raw anger on his face made me smile more.

"Is there something you want to say to me?" he asked, his knicker clearly in a twist.

I shook my head, grabbing a towel and swinging it around my neck. "Not at all. Is there something you wish to tell me?" I couldn't stop myself from grabbing a fork and taking a big bit of Feighlynn's delicious enchiladas right out of the pan, smiling widely with a mouth full of food.

His eyes followed the action. "Actually, there is." He squared his shoulders. "I don't know what this is you two have going on, but Fay isn't someone you can take advantage of, even if she's living on her own. I will not let some thug exploit or hurt my wife."

"Ex," I reminded him, crossing my arms over my chest. "You keep forgetting that 'ex' right there. She's your ex-wife, and I'm not exploiting anything. Well," I smirked, looking down at the leftovers from dinner, "maybe her cooking skills, but I think she knows that."

His fists clenched at his sides as he tossed away the dirty towel onto the pile of clean ones. "She is the mother of my children, and the woman I spent most of my adult life with. Two letters will not change my love or concern for her."

"No?" I should probably keep my mouth shut and not escalate this further, but my possessiveness is blooming, as well as this desire for justice and the need to protect her from this scumbag. "Your cheating and leaving her for another woman sure changed her love for you." I'm assuming that, but I'm sure I'm right. My Lynn didn't look too pleased to see him here again tonight.

"You don't know what you're talking about," he sneered.

"Maybe so," I shrugged. "What I know is, that woman is fucking amazing, and there is nothing you can do that can scare me away from her. But, hey, I'm not one to do the same as what you are trying to do, so if you think your cheating love is enough to win her back, I won't try to stop you. Just know I'm not going anywhere unless she wants me to."

***

Nick

"You're back already?" Jessie looked surprised as I walked back into the apartment, holding a pink bag with whatever Fay packed for our daughter.

I smiled sadly, feeling lower than I ever have before, but not wanting it to show for Jessie. "Your mom had company, so I just got you some things you might need and came back."

"Company?" Jessie looked confused. "Was Aunt Kate over?"

"No, I sighed, walking to the kitchen to find the liquor bottle I had stashed in the freezer. "It wasn't Katherine."

"Then who?" Jessie pressed.

I placed a hand on the counter to keep myself steady as piping fiery anger coursed through me again. "Just a neighbor," I gritted through my teeth.

"Huh," Jessie murmured nervously, no doubt sensing my mood. She picked up the bag and twisted the handles in her hands. "So, we're not going to Preston's game tomorrow?"

That game. I had forgotten the reason for going over there in the first place because of the scene I had walked into. My *wife* kissing and getting groped on by some deviant-hoodlum. I'm going to have my secretary do a background check on him tomorrow. I'm sure I can call in a favor through Albert Milton at city hall on Monday too. I have this new neighbor's address, so looking up his other information should be easy.

Jessie and standing anxiously, waiting for an answer.

"I think your mom already has a ride."

"Oh." She looked disappointed. If I told her exactly what it was her mother was doing, I'm sure she would be even more disappointed than she is now. I won't be the one to tell her, though. That would ruin any chance of getting on Fay's good side. "That's too bad. I wanted to see Pres play."

"I'm sorry, sweetie."

Fay. My Feighlynn. That punk was calling her Lynn? That's never been her nickname. Never or for anyone. She was always Fay. He acted all big and bad, like her house was his. He looked like some dumb dog, pissing all over what he thought was his territory. He can't know her too well yet, or he would call her by her real nickname. Not something ridiculous like 'Lynn'.

And damn it, and the way he was all over her. She had red marks all over her damned neck. He really might be part dog. He acted just like one. She already has one annoying dog. She doesn't need two.

I poured the bourbon into a plastic cup, a fast food freebie that once came with a happy meal or something. I scowled, recognizing and remembering the cup instantly. And that Fay kept it because it had puppies and kittens all over it. We couldn't have a real dog back then, and she was completely happy just having pictures of cartoon ones on a cup. She drank out of this thing every day for about a year until I got my first real paycheck at my job and replaced our plastic dishes with real ones. Even then, she would gravitate to this cup from time to time, until I told her it looked trashy. Then she retired it to the back of the cabinet until it ended up boxed up in the garage.

Why didn't I just let her use the damned cup in peace? Why did I have to ruin that for her?

As I turned the cup in my hands, I was too consumed with my memories of happier times to drink.

"Daddy?"

"Hmm?" I turned to stare at my daughter. She was looking at me with so much concern.

"Are you okay?"

She gnawed on her bottom lip with worry, and she looked so much like her mother that I choked on a sob.

"Daddy?!"

"I'm okay," I rasped in a rough voice. When she came to comfort me, I wrapped my arms around her, thankful for her warmth. "I'm just a little sad."

"Because Preston didn't invite you to his game?"

"Yeah," I laughed humorlessly, wetness filling my eyes. I looked up at the ceiling, willing the tears not to break free. "I'm just worried I won't ever get forgiveness. I messed up so much, Jessie. I ruined everything."

"Daddy," Jessie said softly, and I suspected she may cry too. "If you want forgiveness, earn it. Mama says that. Sorry doesn't always fix a problem, but actions can. Why don't you show Preston that you're sorry?"

I buried my nose in my daughter's hair, smiling sadly because she is way too good of a soul to be saddled with a father like me. But she was right. My sweet daughter is still the light in my every day and the voice of reason in my madness.

"It's not just your brother I'm scared will never forgive me, but your mom too."

"That's silly," Jessie smiled softly. "Mom doesn't hold grudges."

"I really messed up, though, sweetie."

"Yeah," her smile turned sheepish. "I forgave you for leaving. I'm sure they can too."

Jessie was still right, or maybe I just am fool enough to believe that I can be forgiven still. I just need to show Fay that I've changed. I need to show her I'm sorry. All the mistakes that led up to our divorce, even before Arlene and the cheating. I need to show her I'm a changed man now.

Starting with being there for our kids.

I need to go to that damned game.

"Do you know the details about your brother's baseball tournament?"

"I can look at the school's website. They should have it under the athletics tab. Why?" Hope gleamed in her eyes.

I smiled softly. "Let's leave the unpacking for Sunday. Pack a bag. We're going to your brother's game."

Chapter Fourteen

Good Company

"Honey, I'm home!" she called out, and I heard the door closing loudly just after.

I was sitting in my office at home, rubbing my head from the stress of the past few days. The firm had just taken on a new client, and the case was proving to be difficult. More difficult than they originally led on. I've had my nose in law books for days and have gotten very little sleep. I didn't even have the energy to answer her.

"I see you haven't moved." Fay popped her head into the doorway, looking at the stack of books on my desk. "The kids were safely handed off to Kate. She said she'll bring them back after they get back from my parents. We have the week to ourselves!"

She had so much energy, and that triumphant glint in her eyes. Even though I was stressed and tired, I smiled tightly at her. "You should have gone too. I know you wanted to. I'm sorry I had to drop out." We were all meant to go visit her family, but I just had too much to do here to take any time off.

"It's not your fault." She skipped into my office, coming around the back of my chair. I leaned back and groaned as her fingers kneaded into my stiff shoulders. "We can go anytime. This was a once in a lifetime opportunity for me to get time alone with my husband."

"I will not be very good company," I sighed.

She giggled sweetly. "Are you ever?"

I scoffed, turning to look at her in offense, but then smirked, seeing that playful look on her face. She was teasing me. "I have my moments."

"Really?" Her eyes narrowed in challenge. "Prove it."

I looked back at my desk and the stack of papers I still had to review. "I wish I could."

"Wish granted," her tone was firm. She swiveled my chair around, then grabbed my hands and pulled me to my feet.

"Where are we going?" I asked warily.

She looked back at me with that mischievous grin, leading me straight to our bedroom. I knew that look.

"Fay, I really have to get this case figured out." If I lose this case, it will cost the firm a lot, and I could lose my job. That's why I've been so stressed.

"You've been staring at the same page in that book for three hours now," Fay said stubbornly. "What you need is to relax and refresh, then go back with a new set of eyes. Spend three hours with me, then turn the page."

She was right. I had been re-reading the same lines repeatedly, but the words weren't sinking in.

The moment we entered our bedroom, Fay pulled me towards the bed and undid the buttons on my shirt. I stared up at her beautiful face, clean of makeup or anything superficial. She was glowing naturally, and it warmed me instantly. Her presence was like the sun.

When she leaned down to kiss me, right before her lips touched mine, I murmured, "I love you, Fay."

She smiled sadly at me, that glint in her eyes gone as moisture replaced it. SHe leaned in close, right next to my ear. "But you told me you were in love with someone else."

Dread washed over me, making my inside freeze over. Suddenly, our comforting, warm bedroom, full of love and peace, was transformed into the sleek, cold one of Arlene's. I used to think this apartment was high end and exciting. Now it fills me with nothing but contempt.

When she pulled away, it wasn't my tiny, loving wife standing before me anymore, but the woman I chose over her. She had her signature confident smirk on her face, wearing one of her black robes that exposed most of her legs.

With a soft cackling laugh, she lifted a leg and pushed me back onto the bed with a sharp heel on my bare chest.

"You chose this," she sneered.

Right as she was about to drop the robe, I gasped loudly, scaring myself awake. I broke out in a cold sweat all over my body. The sweat soaked my new sheets.

Looking around the room, I felt disoriented until I realized I was in my new condo, not Arlene's apartment. Boxes were stacked near the closet, and my suitcases were still lined up on the other side of the bed. It was dark outside, but the dawn was breaking.

"Damn it," I muttered, dragging my hands down my face. "Shit."

What started out as a happy memory, one from when the kids were still very little and I was new to the law firm, quickly turned into a nightmare.

I wish it had remained the dream of a memory from happier times. What started as a shitty week turned into a great one as Fay helped me to stay focused and keep a steady head. She had sacrificed her entire paid vacation, that was meant to be used to visit her retired parents in Florida to be my rock.

"I'm such a damn fool." I dropped my head in my hands. I tried to hang on to that image of Fay as she smiled back at me, leading me to a place I could find peace, but all that I felt was guilt and remorse.

***

Preston

"Hey, Micheals!" The assistant coach, Coach Anderson, stopped in front of me as I was getting my cleats on. "Your mom's coming today, right?"

With a slight frown, I answered, "Yes, sir. She should be."

"Good. Good." He slapped my shoulder. "You're going to do great today." He slapped my shoulder one more time, then kept walking.

Mason, a senior I'm friends with that happened to be sitting beside me, laughed. "It's true. I feel bad for you," he snickered.

Other guys were smirking and laughing softly under their breath. "What?"

"Oh, nothing," Carter gave me a knowing look. "Just that Coach Anderson has the hots for your mom."

"Are you fucking serious?" I groaned. "Is that why he keeps asking me those questions?" The coach was asking me about my parents' divorce and shit like that since we got on the bus yesterday. I thought he was just a creepy, over-concerned coach, but now it makes more sense.

"Yep," Mason said. "I heard him talking about your mom to the head coach last night after you went to your room."

"When did he even meet my mom?"

"Last spring at the awards dinner," Carter said. "And at the chili fundraiser. He talked about both."

"That's so creepy."

"Eh," Mason shrugged. "Make the coach your step-daddy. That's a sure way of getting on varsity next year."

"Huh," was all I could grunt out. There were two juniors on JV that should have been before me to move up to varsity with the injury. I thought I was asked first because I was better, but maybe not.

Coach Anderson isn't a bad guy, at least not that I know of. I just don't like it. The idea of him trying to hit on my mom makes me want to throw up. He's at least two or three years younger than mom and slaps my shoulder too much. Plus, the other players call him hot links because he's got fat fingers that he's always waving around as he yells at us.

"Hey man, my stepdad is a dick. I would trade him for hot links any day."

"I don't think my mom is looking for a step dad for me right now." I wouldn't mind if she dated. I actually encourage it. It would keep dad from messing with her.

"I can be your step daddy," Carter wiggled his eyebrows.

"Fuck you." I threw a towel at him as he dodged it and laughed.

We had to be at the field to warm up, and were still bull shitting with one another, more of the guys teasing me about becoming my step dad and crap like that.

I was wishing I had told my dad about this game. I don't want him with mom again, ever, but him being here would at least keep other ass holes like him away from her. Hopefully, she found a good friend to come with at least.

"Hey, isn't that her?" Mason asked, pointing at the stands as we walked to the field we were assigned to.

I looked over, and sure enough, my mom was sitting at the center of the bench, wearing a shirt with my face on it.

That wasn't what threw me off. It was our new neighbor from across the street sitting beside her.

"Oh shit," Carter laughed. "I guess it's JV next year for you."

***

Feighlynn

"There he is!" I said excitedly, pointing at Preston walking to the dugout with the other boys and his coaches. I waved excitedly. Preston gave me a tight grin and a slight wave back.

"I think he likes your shirt," Sherry, a mom of one of Preston's friends, laughed.

"He's embarrassed," I giggled. "Maybe I should have just worn school colors instead."

"I like the shirt," Vin placed his hand on my shoulder, making butterflies flutter in my chest. "He may feel embarrassed, but his mom, being his biggest fan, is something he's going to remember."

Sherry sighed with a dazed grin. "That's so sweet."

She and the other moms were stealing glances at Vin every chance they could. Even some dads were looking at him in that way men look at other men when they were impressed.

I was impressed beyond words when I saw him this morning. After dropping Kevin off with a neighbor to be watched while we were away, I came back home to find him on my front porch, wearing the sexiest white shirt and leather jacket combo I'd ever seen. Just like out of an action movie.

When he took that jacket off and I could see his tight-fitting sleeves, and all they were trying to contain, I nearly convulsed right then.

Everything he does today has me ready to combust. I had a very restless, frustrated sleep last night, so that could have something to do with it.

Last night, the mood was tense after I returned to the backyard with a bag for Jessie to give to Nick. I don't know what was said between them, but Nick was beet red, angrier than I'd seen him in a long time. Vin was smiling tightly, looking all kinds of yummy stretched out in a chair, dripping wet and eating the rest of the enchiladas right out of the pan.

After Nick left, the mood didn't really return. Not like it was before. Vin was still playful as he helped me clean up the mess, but after the dishes were done, he simply kissed me, asked what time to pick me up in the morning, then went home.

I laid in bed for hours after, tossing and turning, wishing Nick would stub his toe for his interruption. Again.

The long drive didn't help either. At some point in the first hours, Vin's hands made its way to my thigh, and then never left. Even when we stopped halfway for gas and breakfast, he kept one hand on me at all times. Either on my back, or around my shoulder. He tangled his legs with mine under the table as we ate.

Now, he has his large thighs in his washed denim pressed up against my legs, and a hand holding the seat behind me. I can smell his cologne every once in a while and it makes my mouth water.

Vin caught me staring at him and gave me one of his lazy smirk before bumping my nose with his finger. "What are you thinking about?"

"You," I said honestly.

"Me?" He acted surprised. "What about me?"

"You're cute," I poked his nose back.

"You're the cute one," he whispered in my ear, making the hairs stand up on the back of my neck. "You were fucking adorable singing along to every song the entire way down here."

"I'm good company on road trips, huh?" I laughed.

"You're great company all the time."

My face grew warm as he gave me that look. My panties can't handle that look today.

"So, Fay," Sherry said, breaking the moment for me and Vin. "How long have you two been dating?"

I bit my lip, wondering how to answer. Vin must have sensed my dilemma because he answered for me.

"Not long. I just moved back to town from Fort Bragg after getting out of the Army. My mom is Feighlynn's neighbor."

"Oh, how sweet? So you were in the Army?"

"Yes ma'am. I just retired."

"Well, thank you for your service. What do you plan on doing now?"

I was curious about this too. I stared at his handsome face, waiting to hear his answer.

"As of yesterday, I'm the head of court security for the city. I start next week."

"Wow." I grinned teasingly. "You're a professional hero again."

"More of a babysitter," he laughed. "It's an office job."

Court security? That means he will work at the courthouse. I wonder if that means he will see Nick a lot? That will be interesting. I should warn Vin later about Nick's job just to avoid any unnecessary drama.

"MOM!" I suddenly heard a high-pitched, familiar voice behind us. Me and every other mom turned around, but it was my daughter coming down from the parking lot.

"Jessie?" Why is Jessie here?

Then I saw Nick closing the door to a car with rental tags.

"Seriously?" Vin grumbled under his breath. I sent him an apologetic look, wondering what to do.

Sherry leaned over and whispered to me, "I thought you said your ex-husband wouldn't be here?"

"He wasn't supposed to be."

Chapter Fifteen

Looks Great on You, Mom

"Mama!" Jessie ran in for a hug as I waited for her at the bottom of the bleachers. "Did we miss anything?"

"No, no. They haven't started yet."

I held her tightly while watching her dad walk steadily down to the fields. He had on a polo with the school insignia on the breast, and his usual slacks. His eyes flashed at Vin for a moment, narrowing slightly, then looked back at me and Jessie, his expression softening to a friendly smile.

I felt like everyone was watching his approach. Some of the other parents knew about our divorce, and the way he left me last year. I felt like they were waiting for some kind of soap opera to play out.

This was Preston's first varsity game. I really didn't want to take the attention away from that.

"I didn't know you both were coming down," I said with a friendly grin when Nick got close. "You didn't mention it."

Jessie, who was looking at Vin with a curious expression, turned her pretty little face up to me. "Daddy said he didn't want to miss Pres's game either, and since you already had a ride, we flew down!" She looked over at Vin again when he mentioned the ride, and he nodded with a gentle smile back. I can't even imagine what's going through his head right now.

"Wow, you flew!" Sherry said loudly, breaking some of the tension. "What a lucky girl! We were stuck in a sweat-smelling car for over six hours getting here."

"Must have cost you a pretty penny," Sherry's husband said, shaking Nick's hand.

"I used my miles, so it wasn't bad," Nick shrugged.

"We flew first class, mama! They gave me orange juice and cookies!" Jessie's face was pure excitement. Despite the circumstances, I'm glad her father spoiled her a bit.

Nick looked me up and down, a smile stretching on his face as he lingered on my shirt. "That's cute. How did Preston take it?"

"I don't think he's noticed yet." I looked over at the field, and saw Preston talking with the coaches, stealing glances our way.

Nick looked down at his own shirt. "Maybe I should get a shirt made too."

"That would be a sight," I scoffed. I couldn't even picture it in my head.

"Where's your car?" Jessie looked around the parking lot. "We couldn't find it."

"We took mine." Vin stood up, coming down the bleachers, stepping over each descending bench with his thick legs. People were watching again, ready for whatever was to come next, but I couldn't stop staring at Vin's legs long enough to care much.

That frustration in my belly was coming back, and this was definitely not the time to be lusting over Vin. No matter how good he looks in his fitted white shirt with his tattoos and muscles bulging out, and his faded, butt-hugging jeans.

"Hi, Jessie. It's good to see you again."

Jessie smiled shyly at him, and by the sparkle in her eyes, I could tell she was shy for more reasons than just Vin saying hi. She is my daughter, after all. "It's good to see you again too."

Vin's smile stretched as he held a hand out to shake hers. She hesitantly took it, then tucked herself back into my side.

"Kevin," Nick nodded tightly, tucking his hands in his pockets.

"Nick," Vin responded curtly, his gentle expression slipping away. He rested a hand on the small of my back, and those frustrated feelings inside me resulted in my belly clenching again. I could smell his cologne, and after wondering how he was taking my ex being here, it was reassuring to feel his hand on me. "You should have said something last night about coming to the game. I would have brought extra bleacher pads." He smiled down at Jessie. "You can have mine."

"Thank you," Jessie smiled shyly, looking at the seats fastened to the bleachers, then back at us. "Um, you saw my daddy last night?"

Did Nick not say anything to Jessie? Maybe he was leaving it for me to explain, even though I thought Jessie already knew. She saw the flowers and the note.

Vin tensed, so I answered the question instead. "Vin and I were having a date at home when your dad came by last night to get you clothes." I kept my voice level, but when I saw her eyes widen when I said 'date', my breath caught in my chest.

She looked at Vin again with a confused look, and then it was like everything registered in her mind. "You were the one who sent mama flowers?!"

Vin rubbed the back of his neck. "Guilty."

"Oh!" Jessie looked shocked for a second, then her face fell. She turned around and stared at her father in a way that made my chest just sink. "I didn't know."

Nick just smiled calmly, his hands still in his pockets and a tenderness in his eyes. "I know, sweetie. It's okay."

It got tense for a second, the awkward silence stretching to a full minute.

Then Sherry, praise her soul, said loudly, "Take a seat, you guys. I can't see past your butts!"

***

Vin

This is awkward. I didn't know how to fucking act when I saw this douchebag strolling up like he owned the place.

We fumbled for a second going up the bleachers, Lynn's daughter taking the seat that I just left while Lynn sat back down in hers. There wasn't much extra room, only a spot by Jessie, and Nick hurried to take it with a smug expression before I could.

"Here, honey," Sherry, Lynn's friend, moved up to the seat in front of her, opening up the spot right beside Lynn. "It won't hurt me any to sit by my husband for once."

"Thanks," I said appreciatively. I was about to take the spot in front of Lynn and just lean back against her legs, but I guess that would be too much. Especially in front of her kids.

The need to show this prick she's moved on is making me jittery, though. I want to just fucking grab her and kiss her senseless, making him watch as her cute little moans escape her lips and I devour them.

Her son and daughter wouldn't appreciate that, especially since we have every other parent on these bleachers waiting for something just like that to happen. Embarrassing the crap out of them would be the worst impression I could make.

So, I grabbed Lynn's hand instead, reveling in the minor victory of sitting beside her while her ex-husband glared a few feet away.

Lynn smiled sweetly at me, still looking adorable, with a hint of worry in her eyes. When her daughter looked down at where our hands were joined, I guessed that was why.

"So, Jessie. Do you play any sports?" I asked, to try to lighten the mood.

She bit her lip and nodded, looking like a younger version of Lynn. She was shy, and not as talkative yet, but she definitely had her mother's features.

"I do dance," she whispered.

"Dance? Wow! What kind of dance?"

"Jazz mostly." She leaned on her mom's shoulder, but looked less hesitant about me now.

"I took a ballet class once," I confessed with a sheepish grin.

"You did not," Lynn huffed, a wide smile spreading on her adorable face.

"Ballet?" Nick scoffed, still stealing glances at my hand locked with Lynn's. "How masculine."

I shrugged, feeling unashamed. "My football coach in high school had all his receivers take the class."

"You know, I heard that somewhere," Sherry exclaimed. "I read that most NFL players include ballet in their training."

"I did ballet," Jessie said enthusiastically. "Mom signed me up for ballet when I was really little, and then I moved to jazz and hip-hop when my friends did."

"She's on a competitive team," Lynn bragged with pride written all over her. "She's going to Disneyland this summer to perform after a competition in Anaheim. She's very excited about the trip."

"Wow. That sounds like fun. I love the dole whip at Disneyland."

"I do too! Mama and I had a competition to see who could eat it the fastest last time, and we both got terrible brain freezes. Pres ended up taking them away from us, so we never got to see who won."

"Preston's a little worry wart," Lynn laughed. "He found some article later about someone that died from a brain freeze."

"Nuh uh. That can't be real."

"It was real," Jessie giggled, sounding just like her mom. "Every time we got ice cream, he would bring it up and show us on his phone."

"What a way to go," I snorted. "Imagine what it said on their tombstone."

"Cause of death, ice cream," Lynn giggled with her daughter, and I laughed just watching them.

"Laughing at something so morbid is twisted," Nick muttered.

I sighed, rolling my eyes. The girls' laughter died, and I had the sudden urge to punch the dude in the face. Jessie looked guilty now, and Lynn looked annoyed. She just kissed the top of her daughter's head.

It grew tense again, thanks to the douche bag, but then the players finished their exercises and Lynn's son started heading our way. He had a hard expression on his face. I hoped it wasn't because of me.

"Look, it's Preston!" Jessie said, getting excited and pointing to the field. She stood up and waved wildly, and his face softened. How could it not? His kid sister was as freaking adorable as their mother. "Pres! Surprise! We came!"

"I see that," he muttered, sending a pissed-off look towards his dad. I breathed a sigh of relief, glad it wasn't my presence ticking him off. I felt more pressure to meet this boy again than I did at yesterday's interview. Preston is obviously his mother's protector now and takes the role seriously. I want him to know I plan on taking the same role, and being just as serious about it too.

"Like my shirt?" Lynn asked, pointing to it with her free hand.

Preston looked at her other hand joined with mine, then the smallest grin appeared, lifting the corners of his lips before his eyes glanced at his dad, then at me.

"I love it," he smirked. "Looks great on you, mom."

***

Arlene

"Your call can not be completed. Please hang up and try again."

I huffed in frustration, clicking off my phone and throwing it to the couch.

It's been almost a week. An entire five days have passed since Nick left, and he still hasn't called to apologize, or even to see how I have been. I thought this was a silly little fight that would pass once he got bored with staying in a hotel, but then I got notified by my doorman when I got home yesterday that Nick had come by with movers to collect the last of his things.

No wonder he wasn't at work yesterday. I thought it strange at the morning meeting, him not being there, but then Stevens mentioned Nick's absence being because of his move.

I can't even describe how embarrassing it was to hear that announced so publicly in our place of work. Everyone knew we were living together, and some had even gossiped behind my back about being the reason for his divorce. The office talk was excruciating the entire rest of the day.

I had to cover a meeting for Nick too, with one of his friends at City Hall. Nick was ignoring my calls, so I thought that if I flirted with his friend a bit, he might mention it to Nick and incite a call back. It didn't though. I felt like a fool afterward, the man not showing any attraction to me whatsoever. Even some random man looking more fit to be in the police station than the city manager's office wasn't affected by me at all.

Is the reason that Nick lost interest in me because I no longer hold any attraction to others? I've gone to extreme lengths to keep my appearance as it is, spending hours each week with a trainer at the gym, getting massages and treatments, and visiting the salon at least once a week. Has all that been in vain?

I got up and paced around my living room, chewing on my freshly manicured nails, even though my stylist just scolded me for them becoming so brittle and said they were about to break. When I couldn't take the agonizing silence or my racing thoughts anymore, I picked my phone up to call him one more time.

It connected, but went to voicemail this time. I shrieked in anger, tossing my phone across the living room.

Everything feels like it is falling apart. Nick was, who knows where, refusing to talk to me, and I don't feel like I could show my face at the office again. Not like this. Did he tell people we broke up? Are we broken up? Is that why the gossip was so bad?

Now, I'm just the home-wrecking whore of a lawyer that is after everyone's man and ruining lives. I'm no friend to women, or at least that's what I kept hearing in whispers and muttered conversations all day yesterday. Even my secretary was cold to me.

I don't know how much more of this I can take. I didn't seek a married man. He was the one that made it clear he was available to me. Yes, he was married. Yes, I knew. But I also wasn't the one that tried to take him from his wife. He was already looking to leave.

Why do women get the brunt of the blame in society? I didn't steal a married man or break his home. He broke that himself. I was just his tool. When a criminal hurts another person with a hammer, you don't put the hammer on trial. You put the one who used it.

What I hate most out of all of this is that I still want him. Even if I was being used, I enjoyed feeling needed. It made me feel like I was loved.

A tool can never be loved.

Chapter Sixteen

Baby Ducks

Feighlynn

"That went better than I thought it would," Vin breathed into my ear.

Goosebumps rose on my neck, and the frustrating ache clenched inside of me. His breath smelled like mint. I bet mine smells like coffee and beef jerky. I resisted the urge to cover my mouth or kiss him. Two extremes that were not acceptable for the setting.

"Preston liked my shirt!" I laughed lightly, trying to aim my breath towards the ground.

"Of course he did," Vin chuckled. I felt my face heat with his eyes staring at me in that swoon-worthy way.

I had to keep reminding myself there were other people around. Other people, including my ex husband.

Preston was talking to the younger coach, who didn't look happy. Preston was still smiling, though, so whatever they were talking about couldn't be that bad.

The head coach was blowing a whistle, walking around with a clipboard while snapping commands at a group of boys doing warm-up drills.

"No way," Vin huffed, staring at the field.

"What?"

"I know him," he pointed to the head coach. "He was the assistant coach for my football team in high school."

"No way. What a small world!"

"Yeah, that's crazy."

"You played football?" Sherry's husband asked. "What school?"

Vin started talking with the other dads about sports, Sherry's husband, and a few of the others actually knowing who Vin was from high school days. Apparently, his team was really good back then.

His sudden camaraderie with the dads helped to decrease the tension dramatically. For everyone but Nick, who just stared at the field with a bored expression.

That changed when the game actually started. The game was a good one. All the parents, Nick included, got into it, cheering and yelling loudly with every play. Despite his faults, Nick was a good father. The pride on his face when Preston got his first home run was unmistakable.

"Damn, that was a good game," Vin said after they won.

"Mama, can I go see Preston?" Jessie asked when other siblings ran onto the field.

"Sure. Just don't get in the way."

"I'll come too," Vin said. His pants stretched across his thick leg muscles as he stepped down from the bleachers. "I'm going to say hi to the coach."

Jessie and Vin chatted as they walked onto the field. She seemed comfortable with him now, to my relief.

"So," Nick stood awkwardly beside me as the other parents cleared out. "What's the plan now? Are there more games?"

"Not for them. Not today anyway. I think there's another game next weekend closer to home. They still have to stay and watch the other teams, though. They'll get back home tomorrow."

"Huh," he slid his hands in his pockets, staring at the ground. "So, what about you? You're probably heading back now?"

I sighed. He just had to make this awkward again. "Actually, no. I'll be heading back tomorrow too."

His frown deepened towards the ground. You could have cut the tension with a knife.

"Could I persuade you to fly back with Jessie and me?"

I froze. "Excuse me?" I had to have misheard him.

His eyes swept up to me, pain etched in their corners. "Fay. Please. Don't stay here with him."

I scoffed in disbelief. A choice number of things popped into my head to say, but for once, my brain had a filter and none of them slipped out. Coldness spread over my body.

"Have a safe flight, Nick." I descended the steps.

"Fay, wait. Please, just consider- " He reached out to grab my arm, but I jerked it free.

"Not here," I said coldly. "Not at Preston's game. If you have something to say, it can wait until we are alone."

I would not draw attention to us and take away this victory for my son. I don't know what Nick is thinking. That he has any right to dictate who I spend time with or what I do. It's disrespectful to not just me, but Arlene. How can he ask that of me when she's likely waiting for him back home?

His eyes remained pleading, but I just turned my back and walked away, trying my best to hide the contempt I was feeling.

***

Vin

"How're the tacos?"

Lynn smiled and shrugged. "Good. Needs salt." She picked up a lime and squirted it all over her next taco before sprinkling salt on top.

We were sitting on the Riverwalk in San Antonio, eating at a cantina while watching the boats pass by. Ducks were swarming around the edge of the water, desperate for a bite of someone's food. I thought Lynn would love it, but she's been a little distracted all throughout the meal.

My happy little road-trip partner hasn't been so happy since we left the game. She has been deep in thought and unusually quiet.

Honestly, it's been ever since I left her and her ex-husband alone. It was nice catching up with an old coach of mine, and I think I won over a lot of points with her kids, but she's been tense ever since. I should have grabbed her hand and dragged her with me.

Slapping my hands on my thighs, I sat back in my chair to watch Lynn's small mouth try to fit around her taco. It impressed me when she easily fit half of it in her mouth. Really impressed. I'm glad I had my napkin on my lap.

She looked up at me with a full mouth and gave me a questioning grin.

"You're cute," I smirked.

"Nu-mh mhh nmmh," she mumbled with her full mouth.

I laughed, "Yes you are."

She looked at me like I was crazy, which just made me laugh more.

She forced herself to swallow, then said, "You're pretty good looking yourself. Some of those other moms couldn't take their eyes off you."

I shrugged. "I didn't notice. I was too busy watching you."

Her cheeks flushed over, making her look even more adorable. Then that dejected expression returned seconds later, and I could take not knowing why any longer.

Leaning forward, I used the edge of my cloth napkin to wipe access salsa from her lips, making her lips turn up in one of her shy smiles. I ran my thumb over her pillowy lip, then asked, "Is something bothering you? You've looked a little sad since we left your kids."

She leaned into my touch, and I swear my heart was going to hammer out of my chest. Her sweet, apologetic face was so fucking cute.

"I'm just a little off, I guess," she admitted.

I pressed my lips together, then cautiously asked, "Because of something I did?"

She quickly shook her head. "No. You've been great. Preston told me you saved him from another year on JV. You, knowing the coach was awesome to him."

I smirked. His coach mentioned his assistant having a little thing for Lynn and being disappointed to see her with a date and her ex-husband. Seeing the other coach's face when I shouted we were dating was more than satisfying.

"Then what happened? Are you tired from the drive, or...." I hesitated for a second. "Or.... did your ex do something?"

She frowned, and I knew my suspicions were spot on.

"He just said something I didn't like." She sighed, sitting back in her chair and staring off at the river. "I shouldn't even be letting it get to me, but the nerve of the guy.... Every time I think of what he asked me, I get mad all over again."

"What did he ask you?"

She gnawed on her lip for a second. "He wanted me to fly back with them." Her face turned apologetic. "He didn't want me to stay here with you."

Scoffing, I crossed my arms, not knowing whether to be happy my presence was bothering him that much, or if I should go punch his lights out for upsetting Lynn like this.

"I don't get it. He's with his girlfriend and has the life he always wanted now. Why can't he let me be happy, too?"

"Because he's not over you," I said flatly. It's written all over the asshole's face every time I see him. He might have a girlfriend, but he still calls Lynn his wife. He's not over her. At all.

"He left me," she muttered. "He was over me before we even separated. I think he just doesn't want me to be happy sometimes. Maybe I've been too much of a pushover with him, even after our divorce. I tried to keep everything civil and friendly for the kids' sake. Now that I'm ready to move on, why can't he extend me the same courtesy?"

"Because he's not over you, Lynn. I'm not just saying that. It's clear as day."

"No," Lynn curled her fingers on top of her bottom lip. "No. He's been in a serious relationship with Arlene for almost two years now."

I shrugged. "My ex tried to pull this shit with me for years after we divorced. Even when he was with the guy she cheated on me with after our divorce was final, she would reach out to me constantly to take her back. Cheaters have regrets. I don't think your ex is any different."

"Maybe." She didn't look convinced. "Not likely, but maybe. You haven't seen his girlfriend. She's beautiful, successful, in shape and driven. I'm the boring house wife that would rather eat a bucket of nachos than look at a treadmill."

"What if you ate the bucket of nachos while using the treadmill?" I laughed.

"Oh, two birds, one stone!" She looked excited. "I'd rather float in the pool with my bucket of nachos, though."

"I would too," I grinned. "I don't think you realize how cute you are, Lynn. You're fucking perfect. Success and a gym membership don't make the perfect woman."

"You're sweet to say that, but I still don't think Nick feels that way about me."

"Okay," I said levelly. "What do you think he's trying to do then?"

"He was the controlling type. He liked everything a certain way and in order. I think he's just trying to keep me in line or something. That's why it's bothering me so much."

She really didn't see herself the way others do. She's the perfect woman.

She's mine now though, so I guess it doesn't matter what the hell her asshole of an ex thinks. He's not getting a chance now that I'm in the picture. I'm not an idiot like him. I won't be giving up on a woman as perfect as she is. Not with the way she makes lasagna, or the way she giggles. Her smiles and jokes, and the way she sings off-key in the car. Then there was her soft, small but curvy body.....

Nick was seriously an idiot.

"Well," I leaned forward, putting a devious smile on my face, "are you going to let the dickhead ruin our weekend?"

She bit back a giggle, then sighed. "No. You're right. We're here to have fun. Not pout about jerks." She finally smiled down at the ducks, reaching for a tortilla to feed them a few bites. "Are you hungry, baby duckies?"

"Those are full-grown ducks," I chuckled.

"No, you're not," she pushed her lips together and said in a baby voice. "You're all cute little baby ducks that need to eat lots of food to fly south for the winter."

"I think we are south, and it's spring," I pointed out.

"Don't listen to him," she tossed them a few more bites.

Seriously. So fucking adorable. It wasn't even fair.

I watched her adoringly until a server came by with our check.

"Ready to head to the room?" I asked after slipping my card into the bill book, beating her to the punch.

She bit her lip, looking nervous again, but for a different reason. The way her eyes swept down my chest and then back to my face had me ready to throw her over my shoulder and run to the hotel now.

"Sure," she said meekly, then turned to the growing crowd of ducks. "Goodbye, baby ducks."

"So cute," I murmured. Others were watching now, and I felt like a star with her sitting across from me. Her positive energy was back in full force, spreading sunshine to everyone who drew near.

I was planning to bask in her light all night long.

CHAPTER SEVENTEEN

No Filter

"Wow! This is nice!" Lynn looked around the room with wide, excited eyes as we walked in. "I didn't know that they would upgrade us like that. How lucky!"

"Yeah, that was a pleasant surprise. Lucky."

Luck had nothing to do with it. I called the hotel that she told me she reserved this morning and paid for the upgrade. I wanted the best for her, and the hot tub on the balcony was a huge selling point. The cost was double the price of the double room she had originally booked. Two beds to one king to share made me hesitate, but if she was against it, I would sleep on the couch.

When the attendant told her we had been upgraded, and told her it was to a king suite, she had the biggest, sweetest grin on her face. I don't think she minds sharing a bed at all. All I had to worry about then was her seeing the price difference and the bill saying it had already been paid. It turned out that I didn't have to worry about that either.

She had gotten a call from one of her kids when it came time to sign for the room. I told her to take it and finished the paperwork so she will be none the wiser. The attendant thought we were married, so signing for her was a breeze. I enjoyed being thought of as her husband too.

Our agreement for the trip was that she would pay for the hotel, and I would pay for the extras, like food and fun. I'm keeping my part in the upgraded room to myself.

She looked out the sliding doors to the balcony and squealed adorable when she saw the hot tub.

"Want to get in?" I asked, dropping our bags on the bed and coming up from behind her.

She blushed as I wrapped my arms around her waist. "Not yet," she said shyly.

"Yeah?" I couldn't stop myself from running my nose along the pink flush painting her neck. She was so warm and smelled so good, like flowery perfume. "We're definitely using it later, though. Right?"

"What if I didn't pack a bathing suit?" Her voice was sensual and airy.

Fuck. A wave of excitement moved down my back, settling right in a part of me that was pressed against her back. I had to take a tiny step back, clearing my throat as I collected myself.

"I can let you borrow mine," I suggested with a smirk.

"Hmm, then what will you wear?" I could hear the smile in her voice.

"Nothing," I whispered right against the hollow of her ear.

"Wow," she gasped. "I... I want to get in right now."

She covered her mouth quickly, and I realized she didn't mean to say that out loud. I laughed, nuzzling my face into her neck and holding her tight to keep her from getting away.

"As much as I would love to get naked in the hot tub with you right now, it's still bright outside, and someone might look up."

"I was joking!" Lynn tried to twist away, but I just held her tighter.

"Sure you were," I chuckled. "What kind of action hero would I be if I didn't get the woman naked in the hot tub by the end of the night?"

"I won't be naked. I'm wearing your swim shorts," she reminded me gruffly.

"Oh. Yeah," I chuckled against her neck. "I forgot."

She sighed. "My poor panties."

She then quickly covered her mouth again, and I burst into more laughter, unable to hold her any longer as my laughter got out of control.

"What's wrong with your panties?!"

"Nothing!" She grimaced, walking off towards the bathroom. "Nothing at all!"

"Uh huh," I plopped down at the end of the bed with a wide grin, my eyes fixed on one part of her right at her center. "Need some help?"

"Nope!" She closed the door loudly, then I heard her curse in the sweetest voice under her breath. "As if being sweaty wasn't enough," I heard her grumble. A minute or two later, the shower turned on.

Fuck, she was driving me crazy. I adjusted my pants, the area around my zipper getting uncomfortable and tight.

"Um," Lynn poked her nose out from the bathroom. The door barely opened a crack. "Can you, um, bring me my bag?"

I smirked, leaning back to place my hand on it. "This one?"

She nodded, biting her bottom lip. The door opened a little more, and I could see the reflection of her naked back, round ass and all, in the mirror.

Fuck, my excitement was just calming down too. Seeing her biting her lip, and knowing she was fucking naked that close to me.... Standing up right now would be an issue.

"I don't think I can," I murmured, trying to look anywhere but at the crack in the door.

"And why not?" She was glaring at me in the most fucking adorable way.

"Ah," I bent over, pretending to stretch. "We did a lot of walking today. I'm a little tired. My feet don't want to work yet."

She stared at me, like she couldn't believe that I just denied her, her mouth opening in the cutest little "o".

I sighed, taking one more look at the mirror behind her. Damn, this boner wasn't going away soon.

"I can see your reflection in the mirror, Lynn," I confessed.

Her eyes went wide, and she turned around and yelped so loudly, I couldn't help but to laugh. She forgot to close the door in her rush to grab a towel to cover herself.

She looked mortified, and I felt guilty for all the teasing.

"My poor underwear," I exclaimed, then stood up with her bag in hand, walking towards the open door.

Her eyebrows knit together. "What do you.... Oh." She looked down and saw the strain in my jeans. "Wow."

"Wow to you," I husked, leaning into the door frame. "Want to try on my swim shorts right now?"

"Maybe." her eyes were still on my junior.

I took that as a green flag to do the same, sweeping my gaze down her compact frame. The towel was bunched in her fist at her chest, and she was spilling over it. Her legs were smooth and delicious. Looking at her would not make junior go down any faster.

"Here." I held the bag in front of her eyes, blocking her stare. "You needed this?"

"I think I need something else now," she murmured. Her eyes went wide, and her lips pressed together. "What is wrong with me?" She groaned. "Where's my filter?"

I was done. To hell with being patient, being reserved. To hell with waiting for the nighttime. She wanted me, and I sure as hell wanted her.

I dropped her bag to the ground. "You don't need a fucking filter," I growled. "I'll give you what you really need." I pulled her to me, grabbing her small face in both of my hands, trying to be as gentle as I could. I angled her face to brush my lips softly to hers.

"Yes," she whispered roughly.

A smile crept to my lips before they came forcefully on hers. I devoured every gasp and moan. She tasted like tacos, zesty lime, and cilantro still coating her lips.

Her hands slipped from the towel, rising to my neck. The towel fell into a pool at her feet. I groaned, unable to resist. My hands slid down her bare back, squeezing her ass before lifting her into my arms. Her legs circled around me, and that's when I noticed her bald, and oh-so-fucking perfect pussy wetting the front of my shirt.

"Fuck, Lynn. You know where this is heading, right?" I groaned, carrying her to the bed. "You got to tell me now if you want me to stop."

"Don't stop," she begged. "Please."

"Fuck," I hissed. Her airy voice was making me delirious.

I laid her on her back, then stood to pull off my shirt. I took a second to admire the slick spot she left on it, smirking and showing her. She bit her lip, muttering an "oops".

Holding her gaze, I lifted the shirt to my face, inhaling her lusty scent. She squirmed and made the cutest fucking mewling noises.

As I was kicking off my shoes, dragging off my belt and kicking off my jeans, I admired every inch of her body. She was so gorgeous. I knew she was, but seeing her completely naked, needy and on full display for me, just me....

Fuck.

This woman was now mine. Completely.

***

Feighlynn

Was this happening? Was this really happening?

That frustrating ache in the pit of my belly was making it impossible to lie still.

Vin.

Oh my golly, I've never seen a sexier man in my whole life.

He dug around in a pocket of his bag, making my eyes go wide and my mouth drop slightly when he pulled out an entire row of condoms. At least six total, still stuck together. He dropped the foil packets on the bed and moved his bag to the ground.

"I don't think you brought enough," I joked, reaching for the packets to see them. It's been a long, long time since I've seen condoms.

"I don't think I did either," he said in a dark, raw voice that made my toes curl.

He leaned over me, and my arms instantly wrapped around his neck, hugging him close. His large, hard body felt so good pressed into mine. His lips moved with mine, driving me into a crazed frenzy.

I needed more. The ache in the pit of my belly was driving me into madness.

His hands were massaging and squeezing my breasts, my hips. He made me feel desired. Wanted. Needed. When his thick fingers found my opening, my back arched and I let out a garbled cry.

"Fuck, you're so wet," he moaned into my skin.

His fingers moved in and out of me a few times, then he rubbed the moisture they gathered around my clit. It was a frustrating, sweet rhythm, pumping in and out at a painfully slow pace, then circling my sensitive nub as I writhed beneath him.

Then he took his fingers away completely and brought them to his lips. Staring down at me, he sucked those two fingers into his mouth, running his tongue between them.

"Ngh," I groaned, bucking my hips.

"I knew you'd taste so fucking good," he husked.

With hooded eyes, he looked down at my body, exploring inside me with those thick fingers again. I thrust my pelvis against his hand, moaning when his palm created delicious friction in all the right places.

His mouth found one of my nipples, making me buck like wild. He groaned, sucking harder. His tongue was teasing my peak. It pulled at where his fingers were exploring me.

Then his mouth started moving south, leaving a wet trail from open-mouthed kisses. I stared down at him, watching the predator look in his eyes. His shoulders and back were taut, making his muscles swell in the yummiest way.

"So yummy," I breathed out loud, voicing my filterless thoughts again.

His hot breath caressed my body as his lips curled up. "You're so fucking yummy, baby."

Baby. No one has ever called me baby. It made my insides clench.

When his kisses met the sensitive skin right above my sex, those green eyes met mine. He held my stare as his warm tongue stroked my slit. His fingers were curling inside of me, and his tongue was teasing me gently from the outside.

"Mmh," he groaned, gently sucking on my nub.

His fingers moved more fervently, curling and stretching me inside. His tongue was concentrating on my bundle of nerves, sending mind-numbing currents of pleasure through my center. My legs shook. He had a hold on one of my thighs, pushing it into the mattress to keep my legs from closing. His fingers digging into my soft flesh even felt good.

When my back arched, bending high off the bed, and my eyes were rolling back with delirium, he groaned and sucked my nub even harder. His fingers and tongue were wild, driving me to that edge.

"YES!" My leg hooked around his neck, holding him in place as dots danced in my vision. My inside exploded all at once, making shivers wrack my body.

"Fuck," he groaned, lapping up everything.

As my legs calmed, he slowed and just stared at the mess he had made of me. His satisfied smirk made my knees feel weak. My entire body felt like jelly.

"Mine," he met my eyes, the intensity in them making my heart race. He held my gaze, then planted a long, sensual kiss right over my moist lower lips. "This pussy is mine now, Lynn. All mine."

I nodded, eager to agree. He could have it. He treated it better than anyone ever could. Even me.

"All of you, baby," he moved his body up the bed, his chest rubbing against mine as he held himself above me. "I want all of you."

"Vin," I whined, wiggling beneath him.

"Say you're mine," he demanded in a husky voice.

"I'm yours," I moaned. "Please-"

His lips cut off my pleas. I groaned, tasting my moisture mixing around my mouth with his tongue. I've never tasted myself before. Ever. Why does it turn me on so much?

"You're all mine," he growled deeply. "This is just the beginning."

My mind was in a haze. I couldn't comprehend what that meant, but I was eager to find out.

He sat back on his heels, reaching for the foil packets beside my head. My eyes went wide when he moved his boxers down his waist.

I had a decent idea of what I was getting into. I saw the strain on his jeans. I sat in his lap in the pool yesterday. Seeing it, having it right in my face, was still a shock. A huge shock.

"Wow."

His confident smirk erupted into airy laughter. "Damn," he chuckled, tearing the foil with his teeth. "You make me feel ten feet tall."

"Are you not?!" My eyes were still on his thing, watching as he pulled the rubbery material over its firmness.

"Fuck, you're adorable," he groaned.

He leaned back over me, adjusting himself to press against my wetness. He was cradling my face in his hands, staring at me with so much affection it made my face burn.

"You're beautiful, Lynn. Inside and out." He rested his head on mine, nuzzling his nose against me.

I closed my eyes, letting myself believe his words. He makes me feel beautiful. My mom's body, with stretch marks and cellulite, feels twenty years old again with him.

His hands roamed, caressing my soft skin. I pushed my chest into his grabby fingers and moaned as they continued down to my waist.

"Every fucking inch of you is beautiful." He lifted my thigh to hook over his hip. "And you're mine."

"Yours," I breathed, brushing my lips with his.

With one powerful thrust, he filled me. He swallowed my cries as I adjusted to him. His hands were digging into the skin of my thighs, holding me still. His breath was as ragged as mine.

We were connected. Completely. It was like our hearts were beating at the same speed. The same rhythm.

His lips were moving with mine, and he slowly moved. My legs curled around his waist, my back arching off the bed. He was reaching a place so deep I didn't know if I was trying to get away or begging for more.

"Fuck," he groaned. His whole body was strained, like he was holding himself back.

The painful stretching got sweeter and sweeter with every thrust, and soon I was meeting him eagerly. I wanted more.

He sat back on his heels, holding my legs to his chest. Watching him get lost in the pleasure of making everything in me clench.

Just when I thought it couldn't get any better, he started kissing my instep. He ran his tongue up the underside of my foot and sucked my toes into his mouth.

I bucked, screaming out, feeling the tug deep in me. My insides were quivering.

I had never, ever felt anything like that before.

He stared down at me with hooded eyes, that predatory expression on his sexily handsome face. His teeth scraped against the pads on my toes and l couldn't take anymore.

Screaming out my orgasm, my legs shook violently. He groaned, relentlessly pumping into me through my climax.

When my legs stilled and I released my death grip on the sheets, he leaned back over my body. He crashed his mouth to mine, devouring my lips. He wrapped his arms around my waist, lifting me off the bed.

I was suddenly on top, straddling him, grinding my body into his as my sex squeezed his massive length. He had my butt in his hands, guiding me, thrusting upward and making everything so much more intense. He was impossibly deeper. It felt like he was about to break through, but I loved it. Everything was so new. So intense. So mind-numbing and amazing.

"Fuck, baby. One more time. Cum for me one more time," he growled, intensifying his assault.

"Vin," I groaned, quickening my pace.

The build-up was about to explode once again. Everything was too intense in this position. Seeing him lost in me was tipping me over that edge.

"Vin!" The dams were about to burst. I couldn't keep it in.

A guttural growl rumbled in his sexy, muscled chest. His legs flexed behind me. He pulled me in for a kiss, and as I was crying my release against his lips, I felt the pulsing strains of him doing the same.

"Fuck, baby," he grunted, holding my ass still firmly against him until his body relaxed. I collapsed on his chest, spent and feeling the best kind of relaxed.

"Wow," I gasped, still trying to catch my breath.

"Wow," he kissed the top of my head. His hand pressed into my back, and I felt totally enshrined in bliss and his comfort. "You okay?

"So okay," I murmured. "My body feels like jello."

"Mmh, let me see." His hands moved to my sides, then I squealed as he squeezed me.

"Stop!" I laughed hysterically, thrashing on top of him.

His deep chuckles vibrated between us. His fingers quit their assault, and he hugged me tight.

"Your mine," he husked deeply, his lips teasing my jaw. "You're my girl now, Lynn. You know that, right? No take backs."

I giggled at his playful tone. I folded my hands on his chest and rested my chin on them. "Then you're my man?"

He smiled widely, kissing my forehead. "I'm your man."

***

"The sun is finally going down," I said, staring out the balcony window at the pinkish sky. I was lying across Vin's lap as he rubbed soothing circles up and down my back.

"Ready to use the hot tub?" he laughed softly.

"Not yet." I rolled over to stare at him. We used half the foil packets he brought, and as great as a hot soak would feel right now, there's something I need even more. "I'm hungry."

"Are you hungry, or *hungry?*" He wiggled his eyebrows.

"Regular hungry for now," I giggled. "I need food."

"Yeah? I guess we worked up an appetite. Want to just order room service?"

I bit my bottom lip, thinking for a few moments, then shook my head. "Let's go out. The baby ducks are hungry too."

Chapter Eighteen

Ducks

"Where'd all the baby ducks go?" I observed the river as we walked hand-in-hand through the Riverwalk trail.

"It's late. They're probably sleeping somewhere," he pulled against my hand, pulling me against his frame and wrapping his arm around my shoulders.

The height difference made me fit perfectly into his side. I felt my face heat at the protective way he was shielding me from the people passing in the busy crowd. Even after the past few hours in the hotel, I'm still getting those frustrating butterflies at his slightest touch.

"Where do you want to eat?" He grinned down at me, those green eyes of his catching the gleam from the lights strung up all around. "Tacos again?"

"No," I laughed. "Mexican food for dinner two nights in a row?"

"Plus, we had it for lunch," he leaned down to whisper in my ear, "and I ate taco after that, too."

My face had to have turned bright red. I giggled at his dirty joke. "You can't say that!"

"Why not?" he chuckled. "It's true. I plan on going back for seconds later."

Well, crap. There goes my new pair of undies.

The path got narrower, and Vin had me walking in front of him with both arms around me to guide me. I think he was looking out for me to keep me from falling in. I kept stumbling around as we laughed and teased each other. The stone pathway trips you up if you aren't paying attention.

We passed a corner of the Riverwalk with a couple of tightly packed restaurants. I was lost in Vin, staring back at him, trusting him completely to guide me as I laughed at another crude joke. That was when I heard a chorus of voices yelling out, "Miss Micheals!" all at once.

I looked around frantically, confused when I heard my last name.

"There," Vin pointed at the restaurant we just passed.

There were about two dozen teenage boys leaning over the railing on the patio of a restaurant, yelling for me. My son was at the center of them. Preston almost looked smug looking down at us.

"Come on, Preston's mom," one boy yelled. "Come eat with us!"

I looked at the name of the restaurant and laughed. 'Dicks' was not what I had in mind. At least....not for a restaurant....

"What do you say?" Vin smirked. "Does dick sound good?"

"Quit," I slapped his chest.

"I meant the restaurant," he husked in my ear. "What were you thinking?"

I bit my lip, knowing my blush would not fade soon.

"Come on, mom!" Preston yelled. "We've got two extra seats!"

Lord, I can not believe that I'm going to be eating at a restaurant called 'Dicks' with my son and the man I just spent the better part of the afternoon showing my naked mole rat to. This ought to be fun.

***

Vin

"Pop a squat, Trude," Coach Cabrera slapped his hand down on the empty seat beside him.

I tried not to laugh at the ridiculous paper hat he was wearing on his head. Most of the kids had on the crudely made paper hats, all with different offenses written on them. *BED WETTER, BOOGER MUNCHER, I SUCK MY THUMB,* were just some things written on the front of the hats. Coach Cabrera's hat said *OLD FART.* The coach sitting beside him, Anderson, I think his name was, didn't have on a hat. I guess he wasn't as good of a sport as his boss.

"I like your hat," Lynn giggled, pressing her lips together as her eyes smiled adorably.

"Thanks. I think we need to get y'all some too," Coach Cabrera started snapping his fingers for a server.

"You're going to love this, mom," Preston said loudly to her, talking over the noise of his friends. He had on a hat that said *MAMA's BOY.* "They have to be rude to you."

I laughed, catching that from when we came in. The host asked "what do you want?" Then just pointed to the door leading out, waving his hand like he didn't have the time or care to lead us here. Even the door was labeled push, even though we had to pull it to get outside. Lynn looked fucking adorable, trying to force it to open the wrong way.

The server, a college age girl smacking away loudly on a piece of gum, walked over with a bored expression. "What do you want now?" She grumbled.

"Hats! Hats! Give 'em hats!" One boy yelled loudly.

The server curled her lips in distaste. "I'm busy."

"Let me do it!" Another boy yelled, his hat saying *COOTIE KING.* He got up like he was about to walk to a stack of paper sitting on a counter not far away.

"Eww, no. Keep your cooties to yourself." With one last eye roll, she walked over to the pile of paper and started writing on two large sheets aggressively with a sharpie.

"Where's your hat?" Lynn asked the assistant coach.

He had a bored, irritated expression, but perked up as she spoke. It irritated the shit out of me.

"I, uh, guess I got overlooked."

"Nuh, uh. You said the hats were stupid," the teen sitting next to Preston said with a small smile.

The assistant coach's face turned sour again.

"Aw, I think it's fun. You should get one," Lynn laughed softly, adjusting the hat on her son's head. Preston was totally a mama's boy. He looked proud even while his friends started to snicker and tease him.

"Maybe I will," Anderson murmured, looking back at the server. "Hey, um, can I get one of those too?"

She scoffed, rolling her eyes, but got another sheet of paper ready.

The assistant coach smirked until he saw my arm slip around the back of Lynn's chair. He was smitten. Anyone could tell, which I suspect was what most of the boys were snickering and whispering about now. Even Coach Cabrera looked amused.

He can have a crush, but I'm not giving him an in. I spent all afternoon making her scream she belongs to me. Those weren't empty words. She's mine.

The server walked back over, three tall paper hats in hand. One said *MILF*, which obviously went to Lynn. Preston looked mortified, which had even me laughing.

The other two hats were obviously for me and the shithead assistant coach. One said *MUSCLES FOR BRAINS*, and the other said *I'M WITH STUPID* with an arrow pointing down.

Anderson reached for the muscle one, but the server snatched it out of his reach with a disgusted grimace. "It says muscles, not flab," she sneered, then placed the muscle hat on me and the stupid one on him.

"It fits you so well," Lynn giggled, staring at me.

"Yours does too," I smirked, then leaned in and whispered in her ear, "but only I get to do that to you."

"Stop," she hissed, her cheeks burning with timidity.

"Sorry. I got muscles for brains," I pressed my lips to her ear, relishing the way her body leaned into mine. I had almost forgotten that there were kids around. For a second, it was like we were lost in our own little world.

"Gross. Can you both not?" Preston grumbled.

"Oops," Lynn giggled, leaning away slightly. I didn't move away from her, though. I was still leaning over her chair, even knowing her son was watching.

He wasn't the only one watching. A very grumpy coach with a stupid hat was watching my exchange with my girl with a disgruntled face.

"Sorry," I looked at Preston, my expression not showing any remorse at all. "I was just telling her I liked her hat."

"Sure you were. Then maybe you should switch."

I laughed, but complied, switching Lynn's hat with mine. "I've always wanted to be a MILF."

"You're dating one," Preston's friend said, right before Preston punched him in the shoulder.

"How long have you two been dating?" Anderson asked, looking so awkward with the paper hat.

"A few weeks now," I looked at Lynn. "I asked her out the second I knew she was single."

"You asked me out after eating my lasagna," she laughed. "It was the food that pulled you in."

"No, your cooking is a bonus." I smirked. "It was your laugh that got me."

"My laugh?!" She looked more than flattered. "No. I know it was my lasagna."

"That was probably the best lasagna I've ever had," I grinned.

"Now you got me craving lasagna," Coach Cabrera slapped his hand down on the menu right when the server came.

"Uh, we don't serve that here, old fart. How about a spit burger instead?"

After the server took Lynn's order, she excused herself to the bathroom to wash her hands. I was laughing with my old coach as the server and another server messed with every one of the kids. That was when Preston moved down to his mother's seat, and I knew he had something to say.

I looked at him expectantly, a friendly smile on my face as he kind of sized me up. I still had my hand on the back of Lynn's chair, which was the last thing he started at.

I rested my hand on his shoulder, since it was just a few inches away now anyway, and asked, "Got something on your mind?" My tone was light, but I was nervous as heck. He was his mother's protector. If I pissed him off or got on the wrong foot with him, it would be detrimental to my relationship with his mother. That was something I wasn't willing to bet on. I wouldn't lose the first great thing to happen to me in so, so long. I don't think I did anything to set the kid off yet, but his stare still made me nervous.

"You really like my mom?" He finally asked.

I felt like I was sitting on fucking pins. I had to work extra hard to keep from moving around in my seat. He was sixteen, but the boy had a stare that would shake a hardened criminal. He's been the man of his house since his father left, and it shows.

"I like your mother a lot," I answered honestly. "She's an amazing woman."

"I know she is," he said confidently. "She's the kindest person in the world, which is why she still puts up with my dad's bull shit the way she does. She's been played and hurt enough, so if you are not serious about her-"

"Let me stop you right there," I squeezed his shoulder. "Preston, I'm so fucking serious about your mother, you wouldn't even believe. I've been where your mom is at. Exactly where your mom is at, only I never had kids. I know what you are worried about, I promise you, I'm never going to play with her. Not like you're worried about." I smirked, then added, "We had an awesome water gun fight in your pool last night, though."

He looked shocked for a minute, then laughed dryly. "Really? Mom got you to have a water gun fight with her?"

"Oh, I brought the water guns. She just supplied the water."

"Huh," he laughed, his serious expression melting away. "I bet mom loved that."

"Loved what?" She asked, just coming back out and hearing the tail end of the conversation.

"You had a water gun fight last night?" Preston got up from his mother's chair and helped her push it in after she sat back down.

"Oh, yeah!" The cutest smile broke on her face. "I totally won!"

"You think you did?" I chuckled. I know I was the real winner. I got her.

***

Nick

"We're home!" Jessie sang out as I unlocked the condo door.

Flying for the day only had us traveling light. I only had my keys and wallet, and she had a small backpack. It was a quick and easy flight back. Not baggage checks or claims, and nothing to lug around.

Why do I feel so much weight on my shoulders then?

Ever since we left the game, I've felt like complete garbage. The way Fay looked at me.....

My heart sinks in my chest just thinking about it now.

"Can we order more pizza, daddy?" Jessie asked, skipping around boxes to head to her room.

"Sure, sweetie. I'll make the call."

She stopped her prancing and stared at me as I opened the cabinet and brought down the bottle of Johnnie Walker and poured myself a glass. I've been trying to hide my mood, but coming into this condo that I was hoping to share with her mother after being so Fay was so hostile to me was what tipped me out of my facade.

"Daddy?" Jessie walked hesitantly over to me. "Are you mad?"

She asked me in the car several times on the way to the airport, asking if I was mad at her for thinking some flowers Fay received were from me and not that tattooed asshole she was with.

I was pissed, but it wasn't at Jessie. I was mad at myself.

"I'm not, baby girl. I'm just tired." I hugged her to my side.

I closed my eyes for a moment as I picked up a lingering scent of her mother's perfume on her. A choking sob almost broke free, but I swallowed it down.

"Daddy?"

"I'm fine," I forced a smile. "Really. Why don't you see if you can get a head start on Preston's room? He'll be here tomorrow. I'll come help after ordering the pizza."

"Okay," she said meekly. I knew she was still worried, but I didn't know how to put on a better act than I already was.

I felt miserable. I knew it was a long shot, but I still wanted Fay to come back with me. She's doing who knows what with that ballerina jerk right now.

As I pulled out my phone, I stared at my call log screen, scanning over all the red lines from ignored calls, mostly Arlene's, telling myself that I was looking for the number for the pizza place.

I knew who I was really looking for, though. When I saw her name appear, my finger hesitated over the call button.

That sinking feeling in my chest was too hard to ignore. I pressed call. My knees gave out, and I sank to the floor when a male voice answered.

"Hello?"

It was him. Why the hell did he have my wife's phone?

"Hello? Hey, is this Nick?" he snickered loudly on the other end of the line.

Just when I thought I couldn't feel any worse, another familiar voice came through.

"It's my dad? Let me have it. Go help mom. She's going to fall in, trying to feed the ducks."

He was with Preston...

"Hey, dad. Sorry. Mom left her bag here on the patio of the restaurant while she ran off to feed duck french fries. Do you need something?"

I was stunned for a moment, but then found my voice. "Um, yeah. Hi, Pres. I just.... I just wanted to let your mom know we got back safe."

"Okay. Cool. I'll tell her."

"Thanks," I muttered, holding my hand over my eyes like I could hold in my tears. "Um, Preston?"

"Yeah, dad?" He sounded distracted.

I took a shuddering breath, then said, "I... I love you, son. See you tomorrow."

"Yeah. I love you too, dad. Bye."

CLICK

My hand fell to the floor as the line went dead.

My wife and my son. That man... He was winning over everything I had lost in this divorce. I have never felt more defeated in my entire life.

Chapter Nineteen

I Got You

Vin

"That was fun." Lynn twirled in a circle on the less crowded trail leading to the hotel. "Preston has good friends."

"Preston's a good kid," I smiled. "You did a good job with him."

"Eh, he's more of a parent than me most of the time."

I chuckled, knowing what she meant. I saw endless examples of his maturity and how he looked out for his mother in so many ways tonight. As a man that also grew up with a single mother, I was impressed.

"She's a natural drunk. No alcohol needed," Preston had said to me after getting off the phone with his dad. I had barely grabbed his mom in time before she fell face first into the hoard of hungry ducks. "If she's near water, she's going to fall in if you don't watch her." He then warned me about her distracted driving, and not to let her listen to her books while she drives.

I took mental notes throughout dinner about how he treated his mom. He seemed like the parent most of the time.

"He likes you, you know," Lynn bumped her shoulder against mine, looking all cute and smug.

I wrapped an arm around her shoulders, feeling pretty smug myself. "What's not to like?"

"I don't know. I have no complaints yet," she giggled.

"That's good to hear. Please let me know if you ever do." I kissed the top of her head.

Dinner was fun, even with that bump-on-a-log assistant coach glaring at me the entire time. Lynn was the life of the party, getting most of the kids to play some type of charades game on her phone while we waited for the food. Even the staff couldn't be jerks to her. It was in their job description, but not one of them was a dick to my girl after the drinks came.

"It's so pretty out here at night," she said, looking up at all the hanging lights. "There's not as many people as earlier, either."

"They gather at the bars and clubs the later it gets. We're getting far from the mall, too."

"You know," she twisted back to stare up at me, grabbing my hand on her shoulder with both of hers. "I haven't been to a bar or a club in a long time."

"Me neither. Well, maybe bars, but only the restaurant ones. I'm too old for that shit." I used to have to pull my soldiers piss drunk out of bars in the middle of the night when they would start causing trouble. It turned me off to the whole idea of partying.

"You're not old," she droned.

"I felt old around all those kids tonight."

"Really? They all seemed to think you were the coolest thing ever. They couldn't get enough of your stories about their coach and the army."

I chuckled softly. "Only old men tell stories like that to the younger generations."

"Nuh uh. You're too sexy to be old," she said, then quickly covered her mouth with her hands.

"You think I'm sexy?" I teased her.

She sighed, dropping one hand and grabbing my hand with her other. "Who wouldn't? I didn't mean to say that out loud, though."

"I like that you have no brain to mouth filter." I hugged her to my side. "It's one thing that makes you so sexy." I wiggled my eyebrows to drive my point home.

"It's not sexy," she smiled, biting her bottom lip.

I shrugged. "Sexy. Adorable. The cutest fucking thing ever."

"You're sweet," she giggled. "Fine. If you don't mind my filterless mouth, I won't mind it either."

"You shouldn't. I like your filterless mouth." I bent to gently place my lips on hers. "I like it a lot."

The lighting from above danced on her gorgeous face, and her eyes twinkled.

"I like your mouth too." Her eyes glanced at my lips. She then whispered, "I really like what you did with it earlier."

A fire lit inside of me. "What did I do earlier?"

Her face turned the prettiest shade of pink. "You know."

"Did you suddenly gain a filter?" I laughed softly.

She stubbornly set her jaw. "No. That's just.... Dirty."

"Dirty, but delicious," I whispered, kissing her one more time. "I plan on doing it again when we get back to the room. Maybe in the hot tub this time."

She squeaked, making a smug smile spread across my face. Fuck, she was adorable. I wanted to put my dirty mouth all over her, right here, right now.

That was probably a bad idea. My kisses and groping were getting worse by the second. It was less crowded, but there were still people around.

We passed a bar with salsa music playing, signs for margarita specials posted outside. Lynn turned her head, clearly intrigued.

"Mmh, margaritas," she got all doe-eyed at the sign. She was craning her neck to see inside. It was clear what she wanted.

I guess my dirty mouth can wait another hour.

"Want one?" I started steering us to the bar, already knowing her answer.

"Maybe one," she beamed. Then she pursed her pouty lips. "Do you think we can get one to go?"

A shit-eating grin broke across my face. "Probably not. It doesn't matter, anyway."

"Why?"

"Because your mouth and mine will be busy with other things the second we get back."

Her eyes flickered to my lips as she bit her own. Fuck, I didn't want to wait, but teasing her was too much fun.

One kiss. One more deep, spine-tingling kiss. Then I'd be fine until we got back to the room.

***

Feighlynn

"Two house margaritas on the rocks," Vin ordered after leading us to the bar. He looked at me for a long few seconds, assessing me, then added, "Actually, make hers a strawberry one."

"Strawberry?" I giggled. "Why strawberry?"

He shrugged, a true action hero smile on his handsome face as he leaned against the bar. "You look like a strawberry margarita sort of girl. That, and you were staring at the picture of the strawberry one the hardest."

"Oh," I laughed. "It was the prettiest."

He wiped a hand down his face, like he was hiding his smile. "Fuck, you're adorable."

He keeps saying that, and I'm believing it more and more.

The margaritas came and were good. Fantastic, but really strong. I was getting warmer and warmer with every sip. Mine was sweet and garnished with two strawberries. I tried to offer one strawberry to Vin, but he shook his head. He waited until I popped one in my mouth, then leaned over to kiss me, sucking the juice off my lips.

My mouth dropped.

Vin smirked, licking his lips. "It tastes better like that."

My thighs clenched. "Did you have to go to some special training to learn to be that... that....?"

"That what?" He chuckled. "That smooth? That charming?"

"Sexy," another word vomit slipped out, but the alcohol was making me not care. "My panties can't handle much more of you."

He coughed on his drink and adjusted himself on the stool he was sitting on. "Fuck, I don't know if mine can handle much more, either."

We teased and flirted some more than we sat and drank. I ended up ordering a second, and then a third margarita, while Vin drank Dos Equis. The bar livened up the later it got, and eventually people started dancing on the small dance floor on the pavilion outside. A live band was playing slow and smooth Spanish music, the deep tremor of the lead singer setting the mood.

It felt romantic. With the lights and the setting of the Riverwalk, and with my action hero date, I felt like I was in a romance movie.

I was mesmerized for a while, feeling tipsy and watching the band and dancing. The people on the dance floor were swaying softly, their heads bowed together as they swung and ground their hips.

"Do you want to dance?" Vin asked me, watching me intently.

"I thought you didn't dance?"

"I never said that?" He smiled before taking a swig of his beer. "I said I don't go to clubs and bars. Doesn't mean I never did."

"So you can dance?"

He shrugged. "I took ballet."

I giggled at the reminder. I could just picture this big, hard-muscled ex-soldier in a tutu and tights.

Looking back at the dance floor, seeing those couples moving together, it became harder to picture Vin dancing. Maybe because I couldn't picture myself out there dancing like that, and I didn't want to picture him with anyone else.

"I can't see it," I tilted my head at him. "You're so tall and muscly. I can't picture you dancing like that."

"Well, I'll have to show you then." He stood up and held his hand out for me, a confident smile on his wet lips.

I blushed, feeling self-conscious about the idea. I never had the chance to try dancing like these people were dancing right now. It wasn't something Nick would ever agree to do, and I never had the chance to do it with anyone else.

"Come on," Vin leaned in and whispered deeply. "Trust me."

I did trust him. As much as I feared falling on my face or tripping on my own feet, I trusted him to catch me if I did.

"Okay," I whispered, taking his hand and letting him lead me to an open space on the dance floor.

My heart was pounding, and it was only partially from the fear of dancing in front of so many people. It was mostly just from being in this moment with Vin, his authoritative confidence that had me wanting to give him all my trust and control. It was exhilarating, feeling open with someone like him.

"Do you want to stand on my feet?" He leaned down and asked, his green eyes shining into mine.

It was a teasing remark, but I was actually tempted to take him up on it. He was so much taller than me, and I felt that height difference standing with our bodies this close together.

"I'm sure I'll step on your feet plenty."

He chuckled, gliding his hands down my arms until they met mine. He rested my arms around his neck in a smooth motion, then slid his hands down to my waist and lower back. "You won't. I got you."

Got me, he did.

He pressed my body against his, his firm muscles making my mouth go dry like I was thirsty. Then he swayed, his hands on my back guiding me, forcing me to move with him. I was like his puppet, moving at his command, and loving every second.

His eyes looked hooded in the closeness of our bodies, his head dipped down to mine. His mouth was partially open, his tongue pressing against his teeth. He looked so sexy, so sensual. I felt sexy in his arms.

As the music wrapped around us, all the other people faded away. It was just him and me, moving to the erotic beating of our hearts pounding in our chests. I felt connected to him. Connected in a way that was so intimate, it felt sinfully right.

"I told you I got you," he husked, his mouth just a breath away from mine.

"I knew you did," I smiled softly, lost in his expression. "I trust you."

"Good," he rested his forehead on mine, closing his eyes like he was soaking me in. "You're my girl, Lynn. I've got you. Always."

My heart skipped a beat. "That's a heavy statement."

"It's a promise."

Then, his mouth was on mine, and I melted into him more.

His promise was making me more drunk than the alcohol could, and I wanted to intoxicate myself more and more. I believed him. This didn't feel like something light, or just a casual partner to date and have fun with.

There was something deeper here. Something that reached deep down in me and healed that those parts of myself I didn't even realize had been broken.

I spent most of my life catering to others. To Nick, and then my kids. Even to my dog and neighbors before I thought of my own needs or wants.

Vin made me want to be selfish. He made me believe I could be. That even if I gave in to all the things I didn't realize I wanted in the past, he would be there with me to keep me safe through it all.

Like dancing tipsy in a random bar in a city a few hundreds of miles away from home. I never would have done something like this before, not wanting to worry my kids or anyone else.

I was safe with Vin, though. He had me.

CHAPTER TWENTY

Fallen

After dancing until my feet were sore, Vin and I took our sweet time walking back to the hotel.

We were slow at getting back, not because of the scenery or because of any more margarita stops, but because every two seconds I had to reach up and start kissing him as I remembered the way he held me while we danced. Everything about him drew me in, and I know I was having the same effect on him too.

At one point, we walked under a bridge with no other people around, and he spun me around and pinned me against a rail, kissing me so passionately that it made walking uncomfortable the rest of the way here.

When we got back to the hotel room, things got heavy fast. Our frustration was at its breaking point. As soon as the door latched shut, he had me pinned against the hall and both of our pants were off in no time.

I had never done that before. Make love while pinned against the wall. Ever. He held me the entire time, roughly taking me in his arms with nothing more than a wall behind me for support. He made me feel small and desired. He had total control over me, and I loved every second.

Now, we're sitting in the hot tub on the balcony, staring out at the night view. I still felt small and cherished in his lap as he caressed and snuggled against me.

"This is nice." I leaned back against Vin's chest in the hot tub, the bubbles from the jets rumbling around us.

"So nice," he kissed the back of my neck, making me bite my lip and moan softly. "Everything about this trip has been nice."

"Not quite everything," I laughed humorlessly, sinking a little more into the water as I remembered our surprise before the game. "The second half of it has been perfect, though."

"Yeah. Having an ex show up without warning is never fun."

"Hmm," I nodded, leaning into him as he continued to kiss my neck. "Thank you for everything today," I whispered.

"For driving you here," he chuckled. "It was my pleasure, especially after hearing from Preston how distracted you can get."

"Jeez," I scoffed. "Not just that. I mean, for everything today. For the first time since I can remember, I felt.... I don't know. Taken care of? It was nice to let loose like I did."

He tightened his hands on my waist and twisted me in his lap, causing me to straddle him in the giant tub. He had a giant smile on his handsome face. Beads of sweat were forming on his forehead, and started dropping as his smile lines disturbed them. How can a single man be this sexy?

"You really know how to make a man feel like he just grew a couple of feet. You know that, right? If you don't watch out, I'm going to get an enormous head."

"You were already super tall," I giggled. "I felt like I was dancing with a giant tonight."

"Well, this giant enjoys taking care of you." His eyes shone with sincerity. "I want you to never have to worry when you're with me."

"You're doing a good job then." I wrapped my arms around his neck. "Like my own action hero," I giggled.

"You know what else action heroes are good for," he smirked, pressing his firmness against me.

I whimpered as he ground against my sensitive flesh. The hot tub took away most of my soreness from our earlier activities, and then the dancing, but my naked mole rat was still a little tender.

Not that it mattered. I still wanted him.

"We probably shouldn't do that in the hot tub," I said softly, already melting into him.

"Probably not," he laughed. "But that doesn't stop me from wanting to."

"You could just take me on the wall again," I suggested.

"Liked that, didn't you?" I felt his breath on my neck from his silent laughter.

"It was nice," I sighed dreamily.

His large biceps holding me in place and the rest of his muscles contorted around me were as pleasurable as the actual pleasure I felt from the sex. Even now, my hands are taking on a mind of their own, traveling across his chest and down to his abs to feel the taut planes of sexiness.

"Mmh, I like your hands touching me," he rested his head back on the edge of the tub.

I took that as a cue to explore a little more. I leaned back on his knees, skimming my hands lower until they reached a delicious tapered contour that led down to his most impressive muscle of all.

He was hard and ready, feeling so smooth, like a velvet rock as my fingers wrapped around his girth. His mouth opened to a soft 'o', and he made this satisfied noise in the back of his throat.

My hand pumped his full length, slowly and intentionally going up and down. No matter how slowly or smoothly I moved, the water was still sloshing around us. We really shouldn't be doing this in a hot tub on a balcony overlooking the busiest part of the city, but I no longer cared.

He opened his hooded eyes to stare at me as I got more enthusiastic about my movement. Seeing his pleasure was too rewarding to let up now.

Then I got even more brave.

I pushed up on my knees, lining my body up with him, before I slowly lowered myself back down. It stung just for a second, and then the fullness of all the pleasurable sensations took over.

"Fuck, baby," he groaned, sitting back and letting me do all the work.

Riding him and watching his face as the friction fought against the slickness between us was everything. It drove me to ride him harder. Water was splashing out on the balcony, but I didn't care. I could feel that sweet spot tingling inside of me as it took its proper beating, and I was chasing my release while watching him get close to his.

"Shit," he suddenly grabbed my hips, forcing me to stop. "You're going to make me cum, baby."

"Then cum," I groaned, trying to move once again.

"Hold on," he lifted me up and off him, then quickly got out of the hot tub.

My eyes glazed over, seeing his member at a full salute, slick with more than just water. When he came back out holding a condom to his tip and rolling it down, I suddenly realized why he stopped me.

"See," I laughed softly as he got back in. "I don't have to worry about anything. You take care of it all."

His face was serious as he picked me up and placed me back on his lap. Every movement between us was so natural, it almost surprised me.

"I want to take care of you, Lynn. That's all I want to do. All I can think about."

I bit my lip, suppressing a moan as he slid back into me. "You mean, as in sex?" This almost sounded like a deeper confession than he just wanted to take care of me in bed, and I wanted to be sure.

I was falling for this man. More and more by the second. He was mending all the parts of me I didn't even realize were broken, and I'm scared if our feelings are not the same, I could just end up hurt again. After the dancing, and the dinner with Preston, I knew where I stood. I held my breath, hoping he felt the same.

"No. Not just when we have sex," he husked, his serious expression staring up at me. "I want to take care of you in every way." He nuzzled his face against mine as he slowly moved inside me again. "I'm your action hero, baby. Remember. I'm here for you. I'll even save you from falling in with the ducks when you need me to."

"I wasn't going to fall in," I argued weakly, the pleasure already overtaking me again.

He laughed softly. "You were falling then, just like you're making me fall now." I leaned up to look at him, confused. "I'm falling for you, baby. Head first. Now, quit distracting me so I can finish making you fall, too."

Too late. I've fallen.

***

Vin

I couldn't stop smiling every time I looked over at my sleeping girlfriend sitting in the passenger seat of my car.

Poor girl. I didn't really give her any chance to rest last night. I drove my point into her on repeat throughout the night; that she was mine and no one else's. Her perfect little body kept up all the way, but no amount of caffeine or sing-along songs could keep her eyes from closing once we hit the road.

I was tired too, but seeing her was all the energy I needed to keep going. My car was trashed with her food wrappers and water bottles, plus insignificant items here and there that she kept pulling out of her purse yesterday, like notepads and tissue packs, but I have never been happier to have such a messy car.

We were almost home now. After last night, I wish we were going home together. I know that will be impossible for a while. A long while, most likely. Her kids were still her priority, as they should be, and I know she's going to do what is best for them.

Still. Living across the street from her is the next best thing. We can still take our daily walks with Kevin.

Shit. I forgot I start my job tomorrow. I guess the morning walks will be harder to do. I have to be in the office by eight in the morning before the first court hearings.

That made me think of another issue Lynn brought up last night.

While we were cuddling in the sheet, between rounds, we were talking about work and she brought up what her ex was. He was a lawyer, and she warned me I would likely see him at court often. She said his firm even worked closely with several government offices, so I might not just run into him in court.

I'll have to ask Milton about him later. I don't want to make life harder for Lynn by causing more strife with her ex, but I sure as hell will not pussyfoot around the man.

He clearly still had feelings for his ex wife. I wasn't backing down for him, but I also had to tread lightly because of their kids. Preston didn't seem close to his dad, just Jessie sure did. She was a daddy's girl if I ever saw one. It made me jealous. She looked so much like Lynn. It made me crave to have a daddy's girl one day too. One just like the beautiful sleeping woman snoring lightly in my passenger seat.

We had time. I was serious about her being mine. I'm never going to be stupid enough to let her go.

When I got to the outskirts of our neighborhood, I gently shook her to wake her up.

"Wake up, baby. We're almost home."

"Five more minutes," she grumbled, rolling over to lean her head against the car door.

Damn, she was so fucking adorable.

"Kevin is waiting for you," I laughed softly.

She groaned, then stretched. I had a hard time focusing on the road with her cute little moans filling the confined space as she stretched and arched her back.

"We're really almost home?"

"Yeah," I chuckled deeply, reaching over to rub her leg. "You slept almost the entire drive. I was lonely."

I meant to tease her, but her adorable regretful expression made my heart race instead.

"I'm sorry," she said with sleepy eyes. "I didn't get much sleep last night."

"I know, baby," I rubbed her knee. "I was just teasing you. It's my fault you didn't get any sleep."

Her eyes narrowed playfully. "You're right." She couldn't hold the scowl for long before she burst into a fit of giggles. "It was well worth it. You can keep me up all night whenever you want."

I bit my cheek, running through my next question several times before letting it out. "Even tonight?"

She looked shyly over at me, biting her full bottom lip. "Sure. I don't see why not. The kids won't be home until tomorrow after school."

I was mentally pumping my fist in the air, but tried to keep my excitement contained on the outside. I gently squeezed her knee again, and said, "Good. I wasn't ready to let you go."

CHAPTER TWENTY-ONE

Lunch Plans

"I'm not ready for you to leave," Lynn whined, her arms wrapped around my waist, lying on top of me.

I've been pinned in place. Not just by her, but her dog lying on my legs, making moving impossible.

I'm loving it.

Damn, she was so adorable. Even more when she was just in an old t-shirt and her hair was all messy from sleep.

"I'm not ready to leave either, baby. Maybe I should just not go. I can call in sick or something."

She pressed her lips into my chest to hide her smile. "Missing your first day. What a model employee."

"I think my boss would understand." Especially if he saw her like this, but that would never happen. I'm gatekeeping this woman's just-out-of-bed appearance for myself.

I couldn't bring myself to let her go yet, so I just enjoyed the feeling of her in my arms for another ten minutes before starting getting out of bed again. Lying there and cuddling her, kissing her sweet-smelling hair, I thought of all the ways I can prolong my time here. What parts of getting ready for my first day of work could I cut out?

I didn't need a shower. Did I really *need* to brush my teeth? Or do my hair? Could I just wear a hat?

I could rush to the courthouse and make it just in time if I didn't stop to eat breakfast at all. Mom won't like me leaving without something to eat, but it's a sacrifice I'm more than willing to make for this woman. To prolong this blissful weekend with her.

Shit, it would be so much easier to just leave from here, but I had no more clothes to change into. I needed to at least run home for that.

"I really need to go now, baby," I kissed the top of her hair. "I don't want to, but I do."

"Okay," she sighed, leaning up to smile sweetly down on me. "I guess I can let you go. If I have to."

"I wish you didn't," I groaned, squeezing her one last time.

As she was pressing her lips to mine, they lifted in an excited smile. "Do you get a lunch break today?"

I chuckled, following her train of thought. "I think they have to give me one. Why? What do you have in mind?"

"Well," she wiggled excitedly, making parts of me involuntarily excited too. "There's a good pizza place near the justice center. Or a good sushi place near the library. Or burgers... I know!" She lit up. "There's this sports bar with an outer space theme. My sister and I have gone for drinks a few times before shows at the theater. I've always wanted to try their lunch menu."

"A space themed bar?" I chuckled, knowing what bar she was talking about. It was quirky, and near the parking garage of where I'll be parked. "Sounds fun. I'll message you when I get to work and let you know what time I take lunch."

"Yay!" She straddled me, kissing me deeply. We both had morning breath, but neither of us cared. Her kisses are sweet enough that the morning breath didn't bother me one bit.

When I finally got my reluctant ass out of Lynn's house and got ready enough to speed to work, I didn't let the prospect of me getting a speeding ticket diminish my good mood. I was still all smiles as I skipped the busy elevator and took the stairs two at a time to the fourth floor, where I was meeting the retiring manager, Jerry, who would brief me for the next two weeks on my job duties.

Milton was in the meeting room too when I walked in, making for a few minutes of teasing banter before we actually sat down to discuss my duties.

This job would be easy compared to the places I served in the past. I was just a babysitter for the security teams, and everything seemed to run smoothly already.

Before Milton went off to leave me with Jerry, he asked me about my weekend with that knowing glint in his eyes.

"Do anything fun? Any, you know, dates or anything?"

I chuckled under my breath. "You could say that." I scratched my chin, rough from not having the time to shave.

"I take it your date with your neighbor went well then?"

"I'd say so. It lasted until...," I checked my watch, "about an hour and a half ago."

"You stayed with her the entire weekend?" Milton sat up straighter, ready for the details.

Jerry chuckled, watching us. "You seem almost as excited about the man's dating life as he is."

"You don't know this guy like I do, or you would be excited too."

"What's that supposed to mean?" I raised my eyebrows at my old friend.

Milton shrugged. "You're you. You must really like the chick to spend the entire weekend with her."

"When I was single, I could spend the entire weekend with a girl, and it could mean nothing," Jerry scoffed, then looked at me. "And I'm not half as good looking a mother fucker as this guy."

"Trude isn't like that. He's tried and trude, the prude," Milton snickered at himself.

"Damn, I haven't heard that in a long time," I laughed.

Milton looked at Jerry and said, "Trude doesn't do bachelor life well. He never took women home from the bar or anything. I was worried his man parts wouldn't work anymore if he ever found a girl that would change him from his prudish ways." He wiggled his eyebrows at me. "Go on. Tell me it still works."

I sat back and smirked, not giving up any details. The details of my time with Lynn were none of his business.

"Come on," Milton leaned forward. "Give me something."

I chuckled. "Fine. We had a date Friday night at her place."

"Yeee-eah you did," Milton interrupted, dropping his tone suggestively.

"Shut up. It wasn't like that. She cooked, and then we had a water gun fight outside before I went home."

Milton looked at me like I was crazy. "What? Are you twelve?"

"Maybe," I smiled widely. "It was seriously the best date I've ever had."

"Man, I've been there," Jerry laughed softly. "My wife has one of those soft dart guns she stole from the grandkids. She keeps that thing in her chair in the living room to shoot me if I snore on the couch. Sometimes I fake sleeping just because I like to hear her giggle when I *wake up* in a panic." He smiled fondly at the memory. "Your girl sounds like a keeper, young man."

"She is." I'm keeping Lynn forever. I know it already.

"Yeah, yeah. I get it. But did you seriously just have a water gun fight from Friday night until this morning?" Milton didn't seem content with just the water gun details.

"No. On Saturday, I went with her down to San Antonio to watch her son play in a tournament for high school baseball. I met both her kids officially for the first time. We got back late last night, and I stayed with her until this morning." I smiled after running through the cliff-note version of my weekend.

"I guess it works," Jerry laughed to himself. I just snickered.

"You even met her kids?" Milton seemed surprised. "Did they like you?"

"I think so. Her son, for sure, did."

"Huh," Milton seemed thoughtful now. "So, it's serious?"

"Pretty damn serious. I like her a lot."

"Well, I'm happy for you then. You deserve someone that can make your thing work again. I thought your ex made it shrivel up for good."

"Screw you," I scoffed.

"I'm just messing with you," Milton laughed. "So, when do I get to meet her?"

"Why the hell would you meet her?"

"Because I'm your friend," I faked being offended.

"So?"

"Come on, man. I've got to see the woman that the tried and trude prude into a smitten kitten."

"A kitten?" I scoffed.

"You have got me curious now too, and I don't even know you like that, prude Trude," Jerry laughed.

I checked my phone, and there was a text from Lynn, a reply from mine I sent letting her know when I got here on time. She was asking about my lunch break.

"I have plans to meet her for lunch today." I scratched the back of my head.

Milton and Jerry exchanged a look, then Milton asked, "Where are we going?"

***

Feighlynn

"Be a good boy." I squatted down and scratched between Kevin's ears. Then I hugged him tightly, a burst of excitement shooting through me.

I feel like a teenager again. I'm giddy and eager to see Vin, even though it's only been four hours since he left in a rush for work.

He was so funny to watch as he was rushing from his house to his car. I was just starting my walk with Kevin, and even though Vin was running late, he still pulled up beside me and demanded a kiss.

A few neighbors saw us, but that's okay. Now that my kids are aware, it's not like I want to keep dating my sexy neighbor a secret any longer.

I think after this past weekend, we're both fully committed to dating one another. I wasn't sure before, but hearing him demand that I say I'm his as he relentlessly took me repeatedly had a lasting effect. I really felt like I am his and he is mine.

"Eek!" I squealed, squeezing my dog tighter. He barked and licked the side of my face, excited too, though he did not know why.

"Okay, boy. I really need to go."

Vin will go to lunch at one. I have little time. I wanted to get there a bit early to get a big table. He said he was bringing his boss and a few officers, too. I offered to just stay home so he could bond with his new colleagues, but he insisted I be there.

I was nervous about meeting people he would work with. I'm trying to keep a casual mindset about the whole thing, but it seems like something a new girlfriend shouldn't intrude on.

But then again, we aren't two young ducks anymore. I'm already committed to this, and I know he is, too. I guess that makes it less weird, and maybe even a little romantic. He still wants me to meet him, even if others are around.

Jeez, I hope I don't do something stupid, like squirt mustard down my shirt or sneeze in the chip bowl. Nick used to coach me before we would meet with his work friends for anything, just to ensure I didn't step out of line with my filterless mouth. I don't think Vin cares as much about public opinions, but my experiences with Nick still leave a sour taste in my mouth.

As I was grabbing my bag and keys and headed for the garage, the doorbell rang. Kevin went nuts, like he always does. It took me a second to calm him down and pull him back.

"It's just a delivery!" I told him, knowing the mail carrier stops by about this time almost every day.

When I knew he was done with his protective fit, I cracked open the door, staring down at the mat to see what package was left.

Instead, I found a pair of men's oxfords. I followed the legs to the shoes up and had to resist the urge to groan when I saw Nick standing there.

"You're not a package," I said almost accusingly.

"No. I am not. You sound disappointed," he smiled.

I am, but saying that would be rude. "Do you need something?" I said instead. "I was just about to leave."

That took the smile right off his face. "Oh, uh, leave for where?"

I quirked my lips to the side of my face, not sure if I wanted to tell him. I haven't seen or talked to him since Preston's game, and I didn't really want to talk to him now. "I have lunch plans," I simply said.

"Oh." His shoulders slumped forward slightly, his face full of disappointment. "I was stopping by to see if I could take you out to lunch. I guess that wouldn't work then."

"Nope," I sighed, not sure why he would want to have lunch. We've not had lunch or done anything without the kids involved together since we separated. "I'm sorry, Nick, but I really have to go. If you need to talk to me about something, can it be later?"

"Sure. What about dinner? Tonight?"

"It's a Monday night. The kids will need laundry done and I have a list a mile high of other things I need to do for them. Can I just call you sometime tomorrow?" I checked the time on my watch. I had an hour still, but the traffic during lunch was sometimes a pain. I needed to leave soon to make sure I got there early.

Nick shuffled awkwardly on his feet. "I'd really like to talk to you sooner rather than later, Fay. This is, uh, kinda important."

"Important or not, I don't know if I'm comfortable meeting you alone for any meal. Arlene wouldn't appreciate it either."

"That's kinda what I wanted to talk to you about," he mumbled. "I'm... I'm not with Arlene anymore."

"Oh," I said awkwardly. "I'm sorry to hear that."

"Yeah," he shifted nervously on his feet again. "I'm not sorry to end it at all. It was a mistake."

A mistake? The break up was a mistake, or did he make a mistake with Arlene where he got kicked out? Is that why he needed the condo?

I didn't have time for this.

"Are you just needing someone to talk to about the breakup?" I asked, going out on a limb. I was growing anxious about the time and wanted to finish this quickly. "If so, I can call you after I get done with lunch, but I really need to go."

His brows shadowed his eyes as he frowned. "Are you meeting *him?* That guy?"

I bit my bottom lip, sensing his hostility towards Vin. It's unwarranted, and I wasn't sure how to tell him that.

"Fay, please," Nick took a step forward, reaching out to grab my hand. "Please, stay and talk with me. Don't go see him."

Chapter Twenty-Two

Déjà Vu

I pulled my hand out of his, taking a step back. "Excuse me?!" I felt like a trout, opening and closing my mouth in stunned anger. First, he had an issue with me driving back with Vin, and now he's trying to prevent me from going to lunch with him. "Where do you get off trying to keep me from spending time with the man I'm seeing? What the hell is wrong with you?"

"Now, wait," he tried to push inside the house, but I stayed firmly in place, blocking him. "Let's talk about this inside."

"No! I already told you I'm not comfortable being alone with you right now and there's no reason for you to come into my house."

"Our house," he tried to correct me.

"My house!" I snapped back. "It's mine, free and clear, after *you* left it. I'm sorry your relationship with Arlene went south, but quit trying to get in the way of mine."

"That's ..." He pulled at the hair on top of his head, taking a few frustrated steps back, then coming to face me again. "I'm trying to tell you I want you back, Feighlynn! I mean, damn, I made a fucking mistake! I should have never left you! I realized it the second I did I was making the wrong choice. I should have chosen you!"

A cold, tense silence stretched between us. Again, angry shock made my entire body go rigidly tense. How dare he. After all this time, how dare he try something like this? I sat back and pretended everything was completely okay when he ran off to be with his mistress. I never tried to stop him or guilt him into staying. How dare he think he has any right to stop me from moving on?

"So now that things aren't working out with your girlfriend, you're wanting to come back to me? Is that what this is?" I felt the icy venom in my tone. I didn't care.

"No," he quickly shook his head, trying to reach out to me again. I jerked away, avoiding his touch. The pain that flashed in his eyes had no effect on me. "No, Fay. That's not it. I realized my mistake the second I left this house. I knew Arlene wasn't what I really wanted. I knew it was always you. All I'm asking for now is a second chance."

"You're crazy." He had to be clinically insane to be pulling this stunt right now.

"I might be crazy, but that's because I'm still in love with you. You're still my wife."

"Your wife?!" I scoffed. "We divorced. I am no longer your wife and your mistakes are no longer my concern."

"Please Fay," there were tears in his eyes now, but again, it didn't move me at all. I felt nothing but bitterness for this man. "There has to be something left in you. Some part of you that still loves me."

"Not a single cell in my body still loves you, Nick. Not one," I said coldly. "I know I've been amicable through the whole divorce. I've played nice and I've been the one to bend through it all. I tried to make things as easy as possible and remain as civil as possible. But none of those things I did for your sake. Not one. I did those things for the sake of my kids. If you somehow mistook my friendliness and civility as any affection I might have left for you, I'm sorry. All my affection died for you the moment that you confirmed you cheated on me. There's no way I was ever going to recover from that with you. Now, if you excuse me, I have a date to get to."

With that, I calmly, but firmly, shut the door on his shocked face, picked up my stuff, and headed for the garage.

As I was pulling away, I saw Nick sitting on the top step of my porch, his head in his hands as his shoulders shook. I felt no remorse. No regret. Nothing but anger for the fickle, cowardly man that once again tried to steal my blooming happiness because of his own selfish agenda.

***

Vin

"Is everything okay?" I whispered in Lynn's ear.

She smiled up at me, nodding her head. Her smile didn't reach her eyes.

Lynn was already here waiting by the time me and my new colleagues arrived. She had gotten a table and was just waiting in the front as they set it up, pulling three tables together to accommodate all of us.

I saw her through the glass doors before we came in, and I could tell right away that something was wrong. She was staring down at the ground with none of her adorable quirks showing. She was singing to herself, or talking excitedly to the hostess, or even looking at her phone with that cute look of concentration she gets whenever she was going through emails or texts. She was just staring blankly at the ground, no emotion at all on her beautiful face.

When we walked in, she instantly perked up, acting like her usual self, but I knew her well enough now to notice the tension in her movements and the way her smile seemed forced. I don't know what changed in the time I left her this morning, but something did, and it is worrying me.

I couldn't press her here, so I just kept a hand on her thigh as we sat with Milton and Jerry, and five of the other security officers I'll be working with.

"What are you two lovebirds whispering about over there?" Milton asked, hiding his smile behind his draft beer.

"Mind your business," I retorted, squeezing Lynn's thigh one last time before wrapping my arm around the back of her chair.

Lynn just laughed softly, her smile still not fully reaching her eyes and making them crinkle in the corners like they usually do.

"If this dude ever gives you a hard time, Lynn, let me know and I'll set him straight for you," Milton snorted.

"Sure you would," Jerry patted his shoulder, then winked at Lynn. It made her giggle, which I appreciated.

"Y'all are funny," she said as she leaned into me. "So, you and Vin were in the Army together?"

"We grew up together," Milton said. "We joined the Army together, but I got out as soon as I could. This mother fucker became a lifer. He was made for the military. Mr. Tried and Trude."

"Don't start with that shit again," I muttered, feeling a bit embarrassed, and maybe nervous. I didn't know what kind of shit was about to come out of Milton's mouth.

"Tried and Trude?" Lynn looked curiously up at me.

"Tried and Trude the prude," Milton started snorting, laughing.

"You're a prude, huh?" Lynn smiled, and this time it reached her eyes, making my heart beat rapidly at how breathtaking she looked. "I never would have pegged you as a prude."

"Oh, ho, ho," Milton snickered loudly. "So his junk does still work?"

"Shut the fuck up!" I threw my napkin across the table at him.

Lynn was full on laughing now, lighting up the entire restaurant. Gawd, she looks the prettiest when she's laughing.

"Look at you," Milton scoffed. "I'm glad Trude finally found a woman that can make him smile like that."

Fuck, I probably looked like a fool just now, staring at her like I was. I couldn't help it.

Lynn blushed, looking at me from the corner of her eyes with a shy little smile. I don't care if I look like a fool anymore. How could I not be infatuated with a woman like her?

Milton asked Lynn questions about her work, getting to know her more while I talked to Jerry and the officers I would work closest with. I still had my arm around Lynn, and she was still leaning into me, but it felt so natural that we easily carried on our separate conversations.

"Jeez, I swear you look so familiar," Lynn said to Milton at some point. "The more we talk, the more I get this sense of déjà vu."

Milton's smile faltered for a second before he pasted it back on. "We might have met a few times in the past. At city events and such."

Lynn quirked her head to the side, tilting it adorably as she thought deeply for a few seconds. And then it was like something just dawned on her.

"Oh," she whispered. "Huh."

Her eyes quickly flashed to me before looking away, and then she put back on that forced smile.

"Small world," she whispered.

"Not too small." Milton seemed apologetic somehow. "Kevin is a good guy. I'm happy for you both."

She nodded, looking much like she did when we first showed up. Her smile wasn't reaching her eyes again.

I was curious about what they were talking about now. It was clear they had met before, but judging by the mood, I knew not to bring it up in front of others or ask questions. Luckily, Milton was already giving me that look, saying he would fill me in on everything after this.

When everyone finished eating, Milton and I battled it out for the tab. He won, saying he would just take it out of my first paycheck.

"I guess I'll see you later," Lynn said to me as she stood from her chair, getting her purse from the back of it and putting it over her shoulder.

"Let me walk you to your car." I rested my hand on her back. I then looked at Milton. "I'll be right back."

He nodded, already knowing I wanted to talk to him before heading back to work.

Lynn thanked Milton, then said bye to everyone else before I escorted her outside.

"Where are you parked?" I asked as she fished her keys from her purse.

"Right there," she pushed the button on the remote, unlocking her SUV parked on the street a few spaces from the front of the restaurant. "Thanks for lunch. I had fun." She wrapped her arms around my waist, giving me a quick hug.

I held her in place before she could pull away from me. I waited for her to stare up at me with a curious expression before I again asked, "Is everything okay?"

Her smile fell a little, then she bit her bottom lip. "Was I acting weird? I'm sorry."

"Don't be sorry," I squeezed her waist. "I'm just concerned, babe. You weren't your normal happy self."

"Yeah," she sighed, resting her chin on my chest as she stared up at me. She looked like she was debating on telling me something, her mouth opening and closing every few seconds. Then she finally told me what had happened. "Nick showed up at my house right as I was leaving. He just.... He just really got under my skin."

"How?" I asked flatly, trying not to show my irritation, but I knew it was leaking through. I wasn't irritated with her, just with her ex, that seems to show up every time we have plans together. It's starting to really piss me off.

"I can tell you about it later. I told him off pretty good before shutting the door in his face, so hopefully it won't happen again."

That small explanation did nothing to quell my irritation, but I didn't want to press her if she wasn't ready to tell me.

"Can you text me when you're ready to walk Kevin tonight? You can tell me then?"

She bit her lip and nodded. There was worry on her face, and all I wanted to do was kiss it away until she was giggling again. Then I wanted to go find her ex and put him six feet under.

I settled on kissing her, deeply but quickly, since the others were filtering out of the restaurant now.

"I'll see you later." I kissed her one last time before closing her door.

I stood on the sidewalk and waved back at her as she drove away. I had so many thoughts running through my head, many of them murderous. This need to protect Lynn from anything that could hurt her or make her unhappy was rising in me. I just wanted to deal with her issues and make them go away. Her having kids with this bastard was the only thing stopping me from landing my fist in his face the next time I saw him.

"You got a good one." Milton stood beside me.

The others were already walking back towards the courthouse, talking among themselves and paying Milton and me no mind. It was just us after they crossed the street.

"I know I do," I murmured. "So, how do you two know each other?"

He tensed a bit, and I felt I already knew the answer before he said it.

"Her ex-husband and I work together quite a bit."

I nodded, since he was just confirming what I already assumed.

"He is still crazy about her. You know that, right?" Milton confirmed the other thing I had already picked up on.

"Oh, I figured. He lost her, though. That woman is mine."

Chapter Twenty-Three

Natural Mom

Feighlynn

"Hey, guys!" I said excitedly, maybe a little too excited, as my kids walked through the door, just getting home from school. "I missed you!"

Preston gave me an odd look as I hugged Jessie. I tried not to read too much into it and kept up the upbeat vibe.

"I've got dinner in the oven! Meatballs!"

"Yay!" Jessie cheered and giggled as she skipped up the stairs.

Preston hung back, still staring at me. "Everything okay, mom?"

I frowned at the question. "Why wouldn't it be?"

"Because," he scrutinized me again, "you're hyper. Something happened."

I couldn't deny something happened, but I also wasn't ready to talk about it, especially with my kids.

"Go put your stuff away," I murmured, busying myself wiping down an already clean counter in my kitchen.

"Everything okay with Vin?"

"Yes. Why wouldn't it be?" I replied.

Preston raised an eyebrow at me. "Because you're acting weird."

"You're acting weird," I retorted. "Go put your stuff away. Bring your game stuff down so it can soak in the basin before dinner."

He sighed, shaking his head, but walked off to do what I told him to do. My son picked up on everything and would still be suspicious, but I couldn't tell him about what his father did today. That wouldn't go over well.

As I was checking the meatballs, Kevin went nuts in the front room. I thought nothing of it, thinking maybe a cat was maybe too close to the front yard, but then the doorbell rang.

I closed my eyes as I sighed, willing for it to not be Nick again. I couldn't be held responsible for what I did if he was back, and I really didn't want to do anything in front of the kids.

"I got it!" Jessie yelled, beating me to the door.

I slowed my pace and listened, growing more suspicious.

"Hey, Jessie!" I heard a much more welcome voice than the one I had expected. "How are you? Did you have a good rest of your weekend?"

"Hi Mr. Vin. I did! I got to pick out a new bed and ate pizza twice."

"That sounds fun," he chuckled. My anxious mood lifted just hearing his deep laugh. "Is your mom here?"

"Right here," I emerged around the corner where I had been hiding and listening in.

Vin had a gentle expression on his face as he took me in. His smile was infectious. I had just seen him several hours ago, but I realized how much I missed him in that short amount of time.

"Hey beautiful," he said, making my insides melt.

Jessie giggled, then turned to skip up the stairs. "I gotta get the washer before Preston fills it with his stinky baseball stuff."

"Oh, no," Vin's smile spread across his handsome face. "Not stinky baseball gear."

"She got one of his jock straps tangled with her leotards during football season, and it scarred her for life."

"Poor girl," he pulled me in for a hug now that Jessie was out of sight.

"I know. I'm starting to save for her future therapy now."

He laughed, brushed his fingers against my face as he gently cupped it in his hands. I closed my eyes as his lips met mine, chasing away so much of the tension I'd been carrying in my body all afternoon.

"Hi," he whispered in a deep raspy voice, resting his head on mine.

"Hi," I giggled. "Long time no see."

"I know. It felt like a lifetime," he teased, still holding my face in his hands.

It was crazy how decompressed I felt now, just standing there in my doorway with him. I had spent the better part of the afternoon in this awkward state of depression and anger. The thing with Nick happened right before lunch, so I had little time to process before then. Then, seeing Vin's colleague, it just magnified my irritation with my ex. It felt like Nick was ruining everything that had to do with Vin for me.

But he couldn't ruin this. This moment with Vin now, where the entire world and the problems in it faded away. So all that was left was the man before me, holding onto me and making me feel like I was someone special.

"How was work?" I leaned into his touch, focusing on the now and not the past.

"It was good." he slid his arms down to wrap around my waist. "Lunch was my favorite part of the day."

I laughed softly, feeling the same way. "Mine too."

He sighed, then asked what I knew was coming. "So, you wanna talk about it?"

He didn't need to explain what "it" he was referring to. I knew he would be curious. If I was in his shoes, I would be too.

"There's really not much to talk about. Nick showed up before I left, saying all kinds of nonsense. I told him the truth and left."

"The truth?" Vin raised his eyebrows.

I softly let out a weary sigh, then told him, "He told me he wanted me back. I guess he and Arlene broke things off. He was adamant about me hearing him out, but I told him to kick rocks and leave." I stared up at Vin through my eyelashes, catching the tightness around his eyes. "It's been irritating me all day, though. I wanted to kick him."

"Maybe you should have," Vin said in a dangerously low voice.

"Maybe I should have," I agreed.

"I can always do it for you," Vin offered.

"That's sweet," I laughed dryly, "but I think I said what needed to be said. I even cursed at him."

"Oh no," the corner of Vin's lips curled up in amusement. "Not cursing."

"My words packed quite the punch," I lifted my chin.

"Oh, I bet. Especially with cursing."

"You're teasing me." I narrowed my eyes.

He chuckled softly. "No. I just think you're cute. I'm trying to just picture you saying any curse word to your ex instead of focusing on how much I want to beat his ass for making you upset."

A blush burned on my cheeks. "It's not that big of a deal."

"It is, Lynn. I'm laughing because you're cute, but I really just want to punch him in his arrogant face."

I pursed my lips. "He has an arrogant face, doesn't he?"

"So fucking arrogant," Vin smiled.

He rested his head on mine again, making the moment stretch into this warm, fuzzy feeling. I was so irritated earlier, upset with not just Nick, but even myself for making Nick think I was a pushover to begin with. I didn't feel like a pushover with Vin holding me. I felt like I could do anything.

***

Preston

"What the crap," I muttered under my breath after hearing what dad did to mom today.

I know I shouldn't, but I was listening at the top of the stairs to their entire conversation. When I heard the doorbell ring and Vin's voice filtered up all the way to my room, I couldn't help myself. I honestly thought that he was the reason for mom's bad mood.

Mom always acts the same way when she's down. She acts overly chipper to the point she looks awkward. We had to see it for months after dad left. Seeing her act that way again after spending the weekend with our new neighbor, I thought he had set her off. I did not know it was my dad.

"What are you doing?" Jessie asked, coming into the hall with a laundry basket full of clothes.

"Uh, checking to see who was at the door," I murmured, then narrowed my eyes to her basket. "I called dibs on the washer."

She stuck her tongue out at me, then hurried down the stairs. I chased after her, forgetting that mom and her boyfriend were being all kissy face at the bottom. Vin and mom leapt apart from one another, guilty expressions on their faces. It was laughable, but I didn't have time to laugh if I was going to beat Jessie to the washer.

"Hi Vin. Bye Vin," I yelled, chasing my screaming sister.

"Mom! He's trying to steal the washer!"

"Mom! I called dibs!" I yelled back.

I caught Jessie right as she was running with her hand full through the kitchen. She screamed, then laughed as I tickled her sides. She tossed the basket in the air, so dirty clothes went everywhere.

"STOP!" Jessie howled.

"Say it. Say I get the washer!"

"NO!" She kicked and bucked, unable to throw me off.

"Preston," Mom had her disapproving tone. "Quit. You don't even have your laundry together yet."

I stopped tickling Jessie, but held onto her arms so she couldn't get her stuff and get it in the washer before me.

"Mom, she had a washer at dad's. She had all weekend to do clothes. I have to wash my uniforms."

"I don't want to use it after you wash your nasty cups, you jerk!" Jessie tried to twist free.

"Then do the laundry tomorrow!"

"No! My favorite jeans are dirty."

I scoffed, then looked at mom pointedly, hoping she would see how unfair Jessie was being.

"Let your sister go," mom said firmly. "Jessie can wash her jeans on the quick cycle while you soak your stuff in the basin. You know grass stains need to soak, anyway."

I pressed my lips together, then admitted, "My favorite jeans are dirty too."

Vin, who was leaning against the counter watching us with an amused grin, laughed softly. Mom shook her head and sighed, but didn't look that upset. She was back to her normal self.

"Why don't you wash your jeans together?" Mom offered.

"Eww, gross," Jessie gagged as she gathered her clothes back in her basket. "His clothes smell like a boy."

"I am a boy, you dork."

"That's why you smell so bad!"

"Guys," Mom laughed, shaking her head. "You're both being silly."

"No, she is!" I pointed at Jessie.

Jessie huffed, turning her nose up as she walked towards the laundry room.

"Why don't you just use the washer at my house?" Vin offered. "It's right across the street and empty. Mom only does laundry on Thursdays, anyway."

"At your house?" I lifted my eyes skeptically. "Isn't that weird?"

"Why would it be weird? It's resourceful," he shrugged.

I looked at mom, and she shrugged too. "If you want your jeans washed now, it's your only option." She then grinned at Vin. "And then you and your mom can come over for dinner. We're having meatballs!"

Mrs. Velma couldn't come for dinner. She said her favorite show was about to come on, but mom had me take her over a plate of spaghetti and meatballs with garlic bread and salad when I went to switch my laundry. She was grateful and was quickly distracted by a soap opera. It felt weird at first going into their house with my dirty clothes, but she didn't pay any attention to me, so it felt normal pretty fast.

Vin stayed at my house, helping mom in the kitchen as she set up for dinner. Every time I walked in they would jump apart, mom with a red face and Vin looking smug. They were worse than the couple at my school. If mom didn't look so happy, I would have thrown up ten times by now.

Dinner was fun. Just like in the restaurant in San Antonio, Vin took care of mom, helping her to serve her food and pouring her water. He did the same for Jessie, who sat across from him, too.

We talked. We laughed. Mom more than anyone. What usually would be a twenty-minute dinner turned into two hours, but no one seemed to notice or care.

Then, there was the way Vin would look at mom. Jess and I both noticed it. When mom would laugh, giggle, or get engrossed in any part of the conversation, Vin would stare at her with eyes like he never wanted to look away. He would smile and wrap an arm around her chair, or lean in to get a closer look at her.

Sometimes he would notice Jessie or me catching him and sit back nervously, an embarrassed look on his face. No one could deny that he really liked our mom. Jessie even whispered it to me when Vin got up to get mom a napkin when she spilled sauce on the front of her shirt.

I had never seen mom happier. She wasn't fluttering around, trying to serve him. She wasn't flustered or trying to mask her usual playfulness. She was herself, and completely at ease.

She could never just be herself with dad. Even at their best, she would still have to cater to my dad's needs, while many of hers were overlooked. Even what we ate back then was cooked to my dad's tastes.

He hated spaghetti and most other Italian food, so we never ate it, even though mom loves it.

Vin went on and on for about ten minutes about how good the meatballs were. I think he had three helpings, and even ate the leftovers from mom's and Jessie's plates.

Eventually, Jessie had to go do her homework, and I had to get my laundry from the Trude's house. That left mom and Vin alone in the kitchen, doing dishes side by side. As I was leaving, mom was showing Vin how to blow soap bubbles through her fist. Kevin was jumping at her feet, catching them in his mouth.

Vin was exactly what my mom needed. She could be herself with him, and he seemed to like every single one of her quirks. I was worried dad would sneak back into mom's life, but I don't think Vin would let him. Vin himself said that he wanted to punch dad in the face, and mom didn't seem opposed to the idea.

I might punch dad in the face next time I see him. Vin probably can't, but dad couldn't do anything to me.

When I got back to the house with my full, clean laundry basket, Jessie shushed me right as I was walking through the door. She was hiding around the corner of the foyer with a mischievous smirk on her face. After jerking the basket from my hands and setting it on the ground behind her, she grabbed my arm and yanked me to hide behind the wall, too.

"Shh," she pressed her finger to her lips, then pointed around the corner towards the kitchen.

Music was softly playing, as it usually was when mom did dishes, but then I noticed that, other than the music, it was completely quiet. I hesitantly looked around the wall, peeking into the kitchen, and that was when I saw Vin and my mom dancing. Her arms were stretched up to wrap around his neck and he was bent over to rest his face against her.

When they passed by the entryway gap, I saw my mom's feet on top of his, like a toddler dancing with an adult. Considering how tall he was and how short she was, it worked. It almost made me laugh out loud. I had to quickly cover my mouth with my hand to stifle it.

"That's so sweet!" Jessie whispered right in my ear. "Do you think he will let me dance on his feet, too?"

"Yeah," I chuckled. "I totally think he would."

CHAPTER TWENTY-FOUR

Every Woman's Type

Nick

I groaned, parking my car in the garage next to the courthouse. I still had a splitting headache. The aftereffects of drinking myself to sleep every night and then waking up after just a few hours of fretful sleep.

I keep having horrible dreams. Dreams that start out as memories from the past that shift into nightmares. Those memories slowly transform until it's no longer me with my wife in them, but her new boyfriend instead.

Last night was worse. It was the first time I picked Jessie up after school all week, the first day I felt like I could hide my pain from my daughter. That was until she asked if she could dance on my toes.

I had no earthly idea what she was talking about until she described it to me. The way she talked about it, I knew she had seen it done recently. Foolishly, I thought maybe one of her friend's little siblings danced on someone's feet and Jessie saw it, or maybe she got it from a movie.

When I asked, she suddenly got nervous, biting her lip and looking guilty. I knew I shouldn't have pushed further, but there was some deep part of me that was just begging for punishment.

She confessed to seeing Fay's new boyfriend dancing with Fay like that. In my kitchen. In the home that I built with her.

That sent me into a downward spiral again.

I tried to keep it together, hiding my depression from Jessie throughout dinner, but I could hide the pain I felt when I dropped her off at home and I saw Fay with the bastard. He had that dog *I* bought for Fay on a leash in one hand, and his other arm wrapped around my wife's shoulders.

When he kissed her right there on the street for anyone to see, both of them lost in their own world, it felt like a knife in the gut. I couldn't even breathe. I could barely wish Jessie goodnight, sending my worried-looking daughter inside with a forced smile before I broke down. I pulled off down the street, parking in front of a vacant lot with overgrown shrubs along the street to give me some cover as the waterworks started.

So many thoughts went rushing through my head, so many guilt-filled memories. The last Christmas party I threw in our home before the divorce, where I snuck outside with Arlene while my wife was waiting on guests and being her normal, wonderful self. She was the light of the party, but I set my sights on my affair instead of her.

There were so many late nights I spent with Arlene telling my wife I was working instead. How did Fay feel waiting up for me all those times? I could still picture her numb expression every time I came home and headed straight for the shower.

She knew. I tried hard to hide it, but looking back, I could remember her expressions so clearly. At first, she would look pained, but over the weeks, then months of my disloyalty, she detached, going numb.

Fay said her love for me died when I admitted to the affair. That's not true. I can see that now. She had months to stifle her love for me. I killed it, slowly and painfully. She cleared her heart completely of me, and now she was replacing me with someone else.

I don't know how I can ever forgive myself for what I did to her. Feeling this pain now, I can't even imagine how much worse she felt.

Staring up at the roof of my car, sinking into my own despair, a familiar giggle sounded outside the window. I looked over to see my wife and her boyfriend walking down the street, oblivious to my presence. Or, I thought, they both were.

Only one of them was oblivious. As I sat staring, glaring, wishing the tattooed asshole kissing the back of my wife's to drop dead, he glanced over, and his eyes met mine. It should have been too hard to make out the features on my face because of the tint in the windows, but that asshole managed it somehow.

He smirked, then bent down and kissed my wife right in front of me. Right there outside my damn window. Her dazed expression, eyes fluttering, lips puckered and red as she stared tenderly up at him, almost sent me into a rage. I've never been a violent man, but I considered it at that moment.

When I got back to my condo, I downed half a bottle of Johnnie Walker. I passed out in my recliner, then jerked awake a few hours later when my dream of the last time I made love to my wife turned into a nightmare of that bastard taking my place. In my house. In that home I had built with my fucking wife, then threw away for nothing. For a momentary lust that I thought was genuine affection. It was nothing but a fleeting passion that dwindled into guilt and sorrow.

I couldn't sleep after that. Fear of that nightmare coming back kept my dreary eyes from closing until the sun came up and I had to get ready for work. I drank half a pot of coffee before leaving, after getting sick twice, but the exhaustion and headache remained.

To complicate things further, I am now heading to a case that Arlene and I were partnered on.

Arlene had been hovering, making a nuisance of herself in the office. It's becoming increasingly annoying. Her attempts to get my attention have become disgracefully pathetic, and sometimes even degrading. The fact that I left my wife for her sickens me more and more each day.

Now, I have to sit beside her in a packed courtroom until it's our turn to appear before the judge. If it wasn't for our client paying the firm an arm and a leg to have both of us there, I would have called in sick and let Arlene do it herself.

I used the excuse of having a headache to avoid small talk with Arlene as she tried once again to ask what I was doing after work. I remained friendly and professional to our client, but was dreading this entire ordeal. An arraignment for something trivial like this is not usually in my job description, but high-profile clients don't care.

Arlene kept trying to press up against me, tangling her leg with mine until I moved it, or stretching awkwardly to lean over and breathe on my neck. It was getting beyond irritating, so I had to eventually move over to the other side of our client, muttering an excuse about wanting her to feel supported on both sides. I added in some nonsense about keeping her protected from the true criminals, which earned me a grateful smile from our client, but a vengeful glare from Arlene.

I didn't care. She was becoming a pest. Whatever I saw in her before was no longer there. Her desperation destroyed any attractive qualities she once possessed for me.

As we sat and watched, the pleas of the offenders called first. No one enjoys these types of court hearings. Everyone had already come to court ready to argue, and watching the judge flippantly hand down rulings without caring much for the backstories the offenders prepared builds the adverse tone in the courtroom. Things can get heated pretty quickly.

A man with DUI charges was next to appear before the judge. He started in on the judge before his lawyer even got to his feet, complaining about having to pay for an Uber because of his suspended license. The judge was merciless because of the man's combativeness. Eventually, the man lunged for the judge, resulting in the entire courtroom erupting into chaos.

A woman screamed, and babies started wailing as people jumped away from the first few rows. The two bailiffs rushed to contain the man, but he was large and started throwing punches at them.

One bailiff had the offender by the elbow, trying to pin him, but the man kept throwing him off. They fought for about thirty more seconds before the judge's chamber door swung wide open and the last person I ever wanted to see came barreling in.

My wife's boyfriend, Vin, I believe, was his name, was in a pair of slacks and a polo, not your typical bailiff attire, but he had the look of someone in charge. He had on some sort of utility belt with a handgun and compartments for other gear you would see a police officer typically carry. No one but a qualified security personnel or officer could be in the courthouse with a weapon, which had me wondering why Vin was there. I thought he was in the military. Did he work for the city somehow?

He made quite an impression, storming over to the offender and throwing him on the ground like he was nothing more than a sack of potatoes. He came in so fast that the man didn't have time to react any more than let out a scream as he was tackled.

Vin dug his knee into the man's back, then had both hands secured in one of his hands within seconds. His bellowing commands to "stay down" and "comply" could be heard clearly by everyone. The man had a fearful expression, and I couldn't blame him. Vin could exceedingly overpower him, or any other man, for that matter.

A fact that had me vastly irritated and somewhat afraid. I had a wave of fear pass through me, watching. I was suddenly thankful I didn't challenge him yesterday out on the street.

The collective gasps in the room turned into applause as Vin placed the man in handcuffs. He hauled the offender up to his feet like the man weighed nothing. He forced the man to stand as the two bailiffs collected themselves. One hand was on his neck and the other held the cuffs.

After making sure everyone else was fine, Vin escorted the offender out with the bailiff.

"Wow," our client whispered loudly, with a hand covering her mouth. Her eyes were wide with excitement. "I bet he can toss a woman like that, too. Lucky her, whoever she is. I'm jealous."

That brought back one of my nightmares from last night, making my head pulse painfully as my chest tightened. Fay was a tiny woman. Her boyfriend was a giant. The difference between him and me made it so much more painful to imagine.

"No kidding," Arlene scoffed, staring after my wife's boyfriend, too. "I think I know him."

My eyes widened in surprise. "You know that man?" I pointed in the direction he had left. "How?"

Her eyes sparkled, a smug grin lifting the corners of her red lips. "Oh, I just ran into him by chance last week. Maybe I should ask him for drinks to thank him for his service here today? He didn't have a ring on."

"Like that would have stopped you," I scoffed.

Our client's eyes widened, and I realized too late that I had said that in the wrong company.

"I mean, because the man was clearly, um, her type," I tried to cover for myself.

"I think that man is every woman's type," the client laughed, biting her lip as she stared into space.

Our client seemed satisfied with that excuse, but Arlene most certainly did not. She didn't bother me after that. She just glared and huffed at me until we left.

I didn't have the mindset to care about Arlene's feelings. As I drove home that evening, images of my wife being tossed into bed haunted my every thought.

I stopped by the liquor store once more to pick up another bottle. It was going to be another sleepless night.

Chapter Twenty-Five

Wrong Snake

Arlene

How dare he. How dare he treat me this way?

"Like that would have stopped you..."

How fucking dare he.

I thought it was bad enough that he was ignoring me and choosing to end things the way he did. I thought this was a minor tiff. Something that would blow over once he got over whatever caused him to become the malcontent ass he was being.

He left his wife for me. I didn't tell him to. He did that on his own. To think he has been holding such odious thoughts towards me because of the action *he chose* took me by surprise.

No one held a gun to his head and told him to cheat on his wife. I didn't have to do much at all. His discontent in that life drew him to me, not any effort I made. To think he was now holding me in such contempt for his own misdeeds....

It disgusts me.

I almost got my hopes up for a second, too. When he got all crazed in the eyes and demanded to know how I knew that barbaric man in the courtroom, I mistook it for jealousy. I thought he was finally coming around and just needed an extra push.

Yes, the giant gentleman that intervened in the chaos would normally be any woman's wet dream, but I held no genuine interest in the man. He may be fun from a *toss around in bed,* as our client said, but my interest was still set on Nick.

That was until he made that comment.

I've been getting more and more frustrated with each passing day, refusing to be the joke of the office because of that fickle man. I loved him. I truly did, but that man I fell for was a decisive, tenacious man that knew what he wanted in life, and wasn't afraid to take it. He once seemed so unyielding and strong.

Now, I can finally see that I was projecting my desire onto him. I saw what I wanted to see. The person I thought he was is far from the man who sat in that courtroom with me today.

I thought I had found a family in him. Not just him, but his daughter. Jessie was the loveliest child I had ever met, and I thought that reflected her adoring father. Maybe it wasn't his influence, but her other parent that made her the sweet and sensitive girl she was. I definitely do not see any of those traits in Nicholas.

I was done. As much as I wanted a family and someone to chase the loneliness away with, I was losing myself in my attempts to secure a man that was truly not worth my time.

Walking into my apartment, I dropped my keys and bag on my table and fished out the printed email I had been holding on to for the last few days.

A friend from college was opening her own firm in Chicago. She heard of my divorce and reached out to me a few months ago, but back then, I was with Nick, still dreaming of a future together.

I now realize that the future I imagined will never come to be.

My eyes scanned over the offer of partnership from my friend, and my heart clenched with fear and excitement of a new future I could face head on soon.

Then, my heart sank thinking about one person I wasn't truly ready to run away from just yet.

Jessie.

I really love that girl. Truly and fully. I know now seeing her again might be impossible through Nick. I don't want to lower myself to ask him for that closure.

There was one other person I could ask.

A knot formed in my stomach at the thought of asking Feighlynn for this favor after the part I played in the end of her marriage. But also, there was this small part of me that was hopeful she would be gracious like she had always been in every other aspect pertaining to my relationship with her ex.

Jessie had to have gotten her golden personality from someone. Feighlynn might just give my undeserving self a chance to tell her daughter goodbye.

***

Feighlynn

One Month Later...

"Look at you, all smiling and happy," my sister smirked, tossing a peel from the orange she was eating at me. "Makes me want to vomit."

I huffed, tossing the peel back at her face. I tried to act sour, but the smile just wouldn't leave me. "Vomit at your house, then. Quit raining on my parade."

"I'll vomit on your parade," she laughed. "Even after a month, you're still all squeals and giggles, you freak. It should be illegal to be as happy as you."

"That's rude," I scoffed.

"It is rude! Rude of *you* to act all perky around your sister who came over to hide from her husband and kids. Wipe that smile off your face and complain with me!"

I rolled my eyes, trying not to laugh. Kate came over after finding out her husband signed her up to host a luncheon for his work on the same weekend their oldest was going to have his first t-ball game. She wanted to vent and complain, but I've done her the injustice of not having any complaints of my own to add to the mix.

"What can I say?" I murmured, taking extra care in cutting her caesar wrap in half at an angle, so I could rearrange the two pieces to form a heart. "For once, my only complaints will just sound like I'm bragging, so I'm choosing to keep my lips sealed."

Kate stared begrudgingly at her plate as I slid it in front of her, glaring at the heart-shaped food before ripping the two halves apart.

"Bragging? Like what? His snake is too big or something?"

"Why do you always have to refer to naughty bits as animals?" I stifled my laughter.

"Quit avoiding my questions," she growled, taking an angry bite of the wrap.

I pressed my lips together, then shrugged. "It is hard to get moving on Mondays."

"Wo-ha-how. That big, huh? Are you walking around bow-legged after your kitty takes a beating all weekend?"

"Shut it," I said before taking a bite of my lunch.

"Geez, it's Friday. Is your kitty ready for the abuse?"

"My kitty is perfectly fine, thank you."

"Speaking of your kitty, is it time for another trip to the groomers? By groomers, I mean your bathroom with my waxing kit?"

Lifting my chin, I said, "Nope. I'm taking care of my own kitty. Thank you very much."

"*You're* waxing it?"

I shook my head. "Nope. I went to a salon two days ago. The naked mole rat is naked again."

"Ah, I would have done it."

"You just like hearing me scream," I chuckled.

Vin and I have been going strong for the last few weeks. We've fallen into a routine of him walking Kevin with me every night, usually after eating dinner with me and the kids. It's crazy to me how normal it feels.

His mother is set in her own routine, which rarely includes Vin. She almost forgets her son is living with her sometimes, but every once in a while, she gets total clarity and will make dinner for the both of them. Those evenings are the ones where he misses dinner with us, but he always rummages around for leftovers after our walk.

I'm not entirely sure Miss Velma understands we are dating. She still treats me the same as she always does when I see her outside, and never mentions her son to me. The poor woman doesn't keep most thoughts about her these days.

Because of the kids, Vin doesn't stay over during the week, but as soon as the weekend comes, he doesn't leave. From Friday evening to Monday morning, he's with me, hence the bow-legged bald kitty walks on Monday.

The past month has been amazing. I'm falling for Vin more and more every day. Every touch, every smile, every look had my chest tingling in the best of ways. I have no complaints.

"Speaking of wanting to inflict pain on someone, how's Nick handling your anaconda wielding action star?"

"Action hero," I corrected her. I shrugged. "Nick has said little lately. I actually haven't talked to him in a few weeks."

"Huh," Kate stared at the contents of her wrap, like she was judging the lettuce for not being more chicken. She isn't a fan of vegetables. Even lettuce. "I thought after declaring himself, he wouldn't have given up so easily."

"He did. I really haven't seen him or talked to him. All communication goes through the kids."

"That's good, I guess." Kate picked out a sizable chunk of lettuce, side-eyeing me like she was waiting for me to protest. I just snatched the chuck from her fingers and tossed it in my mouth. I don't know why she hates eating green foods. They're delicious.

Kate went back to complaining about her husband, saying she was going to sign him up for crossing guard duty and to referee every t-ball game he had off for the rest of the season as payback for volun-telling her to do an event so massive. I volunteered to help her with the luncheon so she could watch the game. Then I'd hold down Wes, so

Kate could wax his animal parts after the party was over. She liked that idea a lot.

"Are you going to invite Mr. Anaconda too?" Kate asked me, wiggling her eyebrows.

I laughed, almost falling off my stool at her new nickname for him. "Please don't call him that to his face."

"I have to meet him first!" Kate laughed dryly. "Seriously. Invite him. I need to meet the action star."

"Action hero." I checked my watch. "He gets off early most Fridays. If you stick around long enough, you might get to meet him today."

"Oh, goody," she clapped her hands together. "Avoid all my motherly and wifely duties and I get to meet the Anaconda himself? My day suddenly got a lot better."

"Did it not get better just from being in my presence?" I scoffed, acting offended.

"No. You give me a headache," she smirked.

"How rude."

We were giggling and teasing each other like we always did, carrying on in the kitchen, when I heard Kevin's usual barking when someone got close to the house. He was pacing and jumping on the front window, showing whoever was out there was getting closer and closer.

Kate perked up, clapping her hands excitedly. "Yes! Mr. Anaconda is here!"

"Maybe?" I checked my watch again.

It wasn't even two yet. Usually, if Vin was going to get off early, it would be at three when the courthouse building closed to the public. Then he would usually stop by his house first and get changed for the gym, then come ask me to join him.

I always join him, but only because he buys me the most unhealthy smoothie his gym's cafe makes. Then I get to watch from the exercise bike as he lifts heavy weights. I sip my drink and smile to myself, watching his muscles work. It's very rewarding, and now I can tell people I go to the gym.

Kate jumped up and beat me to the door, looking out the keyhole with an overjoyed smile. That smile slowly slipped off her face, causing me to become concerned.

"What? Who is it?"

"Heh," Kate looked angry now. "A different snake."

"Who?" I pushed her out of the way and got up on my tiptoes to peer out. Then I gasped softly.

Arlene was the one on the other side of my door. After Nick said they broke up, I never thought I would have to see her again.

"What the hell is she doing here?" Kate sounded ready for a fight.

Gosh, I hope I didn't have to bail my sister out of jail today, because if Arlene came here to cause a fuss, my sister was not going to just sit back and watch.

CHAPTER TWENTY-SIX

Find Your Happy

This was awkward.

It's been over half an hour, maybe longer, and nothing has truly been said yet. After offering her coffee, and then water, we've so far just muttered tense greetings and light inquiries about each other's day.

She seemed more animated hearing about the kids, smiling when I mentioned Jessie's dance recital coming up. Once that topic awkwardly faded away, thanks to Kate huffing, "why do you care?" the conversation died again.

Now, Arlene was seated on the couch opposite me, flinching every time my sister made a loud noise in the kitchen. Kate was intentionally banging around in there, making her presence known even after Arlene asked to speak to me alone. I had to keep pressing my lips together from the urge to laugh.

Kate was much more upset than I was by the sudden visit from my ex-husband's affair partner. I'm indifferent. Months ago, this may have upset me more, but now I'm just curious why she would show up here out of the blue.

"So," I broke the silence, since she seemed to be still contemplating how to start, "what brings you here? Just in the neighborhood or…."

Arlene made a face at my attempt at breaking the ice. I guess my bad jokes aren't her thing.

"No, I wasn't in the neighborhood," she responded in a careful tone. "No, I wasn't in the neighborhood," she responded in a careful tone, her eyes flashing hesitantly at me, "since your last Christmas party where I was invited."

I smiled tightly. "I figured. It was just a grim joke. I meant nothing by it."

Arlene's eyes opened wide in surprise for a split second, until Kate dropped a pan loudly on the tile floor, making Arlene jump and huff.

Her response made me think she assumed I meant something malicious originally. Maybe she was assuming I was asking if she had been visiting this neighborhood often with negative connotations.

"My bad!" Kate yelled, and I couldn't help but to laugh.

"I'm sorry," I told Arlene. "Kate is protective. I'm sure you understand how siblings can be."

Arlene had a hard expression passing over her face, but her eyes looked sad.

"No. I have no siblings. Just a mother I no longer speak with. I'm afraid I don't entirely understand that protective bond between family members."

"Huh." I wasn't sure how to respond to that. "Well, I guess you didn't have to worry about sharing clothes, toys and other things with others then," I laughed awkwardly.

It wasn't until I heard Kate snorting and snickering in the other room that I realized what I had just said and how passive-aggressive it must have sounded.

Arlene, lips pulled tight in a grim expression, so I hurried to clarify, "I didn't mean- "

"I know," Arlene cut me off. "I knew what you meant. No need to specify the irony in that statement."

I sighed, feeling exhausted from the five minutes we'd already been sitting here in this weird tension. "You know what the opposite of irony is?"

Arlene raised her thin eyebrows.

"Wrinkly."

She stared stoically at my poor joke, and then her face split into a reluctant grin. She laughed behind her hand, shaking her head.

"I was right," she snickered, the tension draining from her features as she laughed. "Your daughter is far more like you than her father. Thank God."

I cocked my head to the side, curious about what she meant, but before I could ask, another knock sounded at the front door.

We both looked over as the door swung open, my new guest needing no invitation to enter. He knew he was welcome.

I couldn't stop the beaming grin from erupting on my face at seeing Vin, still looking official in his work clothes.

"Honey, I'm home-" Vin stopped short, seeing Arlene and I seated in the living room across from one another. "Oh, am I interrupting something?"

"Is that the action star?!" Kate poked her head out of the kitchen.

Vin smirked, giving me a side eye before coming over to the couch I was sitting on and leaning over me. "You call me that to other people, too?"

I giggled as he wrapped his arms around my shoulders and kissed my cheek. "Only to my sister. You have a problem with that?"

"Not at all," he chuckled, kissing my cheek one more time before straightening up. "Hi Lynn's sister," he waved through the opening g to the kitchen.

"Hi Mr. Anaconda!" She sounded too enthusiastic, calling him that.

I sighed, wanting to knock her down to the ground and force-feed her green stuff until she puked.

"Mr. Anaconda? Haven't heard that one yet." Vin lifted an eyebrow at me.

"Ignore her," I groaned.

He laughed, then looked at Arlene. His smile dropped quickly as he studied her. Arlene looked surprised to see him, wide-eyed, with her mouth gaping. I guess it would be weird and surprising meeting my boyfriend in this situation.

"Huh," Vin mumbled, "Hello."

He sounded so stiff compared to when he was speaking with Kate.

Arlene found the ability to close her mouth. It was hard to read her expression. She seemed a little sad as she shifted awkwardly, crossing her legs and fidgeting with the accent pillow. Her long red nails were pulling through the pillow's fringe.

"Hello," she nodded in greeting.

Something about Vin's demeanor suggested he wasn't open to any further conversation with her. But his eyes softened when he looked back down at me.

"Is your company staying for long? I was thinking about taking you to go grab a smoothie?"

I laughed softly. He knew I was never going with him to the gym to actually workout, but he still liked it when I was there. Probably because I text him inappropriate comments and observations the entire time.

"How long until you have to leave?"

He played with the hair falling down my back. "However long you need me to."

"Aw," Kate came out of the kitchen. "We'll all be heading out of here in about thirty minutes. Uninvited guests included." Kate threw a severe glance at Arlene before putting a smile back on her face and linking her elbow with Vin's. "I can walk you out. Give them a chance to finish."

"Well, alright," Vin smirked while staring back at me. I waved my fingers, trying not to laugh. Kate was undoubtedly going to give him the third degree for the next thirty minutes. He didn't seem to mind.

Arlene watched as they left, visibly relaxing with Kate no longer in the house.

"Sorry," I sighed, smiling gently as I shook my head. "I know my sister's a lot."

Arlene's lips twisted in their corners. "I was more surprised to see your, um, boyfriend." She sent a blank stare towards the door, then muttered, "It all makes sense now."

Makes sense?

I smiled tightly, not sure if her musing needed my reply.

She sighed, letting out a long, heavy breath, then met my gaze. "I apologize. I know you have no obligation to sit and speak with me. I just...."

Her eyes turned vacant again, and the silence stretched for several long seconds before she met my eyes again.

"I don't know if you are aware, but... But Nicholas and I... we ended things several weeks ago."

I nodded. "I was aware." I was about to add that I was sorry to hear that, but I thought that would be overstepping. Their relationship was none of my business.

Arlene sighed and sat back like she was exhausted. "Of course you were." Her shoulders slumped, and she gnawed on her bottom lip. It was the most vulnerable I had seen her since she got here. Then, when she looked up at me again, I saw such thick emotional turmoil, it was like I could feel it myself. "I'm sorry, Feighlynn. When... When things started, I never considered you, and was purely selfish in my meager pursuit of boosting my ego. I never thought things would progress the way they did, that is until..." she looked hesitant, but continued, "until I saw your life here," she looked around the house. "I saw how happy you were and wanted more of what you had."

She paused for a long time, staring at a picture of me and my kids above the mantle. I used to have a picture of us with Nick there, but that went away after he left. I didn't have a single picture of Nick in this room any longer, but Arlene's longing expression remained as her eyes swept over each image of me and my kids.

"I can not have children," she admitted in a broken whisper. "That's what broke my first marriage. Well, it was the largest factor, at least. I always wanted children, but tried to bury that desire. But when I met Jessie, that desire returned, more fiercely than before."

I knew she and Jessie were close. I tried not to let it bother me, and over time, it didn't. I was thankful that my ex-husband's partner cherished my little girl in her own way. It's more comforting now to hear such emotions coming from Arlene, all for my little girl, who I cherish so greatly too.

"I've settled my feelings for Nicholas," Arlene admitted in a rough whisper. She then huffed with a broken laugh. "I realized how pathetic I had become with him. He was never worth the heartache I caused in both yours and my life. What I am having trouble letting go of, though... Is... Jessie." Her eyes turned pleading, moisture glistening in them. "I have no right to ask this of you. I know I do not deserve this closure, but I had to ask. Please, Feighlynn. Please allow me to tell that little girl goodbye."

A tear slipped down her cheek, and my heart went out for the woman who I once thought broke my family apart. I can see now that she was far more broken than we were, and Nick was just a catalyst for change and healing.

I'm happier now than I have ever been with him. I almost want to thank her for making me see how much better life could be without Nick in it. I felt pity for her, because while I was healing, he was breaking her more.

"You love my daughter. Don't you, Arlene?"

She vehemently nodded her head, wiping the pouring tears from under her eyes. "More than I have ever loved anyone else in my life."

More than anyone? The weight of that statement was so heavy and sad, I could feel her pain.

No, she deserves nothing from me, but I do not care about what she deserves. I couldn't live with myself if I broke this woman more than she already was. This request came from her love for my daughter. How could I refuse?

"I'll ask Jessie," I told her softly. "It's ultimately up to her."

Fresh tears fell from the corners of her eyes, and she nodded. "Thank you," she mouthed, air barely making it past her lips.

"And," I hesitated for a second, "and I forgive you. I hope one day you can find exactly what will make it truly happy."

Chapter Twenty-Seven

Interrogation

Vin

"So you're the action hero?" Lynn's sister asked, raising an eyebrow at me with a mischievous smirk on her face.

She looked a lot like my girl, which made me like her from the start.

"You're the sister," I grinned, looking down at her before extending my hand. "Kevin, but Lynn calls me Vin."

"Lynn," she giggled while shaking my hand. "That's cute. No one's called her that before. I like it. She calls me Kate, among many other things."

"Other things?"

She shrugged. "I'm her favorite sister, favorite person, favorite creature in the world. She also calls me 'The Cat Wrangler' as of late."

"Does she really?" I gave her a curious look. "Why?"

"Eh," she lifted her shoulders. "I guess it's more of an unofficial title. You're welcome, by the way."

I was more confused than before, but muttered out, "Thanks?"

"No problem," she laughed. "Gosh, the things we do for our siblings sometimes. Tell me, action hero Vin, do you have siblings?"

I shook my head, "No, it's just me."

"Huh. So, do you know the importance of sharing? Because I need to know how willingly you're going to share my sister with me. I'm a little needy, and if you two get more serious, we might fight over her once or a million times."

"I think I can hold my own," I scoffed.

She frowned deeply. "So you don't like to share?"

I laughed at her serious face. She was a little crazier than Lynn, and definitely not as sweet, but the quirkiness was definitely a family trait.

"I can share, but only for family."

"Clingy, are we?"

"Clingy?" I repeated as we crossed the road towards my house. "I don't know about being clingy. More worried than anything."

She gave me a confused expression, so I elaborated.

"Your sister is adorable. Literally the cutest and sweetest woman I have ever met. But.... She isn't always the most aware."

Kate snorted, "Aware. Ha!" she snickered behind her hand. "She's a flipping airhead. You can say it."

"No," I laughed with her. "She's just too sweet for her own good sometimes. I worry." I thought back to the woman who was sitting in her living room with her. "Lynn doesn't consider herself enough. I learned that the moment we met. I just can't stomach the idea of someone taking advantage of her selflessness."

Kate studied me for a few seconds as we slowed outside my house. "So you want to be the bad guy for her? Is that it?"

A guilty smile lifted my lips. "You could say that."

"A real action hero," Kate laughed. "My sister was right. The name fits."

"Thanks, *cat wrangler*." I still didn't have a clue what that could mean, but Kate got a kick out of me calling her that.

"Okay," she chuckled. "You passed."

"Did I?" I raised my eyebrows. "I didn't know I was being tested."

"Sure you didn't," she smirked. Then she sighed while looking me up and down. "You'll do. You'll do nicely."

"Thanks." I twirled my keys around my fingers, then stared off toward Lynn's house. "So that woman in her living room right now? Would I fail your test if I asked who she was?"

I know I've seen that woman before. She was the snobby husband-grabber from Milton's office. She gave me nothing but bad vibes before, and that wasn't much different this time.

"You wouldn't fail, per se. I guess that would depend on why you were asking." Kate stared pointedly while waiting for my answer.

Even not knowing why that woman was there, I felt honesty was the best answer here. "I met that woman once before. She didn't give a good first impression." I looked at Lynn's windows, trying to glimpse them. "I'm worried about my girl. Leaving her with a snake."

Kate threw her head back, laughing wildly. "Snake," she scoffed, slapping her knee. "Oh, that's great. That's what she is. A flipping snake."

Concern settled in me, and my feet moved towards Lynn's without even telling them to.

"Hey, it's fine," Kate grabbed my arm and stopped me, still trying to control her laughter. "My sis can handle her."

"Who is she?" I asked again.

"Oh," Kate waved her hand, "Just the snake that stole her husband."

My eyes grew wide. "And she's having tea in her living room?!"

"I think it was coffee. Not tea," Kate smirked.

"I'm serious. That's Nick's mistress?! What if she tries to hurt Lynn?!"

"That won't happen," Kate shook her head. "Feighlynn's always handled her ex and his mistress amicably. No one can hate her, even that snake. I think Arlene just wanted to clear the air." She followed my worried gaze to the house. "She couldn't say much with me there. As my sister's official 'bad guy' stand-in, Arlene wasn't talking while I was listening in the other room. I wanted to give them a second so she could finally spit whatever she came to say out and then leave."

Kate looked worried too, despite what she said.

"She won't hurt her?" I asked. "Are you sure?"

"I'm sure." Suddenly, there was a glint in her eyes. "My sister can hold her own. I'm telling you. You should keep that in mind."

I scoffed, imagining my little bitty girlfriend trying to fight anyone, let alone me. "I'll keep that in mind."

We stood out front on my lawn for about ten more minutes, Kate shooting more questions at me. Nothing too serious, until she got to the questions about my previous relationships. I don't make it a habit of talking about my ex-wife, but Kate really dug in on the subject, seeing I was hesitant to answer every question.

Lynn and I had already talked about everything concerning my divorce. I also knew how close Kate and Lynn were, so I was impressed that Kate didn't already know all this information. Lynn didn't share my personal information, which made me fall for her even more.

Kate was Lynn's sister. As much as I didn't enjoy talking about my ex to strangers, I felt like I could to placate her. So, I let Kate know about my ex cheating on me and the events that unfolded afterward. I was deployed and came back to her with another man, and all the dirty tricks she tried to pull to get my paychecks after I kicked her out. It made me not want to date seriously again for a long time. A very long time.

Not until I met Lynn.

Kate seemed happy with my answers, and I felt I had passed another test of some sort.

Eventually, the mistress, Arlene, came out of Lynn's front door, Lynn hanging back in her entryway. It looked like the mistress had been crying, but Lynn looked absolutely fine. Her smile was as kind and genuine as ever.

Kate was right. Lynn was fine.

The door closed, and that snake-like mistress started back a bit, seeing Kate and me watching from my front lawn. She hung her head, wiping under her eyes, and headed for her car.

Kate sighed. "I guess that's my cue. Go get ready for the gym, action hero. It was good to meet you."

"You too," I said as she pulled me into a hug. "Get home safe."

She waved as she ran across the street.

I felt like I had just been in a whirlwind from my brief conversation with Kate. She loves her sister. That was clear as day. I just hoped I had said nothing to put my foot in my mouth that she would relay back to Lynn later. I replayed everything I had said about my ex over and over in my head, but nothing off putting came to mind. Nothing Lynn didn't already know.

"Hey there," Mom greeted me warmly as I went into the kitchen. "How's my soldier today?"

She called me a soldier. I thought for a second she was having a clear day, but she only calls me her soldier when she's living in the past.

"I'm good." I kissed her cheek. "How are you? Did you get out at all today?"

"Oh, I just cleaned around the house. Worked a little here and there," she arranged an already perfect bouquet on the counter. "Do you have any plans for dinner?"

I cringed inwardly, wondering how to explain my weekend plans with Lynn.

"I'm about to take my girl to the gym, then we might pick something up for dinner. Want us to get you something too?"

Mom's eyes lit up suddenly. "Oh, no. You go enjoy your date." She pressed her lips together, like she was trying not to smile too big while she looked at me from the corner of her eyes. "So. Things are getting serious with that girl now, huh?"

I laughed deeply at her eager expression. "Yeah. I'd say they are."

"Well," mom started pruning a rose. "Will there be wedding bells in the near future?"

"Maybe," I smirked. "If I can talk her into it, there will be." I kissed her head as I walked past. "I'm going to get changed. Let me know if you change your mind about dinner."

"I will!" Mom yelled back at me, then I heard her singing the opening song of one of her soaps under her breath.

Marriage. I had thought little about it, but now that mom brought it up, it was in the front of my mind.

Chapter Twenty-Eight

Home

I was so ready for the weekend. Last weekend was too short, with Lynn using Sunday to pick her daughter up early from her father's place.

She explained to me what that snake-like woman wanted that day. She and Nick broke up, and she was moving across the country. She wanted to tell Jessie goodbye.

My woman is a saint. If I was in her shoes, I would have told the bitch that stole my husband to fuck off. Lynn didn't do that. She talked with her daughter and asked if she wanted to meet her father's mistress one last time before she moved. She let her daughter have the final say, then supported her through it before dropping her back off at Jessie's dad's Sunday night.

Lynn didn't stop there. That mistress snake woman had asked Jessie if she would see her off at the airport, and Lynn took her. She went with her daughter to wish her ex-husband's mistress good luck. I took Preston to dinner on Tuesday night while Lynn took Jessie to see the snake woman off. Even Preston couldn't believe his mother went that far for a woman he said didn't deserve it.

She's a fucking angel. There is no doubt about it.

I had one last thing to do before heading home to spend another amazing weekend with my angel of a girlfriend.

"You called?" I popped my head into Milton's office.

"Hey, man," he waved his hand in front of him toward the chairs as he looked away from his computer. "Have a seat."

"Why do I feel like I'm being called to the principal's office?"

He looked over with a cocky grin. "Have you been a bad boy?"

"Fuck you," I scoffed.

He laughed at himself. "I'm just joking, asshole. No trouble here. Well. Not yet. If I get a few drinks in you tomorrow, I plan on causing *some* trouble."

"What the hell are you talking about?"

"I'm talking about this." he tossed a thick card across his desk. Its foiled lettering and intricate script were too flashy for my taste.

"What's this?" I asked, picking it up.

"An invitation to a charity function being held tomorrow. I need you and your girlfriend to fill my table."

"Huh," I tossed the invitation back at him. "I don't want to."

"Come on, dude. Don't make me invite my secretary." He looked over my shoulder to make sure no one was listening. "Two drinks and he's sloppy as fuck."

I leaned back in the chair, folding my arms over my chest. "I have big plans for this weekend. I still don't want to."

Milton scoffed. "You told me at lunch you were just spending the weekend with your girl. Get out of the sack for a night and let her dress up. Women like feeling like a princess every once in a while."

I smirked. "I always make my girl feel like a princess."

"Bull shit," he snorted. "Come on. She used to go to these things all the time. She will love it."

That didn't make me happy to hear. Not at all. I could imagine Lynn now, dressed to the nines and hanging on the arm of her asshole ex. He would have been the envy of every man there.

I hate that. She's mine.

"Look at you." Milton wiggled in his seat. "Getting jealous there, Trude?"

"Fuck you."

He laughed, pushing the invitation back towards me. "You're coming. You know you are. Stake your claim in front of everyone like you want. You can piss all over her heels, so no other men come sniffing. Doesn't that sound nice?"

It sounded nice. Ever since my mom mentioned marriage, all I have been thinking about is staking my claim publicly on my girl. I was growing more and more sure by the day that she was my future.

"I'll think about it," I muttered, picking up the invitation.

"There we go," he grinned. "I'll put you both on the guest list."

"I have to ask her first."

"She'll say yes." Milton waved his hand.

I was about to come back with some smartass retort when an unpleasant thought popped into my head. "Hey, is her ex-husband going to be there?"

Milton looked uncomfortable for a second, then shrugged. "Would it be bad if he was? Wouldn't that be more of a reason to show up with her beside you?"

It did sound tempting. I could rub his nose in my happiness. Happiness he threw away for some snake.

"Fine," I groaned. "I'm going home," I pushed myself up from his chair.

"Home? You mean your girlfriend's house?"

"I meant home." Lynn was my home. Even if I don't live with her yet, I've already decided she was my home. My future.

"Don't forget to ask your *girlfriend*," Milton told me teasingly as I left his office. "Piss on her heels all night long!" He yelled as I walked down the hall.

The receptionist looked at me oddly, but then went back to typing as I got on the elevator.

The entire drive home, I thought about how tomorrow would go if her ex was there. I want to show her off and make her feel like my queen, but I'm not sure how she will take it seeing her ex there.

I called her instead of worrying over it. If she said no now, I could call Milton and let him know she was uncomfortable with it before he solidified any more plans that included the two of us.

"Hello?" Her sweet voice carried through the car speakers, making me smile.

"Hey, beautiful. What are you doing?"

Her little sigh had me pushing the accelerator to get to her faster. "Trying on clothes my sister gave me."

The brief anxiety I felt from hearing her sigh disappeared. She sighed a lot when her sister talked her into something she was unsure of. I laughed gently, wondering what clothes her sister could have given her.

"What kind of clothes?"

"Work out clothes."

"You said you needed some," I reminded her. "Are they that bad?"

"Not *bad*," she said nervously. "They're just not something I would pick out myself."

"I'm sure they're fine," I grinned to myself. She's adorable.

"I don't know," she sounded worried still. "I promised her I'd let you see it first. Then I'm taking it off."

If her sister gave her the clothes, I don't know what to expect.

"I'm on my way to you now, so I'll see you in a few minutes. I'll check them out then. But, hey. I wanted to ask you something."

"What?"

"I got an invitation to a charity thing tomorrow night. Would you want to go? Milton kinda pushed it on me at the last minute, and I wanted to run it by you first."

"A charity function? Like, one of those table events?"

She sounded familiar with these things. "I think so. He mentioned buying a table."

"So it's formal, huh? That should be fun. Yeah, I don't mind going."

"Good. I'll let him know. But there's one more thing. Your ex might be there."

Her silence stretched for several long seconds before she muttered a "huh". She didn't sound as thrilled now.

"We're not sitting with him, are we?"

"No, no," I quickly told her. "Milton wouldn't have asked me if that was the case. He didn't even sound too sure he would be there."

"Well, it should be fine, then. Those events are usually so busy that you don't talk to the same person twice. I don't mind if you don't."

She's a fucking angel. I swear. I couldn't wait to show her off as my woman in front of the people who thought she belonged to another man. Yeah, it might be the equivalent of marking my territory, but I couldn't help myself. Call me a dog, but this dog wanted the world to know the angel named Feighlynn was mine.

"You're amazing. You know that, right?"

"I know," she said cheerfully. "Now hurry and get home, so I can change out of this mess."

I chuckled. "Yes ma'am. I'll be there soon, baby."

She told me to get home so naturally. I couldn't stop smiling the rest of the way there.

***

Feighlynn

"Look what I can do," I boasted as I flexed my nonexistent muscles.

Vin smirked, squeezing my arms. "Nice. You got a little swole going. Lifting those smoothies is paying off."

"I know!" I giggled, biting my lip.

My eyes roamed down Vin's biceps. They were swollen and hard, on full display in his cut-off shirt. Friday evenings have become my favorite, because I get to see Vin like this. Then I get to feel those delicious muscles throughout the weekend, uninterrupted by my weekly obligations.

Vin reached over, resting his hand on my thigh while giving it a gentle squeeze. His eyes flashed at my exposed legs. Kate gifted me the workout outfit I was now wearing, and I could tell Vin approved.

Kate has been more supportive of my new relationship since meeting Vin last Friday. She showed up at my house bright and early to present me with her gift of workout clothes. She said she specially ordered the baby making kind. The kind that pushed my girls and hinny up and showed more skin than I would normally be comfortable with.

After putting them on, I almost changed out of them about ten times, but Kate made me promise to leave them on until Vin saw them. His eyes when he walked into my room after getting off work were enough to keep me in them. I liked the way he hovered close by as I walked on the treadmill sipping my smoothie, too.

"I need to tell your sister thanks," Vin mumbled low and huskily.

"What was that?"

"I said, are you hungry? Want to stop somewhere for dinner?"

I tried not to smirk as I shrugged. "I could eat."

"I could give you something to eat," he mumbled again.

"Oh yeah," I laughed. "What would that be?"

His hand tightened on my leg. His eyes flickered to my thighs again. I tightened my thighs around his fingers, making him groan deeply.

"Let's go back home, and I'll show you."

I giggle, feeling ten different kinds of giddy. He's been referring to my house as our home a lot, and I love it. He's really only at his house to sleep on the weekdays. Even my kids have become used to him being in our home.

"I like it when you call my house home," I whispered shyly.

Vin's heated gaze softened. His hand rubbed my thigh lovingly.

"I enjoy calling your house home, too. It feels like home. More than anywhere else ever has."

I bit down on my lip as I stared up at him, thinking about the weight of what he just said. We haven't been dating a full two months yet, and I already feel more attached to him than I ever have with any other person. Apart from my kids, of course. Even Kate says she's never seen me this happy.

"Move in, why don't you?" I teased shyly.

My heart went crazy at the tender look on his face.

"Is that an invitation?"

With an unsure shrug, I ducked down lower in my seat. "Would that be crazy?"

"Maybe," he stopped at a stoplight and brushed the hair from my shoulder, "but I'm already crazy about you."

Chapter Twenty-Nine

Get It Together

Nick

"You look good, daddy," Jessie smiled sweetly at me as I stepped into the living room.

"Thank you, honey." I adjusted my tie in the mirror, then bent over the couch to kiss the top of her head.

Preston barely glanced up at me from his phone. He was lying across the couch, the same scowl on his face that he had when he got here. That's the only expression I see on him now.

Pursing my lips, I adjust my cufflinks while willing my son to look at me. When he didn't, I sighed, then asked, "Do you have dinner sorted out, Preston? Did you order pizza?"

"Yep." he still didn't look away from his phone.

"How did you pay for it?" I didn't get a notification about my card being used and it was still on the counter exactly where I'd left it.

"Mom's card."

I rubbed my eyes, holding in a groan, before sighing and putting the card back in my wallet. "Why didn't you use my card?"

Preston shrugged. "Mom's was saved on my phone. It's not a big deal."

"It is a big-" I stopped myself before I let my frustration show too much. Jessie's smile had already dropped, and she was looking at us like she was scared we were about to fight. "It's fine," I said to myself more than to him. "I'll just pay her back."

"Why? She won't care. Vin's probably paying for her food all weekend."

I gritted my teeth to keep myself from exploding. Every chance he gets, Preston brings up Fay's new boyfriend. It's like he's just trying to rub it in that she's moved on and I'm alone without her, miserable in my mistakes.

I grabbed my keys, heading for the door. "I'll be back in a few hours."

"Bye, daddy!" Jessie waved after me. "I love you. Have fun!"

"I love you too, honey. I'll try."

I looked one last time at Preston, but he was still staring at that damned phone. If it wouldn't damage things more, I'd take the thing from him.

I was irritated on my drive to the gardens where the charity dinner was taking place. If my bosses were not the ones that invited me to this event, I wouldn't be going. They purchased the table for our firm and it was an invitation I couldn't refuse.

The drive was short. Living downtown, all my drives are short, seeing as everything is within a few blocks from my condo. Even with the convenience of a short drive, I still get hits with waves of loneliness at every turn.

Fay is moving on. I'm trying so hard to accept that, even keeping my distance, but it seems to just get harder and harder as time marches on.

My weekends with the kids haven't been helping. Jessie being Fay's little clone and Preston rubbing his mother's relationship in my face at every opportunity keeps me with a bottle of Johnny Walker next to my bed at night for the rest of the week.

Pulling up in line for the valet, I strum my fingers with annoyance on the steering wheel, itching for something to help wain my irritation now. Staying sober with my kids at the condo isn't the easiest thing.

"Sir," the valet handed me my ticket as I got out of the car.

I grumbled, "Thanks," while passing him a twenty.

The stairs leading up to the building were awkwardly spaced, which was great if you wanted to pause and talk to others, which I did not. I just wanted to get this night over with and get back home to spend some time with my daughter and try to turn things around with Preston.

Memories flooded me of Fay on my arm at these events, hugging and talking in that excited way she does to everyone, even acquaintances she'd only seen in passing a few times. She made these events tolerable.

I tried going with Arlene a few times after the divorce, but it was never the same. Arlene felt like a weight, making events like this drag even longer. With Fay, I never noticed the time passing by. She lit up the room just being in it.

"Nick! You made it," Leroy slapped my back as I walked into the dining area outside of the main conservatory.

Grabbed a glass of wine off the tray from a passing server, I lifted it in greeting before taking a long sip. It was going to be a long night of forced smiles.

"Glad you made it out," Stevens said, lifting his glass too. His wife was hanging on his arm, clearly already drunk.

"Nick," she squealed, holding her hand out awkwardly. I gave it a gentle squeeze.

"Your date arrived before you!" She laughed, tossing her body drunkenly against Stevens.

Another wife tried to shush her, but she just looked glossy-eyed and confused, before giggling again.

I was confused. Were they talking about Arlene? She had left this past week for another job, I had thought.

"You're mistaken, sweety," Stevens whispered to her.

"Am I?" SHe furrowed her brows, then shrugged. "Okay."

Another wife or girlfriend hooked her arm in Steven's wife's, then pulled her away to the bar.

"Sorry about that," Stevens said dismissively, but there was still an awkward set to his jaw. "Let's get you another drink."

The women love this event every year because of the venue. The gardens and koi ponds get them excited as the men talk business and network. Networking with the city's most influential people is why the firm buys a table every year, but I'm not in much of a mood for talking with a fake smile today.

Standing at the bar with Stevens, he pulled me into a conversation quickly with a chairperson of some kind of committee for something that was probably important. I couldn't focus much on what was being said. I just nodded along and smiled at the right times, knowing my boss just wanted me for my smile right now. These older women love a successful younger man, and I'm the only fully single man in the firm right now. I know that was the main reason Stevens insisted I attend.

I was agreeing with some trivial compliment Stevens just gave the chairperson when familiar, sweet-sounding laughter reached my ears, making my heart drop to the pit of my stomach. I went still and almost spilled my wine everywhere, searching for the sound.

Stevens coughed, trying to catch my attention again. He wanted my focus on Miss Cougar-With-Too-Much-Perfume, but nothing could stop me from searching for the source of that sound.

That was when I saw her. My Fay. She was across the room near the cherub fountain, wearing the most gorgeous soft blue dress that exposed most of her back. Her thick, dark hair was swept up high in a ponytail, pulling your attention to her bare neck.

I knew it was her before she even turned her head to gaze up at her giant of a date. He was in a single sports coat and white shirt, not even buttoned all the way. His tattoos were showing open on his chest, making him look like a barbarian. His cowboy boots and jeans were nothing too out of the ordinary compared to the old money cowboys and cattlemen in attendance. Jeans and sport coats were the norm among the older tycoons, but seeing it on him was different.

And the way Fay was staring up at him. Damn, it made me sick. Did she ever look at me that way? I feel like I only get glares and the cold shoulder from her now.

"I'm sorry, chairperson. Let me guide you back to your table," I heard Stevens say, but I still couldn't take my eyes off my wife.

My ex wife.

Damn it.

When the bastard looked at her, it was like he was claiming her for all to see. His eyes were taking her all in, moving over her beautiful face, and then glancing at the alluring curves of her body periodically.

When I saw him lick his lips, eyes lingering on her bare back, I wanted to explode.

"Pull it together, man," Stevens was suddenly in my ear, prying the wine glass clenched in my hands.

"That's my wife," I whispered roughly, fighting down so many emotions storming inside me. "That's my wife!"

"I know it's hard seeing your ex-wife with another man," he gripped my shoulder, leading me a little forcefully back to our table. "I remember the first time I saw my first ex-wife at a restaurant on a date. I wanted to flip tables and the whole shebang, but this is work. Get it together, Nicholas."

"That's my wife," I said again, trying and losing the fight not to stare back at that beautiful back and slender neck.

Stevens pushed me towards the bathroom, telling me to cool down and get it together again. He looked less sympathetic and more agitated, and his mutterings to Leroy sounded harsh.

This was my job. I needed to pull myself together.

I just didn't know how to do that with my ex wife in the same room, looking the way she did in that gorgeous dress. She was lighting up the event without even trying, as she always did, but she was doing it on *his* arm instead of mine.

How do I 'get it together' just like that?

CHAPTER THIRTY

Beginning Of A Nightmare

Feighlynn

"Wow, nice car," the valet boy's eyes went wide, staring at Vin's car.

Vin helped me up from the passenger seat, waiting for me to adjust my dress before tossing the boy the keys. I stifled a giggle at seeing the excitement in the kid's eyes.

"Knock yourself out, kid." Vin took the ticket from the boy, who couldn't have been over twenty-one, and slipped him a fifty. "I just filled her up if you want to take her around the block a few times."

"Really?!"

"Sure," Vin patted his back before helping me up the first set of steps.

"That was awfully sweet of you," I beamed up at my action hero.

"I remember being at that age. I've got good insurance."

I grinned, almost tripping on the hem of my dress as I stared up at him. He was so handsome in his jacket and dress shirt. I had a feeling I would trip on my feet all night.

I also knew Vin would be there to catch me. He caught my shoulders, then rubbed his hand down my bare back. His eyes darkened as his hand rested on the lowest part of my back.

Maybe I'd get Vin to trip up once or twice, too. The way he was looking at me had butterflies fluttering chaotically in my chest. His looks were lethal on a regular day, but dressed up like this, I felt ready to combust with every glance in his direction.

"Have I told you how beautiful you look tonight?" Vin whispered in my ear. His tone was hushed and sexy.

"Once or twice," I grinned, leaning against him.

He kissed me beside my ear, and I could feel his smile on my skin. "You'll be hearing it once or twice more."

"You don't look too bad yourself." I rested my hand lightly on his chest, admiring the hard muscles beneath my fingers.

He smirked, then said, "We don't look too bad for getting ready in thirty minutes."

"That's a record for me. I thought it would take me thirty minutes to just figure out this dress."

I bought this a little over a year ago for another event like this one. An event I was supposed to attend with Nick. He broke the news about Arlene before I ever even opened the garment bag. I felt Nick fading away at that point and picked out something a little more risky than what I normally would have. I'm glad I never wasted this dress on him.

"I helped," Vin said proudly, rubbing his thumb on the small of my back. "I'll be helping you get out of it later, too."

I bit my lip to keep from gaping at his suggestive comment. I was already looking forward to getting home later.

Home with Vin.

Gosh, by next weekend, he could really live with me. I just have to talk to the kids to make sure this isn't something that will cause therapy or anything like that.

"Fay!" I heard a familiar squeal as we walked into the foyer of the event building.

I looked over to see Virginia, one wife of Nick's bosses, coming my way. She already looked intoxicated and had a full glass of white wine in one hand.

"Fay, my lovely. It's so good to see you!"

She walked right up to me, pulling me into an overly enthusiastic hug. I almost fell down, but thankfully, Vin's large hand on my back kept me upright.

"Virginia," I laughed awkwardly. "Um, yeah. It's good to see you too. How are you? How's Ella?"

"Oh, good," she waved her hand. "She's with the nanny for the weekend. Gotta give this mama some time to get her drink on. You know what I mean?"

I smiled through the awkwardness. Cecilia, the long-time girlfriend of one of Nick's other bosses, looked embarrassed for Virginia. I tried to smile and reassure her, but Cecilia never liked me much and just gave me a tight smile. She kept glancing at Vin, though, which I found to be unpleasant.

"Aw, Feighlynn," Mr. Stevens, Virginia's husband, came up and put a hand on his wife's elbow. He grabbed it rather forcefully, which I liked little. He was always a little too rough under the surface with his wife and was all smiles and underhanded compliments to others around him. "I didn't think I would have the pleasure of seeing you here."

"Small world, I guess," I smiled tightly. I had no reason to converse with the toxic man any longer, and didn't want to open up more of a dialogue than he already had.

Mr. Stevens ran his eyes up and down my dress in a way that made me feel yucky. Vin must have noticed, because he grabbed my waist and pulled me against his side.

Stevens' eyes crinkled in the corners, and I couldn't tell if the tension was amusement or concealed irritation.

"We should get back to our table, Ginny," he squeezed his wife's arm, making her wince slightly. "Good to see you again, Feighlynn."

Cecilia wrinkled her nose, gave me one last look, then sent Vin a completely different look before turning to follow her friend and Nick's boss. I breathed a sigh of relief when they were gone.

"Who's the sloshed chick?" Vin asked as Virginia was being dragged away.

He was still giving Mr. Stevens that hard look. Stevens was a hard man to like, especially for a morally conscious man like Vin.

"Nick's boss and Virginia is his boss's wife."

"Oh." Vin looked even more disgruntled.

I laughed at his protective expression. He looked every bit the action hero I deemed him to be, ready to sweep in and save the damsel from the evil rich man with more money than values.

Vin's scowl slipped into a confused expression. "What?" He stared down at me.

"Nothing." I hugged myself against him. "You're just cute."

"Me?" He raised his eyebrows. "I look cute when I'm pissed?"

"Are you pissed?"

He shrugged, scratching the back of his head. "Wouldn't you be?"

"Then yes," I smiled broadly, squeezing his thick waist. "You're definitely cute when you're pissed."

He chuckled at me, then bent to kiss the top of my head. "And you're cute all the time, which I see is going to be a problem the rest of the night."

"What kind of problem?"

He grumbled, lifting my face to his with his fingers under my chin. "The problems that invoke the less sophisticated side of me."

"Ooh, I like the less sophisticated side of you. He's cute when he's pissed."

"He's not cute," Vin growled playfully. "He's a feral mother fucker." He pretended to munch on my neck, making me giggle.

"You two look as disgustingly gross as ever," Al Milton suddenly appeared behind my cute, feral date. If Vin wasn't so tall, I might have noticed him earlier. "Get a room."

"Be nice," an attractive woman with sharp eyes and a brilliant smile gave him a disapproving look. I had seen her at these events before, but never talked to her. She smiled warmly at me, holding out her hand. "Emma Milton. You must be Lynn."

"Hello," I shook her hand, noticing how warm it felt. "I think I've seen you once or twice, but we never got to meet."

"I believe I recall seeing you in the past. It's a shame we were never introduced previously, but I stayed away from the," she flashed a glance at the table where Virginia and Cecilia were mingling with Nick's other colleagues, "the less appealing crowd. Wouldn't want to taint my ears with the nonsense of the vain and egocentric."

I was taken aback for a moment, but she smiled kindly before adding, "Not you, Lynn, dear."

"She's talking about the Leroy and Stevens firm," Al filled me in. "My wife isn't fond of lawyers on a good day."

I liked the backbone of this woman. The way she held her head high and spoke her mind. I couldn't help but giggle to myself, knowing I had felt the same way for years at these functions during the times I had to stomach Nick's bosses' arrogant conversations. Emma's eyes sparkled at me, like she could sense my train of thought.

"It's good to see you again, Em," Vin kissed her cheek, offering her a loose hug.

"Kevin. I heard wonderful things about you in your new role. The rumors of the barbaric bailiff that tosses criminals like they weigh nothing reached even my department on the other side of the city."

"Emma works for the school board," Al filled me in.

"Ah," I nodded. I see now why she has a more authoritative demeanor.

"So, tell me, Lynn. What do you do?" Emma hooked her arm in mine and walked towards the large conservatory.

"I'm a graphic designer, working from home."

Emma and I chatted about work as we began walking through the gardens, but soon we were talking about other things, too. The flowers were in bloom, which I had to stop and appreciate. I love the gardens here, but haven't been in a while.

Emma was warm and laughed often. When I leaned too far over one of the koi ponds and almost fell in, she burst into a fit of giggles, trying to hide them behind her hand, watching Vin catch me at the last minute. It probably looked comical seeing this big, burly man lift me by my waist right before my nose touched the water. I may or may not have squealed like a monkey, too.

"Oh, Kevin," Emma kept laughing behind her hand. "She is absolutely lovely. I don't think you could have picked a better match.

Adorable." Emma pinched my cheek while Vin was still holding me. "I just want to put you in my purse and take you home."

"I'll fight you for her," Vin grumbled, helping to set me on my unstable feet.

"I'm sure you would," Emma smirked, with that sharp gleam in her eyes.

"I told you." Al elbowed her while sending me a wink.

"Told her what?" I asked, smoothing the front of my dress.

"That Kevin was smitten." Emma hooked her arm on her husband's. "Oh, I'm parched after our walk. Let's go find our table."

Vin kept a hold of me as we wove our way out of the gardens and back into the main event room. It was quite crowded now, and I knew the event was close to starting. The hospital the fundraiser was for had slides going on a giant projector above the stage. Images of sick kids in hospital beds were currently flashing brightly on the giant screen. One little girl smiling while cuddling a teddy bear made my eyes burn and my chest get all tight.

"Aw, baby," Vin rubbed my back. "You look like you're about to cry."

"She's just so little and cute. She's too little to be in that big old bed."

"That's how they get you." Al looked back at me with a crooked grin. "Playing on your heartstrings."

"They can take all my money," I murmured as Vin wiped the few drops of moisture that were leaking under my eyes.

"You're fucking adorable. You know that?" Vin smirked.

"I'm telling you, I'm sneaking out of here with her in my pocket," Emma said, grabbing two wine glasses off a tray and handing one to me.

"And I'm telling you, I'll fight you for her," Vin said, flagging down a server with a tray of beer. He held two fingers up and the server nodded, indicating to give him one minute.

"While you two are fighting, Lynn and I might sneak out of here and get some actual food. Did you see this menu?!" Al held up the menu card from the table. "Last year we got prime rib. Who eats eggplants?"

"Well," Emma smirked, pushing her finger to her lips, then glancing down the front of Al's body. It took me a second to understand what she was looking at. "I've devoured an eggplant occasionally."

Al caught on right away, wiggling his eyebrows and pulling her close as she tried to act aloof, coolly drinking her wine. Meanwhile, my face felt like it was burning, and I let out a bashful laugh.

"What are you laughing at? You like eggplant too, don't you?"

I bit my lip, staring into his heated gaze. "Only one, but it's a little too big to eat all the way."

"Lynn!" Emma acted outraged, clenching her pearls. "What in the heavens are you talking about?"

"The same thing you were," Al snickered.

The server came back with two beers for Al and Vin, and when the lights flashed, we took our seats. The table fell into a steady conversation over dinner. Al begrudgingly ate his eggplant parmesan, making a brief show of pretending it was meat. I thought it was delicious, and so was everything else brought to us. When the last course, a fruit tart with vegan whipped topping, came, that was when the hosts began their presentations.

Throughout the presentations of the good work these donations have done for the hospital in the past, Vin was distracting me, feeding me bite after bite of the rich dessert. I ate all mine and most of his, which he seemed to find more than a little amusing.

His eyes kept traveling over my body, and I felt like he was undressing me where I was sitting in this room. I could feel the racy thoughts behind each of his looks, and it was getting to me. I pressed my thighs together, but that only worked while he wasn't touching me. When he rubbed slow, sensuous circles on my knee, I knew my poor panties would be soaked through by the time we got home.

I need to fix myself now before it gets too bad.

"Where are you going?" Vin whispered as I discreetly stood up.

"Bathroom," I grumbled.

He smirked, sitting back in his chair, all smug and proud. Damn it. Why did he have to look so good all the freaking time? My panties were done for.

"Hurry back, or I might have to go looking for you."

Emma and Al gave me a knowing look that made me blush wildly. I hurried off before Vin could say anything else.

In the deserted bathroom, I grabbed a handful of paper towels and headed straight for the stall. I didn't know how effective they would be for the sheer lace I wore, but I had to at least attempt to dry them off.

When I felt more calmed down, especially in the southern regions, and my panties felt mostly dry, I fixed them back in place and went to wash my hands. As I was scrubbing with the sweet-smelling soap, I heard the door to the bathroom open and looked up absentmindedly.

My heart hammered in my chest, seeing Nick there in the doorway with a grim expression on his face.

"Nick?"

His eyes tightened. He took a step inside, so the door swung shut behind him.

"Nick, this is the women's room!"

"Fay," he slurred, and I realized right then that he was drunk. I had never seen Nick drunk like this before. He was getting closer, and I could smell the alcohol seeping out of him.

"Wh-what are you doing?" I felt the cold porcelain of the stand-alone sink as I backed up as far as I could.

"Fay," his lip quivered as he stopped right in front of me. "My Fay."

He tried to grab at me, putting his hands on my shoulders like he was trying to hug me, but I pushed him off and he mis-stepped, falling to the ground. I was about to run out of there when a noise startled me. A broken sob, choking him before a series of groans left his twisted lips.

"I'm so sorry. I'm so sorry, Fay. I should never have left you. I n-never should have-"

As his words became incoherent, his groans and cries got louder. He looked pathetic, and not the least bit threatening.

The door opened again, and this time it was actually a woman. She wasn't someone I recognized, and I could only hope she didn't realize who Nick was when she gasped while catching sight of him.

"I'm terribly sorry," I told her. "I think the stories of the kids got to him. Could you give me just a moment, and I'll get him out of here?"

The woman looked less offended, and murmured, "Of... of course. Do you need some help?"

"Do I ever," I groaned, but shook my head, bending over to lift my drunk and disorderly ex-husband off the ground.

"Oh, my," she clenched her chest as Nick leaned against me and let out a strangled cry. He was trying to say he was sorry, still between sobs, but all he could get out were the 's' sounds.

"I'm sorry. We have kids. I think that's why it affected him so," I said again as we passed by her at the door.

"Understandable. Poor dear." She wrinkled her nose, probably catching a whiff of Nick's boozey scent. It was hard to miss.

He kept grabbing my shoulders, crying against my hair as we walked out to the open area right outside the conservatory. I knew I wouldn't be able to handle him much further, but also knew getting his bosses to deal with his drunken behavior was not the best idea. He is still my children's father, and I would like for him to remain employed.

"Wait right here," I said, guiding him to a bench right out of view of the event hall.

"D-don't leave me, Fay," he sniveled, trying to hold on to my hand.

"I'll be right back. Let me get my bag," I told him, prying my hand from his.

He had my kids this weekend. How the heck was he supposed to be a father while he was this messed up? The more I thought about it as I walked back into the event room, the more irritated I got.

Vin took one look at my face, then shot up out of his seat. I was glad we were off to the side and the room was dim, so not as many people noticed. He was kind of hard to miss under normal circumstances.

"I ran into a bit of an issue in the bathroom," I whispered to him. "Can you help me?"

He looked excited for a second, but then something on my face must have shown that the *something* I needed help with would not be what he was thinking.

With a firm nod, he followed me out of the room, grabbing my hand along the way. I am sure he could feel my tension and probably sensed my bad mood. When we were out of the event room, I walked him over to the bench I had left Nick on, and he let out a frustrated groan of his own.

"What the fuck? Why is he here?"

I sighed, wondering where to start. "I don't know. I mean, I don't know why he followed me into the bathroom but-"

"He did what?" Vin's face went stiff, making a shiver travel through me. Maybe I shouldn't have said that yet.

I backtracked and started stammering about my words, "I mean, I was done. Just washing my hands. Maybe he thought it was the men's. It is dark in here, and he is drunk..."

Right then, the lady from earlier came out of the women's restroom. She stopped to look over at Nick with a pitiful look. "Poor dear. I hope your husband feels better soon. He looked so broken hugging you like that. Take care of those kiddos," she said kindly before walking back to the event room.

"Hugging you?" Vin lifted his brows angrily. "That fucker followed you into the bathroom and was hugging you? What else did he do?"

"What?" I frowned at the hostility on Vin's face. "Nothing! He's just drunk."

"Drunk excuses following you into the bathroom?!"

"Vin! Stop! If you're going to just get mad, then go back to the table, and I'll figure this out." He was making this situation more hostile than I expected. I didn't want to make a scene. I just wanted to discreetly get Nick out of here.

"You want me to leave you alone with him? No!"

Nick laughed drunkenly, shaking his head, which was leaning back against the wall from side to side. "That's right, asshole. Go back to where you came from. We don't want you here."

"Fucking prick," Vin nearly shouted, his giant body moving towards Nick's.

I placed my hands on his chest to stop him. I suddenly wished I had grabbed Al instead. Vin was staring at Nick like he was going to kill him, and the look Nick was giving him in return wasn't much better.

In a drunken slur, Nick said, "Get your hands off my wife, asshole."

"I'm going to beat the word 'ex' into your mother fucking skull, you piece of trash," Vin sneered, clenching his fists.

"Stop!" I begged, feeling like I had just made the biggest mistake of asking Vin to help me with this.

"You're choosing some *thug* like him over me," Nick egged him on.

"I'll show you *thug*, motherfucker," Vin moved around me.

I pulled at Vin's arms as I yelled for him to stop, but it fell on deaf ears. It alerted the guard in the main foyer, who rushed over.

"Wh-what?" Nick tried to get up from the bench, but was too drunk to stand on his own. "You gonna hit me now, asshole?"

"You're begging for it," Vin went to swing, but I put all my weight into holding his arm back.

The security guard got there just in time to help yank Vin a few feet back, lessening the threat of my ex getting killed by Vin's fist. I got tossed to the ground in the process and heard my dress rip a little, but was too high on adrenaline to notice where.

Another guard came and helped me up from the ground before going to help his friend. The two put more distance between Vin and Nick, but it caused enough of a commotion that people filtered out of the event hall to look.

Mr. Stevens was one of those people, and when his eyes landed on Nick, he didn't look surprised.

Vin was talking in loud whispers to the two security guards. They must be security sourced from city hall, because it seemed like Vin knew them. One even called him Mr. Trude a few times.

Could this have gotten anymore out of hand? Vin and Nick's careers may be affected by this.

"You're such an idiot, Feighlynn," I whispered to myself. Why didn't I get someone else to help me?

"I can take care of him from here, Miss Feighlynn," Mr. Stevens approached me, pulling out a couple of bills from his wallet and waving over the attendant for the event. "Find his valet ticket and have someone drive him home," he instructed the young attendant dressed in black slacks and a bright red vest. "This should cover the taxi back."

"Um, where does he live, sir?" The young man looked nervously at Mr. Stevens, who was exuding arrogance and annoyance.

Mr. Stevens looked at me expectantly.

"Pacific Kress. It's right across from the library downtown. I can have my son outside waiting."

Mr. Stevens gave the attendant a look that had him scurrying off to accomplish the task. He paused beside Nick, looking awkwardly down at him like he was trying to figure out where to find the ticket.

"Nick, hand him the ticket for your car, please," I pinched the bridge of my nose, feeling like his mother and not his ex-wife like I should.

"Come and get it yourself." Nick gave me a teasing look that had Vin muttering obscenities again as the guards held him back.

I was done with this. All of it. I marched over to Nick, kicking his legs so he would sit up.

"Give me your wallet," I demanded, holding out my hand.

Nick must have realized how over the edge I was, because that drunken smile left his face and he fumbled for his wallet in his back pocket.

When he placed it in my hands, I dug out a few twenties, then found his valet ticket in the front sleeve. I took the hundreds from the attendant's hands and replaced them with the twenties.

"I'll handle getting this jerk home. Just get me his key."

"Yes ma'am," he nodded, then walked hurriedly to the foyer.

I then stomped over to Mr. Stevens and pushed the bills against his chest. "Wave your money at someone else."

He lifted a brow, looking amused. "I understand your frustration, but he's excessively intoxicated, and you're just a snack of a woman," Mr. Stevens eyed me up and down.

Vin made a noise that was as feral as he claimed to be, but I was getting pretty worked up myself. I was in mom-mode, which was just as scary and way more effective.

"Your *wife* was excessively intoxicated too, but I still somehow doubt she would appreciate you sizing up another woman or calling her a snack. Why don't you quit staring at my breasts and go take care of her?"

Mr. Stevens' eyes narrowed on me, but then he pursed his lips and nodded, turning to go back into the event hall. I gave the same icy stare to the others loitering at the entrance, watching the show, and many of them turned to return to their seats, too.

"Ma'am," the attendant from before came back with Nick's car keys. "The car is waiting for you."

"Good," I tried to smile appreciatively at him, but my heart wasn't in it.

I turned towards Nick, snapping my fingers. "Up. Now. We're getting you home."

"Who's getting him home?" Vin asked loudly.

"I am." I turned my stony stare on him. "If you have a problem with that, you can stay here too. If not, get your keys and follow me. I'll need a right back when I'm done."

He looked like he was about to argue, but something in my expression stopped him. "Fine," Vin snapped, pulling his arm out of the first guard's grip.

"You two, help me get him outside and into the car." I looked pointedly at the guards until they moved. They hurried to either side of Nick, guiding his drunken steps out of the doors and down the steps. I followed behind, and Vin was right beside me, seething. I knew he had a lot to say just by the set of his jaw, but so did I.

"This is not fucking okay, Feighlynn," was all he uttered between clenched teeth.

I scoffed, "No, it's not. I will not cause more of a scene here. We'll talk on the drive to my house."

He went silent after that, and so did I. I didn't want to fight, and I knew a fight was coming. Just not yet.

This entire situation was a freaking nightmare, and I would not let it get any worse.

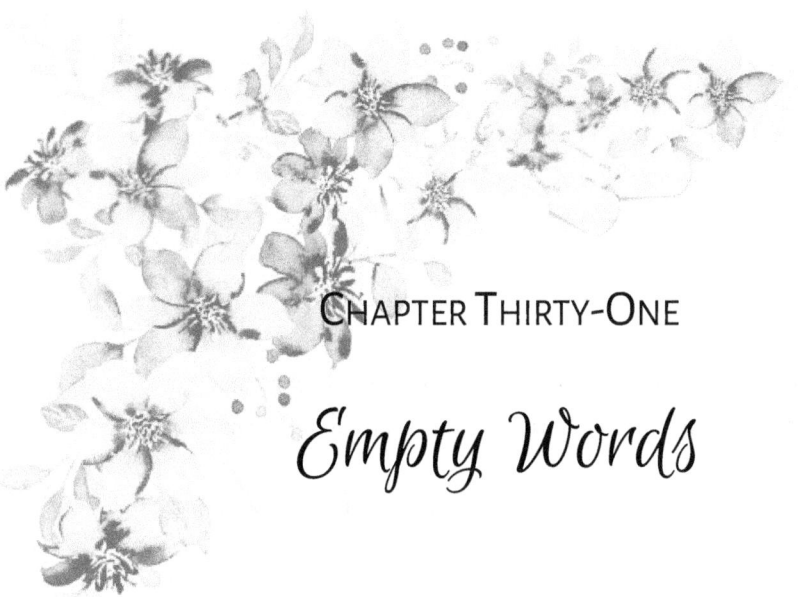

CHAPTER THIRTY-ONE

Empty Words

Vin

I watched on, leaning on the hood of my car as Lynn guided her drunk ass ex to the front door of his building. She wouldn't let me help, giving me a nasty fucking look when I tried.

Thankfully, the doorman seemed to catch sight of her and rushed to open the door before she had to figure out the door code to get in. The doorman opened the door and helped drag Nick through it right as Preston came rushing from the elevator.

"Fucking pathetic," I sneered, feeling the need to punch someone more than ever.

If it wasn't for that look Lynn gave me when she told me to stay the fuck out of it, I wouldn't have so easily let her go upstairs to that bastard's apartment on her own.

Preston looked disgusted with his dad, and I felt a little better knowing he wouldn't let the bastard disrespect his mother more than he already had. Then this sinking feeling made my heart drop to my gut.

Nick wasn't the one Lynn was pissed at right now. It was me.

My stomach still twists imagining that expression on Lynn's face when she had reached her limit.

"You knocked your lady to the ground, Mr. Trude. Pull yourself together," Ivan had hissed at me after yanking me back from that fucker. I thought Ivan was exaggerating, saying whatever to calm the situation. In the red haze that fell over me, hearing that the prick had followed her to the bathroom and forced himself on her, I wasn't really paying much attention to anything else. All I could see was his drunk, arrogant face as the urge to punch it in came over me.

Ten different kinds of regrets and guilt ate away at me while waiting outside for Lynn to come back down. There was a war waging inside of me. The part of me that wants to bust in the condo building and drag my girlfriend out of there before her ex forces himself on her again is barely being kept in check because I know that would only piss her off more.

Preston was there, too. I have no trust in that asswipe ex of hers, but I did trust Preston.

After what felt like forever, Lynn emerged with her kids on her heels. As she walked, I noticed a tear in the side seam of her dress. My eyes narrowed, wondering how her dress got torn. Only the worst scenarios came to mind. All of which didn't help my anger.

Preston gave me a stiff look, then hurried off to his father's car, probably to park it in the parking garage. Jessie had a bag on her shoulder, and Lynn had a gym bag in her hands. The kids must be going back home instead of staying there with their drunk father.

When Lynn dropped the bag on the curb, ten feet away from me. She didn't even acknowledge me standing there staring at her. Jessie looked uncomfortable, and maybe even sad. She smiled tightly at me, then hugged her backpack more on her shoulder.

"You can drop your bag in the car," I told her, wanting to break the silent tension.

Jessie looked at her mom, then Lynn shook her head. "She's riding with Preston," Lynn said, still not looking at me. "She can hold her backpack until he comes out."

Fuck, she was even more pissed than I imagined.

"Lynn, I-"

"Not now," she cut me off. "We'll talk on the way back."

She finally looked at me, but it wasn't an expression that I wanted to see. Her eyes were tense, almost cold. She was always so fun-loving and vibrant. This expression on her face was making me panic on the inside.

I wanted to do something, anything, to break this tension between us, but I had a genuine fear of pushing her too far.

I sat awkwardly on my hood, pleading with Lynn with my eyes. She was back to not looking at me, just staring blankly towards the parking garage with a vacant look in her eyes.

When Preston's mustang pulled out of the garage, my heart hammered in my chest. This talk Lynn and I were about to have alone. I wasn't so sure if I wanted to have it. I didn't know what she was so angry about.

Well, I had a clue, but I think I was fucking justified in getting as pissed as I did. She's standing out in the cold with a torn dress, dragging her kids back home late at night because her ex-husband is an idiot.

"Are you going to be okay, mom?" Preston asked as he got out to help Jessie toss her bags in the trunk. He gave me a look out of the corner of his eyes.

Lynn just smiled tightly, kissing her daughter's cheek before Jessie slipped into the car.

"Drive carefully, sweetie," she waved to Preston.

He gave me one last look before sighing and getting in his car to drive away.

Lynn stood on the curb, watching his car take off, not speaking or moving until he was all the way down the street. Then she finally looked at me again.

Instead of anger, she looked extremely tired. Her eyes were swimming, and her frown was deep. It broke some part of me to see her so despondent. So exhausted and empty.

"Let's go," she murmured after a long stare, then moved to walk past me to the passenger door.

By the time I pushed myself off the hood, she already had the door open and was getting in. I was the one that opened doors for her. She had always waited for me to do it ever since the first week of us dating.

I don't know why, but it made me feel even worse. It felt like she didn't need me. That I had let her down.

I hesitated before getting in, not knowing what was about to go down. Not knowing what she wanted to talk about had my anxiety going haywire.

Every sound in the car seemed extremely loud through the tense silence that stretched between us. The clicking of the blinker, the humming of the engine, the hiss of the air conditioner. All the noises I usually never notice, but now I'm focusing on each one to distract myself from the loud silence.

Lynn sat staring out the window for so long, she was like a statue. Not moving. I kept checking to see if she was even breathing. It wasn't until the last time I checked I saw a tear rolling down her cheek.

"Baby," I whispered, unable to keep quiet any longer.

When I placed my hand on her leg, she squeezed her eyes shut, sending more tears to glide down her face.

"Damn it," I groaned, checking my mirrors before parking off the side of the street.

I leaned over to her, grabbing her face in my hands as I tried to get her to open her eyes. She tried to twist away, but I wouldn't let her.

"Baby, look at me."

"No," her rough whisper was so low, but so fucking loud. "I can't."

My heart cinched seeing her lip quiver the way it did. I wanted to stop it with a kiss. I wanted to kiss away all her tears and all her sadness.

How the hell did tonight get so fucked up? Why the hell did I agree to go to that fucking charity event knowing her asshole ex might be there?

"Please, talk to me, Lynn. Please." I gave in to one urge and kissed a tear from her cheek, only to feel a spasm of pain when she turned her face away.

"I can't Vin. I can't, right now."

"You can't what?" I asked, as my heart continued to sink. "Lynn, please."

"I can't look at you right now," she put a dagger through my heart. "I can't."

"Why?" My voice dropped as I begged. "Because I almost punched him. Baby, he deserved it."

"That's not it! He deserved more than that! But that's not it," she shook her head, trying to escape my hands. Finally, her tear-filled eyes looked at me, piercing my soul. "That's not it."

"Then what is?" I felt empty. What should I do?

She shook her head again. "You really don't know why I'm upset? Really?"

"I really don't," I wanted to yell. "Was it because I wanted to punch the fucker? Lynn, he *followed you* into the fucking bathroom. He forced himself on you. Look at your fucking dress," I grabbed the ripped seam, gripping it angrily in my fist.

That cold look returned to her eyes. "He didn't do that to my dress."

My brows dipped in confusion.

"It ripped when I fell. When I was trying to stop you from punching the father of my kids."

"*You knocked your lady friend to the ground, Mr. Trude. Pull yourself together.*" Ivan's statement returned to me as guilt choked me, making it hard to breathe.

She shook her head again, staring down at the rip in her seam. "Tonight was the first time since we started dating that I didn't feel I could... I could rely on you, Vin. I don't know how to wrap my mind around that yet."

The knife in my chest twisted even more.

Lynn jerked her head out of my hands, and this time I let her, dropping my hands from her face. As fear and shame washed over me, I stared with wide eyes at her tear-stained face. She was still so painfully beautiful. I didn't know what to do. I didn't know how to fix this. I always wanted to fix everything for her. Tonight, she had to fix everything herself.

Damn it, and all I did was make everything worse. She came to get me. She was asking for my help, but I let my temper take over. Damn it.

"Please, just take me to my house," she twisted her body to stare out the window again. "I think our emotions are still too high to talk tonight. You should go home too."

There was a tremor in her voice. If my heart wasn't already torn from my chest, it would have broken right then.

She asked me to take her to her house. Not home, like we had called it earlier, but *her house.* She was putting a line down that wasn't there before.

"You're my home," I murmured to myself, trying to hold on to that sentiment from earlier. They felt like empty words now.....

CHAPTER THIRTY-TWO
Drowned In Loneliness

Nick

Earlier.....

"**S**leep it off, you jerk," Fay hissed in annoyance after Preston helped her get me out of my shoes and jacket and into my bed.

I wasn't as drunk as before, sobering up some on the drive home, but I didn't let that show, knowing being drunk was my only defense against Fay's wrath.

She was taking care of me, too. It wasn't like before, when she would giggle and laugh at my drunken antics before tenderly helping me get to bed. We used to drink together on the nights when the kids were at their grandparents, and she was always playful and teasing.

That was the Fay I was dealing with now. She was furious, but at least she was close to me. Closer than I had felt in months. Confined in the space of my car, the reality of that sobered me up more than anything.

As I was propped on her shoulders, I could smell the sweet scent of her perfume, the same kind she had always used. I could hear every little groan and every muttered insult as she tried to guide my staggering body.

I couldn't help myself but find the smallest amount of satisfaction seeing her anger not only aimed at me, but at her new hoodlum boyfriend, too.

She even protected me from him. That has to mean something, right?

It wasn't until I heard her telling Jessie and Preston to pack their things to go home that the panic set in, and I realized how badly I messed up.

"I.... It's my weekend," I mumbled, trying to lift the sheets to get out of the bed. They were tangled in my arms and took a lot of effort to get off.

Fay turned a hard glare at me. "You want me to trust you with my children after the display you made tonight? Grow up, Nick. Sleep it off and we'll talk about this tomorrow."

Damn it. I messed up. I wasn't as drunk as I was at the event, but I wasn't sober enough not to stumble as I definitely stood from the bed.

If I hadn't been used to drinking heavily as of late, I might have already passed out, but this level of intoxication seemed safe enough for me to still have my kids. I didn't want Fay taking them from me. Not when they were the last good thing left in my life.

"P-please, Fay. Not my kids...." I was panicking. Was I about to lose them, too?

"Geez, dad," Preston came back into the bedroom, taking one sad look at me before helping to pick me up off the floor. I hadn't even realized I was still on it. In my head, I was walking towards Fay, who was watching me with cold eyes from the open door. "You're a mess. Do you really want Jessie to stay here and see you like this?"

"I-I'm fine," I slurred as Preston groaned, picking me up from the floor and setting me back on the edge of the bed.

My stomach twisted, and Preston hurriedly grabbed an empty plastic storage box from the end of my bed and put it in front of me to lose the contents of my stomach.

That was when Jessie reappeared at the door to see what was happening, and I looked up to see the horror on her face. It made my stomach twist again.

No, I didn't want my daughter to see me like this. I didn't want my son to clean up after me and catch my vomit with moving supplies. I didn't want my wife looking at me like I was trash. Like I was the lowest of the low.

I didn't want any of this. I wanted to suffer alone where no one could see me falling apart.

Fay reassured our daughter I was fine, just momentarily sick, and instructed her to finish packing so they could give me time to get better. Jessie pleaded with her mother to stay and look after me, but I didn't want that. I only wanted her to see the best in me, and I was failing miserably.

"G-Go with your mom, honey," I said in a much more sober tone. "I'll call you tomorrow."

Jessie looked distraught, but Fay urged her to go, and she eventually did. Then Fay gave me a pitying look before taking the bile-filled box from Preston's hands and walking into the bathroom with it.

I heard the shower turn on, then the sounds of something being washed as she called out for Preston to go pack.

Preston gave me one last frigid glare before turning to walk out of my bedroom, leaving me alone with Fay cleaning my puke in the bathroom.

She came back out moments later with a washcloth in one hand and my trash can in the other. "Use this to clean your mouth," she handed the washcloth to me. "Your box is drying in the bathtub. Use the trash can if you feel sick again."

I put the washcloth over my entire face, letting the wet coolness sober me further. "I'm sorry," I whispered in a raspy plea.

"Yeah, me too. Me freaking too. Get sober and we'll talk about you getting the kids back tomorrow."

"I'm sorry," I mumbled again, unable to even look at her as I laid back in the bed. The bed we once shared. "I'm so, so sorry, Fay."

It was silent for a long time, so I moved the washcloth, thinking she had left. She hadn't. She was still standing beside the bed, but was staring down at the pictures I had pulled out from storage. The ones that were in that empty plastic storage box I had just emptied my stomach into. They were all pictures of us. Us in our good times.

I got drunk most nights while staring at every one of them, wishing for those times to return.

Fay ran her fingers over a photo of her holding Jessie right after she was born with Preston's toddler body pressed against hers, trying to see his new sister more closely. Fay was radiant, filled with so much love. It was one of my favorite pictures of her.

She then sighed before giving me one last pitying look. "You don't need my forgiveness, Nick. You need to quit torturing yourself."

Then she left, calling for the kids to head out the door. I was left alone, staring at those pictures in my miserable state.

This was the first time Fay had come to the condo. The condo we had talked about buying together for years. I had hoped to build memories to cherish with her again in this place. Now it's going to be stained with the memories of how pathetic I was tonight.

Minutes later, I heard the door open again, and thought maybe Fay had decided to stay and take care of me like she always used to do. I don't know why I deluded myself into thinking that was even a possibility.

Instead, Preston looked in the bedroom, then let out a heavy sigh, seeing I was still awake.

"You're so embarrassing, Dad. Geez. Here are your keys." He dropped them on my dresser. "You still can't stop trying to bring mom down with you, can you?"

As she shook his head in bitter shame, whatever small fragments were left of my dignity disappeared.

The coldness in my condo never felt so harsh as I sat there alone, staring at the photos of the life I destroyed.

Picking up the Johnny Walker bottle I kept hidden in my nightstand drawer, I drowned the loneliness away.

**

Feighlynn

"You're my home."

Those words were haunting me.

I felt terrible. Not just for pushing Vin away like I did, but because of the situation itself. I had been living in a fairytale, but tonight, I got hit with a hard dose of reality just from one innocent bathroom visit.

Well, not really innocent, but the fairytale was real when I stepped into that bathroom with my panties in disarray, then stepped out with a nightmare clinging to my shoulders.

And to make matters worse, I broke apart from all the emotional strain before Vin and I could even talk. My head was still full of irrational thoughts as we were coming back home, and I just didn't want to dive into any more tonight. I didn't want to break down any more than I already had.

Vin's face when I told him to go home made me want to forget the entire night, forget Nick and all the crap he started. It made me want to crawl over to Vin and cry in his arms until all the embarrassment, all the disgust, all the regret, all the guilt just drowned out and all I could feel was him.

I couldn't bring myself to do that just yet.

He was my haven, but tonight, he was the man who wouldn't listen to me and just made an already unpleasant situation worse. And felt so incredibly guilty for putting him there. Putting him in the position to show that side of him. I felt like it was my fault for going to him and not someone else.

I got so used to relying on him; I didn't think there would be a situation where I couldn't.

"I'm sorry, Lynn," Vin whispered after stopping at the curb of my house. "I really am."

The words weren't what got me, but it was the hard set in his jaw and the tightness of his eyes as he didn't meet my stare. He was staring at the rip in my dress instead.

I mumbled some sort of "goodnight" then hurried out of his car and into my house. I could feel his eyes on me then, but didn't have the courage to look back. I only had to fumble with my keys for a second before Preston opened the door to let me in.

Preston's expression when he saw my face triggered more emotions to pour out of me. Pres wrapped his arms around my shoulders and pulled me inside as I broke down.

My son shouldn't have to hold his mom as she sobbed about his dad being an asshole and her boyfriend being insensitive. But there we were. Standing in the entrance to my house, Preston rubbed back and whispered "I got you, mom," until I eventually calmed down.

He gingerly walked me up to my room when I said I wanted to shower and change, but when he left, all I did was lay on the bed, cuddled around Kevin while still wearing my torn dress, listening to the murmurings of my kids outside my bedroom door. I was left in my regrets, letting them eat away with me until I felt empty inside.

Eventually, the house calmed down. I'm sure Jessie was disturbed about the events of tonight, but Preston handled her, too.

My son was picking up the pieces of us left and right. That fueled my guilt further.

Why was I so emotionally triggered right now? Why did I get so emotional about Vin? It wouldn't be the first time I had to deal with a situation that felt like all hell was breaking loose. I can usually put my big girl panties on and not let things get to me the way they did tonight.

Was it because of the shock? Because my boyfriend was about to punch the father of my kids? Was it fear of the repercussions to Nick and Vin's careers that made me get so mad?

I knew none of those things were it. I know why tonight got to me as drastically as it did.

It was because it was Vin. Because the man I was falling for, the first man I felt anything with in longer than I could remember, was the one at the center of it all.

Reality had hit me hard. Knock me to the ground, literally. I had been living in a fantasy, thinking that my boyfriend was perfect in every way, but that wasn't the man who was facing off with my drunk ex tonight.

The Vin I saw was no action hero coming to save the day with his level head, cool demeanor and big muscles. All I saw were the muscles, and tonight that scared me. The feral anger was something I didn't expect.

We were just talking about living together, for Pete's sake. If he had actually punched Nick, how would moving in together work? Jessie is still very much a daddy's girl, and she hates violence. Preston might have been okay with it, but that would just have strained his relationship with Nick more.

All the future drop offs and family events would have been so strained. The kids would never feel a moment of peace. It might already be that way.

Even though I had so many reasons to be upset, why did my heart hurt and yearn for Vin so badly still?

Kevin groaned in doggy annoyance as I reached over him for my purse at the foot of the bed. I pulled out my phone after wiping my eyes on the back of my hand. Kevin sat up and licked my face, making me fumble and drop my phone several times before settling him down enough to unlock the screen.

There, at the top of the notifications, was a missed call from Vin. Then a simple text.

> *My Hero:| I'm sorry, baby. I really am.*

Tears burned my eyes again as I stared longingly at the screen. Why did I tell him to go home? Yes, the kids ended up coming back to the house, but he clearly didn't want to leave things as they were, and right now, all I feel is regret.

So what if he ended up punching Nick? I should have punched Nick, and all things considered, I would have been justified in doing so. So what if they lost their jobs? Nick is a lawyer, and a decent one at that. He could have found a new firm with less repulsive bosses.

And Vin could just come to live with me. We had decided on that anyway, didn't we? I can be a sugar mam. I make enough to take care of feeding another mouth, even one that's as hungry as his. I could take care of him.

I mean, the man is older than me, but considering tonight's events, I'm no longer sure if he is more mature than me or not. More steady on his feet? Yes. Stronger? Definitely. Sexier in every way? Without a doubt. More mature? Surely not. But I doubt there is a man out there that would have been in that situation.

With my phone in hand, I typed up several messages, starting with apologetic, then ranting with exasperation, then deleting everything and simply typing out that I missed him.

That was it.

I missed him, and I was no longer mad. I was just exhausted and empty and wanted him here to hold me and put me back together.

As I went back and forth on what to say, what to type and send, my eyes grew heavier and heavier until exhaustion got the better of me. I knew I would not write anything coherent with my vision this blurry with sleep, so I deleted everything except the "I miss you".

After pressing send, I let the phone fall out of my hands onto the bed, and then cuddled deeper into Kevin, wishing he was a different Kevin lying here with me.

***

Grrrrr...

I woke to Kevin growling in annoyance beside me, moving his furry body closer so I was hanging onto the bed by a butt cheek.

Still groggy, I opened my eyes to get him to move, but then I saw my phone light going off as it vibrated beside Kevin's legs.

As I wiped the sleep from my eyes, I reached for it hurriedly to see if it was Vin. He had been the focal point in my dreams, and I just remembered the text I sent before passing out.

But it wasn't him. It wasn't a number I recognized at all.

"Hello?" I answered when it was close to rolling over to voicemail.

"Hello. Am I speaking with Feighlynn Micheals?" A woman's voice asked me in a direct tone.

I checked the clock. It was three in the morning. Who the heck was this?

"Yes?" I said carefully. "Can I help you?"

"Yes ma'am. I'm a nurse at Carris Methodist. We just had a patient come in with you listed as his next of kin. We're going to need you to come down here as soon as you can."

CHAPTER THIRTY-THREE

Shitty Night

Vin

Last night, after watching Lynn fumble to her door with tears in her eyes, I was left not knowing what the hell to do. I did not know how I could fix this.

The reality of every mistake I made hit me all at once. She trusted me to help her deal with the drunken idiot, but I jumped to anger, and ended up putting her in a worse situation than the one she was originally in.

My fingers were shaking as I sat in my dark car and pressed send on that text message, telling her I was sorry. I couldn't think of what else to say. I was sorry. Sorry that I had made a shitty situation worse out of possessive rage instead of helping her to get his sorry ass cleaned up and home. She had to do it, because she didn't trust me any longer to be around him.

She didn't trust me. That tore me the fuck up inside.

I sat in my car for a while, waiting for a text back. After ten, twenty, thirty minutes of waiting, I gave up and dragged my sorry ass into the house.

I felt like complete shit. I must have looked like it too. Mom was still up, watching some late-night talk show on TV. When I walked in, she looked surprised to see me, then her eyes filled with concern as she took in my entire appearance.

This was a shit time for mom to be observant. I didn't want to explain, but knew the questions were coming.

"Hi, sweetie. I didn't expect you home tonight. Everything alright?"

I rubbed the back of my neck, sighing heavily. "Not really, mom."

She picked up the remote and put the TV on mute. She would not let me run away easily.

"What happened?"

I shook my head. "Nothing, mom. Just a shitty night."

"Did you and your girlfriend get into a fight?"

Damn, she would not let this go. I was hoping I could just head to my room to be miserable by myself.

"Yeah. I messed up," I murmured, eyeing the stairs for my escape.

"I'm sorry, sweetie. Is there anything I can do to help? Do you want me to talk to her?"

"No, mom. I think I got to handle this on my own."

"Well, what about I just make you a bouquet?" She asked hopefully. She really wanted to help. I could see it on her face. "Nothing says sorry like flowers."

I felt the corners of my mouth lift slightly, loving my mom's way of showing support. "Sounds wonderful mom," I walked by her chair, kissing the top of her head. "Flowers would be perfect. I'm going to head up. Good night."

She patted my cheek. "Good night, sweetie."

Flowers from my mom. That was how Lynn and I started this whole thing. Bringing them to her tomorrow while saying how sorry I was would actually be perfect.

Right when I reached the stairs, mom called out, "You still want to marry this girl, Kevin?"

I stopped, imagining my life without her. That thought hurt so badly. Not seeing her smile, hearing her silliness, or her infectious laughter. I knew I couldn't live without her.

"Yeah. I'm going to marry her, mom."

She smiled sweetly, nodding her head. "It will work out. Get some sleep. Tomorrow is a new day."

I nodded, then dragged my exhausted body up the stairs to my room.

I took off my shirt, but it still had Lynn's perfume clinging to the fabric. I kept it on, wanting some part of her with me as I tried to fall asleep. After kicking off my boots and jeans, it didn't take me long to pass out.

***

The next morning, I woke up early, still feeling like shit. I showered quickly, shaved, then checked myself in the mirror, making sure I didn't look as shitty as I felt.

Lynn will walk her dog soon. On Saturday mornings, we usually woke up and did it together. It was a habit, one I wasn't about to break, even though I was on the wrong side of the street.

Mom was still in her room, which was odd. She was usually up with the sun, making breakfast in the kitchen before I left for work. I haven't been home on a Saturday in a while though, so maybe she sleeps in on Saturdays now.

I heard her as I passed by her room. She sounded like she was talking to herself. It was barely seven in the morning. Surely she wasn't on the phone.

"He loves you, dear. Everything will work out. He told me as much," I heard her say.

Was she rehearsing what to say to Lynn? I told her I would handle it, but I guess that didn't stop her from worrying.

Hearing a dog bark, I dropped the thoughts of mom talking to herself and rushed down the stairs two at a time. I knew that bark. Kevin saw a cat, and I know Lynn has a hard time controlling him when he gets excited.

Throwing the door open, I saw not Lynn with Kevin, but Preston.

"Stop it, you stupid mutt." Preston jerked Kevin back on the leash, managing him perfectly fine.

Preston saw me and stopped as I walked down to the street from my house. He was eyeing me skeptically. I know he dragged his crying mom into the house last night, but I wasn't sure how much he knew about the events from the night before.

"Morning," I muttered nervously.

Preston was the gatekeeper to his mother. I knew that well enough to know not to misstep again after sending his mom home crying.

"Morning," he said in a hard tone.

Shit.

At least Kevin was happy to see me. He jumped up, wagging his tail excitedly as I rubbed between his ears.

Preston sighed, jerking on Kevin's leash and telling him to get off me. Then he turned that cold stare back on me.

"Mind telling me what the fuck happened last night?"

My brows knit in confusion. Did Lynn not tell him?

"It was a shitty night," I murmured, rubbing the back of my neck.

Preston scoffed. "Mom wouldn't have cried herself to sleep over a *shitty night*. What happened? Why were you guys with my dad?"

Lynn really didn't tell him anything. I wasn't sure if it was my place. I also knew that I really didn't have an option but to talk to him if I wanted to get to Lynn.

"We went to a charity dinner last night, and your dad was there, too. It was just a shitty night."

"A shitty night," Preston scoffed. "You keep saying that but aren't telling me why."

"Your dad got drunk," I shrugged. "Made a fool of himself."

Preston crossed his arms, looking older than sixteen. He looked me up and down, then said, "That doesn't explain why mom was crying."

This kid....

"I don't know if your mom wants me to tell you everything that happened," I admitted.

"Why wouldn't she?" He lifted a brow.

"Because he's your dad," I said flatly.

"That's even more reason to tell me. Let me deal with him, so mom doesn't have to. What did he do?"

"Kid, you're putting me in a bad position. I really don't want to make your mom more upset than she is."

"So she's mad at you and not him?" He lifted his chin.

"It was a joint effort," I scoffed dryly. "Your dad was a drunk asshole, and I got defensive. That's all I'm telling you. If your mom wants you to know more, she will tell you herself."

Preston stared at me like he was taking my measure. Then he pursed his lips, nodding to himself. "Fair enough."

I sighed, feeling like I had just passed some test. "So, your mom?.... Is she still asleep?"

Preston raised a single eyebrow. "Wouldn't you like to know?"

The kid was pushing his luck with me now. "Is she awake or not?"

His smirk slipped, and he looked back towards his garage like I was missing something. Then I noticed it. Lynn's car was gone.

Preston looked back at me. "She's awake. She's also not home."

"Where is she?" I was worried instantly.

"The asshole is still being an asshole," Preston snickered, shaking his head. "She's at the hospital."

My eyes went wide, fear rising in me. "Is she okay? Did he-"

"Mom's completely fine. Dad's the one who's not."

Chapter Thirty-Four

Texts And Surprises

Feighlynn

"This paper explains the dos and don'ts with his neck brace, and this one is for his cast. Follow up with his regular doctor for pain." The nurse passed me the papers for Nick's discharge.

I leafed through them, looking for the prescriptions, so I could drop those off on the way back to his condo.

What a mess.

I looked back to narrow my eyes at Nick, tired of his crap. He was staring out the window with an empty look in his eyes.

This was in part my fault too, which is the only reason I stayed and agreed to help him get back to his apartment. If I had just gone to bed, or if I'd never sent Vin home to begin with, then I never would have been on my phone to make such a monumental mistake.

The text I sent while I was in a sleepy haze was accidentally sent to my ex. Not Vin, whom I had intended it for.

I still can't believe I did that. While I was deleting and retyping text after text, exiting out of my phone just to open it again, I ended up opening a text from Nick, thinking it was Vin.

Nick texted me almost the same thing Vin had. *"I'm so sorry."* It was the top text in my inbox, and since the message was so similar to Vin's, I messed up. When I typed out and sent *"I miss you,"* it went to Nick. Then Nick, being the idiot he was, decided that meant he needed to come over.

He never even made it out of his parking spot. Nick put his car into drive instead of reverse, then slammed into the concrete wall in front of him.

The security guard that heard the crash came to find an inebriated Nick passed out behind the wheel. He called an ambulance to take him to the hospital, where he was treated for a fractured wrist and a sprained neck.

He was cognitive when I got to the emergency room, and I could see the shame clearly in his expression upon seeing me. But there was also expectation and hope.

When I asked him what he was doing, why the hell would he try driving that drunk? That was when he told me about the texts.

I still can't believe it. My sleepy mistake caused him to nearly kill himself.

"I'll get a wheelchair to escort you both out," the nurse said, eyeing the two of us cautiously. The hospital staff caught on quickly to our strained relationship. Especially after the yelling match we had when I clarified the text was not meant for him.

"I can walk," Nick muttered, swinging his legs from the bed.

"Mr. Micheals, I would advise you to-"

"I said I could do it," he snapped sharply.

The nurse pursed her lips and nodded. I pinched the bridge of my nose, then muttered an apology. She smiled tightly before wishing us luck and walking off.

Standing back, I watched Nick grimace while taking a shaky step on his own.

"Do you need help?"

"No," he grumbled, straightening his back as he took another step, more steadily than the first.

With the cast on his wrist and the brace on his neck, he couldn't help but to shake my head at how stubborn he looked. If he wanted to struggle, so be it.

Even though that was my initial thought, about halfway down the hall, I couldn't take watching him struggle any longer.

"Stop." I held his good arm. "I'm not watching you waddle like a duck all the way to the car. I'm getting a wheelchair."

"I don't need it," he protested through gritted teeth.

"I don't care what you think you need. Sit your stubborn butt right there in that chair and wait for me. I'll be right back."

"Fay, I'm fine. I-"

"Sit!" I raised my voice, not willing to argue any further.

His frown deepened, but he listened. He winced and groaned his whole way down to the seat on the bench. I walked off back to the nurses' desk to ask the nurse from before for that wheelchair.

When I had him in it, no longer protesting despite the sour look on his face, the nurse walked with us to the front of the hospital and waited with Nick while I pulled my car up to the front doors.

Nick stubbornly stood before the nurse could help him, causing both the nurse and me to shake our heads, but neither of us stopped him. It wasn't worth the argument.

"Thank you," I told her once he was buckled in my passenger seat.

She rubbed my shoulder sympathetically. "You're a better woman than me. I would have left my ex-husband on the curb."

I snorted, giving her a grateful smile for the humor that I much needed.

Leaving Nick on the curb was an enticing thought, but I felt responsible. I also didn't want to explain to my kids later why I abandoned their father in his time of need. I had already called Nick's mom, and she was on her way here to take care of him while he recovered. The least I could do was help him get home.

"Just drop me off in front of the condo," Nick grumbled as soon as I got in the driver's seat. "I can get up to my apartment on my own."

"I have to drop your scripts off at the pharmacy and then clear out all the alcohol from your place, so no can do."

"I'm not a child, Fay," he said coldly.

"No, but my babies will not be going back to your place unless I know you're sober. If you don't want me to ransack your liquor cabinet, fine. Jessie and Preston can see you at my sister's on the weekends from now on."

"That's not fair. We have orders in place."

I lifted my brow. "Do you want to go back to court? Because I won't be as compliant this time. Not with my kids, Nick. Do you even remember last night? How drunk you were when I dragged you home? They saw that, Nick. Jessie saw that! If I had left them at your house last night, Jessie might have tried to go with you. How would you feel if she was the one in a neck brace and cast right now?"

He was quiet for a long time, his face full of guilt at the thought. I drove to the pharmacy near his condo, and when I was almost there, he finally spoke again.

"Just drop me off, Fay. Please. My mom can take care of everything else. Just, please, drop me off. I can get up to my place on my own."

"Not without your keys, you can't. I have those in my bag, so you're just going to have to wait." I parked, then grabbed my purse, tapping it smugly before putting it over my shoulder. "Hold tight. I'll be right back."

He huffed, looking away. "You used to be sweet all the time. You changed."

I wanted to laugh out loud. "You've given me little reason to be sweet, Nick." I shut the door, then walked off in a huffy mood.

I would love to just drop Nick off, but I don't trust him not to go right back into his place and drink himself into oblivion again. I know Jessie, and she's going to want to see her dad again soon. She's already texted me asking where I was. Once I tell her what happened to her dad, she'll want to go back to his place.

While waiting in the drop-off line, I pulled out my phone, going to text Preston to let him know we were out of the ER. Instead, my heart sped up when I saw a missed call and a text from Vin.

> *My Hero:| Call me when you can. I really need to talk to you.*

The urge to call him now crept up on me. With Nick outside and the way Vin reacted last night to my ex, I decided against it. I wanted to talk to him. Soon. I just didn't want the first time we talked about what happened last night to be while I was dealing with another Nick situation.

I'll rush through getting Nick taken care of, then I'll just go see Vin in person. It'd be better to explain everything and apologize face to face.

Vin was on my anxious mind as I finished getting the script dropped off and took Nick back to his condo building. I wanted to hurry and get home now.

I used Nick's key card to get into the parking garage, parking in the spot he had reserved for Preston. His car had been towed from the garage, but there were still broken car part bits and glass from the headlights everywhere, along with paint smears and crash marks on the concrete wall.

Nick's eyes looked shocked at how back the damage was. I chose not to say anything, even though it made me feel sick seeing the damage. If I hadn't taken Nick home, my kids could have been there with him when this happened.

I tried to help Nick walk to the elevator, but he insisted he was fine on his own. I didn't argue. It was a short walk and then a quick elevator ride up.

The elevator ride was quiet, just like the drive from the pharmacy to the parking garage. Nick looked all sour and pained while I was busy thinking about Vin and what to say to him when we met. A word slip-up last night when I blurted out that Nick followed me into the bathroom wouldn't be wise. I needed to watch my speech for once.

When we got out of the elevators, I could tell that Nick was already in a lot of pain. The nurse said that his body would be sore for a while. His body locked up from the shock of the impact. His back was probably killing him.

I grabbed his elbow and helped support him out of the elevator, and he actually accepted my help. His pain must be greater than his stubbornness.

Walking him back to his room, I noticed the open bottle and empty glass on the kitchen counter. There was another on his bedside table, only no glass. He was just drinking it from the bottle.

Nick gritted his teeth through the pain while I helped him into bed, then noticed where I was staring.

"That's expensive." Nick glared at me as I lifted the bottle off the bedside table.

"I'll reimburse you," I muttered, walking with it to the kitchen to dump it.

I tossed the now empty bottle in the trash in the kitchen, then dumped the other bottle. I checked every cabinet, even the drawers and the freezer, but found no other bottles. His fridge was well stocked with foods Jessie and Preston like, which softened my disposition, but only a little. He still was the reason last night was such a crap fest.

Sighing, I walked back to his room. "Are there any other bottles?"

Nick was staring at those pictures on his nightstand. I wanted to smash all of them last night, since many of them were just of him and me, but there were some precious ones of my babies too. He was torturing himself with those remnants of the past. Anyone could see that.

"No," he said without looking up. "Just the one here and the one in the kitchen. Happy?"

"No," I scoffed. "Nothing about the last fifteen hours has made me happy."

He closed his eyes, turning his head away from the pictures. "I'm sorry, Fay. I didn't mean to.... I mean..." He pressed his lips together, squeezing his eyes tighter together. When he opened them again, they were glassy and just swimming with emotions. "I can't do this without you, Fay. I can't. I'm trying, but I can't. I fucked up, and don't know how to fix it."

I could feel his pain in every word. I heard the ache in his voice. There was a time that might have moved me. I may have felt sorry for him. But I was where he currently is a year ago. I was the one drowning in my loneliness and pain.

"You can't fix this," I whispered, sitting on the end of his bed. "Because there's nothing there to fix. Not anymore. Not with me."

I picked up a picture of me holding Jessie as a baby in the hospital. Preston was sitting beside me, staring at his sister. It was such a sweet moment. I remember when this picture was taken. I was so overcome with love for my babies, nothing else mattered. Not the pain, the labor, the months of discomfort. Holding my babies was worth all of it.

They were always worth it.

Handing the picture to Nick, I whispered, "They're a different story. When you left me, they were what got me through it all. Focusing on them. You and I can never go back to what we once were. One piece of paper was enough to sever our ties to each other, but nothing can change the fact you are their dad. If you think you need to fix something, do it for them, if nothing else."

Nick's tears spilled over, so I rubbed his back to offer him the only comfort I was willing to give. He set his hand on top of mine on his shoulder, then lifted it to kiss my hand.

"I really am sorry, Fay. I'm so sorry for hurting you."

"Me too," I patted his cheek, avoiding a long cut near his nose. "I need to get home to the kids. Are you going to be okay until your mom comes?"

"I'll manage."

Smiling tightly, I smoothed my thumb over his cut cheek again. "Call me if you need anything. Preston will probably come by later with Jessie. I'll send dinner with them."

"Okay. Thank you."

Standing up, I squeezed his hand one last time before heading out. He needed rest, and I needed to make some apologies myself.

I didn't want to live with regrets like Nick did. Surprisingly, I had none towards my ex. Well, except that text. But I had all kinds of regrets about how I handled things with Vin last night. I would not let things fester any longer.

I headed home, barely putting my car in park before jumping out to hurry to Vin's house. I was bouncing on my feet as I knocked on the door, ready to jump in his arms and apologize until I ran out of breath when he answered.

As the door swung open, I smiled expectantly, but that smile slowly slipped off my face when I was met with a tall, brilliantly blonde woman with sultry eyes and tanned skin.

Leaning back, I checked to make sure I had the right house. Looking over the familiar shingles and brick, I definitely had Vin's house.

"Hi?" the blonde woman looked at me curiously. "Can I help you?"

"Um, hi? Is... Is Vin here?"

"Vin?" she tilted her head to the side.

"Who is it, dear?" I heard Velma's voice.

I let out an anxious breath, feeling reassured I had the right house. Vin's mom just had company. Really pretty company, but this was definitely the right house. I had my doubts for a second, thinking I had gone crazy and driven to the wrong house.

"Oh," Velma smiled widely when she saw me. "Feighlynn! What a pleasant surprise. Have you met my son, Kevin's girlfriend? This is Mindy."

Kevin's girlfriend?

My heart dropped to my stomach and my body broke out in a cold sweat.

The beautiful woman smiled, looking relaxed and not correcting Velma at all. "Hi. It's nice to meet you."

Chapter Thirty-Five

What Can I Do?

Vin

"Okay. Thanks," I muttered into the phone before hanging up.

I've called several hospitals, but couldn't find where Lynn and her ex-husband might be. Maybe because I didn't exactly know what to ask for when I talked to the receptionist. I didn't even know what I was planning on doing when I found them.

Preston said his dad ran into a wall with his car. Preston knew Nick was going to be fine, but didn't know the extent of his dad's injuries. He was waiting to hear from his mom when I talked to him.

I called Lynn and even texted her. I still haven't heard back. Seeing two outgoing texts from me and no reply from her made my stomach twist every time I looked at it. She read my text from last night, but hadn't read my new one yet last I checked. Maybe Nick was keeping her busy.

That thought had my hands twisting my steering wheel, imagining it was his neck.

I needed to get it together before I saw them. I couldn't have a repeat of last night. He was still Jessie and Preston's dad. I get it now. That didn't change how much I wanted to strangle him, but I was going to hold it in. I was going to do better for Lynn.

I bought a bouquet for the prick. You know, as a get well gesture. It was a spur-of-the-moment idea, but the more I looked at the bouquet of brightly colored flowers, the more ridiculous the idea sounded.

No matter how out of line I was last night, that dickwad was still the root cause of all this shittiness. If he hadn't followed my girlfriend into the bathroom and put his fucking hands on her, I wouldn't have gotten too pissed.

No, I shouldn't have tried to hit him. I shouldn't have lost my cool and hurt Lynn, but that asshole still doesn't deserve flowers.

I'll save them for my apologies to Lynn. Nick will get an "I'm sorry" through gritted teeth right before I whisk my girl away.

My phone vibrated, and I got excited, almost wrecking, when I swerved to hurriedly answer it.

It was Preston. Not Lynn.

"Hello?" I tried to keep the disappointment out of my voice.

"Hey. Mom just told me she was taking dad back to his place. I guess they're out of the hospital now."

"Huh," I fell back against the seat. "She called you?"

"Text," Preston said carefully. "I'm guessing you didn't hear from her yet."

"No," I murmured. At least I know her phone worked still. That unlikely possibility crossed my mind once or twice.

Preston was quiet for a few seconds, then said, "Well, she was at the pharmacy. She probably has to do a bunch of crap my worthless dad can't do for himself. I wouldn't worry too much. She'll.... She'll call when she can."

"Thanks," I muttered.

He was probably right. Lynn had her hands full, and she wasn't the woman that multi-tasked easily. Plus, she was with her ex-husband. Calling me back while she was with him might be uncomfortable. Especially after what happened last night.

"You okay?" Preston asked hesitantly.

"Yeah. Just missing your mom, kid. Nothing I can do about it at the moment." There were other ways to help her, though. Lighten her burden for when she gets back. "Hey, I'm going to run and get food and stuff, so your mom has less to worry about later. What will you and your sister eat?"

"Anything but pizza," Preston said dryly. "That's all we eat at Dad's on the weekends."

I huffed in humor. "You got it. If you can think of anything else you kids or your mom might need, let me know. I'm heading to the store now."

Pulling into the grocery store parking lot, I allowed myself to open the chat between me and Lynn. Sure enough, there was a read receipt under my last text, but no response. I understand not being able to call me, but why couldn't she at least send a text?

I was distracted in the store, checking my phone every few minutes. I ended up with a cart full of junk food, plus whatever random shit looked good. I didn't really have a game plan for meals. I was just tossing stuff in as I distractedly walked up and down every aisle.

Premade skewers and stuffed jalapenos ended up in the cart, so I grabbed a couple of steaks. Grilling was easy enough. I could manage that.

After grabbing a bunch of other pomade meals, avoiding the pizzas in the deli, I headed to check out.

I spent an hour in the store, most of that spent staring at my phone, willing it to ring. It never did. Never dinged with a text. Nothing. Surely Lynn was done with her ex by now. Why the hell didn't she reach out to me yet?

Maybe she was still mad about last night. My gut twisted, thinking more and more about how much of an ass I was to her.

The flowers were sitting in my passenger seat, but looking at them now, they didn't seem like enough. The rich blues and reds in the petals were pretty and all, but Lynn wasn't the woman that could be bought with pretty flowers.

Food. The answer to Lynn was something sweet.

I figured the groceries would stay good long enough for me to make one more stop. There was a shop that sold chocolate-dipped fruits arranged in bouquets close to home. I think they sold other shit like smoothies and cookies, too. I knew Lynn would go nuts over a bouquet made of actual food.

"Welcome," the saleswoman greeted me as I walked in.

She showed me everything she had ready to take home, ranging from small bundles of chocolate-covered strawberries to massive arrangements of several fruits. Before I could settle on one, my phone buzzed in my hand and I eagerly went to answer it.

"Excuse me," I murmured to the woman, feeling disappointed again seeing Preston and not his mother on my caller ID. "Hey. I'm finishing up shopping and I'll be there in-"

"I'd come home now," he interrupted me, his voice sounding cold.

"Why?" My blood ran cold at his tone.

He was quiet for a long time, and then asked, "Do you know a woman named Mindy?"

***

Preston

"-I'm heading to the store now..."

Despite the crappy start to our morning, with mom having to leave to take care of my asshole father, I smiled after hanging up with Vin.

I had my doubts for a second last night. Mom hadn't cried like that in a long time, and she seemed so heartbroken when I helped get her to her room.

"Was that mom?" Jessie asked, coming into the living room from the kitchen. "Is she coming home yet?"

I pressed my lips together and shook my head. "No. That was Vin. He's going to the store for mom and wanted to know what we wanted."

"Pizza," she mumbled. She sat on the couch and hugged a pillow in her lap. "I need pizza."

"Nope." I lifted my chin. "If I eat pizza again, I'm gonna hurl. That's the one thing I told him to avoid."

"That's not fair," Jessie pouted.

"Oh, it's totally fair. That's all you want to eat every freaking weekend."

"Because it's good," she said meekly. "Mom and dad always got us pizza from that place when we went into the city."

Ah. I get it now. I know Jessie understood mom was moving on, but she still clung to weird things sometimes. Mom and dad used to take us to that pizza parlor a lot. Dad was always weirdly eager to get that pizza, too.

"I'm sure whatever Vin gets will be good, too."

Jessie shrugged. "I guess." She played with the fringe on the pillow for a few seconds, ignoring Kevin who had cuddled up to her, then asked, "So, you didn't hear from mom?"

I smiled softly. "Yeah. Mom's taking dad back home now and then she'll be back home."

Jessie nodded with a weak smile, then sighed. She got up and headed back upstairs, probably to get ready. The second mom gets home, I know she's going to ask to go to dad's. I'm going to be the one that takes her when mom gets back. Mom's not going back over there to deal with his crap. I think Vin needs some time alone with mom after yesterday, anyway.

I went to wait for Vin or mom in the kitchen. I was busy flipping through a magazine mom had left on the counter of dance shit for Jessie when the garage door opened, and in came mom.

She looked pissed. Not just irritated, but truly pissed more than I had ever seen before.

"Mom?"

She paced around the kitchen, rubbing her hands down her face. The way she was rubbing her eyes, I could tell she was trying to keep from crying. Not sad crying, but angry crying.

"Mom?! What happened?"

She shook her head, "Nothing. I just..." She sighed, looking with red-rimmed eyes out to the front room. Her eyes were on the window, staring past it.

I followed her line of sight and saw Miss Velma out on her lawn with a tall blonde woman. The woman was smiling and laughing with Vin's mom.

The way mom was staring at her....

"Who is that?" I asked.

Mom's lips thinned, her brows knitting together. "Mindy."

I stood wondering what to do when mom sighed heavily again. She didn't look as pissed. Just tired and sad.

"Mom!" Jessie yelled, coming down the stairs. "Mom! How's dad?!"

I saw the struggle as my mom forcibly put a smile on her face.

"Good, sweetie. Your dad's in bed resting. He'll be fine. Grandma's coming to stay with him, too."

"Oh," Jessie fidgeted on the stairs.

I already knew what she wanted. Mom did too.

"Do you want me to take you over there, baby?"

Jessie nodded shyly. "Can I?"

"Sure, sweetie," mom smiled, but it was so sad. Too sad. Even Jessie's face fell when she noticed.

"Mom?" Jessie looked concerned. "Are... Are you okay?"

"I'm fine," mom forced a bigger smile. "Just tired. "Go get ready. I'm going to go change, then we can head back to your dad's. He'll be happy to see you." Mom then looked at me. "Do you want to come too?"

I would have normally offered to drive Jessie myself so mom could stay home. That's what I was planning on, but something told me I needed to stay here and wait for Vin.

"Um, I can come later. I want to finish some stuff up here, if that's okay?"

"Sure it is," mom rubbed my cheek, then headed for the stairs.

When she was gone and we heard her door close, Jessie asked me, "Is mom really okay?"

I sighed and shook my head. "I don't know, Jess. Just go get ready."

She frowned, but went off to do as she was told. She grumbled about everyone being in a bad mood the entire way up the stairs. I just rolled my eyes.

Yeah. Everyone was in a fucking bad mood, and mine just got a lot fucking worse. Who the hell was Miss Velma's friend?

I stood by the front window, watching Miss Velma and the blonde chick named Mindy for a minute until they went back into the house. I then pulled out my phone.

Chapter Thirty-Six

Mindy

Vin

"What?" My heart went still. "H-how do you know about..."

"Some blonde chick named Mindy is at your house right now talking to your mom. Who is she?"

I swallowed past the lump in my throat. "Uh, she's... She's my, uh, ex-wife. Are... Are you sure you heard the right name?"

"Yep," Preston's tone was dry. "I heard it from mom."

"Shit."

What the hell was going on? Why the fuck would Mindy be at my house right now?

"Yeah," Preston scoffed. "Shit."

I ran my hand over my hair, repeatedly, then turned to the saleslady who had been waiting patiently. "I'm sorry. I have to go."

She smiled sympathetically. "Have a, uh, good rest of your day," she said awkwardly. "Good luck," she quietly murmured as she headed back to the counter.

I raced out the door to my car, asking Preston, "Is she still there?"

"Who? Your ex or my mom?"

I groaned. "Both I guess."

"Well," he hesitated. "Mom's here for now. As for your ex, I think she went back to your house with your mom."

Shit. Shit. Shit.

Why the fuck would Mindy randomly show up at my house? What business did she have with my mom? Mom knows what she did to me. Mom knew how badly it hurt and how much of a bitch Mindy was during the divorce.

Except... Mom is confused more than she's not lately.

Fuck.

"I'd hurry, Vin. Seriously. I don't know what the heck is going on with you and mom, but I have never seen her more pissed than I did just a second ago."

My foot went heavy on the gas. "I'm flooring it. Be there soon."

I tossed my phone to the passenger seat as I broke several laws racing to get home. It was still about twenty minutes before I pulled into our neighborhood, and I was in a full panic by then.

Lynn knew it was Mindy. That means they talked. I haven't talked to my ex since the divorce was completed, so I do not know how that conversation would have gone.

When I pulled onto my street, I noticed a coupe outside my house on the street that I didn't recognize. I also noticed Lynn's garage was open, but her car was gone. Instead, Preston was there, looking exhausted.

Instead of parking at my house, I pulled into his driveway.

"Your mom's not here?"

His lips thinned, and he shook his head.

Fuck.

"Groceries are in the trunk." I tossed him the keys. "I'll be right back."

I'd worry about Lynn and where she disappeared to this time. The second I'm done figuring out what the hell my ex is doing in my house before kicking her out.

I pushed open the front door with more force than I intended. The wood rattled angrily after banging against the wall behind it.

"Oh!" Mom pressed her hand to her chest. "Kevin! You scared me!"

I didn't spare mom a glance. I was busy glaring at Mindy, my fucking ex-wife, sitting on the couch like she owned the damn place. She was older. That was for sure. She was a lot blonder than I remember and had that fake mask that older women get when they get work done to hang onto their youth.

Seeing her there, knowing she somehow pissed my Lynn off more than she already was, made my blood boil.

"What the hell are you doing here?" I sneered through gritted teeth.

The corner of her lips lifted in an amused smirk. "Hello to you too."

I was on the verge of snapping. "I'm not in the mood for bullshit."

"What about some coffee?" Mindy pointed to the steaming cups sitting on the coffee table. "Your mom just made a pot."

"I asked you a question." I slammed my hand on the wall. "What the hell are you doing in my fucking house?!"

"Kevin?!" Mom's eyes widened. "What has gotten into you?"

"Me?!" I waved my hands angrily at my ex. "Why the hell is she here?"

"Kevin," Mom tilted her head in disapproval. "I know you two fought last night, but that's no way to talk to your girlfriend. You said yourself you wanted to-"

"Wait." I pinched the bridge of my nose. I couldn't believe this. "Mom, tell me you didn't...."

"Didn't what?" Mom was fidgeting, clearly uncomfortable. "Kevin, I don't understand."

"I know," I rasped. "I know you don't understand, mom. I know!" I was so angry, so frustrated, I felt like I was about to blow.

"Kevin?...." Mom's voice was small, laced heavy with confusion.

I took a deep breath before opening my eyes, avoiding looking at my ex so I didn't lose it again on my mother. "Mom, did you invite Mindy here?"

Mom sputtered, looking back and forth between me and Mindy. "Well... I... Well, Kevin. You... You said... I think you said...."

"She invited me over for coffee," Mindy spoke up, resting her hand on my mom's knees. She patted it gently like she was trying to settle her down. "We were just catching up, but I think I need to go now."

Mom looked more confused, and the range of emotions behind her confused expression made this situation hurt even more. Mom didn't know what she was doing. I bet she was trying to help. She didn't know....

But now I don't know what happened between my ex-wife and my girlfriend, and I'm so scared to find out...

I stood stiffly by the open door as Mindy said bye to my mom. My eyes narrowed when they hugged. Mom had that anxious look on her face that she got when she was really confused but trying to hide it.

Mindy looked me up and down, a sly look in her eyes. She looked amused by something. I didn't give a shit what game she was playing. She was done.

I waved my hand towards the open door, making her smile more as she softly shook her head. Her airy laugh as she walked past me grated on my nerves. As did the smell of her overly sweet perfume. Same shit she used to use. I hated it before. I hate it more now.

"I'll be right back, mom," I said in a much more gentle tone than I was using before.

She looked worried, her eyes darting to the cups of coffee on the table, then at me.

"It's alright," I smiled, trying to reassure her. "It's okay, mom. I'll help you get this cleaned up in a second. I'll be right back."

My smile fell away once the door was closed, and I was left on the front porch with *her*. The last person I ever wanted to see again.

The tension was thick. My anger didn't seem to bother her. She seemed to find it amusing.

"What are you doing here, Mindy?" My voice was low, but laced with all the malice I was currently feeling.

She rolled her eyes. "Jeez. All these years and you're still carrying a chip on those giant shoulders of yours?"

"Answer the fucking question," I snapped.

She sighed, looking at her nails. "Your mother invited me."

"So?" My lips curled in disgust. "That still doesn't explain why the hell you came."

She pressed her fingers to her lips, smiling against them. "She was persistent. Very persistent. I was curious, so I came." She shrugged. "I didn't even know you were here. I figured you'd still be playing soldier at some base around the world."

"Playing soldier?" I scoffed. "You're still a fucking bitch."

She shrugged. "Maybe." She looked me up and down. "You're still the same it seems too. Do they feed you carbs in the Army, or do you survive on protein shakes alone?"

I was about to tell her to fuck off, but then Preston walked back out to the garage to get more groceries out of my trunk. He stared over at us, his brows pulled down, shadowing his eyes.

"Huh," Mindy followed my line of sight. "You have the same car too, it seems. Why is it parked over there and not?...." Suddenly Mindy's eyes went wide, and she turned to look back at me. "Wait. That neighbor woman?!"

That confirmed it. They met.

Mindy shook her head, biting back her cunning smile. "No wonder you're so pissy. She didn't look happy to meet me either. It all makes sense." Her eyes met mine. "You and your neighbor. That's cute."

I sneered, "What did you say to her?"

"Nothing," she grinned. "I think I said 'hi' and maybe 'nice to meet you'."

"I'm not playing here, Mindy."

"I'm not either. Your mom was the one talking the entire time."

She was chewing on her nail, and I could tell there was more. There was something she wasn't telling me.

"And..." Mindy started again. "Well, your mom called me your girlfriend once or twice. Said something about you being madly in love with me. Your short, little neighbor woman seemed surprised at that." Her grin grew. "I guess I know why now."

"Fuck," I muttered under my breath, raking my hands through my hair.

"Hmm," Mindy tilted her head. "Everything makes more sense now. Guess I was worried about nothing."

"You have no right to be worried about anything concerning me," I snapped. "Do you realize how big of a shit storm you created?"

"Oh, I wasn't concerned for you, Kev. Never was. You were never the type to *need* me, or anyone else, for that matter. Your mom is a different story."

My brow pulled down with a mix of anger and confusion. "Mom's not your problem either."

Mindy rolled her eyes, huffing. "If I had known you were living here again, I wouldn't have come. The only reason I did was because your mom sounded like she needed help. I was just planning on making sure she was okay and didn't need to go to the hospital or something, then I was leaving."

"Needs help, how?" Mom was fine when I left. Confused, but that was nothing new.

"I don't know. She just sounded crazy. Like she didn't know which way was up. She thought we were still dating. I got worried and came by. It wasn't a big deal, but I just didn't want to feel like shit later if I saw on the news some confused old lady got in an accident driving on the wrong side of the road or something."

I groaned, pacing on the porch. I should have checked in with mom throughout the day. I should have sent Preston to look in on her, or asked what she was doing when I heard her talking to herself in her room.

She wasn't talking to herself. She wasn't rehearsing what to say to Lynn later. Mom was talking to Mindy. That had to be it.

"Just go," I pointed at her car. "If she calls you ever again, ignore it."

Mindy crossed her arms, eying me. "If I fucked something up with your neighbor, I'm sorry. I really wasn't trying to cause problems for you."

"I got it!" I snapped. "Just go!"

She sighed, shaking her head. "As hotheaded as ever. Don't worry. I'm gone."

She flipped me off, strutting to her car. I stood there sternly, staring until she took off down the road.

When I looked up, I saw Preston watching, too. He was fidgeting with my keys, looking awkward, like he didn't know what to do with them.

"I've got to talk with mom," I yelled over to him. "I'll come over when I'm done. Can you-"

"Groceries are put up," he said before I could finish my sentence. "I'll be in the kitchen."

Fuck. I don't know how much he heard or saw, or what he thought of this shit, but I was suddenly nervous. The kid was a fraction of my age, but when it comes to Lynn, that didn't matter. If her kids started to hate me, it was over. I was done.

With a heavy groan, I headed back in.

Mom was no longer in her chair. She was in the kitchen, bent over the kitchen sink. Her shoulders were shivering, and I caught the soft sounds of her crying.

"Mom," I let my irritation fade away, coming behind my mom and hugging her shoulders.

She dropped the sponge she was using to clean the coffee cups. Her shoulders shook more, sinking forward.

"I messed up," she whispered roughly. "Oh, Kevin," she turned to face me. Her face was dripping with tears. "I messed up. I... I was..."

"It's okay, mom," I whispered, hugging her close as she buried her face in my chest. "You were a little confused. It happens. It's okay."

"No," she whimpered. "It's not."

She's right. It wasn't okay, but it would be. She didn't know what she was doing. Mindy was gone now, and I was sure no matter how confused Mom was in the future, my ex wouldn't be back here. Not after today, for sure.

"I'm sorry, Kevin," Mom cried, her tears soaking the front of my shirt. "She... She met..."

"I know, mom," I held her tighter, kissing the top of her head. "Lynn will understand. It's going to be okay."

I hoped Lynn would understand.

CHAPTER THIRTY-SEVEN

What I Would Change

"But mom, he's..... Yeah?.... Are you sure you don't-.... Okay, mom. Bye."

I was fidgeting on the barstool where I sat and stared at Preston as he spoke to his mom. I tried to call her twice with no luck, but she answered for her son with no issues.

That made me feel more like shit than I already did, but I still sat quietly and waited for him to get off the phone.

Preston sighed as he dropped his phone on the counter. His lips were in a tight line when he looked back at me.

"Sorry, bro. She didn't want to talk about you."

My face fell in my hands. My fingers roughly circled the tension in my forehead. "Yeah. I figured as much."

Preston was quiet, silently standing across from me in the kitchen as I felt like I'm coming apart.

"One day," I muttered. "All it took was one day for every damn thing to fall apart."

"That's because you both have crappy exes," Preston scoffed.

I laughed humorlessly. "Yeah. You're not wrong."

Preston manhandled the dish towel laying across the sink, twisting the fibers between his fingers. "Um, so mom wants me to head over there," he said carefully. "Uh, I guess my grandma finally showed up and was being a jerk about it being dad's weekend."

I nodded, getting the hint. "Yeah. You should go then. Your mom needs no more shit today."

Preston looked around the kitchen, his eyes settling on the fridge. "I'll tell my mom about the food. I'm sure she'll appreciate it."

I smiled weakly. "Thanks. If she... If she needs anything else...." I hesitated, wondering if it was still my place to offer her or them anything still. I sighed, then just said it. "Let me know."

After pushing in my stool and picking up my keys from the counter, I headed for the garage door. I still needed to move my car over to my house, since it was obvious I wouldn't be seeing Lynn today after all.

As I was moving the car, all I could think about was all the things I wish I could go back and change to make this weekend different. Even if I just said no to Milton. I'd be in bed, Lynn lying on top of me right now for a nap, or floating in the pool while she giggled and shot at me with the water guns.

If I had just kept my cool and helped Lynn instead of trying to deck the asshole, we would have gone home together. She might still have had to take the kids, but we had already talked about living together. We could have had a talk already about what that would be like, and I could have spent the day getting closer to them.

I sat in my car far longer than I intended as I thought over everything. It wasn't until mom poked her head outside to give me a worried look that I finally turned my car off and went inside.

She was lucid. Really lucid. She was fully aware of what was going on and what she had done, and it was worrying her sick. I thought I had reassured her enough earlier. She had calmed down and retreated to her room to take a nap. It must have been a quick nap, if she even had one.

"Hey, mom," I kissed her head, smiling gently as I slid past her into the house. "You had a fast nap."

"I.. I couldn't sleep. Kevin... Did you talk with her?"

I tried to keep a smile on my face, but I knew I did a piss-poor job when she gasped and put her hand to her mouth.

"Oh, Kevin," her eyes got glossy again. "I'm so sorry. Is.. is she home? I can talk to her and-"

"It's alright, mom," I took her hands and led her to her chair. "She's just busy doing stuff for the kids right now. I'll have time to talk to her when she's done."

"Are you sure?"

No, but I would not worry my mom more.

"I'm sure." I kissed the top of her head again before handing her the remote. "Your show's about to be on. See if you can rest down here, then when it's over, mind making me that bouquet you talked about?" The flowers were the one thing Preston didn't take inside. They were wilted and pathetic looking from the heat of the car by the time I noticed them again.

"Oh.. Oh!" Mom must have just remembered she offered to do that last night. "Yes! Yes, Kevin. I'll.. I'll start making it right-"

I stopped her as she got back up. "Not yet, mom. Feighlynn won't be back... for a while. She's... she's busy, so there's plenty of time."

Mom looked anxious, but nodded along. As much as I hate seeing her in her confused state, I would prefer it about now. If she was ignorant of what was going on around her, her own mistake wouldn't hurt her.

"I love you, mom," I whispered, smiling as tenderly as I could at the woman who raised me. "I'm going to take care of some things. I'll be in my room."

By taking care of some things, I meant I was going to wallow in misery alone in my room, agonizing again over all the shit I wish I could change.

***

FeighLynn

"I'll see you both on Monday," I whispered to my kids at the door of Nick's condo.

Preston looked upset, understandably so. He walked in when my ex-mother-in-law and I were having a very heated disagreement in the kitchen about whose fault it was Nick wrecked his car into the wall of the parking garage. She insisted I was the one ruining her son's life, and everything going wrong for him is because of me.

First by agreeing to the divorce, and not trying to work through our 'issues'. Our issues, meaning his cheating and wanting to leave me for another woman. How dare I have enough respect for myself to not fight to keep a cheater by my side, in a miserable excuse for a marriage?

Then, after going over the usual tirade of mistakes I made over the years, including vaccinating my kids and bottle-feeding Jessie after having issues with breast-feeding, she went in to how I should have let my kids stay with their inebriated father, because if they were there, he never would have tried to drive to get *them*.

I did not have the patience or the will to correct her about what really happened. It would only make her yell more, and I was reaching my threshold for crap being thrown at me today.

Nick was passed out from the pain medicine by then, so Jessie had to sit awkwardly, watching her grandmother berate me. I ended up asking Preston to come over after the tenth mention of his absence. I didn't want to leave my daughter alone with the woman, anyway.

Nick may be a decent father, but his mother was proving to be a shrew since I divorced him. I'm seeing why Nick never wanted to move back to his hometown after he graduated. I also fully believe he was a big part of why his mom never showed this side of herself to me before. I guess there were good points to his controlling behavior. I didn't have to deal with *her*.

Preston walked into the condo in a rage, hearing his grandmother reprimanding me for not keeping up with my *ex-husband's* laundry. I stood in the kitchen trying to ignore her, keeping myself busy by making a pot of soup for Jessie to take to her father later. Preston went right into yelling at the old woman for talking to me the way she was, and told her if she wanted laundry done, then do it herself.

Jessie and I were both relieved he came. Now I could finally leave without worrying about Jessie being alone with her invalid father and nagging grandma.

Groaning down the hall turned all our attention away from one another for a second to see Nick had woken up and emerged from his room.

"Daddy!" Jessie ran off to help him as he struggled down the hall to the couch.

His mother looked like a different woman, coddling him as he headed towards a recliner.

"She's a freaking bit-"

"Eh," I put my finger over his lips. "No, sir. She's still your grandma. Be nice and respectful." He raised a brow at me, and I couldn't help but chuckle. "Fine. Nice and respectful. Just watch over your sister for me, and make sure the," I glanced up at my ex-mother-in-law, "the witch doesn't gripe at her like she did me."

"I'll knock a witch out," Preston smirked.

I laughed, hugging him one last time around the waist. "Okay. I'll see you-"

"Wait, mom." Preston held on to me, not letting me pull away.

He glanced at Jessie, who was sitting in her dad's lap, drawing pictures on his cast. I couldn't help but to smile at the sweet moment between them. That was the exact reason I couldn't completely hate the man. He was a good father, and I know even Preston thought that right now by the look on his face.

"I'll walk you out, mom."

"I can find my car myself." I rolled my eyes.

Preston laughed softly, shaking his head. "I'm sure you can, but I just... I just want to talk."

My smile tightened. I was sure I already knew what he wanted to talk about, and I wasn't ready to talk about the subject yet. Not when the witch spoon feeding Nick twenty feet away from me right now, acting like she made it herself, got me so riled up.

"I'm tired, Pres. Maybe tomorrow we can-"

"Nope." He reached for his keys on the entry table. "I promised I would tell you something, so I'm going to."

I pursed my lips, wanting to argue, but knew I wouldn't win. Preston was bossy and stubborn. Like his dad. I fought enough with too many people today. I didn't want to argue with him too.

"Fine," I sighed, opening the door. Nick and Jessie looked up, and I waved bye. Nick looked rough, and his eyes were full of sadness, but then Jessie asked him a question about what to draw next and he put a smile back on his face for her.

His mother scowled at me, then explained the ingredients in the soups and how nutritious they were. It's powdered chicken broth and frozen vegetables, Karen, with drop dumplings from a mix boiled in. There was nothing extra nutritious about it.

Right as the door was closing, I felt a small bit of satisfaction when I heard Jessie say, "Mom didn't put the tomatoes in when she made it because she knows you don't like them."

Preston snorted as we walked down the hall. "Jessie knew what she was doing when she said that."

"I know she did," I beamed up at him. "Don't let her sweetness fool you."

"I don't," he scoffed. "I know she can be a brat. She just has everyone else convinced she's not. Kinda like you."

"Me?!" I feigned offense. "I'm an angel."

"An angel until you get on your bad side, then you're freaking vicious." He clicked his tongue and shook his head as we got on the elevator. "It's always the short ones you got to be careful of."

"I'm not that short." I lifted my chin, trying to stand to my full height.

"You look like a midget when you're standing next to Vin," he laughed, but his laughter quickly died into nervous chortling when my eyes narrowed on him. "See?"

I looked away, trying to hide my irritation. "I can't see anything. I'm too short."

"Mom," Preston chuckled, wrapping his arms around my shoulders. "You're exuding short girl energy right now."

"Outstanding energy," I muttered under my breath.

"Sure," he snickered, then sighed. "So, I take it you are really mad at Vin?"

"I don't think that's any of your business," I pulled out of his hold when the elevator doors opened to the garage level.

"Eh, it kinda is. Before kicking out his ex-wife from his house, he bought us groceries for the weekend. I told him I would tell you."

I tried not to let it show, but my ears were perked at the mention of him kicking out his ex-wife. I figured that's who *Mindy, the girlfriend,* was, but that didn't stop me from getting upset.

"He went around all morning trying to find you and dad. I guess he felt bad about whatever happened last night and was trying to apologize to you both. He did not know his mom got confused like she does and called his ex to come over."

I couldn't help myself. I needed to know more. "Why would she do that?" I tried and failed to sound disinterested.

"Well," Preston smirked. "I guess his mom saw how upset he was last night and asked what was wrong. She got confused and thought his girlfriend was the one he had twenty something years ago."

That made more sense than every mad scenario I had played out in my head, but it still made me mad to think about how at home she looked in that house.

And how pretty she was....

And tall.

Darn it, I wish I were tall. Me and my short girl energy can't even keep up with people when they walk too fast. I bet *Mindy* never has that problem.

"Stupid tall people," I muttered.

"What was that?" Preston asked with a barely suppressed smile.

"Nothing," I huffed, marching for my car as quickly as I could. Preston kept up with me easily, looking way too amused.

"Hey, mom," Preston stopped me before I could get in my car. "You really should give Vin a chance to explain, or say sorry, or whatever. I know you're in your short girl anger mode about his ex, but if you saw the way he threw her out, you wouldn't be."

I fiddled with my keys and asked with a mumbled breath, "How did he kick her out?"

The corner of Preston's lips curled up in a crooked grin. "Well, there was yelling. Lots of it. He was yelling a lot about you, though. She said something about being sorry for messing things up with the neighbor girl before driving off, and he told her to ignore his mom if she ever calls him in the future. It was like watching one of those shows Miss Velma gets into. All that was missing was someone getting slapped in the face and someone else unknowingly getting their sister pregnant."

I lifted an eyebrow, wondering how he was so specific.

"What?" He shrugged. "I caught parts of it when I was doing laundry at their house."

"Uh, huh," I smirked, looking down at my keys in my hand.

So, Vin didn't know his ex was there. That made me feel better hearing that. And knowing he kicked her out when he got home.

"Well, I better get back upstairs and watch over Jessie. She might have sweetly locked grandma in the laundry room by now," Preston said before pulling me in for a hug. "Enjoy your next two nights without us, mom. I'll see you on Monday."

Preston had a smirk on his face as he walked off towards the elevators. Both my kids could be mischievous brats when they wanted to me. I wonder where they got that from.

I thought about all that Preston told me on the drive home. I'd start smiling out of nowhere, imagining my action hero tossing his ex to the curb in the most dramatic action hero ways. I was so distracted with my thoughts, I almost took out a stop sign when I hugged the burb too closely, but luckily, I turned the wheel just in time.

I sat straight, both hands on the wheel the rest of the way home, but that didn't stop me from thinking about Vin.

I missed him. Going over everything that happened, there was so much I wish had happened differently. If I had just texted the right person last night, I could have spent today helping Vin chase his ex out with my short girl energy and showing how my smoothie work-out plan was helping to toughen me up.

Vin was looking for me all morning. If I had just called him back....

As I pulled up to my house, the sun was just setting. I'd been gone all day. Was it too late to reach out to Vin now? Would he even be home?

He called me a couple hours ago, but I sent him to voicemail, not wanting to answer in front of Nick's mother. I should have just answered once and told him I would be home to talk to him later tonight. Now, I do not know if he even wants to talk to me after I blew him off all day.

I got out of the car and walked around to go in through the front door. I normally would park in the garage, but I wanted Vin to see that I was home.

When I got to the front porch step, I froze when I saw a giant bouquet of Miss Velma's wildflowers in an intricate vase on my welcome mat. They were gorgeous, and definitely the biggest bunch of flowers she had ever given me.

There was a card wedged between the colorful petals. I lifted it and almost cried, seeing the words scrawled on the outside.

My Lynn, My Love, My Home

I read the card with teary eyes, my breath hitching at every other word.

My Lynn,

Hey baby. I don't know when you get home, or when you will see this. I hope it's soon, because the longer I go without seeing you, the more I feel like I'm dying from not seeing your beautiful face.

No matter how late you get back, please just call me. Please, just let me come see you one time. Let me apologize for all the ways I fucked up last night and today and let me see that gorgeous face of yours once. Then you can go on being mad at me again.

I'll wait. I'll wait as long as it takes, but just let me see you once before I completely die on the inside.

You're mine, Lynn. You're my everything.

Love,

Your Action Hero Vin

Tears were spilling down my cheeks, but I still laughed at seeing the added note at the end.

P.S. I kidnapped Kevin. See me to get him back.

He wrote the soppiest, sweetest note, then had to blackmail me a bit at the very end. I loved it. I loved that I could see him in every letter that he wrote.

I picked up the vase and carried it inside, feeling a swell in my chest as I hurried across the street. There was so much I wanted to change about the last twenty-four hours, but this...

This feeling I had spread through me as I raced to see the man I love made all that fade away.

I felt like I had won. Life through everything it could at us, but this felt like the trial before gaining the greatest gift one could imagine. This felt like we were succeeding in love.

CHAPTER THIRTY-EIGHT

Coming Home

Vin

"He's a hyper thing, isn't he?" Mom asked with a laugh as Kevin ran to get the ball she was throwing once again. "So full of energy."

Mom came alive when I brought Lynn's dog back to the house with me. She was anxious all afternoon, doing nothing but worrying about Lynn and me. One minute with the dog and she was all laughter and cheer.

Mom spent so much time trying to get every perfect flower from her garden in a giant vase for Lynn, that she didn't have a moment to calm herself down. She kept rearranging and adding more to the overflowing vase until I had to ask her to not add any more. Mom just wanted to help in the only way she knew she wouldn't mess up. I love my mom for that.

Mom mopped around, watching out the window with a sad expression. That is until she saw me coming up the driveway with a dog in tow. Kevin sure licked and cuddled the sadness right out of her.

When I went to drop the flowers off on Lynn's front porch, Kevin was in the window pacing the way he does when he hasn't been outside for a while. I fought with myself right there on Lynn's porch steps before I decided breaking in to take her dog for a walk wouldn't be the worst thing I've done.

I let myself in, got Kevin on a leash, then took him around the block like Lynn and I always did about this time. As I was leaning against a tree, waiting for him to get done with his business, I thought over the card I had left in the flowers. The very desperate card, full of all the things I had rehearsed in my head a hundred times today.

It didn't seem desperate enough. I don't know if a single card could convey how much I needed her right now. How much I missed her! How fucking miserable I was having not told her how sorry I was for every single fuck up that happened.

Seeing her face was the only way I was going to get this knot out of my chest and breathe easier. She was the only one that I needed, and I wasn't sure if a single note could get her to come to me.

I was staring down at Kevin as all these thoughts went rampant in my head, and that was when the idea of stealing her dog came to mind.

She has to come get her dog. She might ignore me all day and be too pissed to see in that single damn card how much I needed her.... But she had to at least face me to get Kevin.

I've been pacing in the kitchen, chewing on my nail beds, going from watching my mom play with the dog to staring at the house across the street. I knew she was at her ex's place, and I almost went to go get her, but I knew it would just make things more tense if I did. All I could do was wait.

CRASH

I jumped, wincing when the ear-splitting sound of glass shattering rang out from the living room. Mom had thrown the ball and hit her glass china cabinet in the room's corner. The whole left glass-face door went crumpling to the carpet in a shattering rain.

"Oh, shoot," Mom got up from her chair.

"I got it, mom. You don't have shoes on. How about letting the dog outside instead?"

"Goodness." She patted her chest. "Is his ball okay?"

I chuckled, picking it up from the carnage. "It's fine."

"Good," she exhaled, then took the rubber ball from me. After inspecting it herself to be sure it was safe, she called the dog to follow her outside. "Come on, puppy. I'll throw it for you out here."

She was more worried about the cheap rubber ball than her china cabinet, full of Precious Moments figures. She never acted like she liked Kevin before, but maybe in her own home it was different, since this was her safe place, even at the times she was in her confused state. Maybe I should look into getting her a dog to keep her company during the day while I'm at work.

It took me longer than I would have liked to clean up the mess. Mom stayed outside with Kevin, to my relief. I was worried she was going to come right back in and try to help. I could hear her laughing and yelling good boy through the back window.

As I took dustbin after dustbin of broken glass to the trash, I would look out the window in the kitchen for some sign that Lynn had returned. On the fifth trip, she still wasn't back. With a heavy sigh, I got the vacuum to suck up all the little pieces of glass my fingers couldn't get from the fibers of the carpet.

I had to go over the fucking area for a long ass time. The loud droning of the ancient machine drowned out all other noises, so I didn't realize the doorbell was ringing. Not until whoever it was started ringing the bell and frantically banging on the door at the same time.

My heart raced. I knew... I just knew by the sharp, hurried knocking it was her little fist abusing my front door.

Was she mad? I mean, I fucking stole her dog to get her to see me. It sounded like a solid plan at the time, but now I was second guessing myself.

After swallowing down the giant knot stuck in the center of my throat, I set the vacuum off to the side and moved to the front door. I could still hear mom out back with Kevin, but I heard nothing from the front porch.

I didn't know what to expect.

With a deep breath, I opened the front door, ready to face her wrath. I expected to be slapped or kicked for kidnapping Kevin to get her to see me. I had fucking blackmailed her, for fuck's sake.

Instead, the moment Lynn saw me, she leapt forward, wrapping her arms around my waist. I stood frozen for a second, thinking I was hallucinating or something. Her jumping into my arms was the last thing I expected to happen.

Then the warmth from her body sank into me. The smell of her shampoo filtered through my nose. As my arms encircled her tiny frame, all the anxiety I had felt until this point just melted away.

Not saying a single word, we stood there holding one another, right on the threshold of my house. The house I grew up in. The place I always came back to. It was no longer home. Lynn was my home, and the reunion I was feeling at that moment was so fucking sweet.

"You got my card?" I whispered hoarsely. My throat felt clogged with many emotions.

"Maybe." she nuzzled her face against my chest. I felt her moisture leaking through the front of my shirt, and I knew she was crying.

"Baby," I crooned, grabbing hold of her face. She was so fucking beautiful, even with her eyes red and her cheeks laced with tears. "I'm sorry," my voice came out in an airy rasp. "Last night, I was such an ass. And then today with my ex-"

Her teary eyes narrowed. "Yeah. About your ex...."

I felt nervous again, seeing that fierce expression on her teary little face. But then the corner of her lips lifted in a half-smirk.

"I guess both of our exes are assholes."

I chuckled, hearing her curse with such a cute, teary face. I used my thumbs to wipe the salty moisture from her soft cheeks.

"Yeah. We do, don't we?"

She nodded, resting her chin on my chest. "I'm sorry too."

"For what? Being so fucking adorable?" I bent over and nuzzled my nose to hers.

"No," she giggled, and it was music to my ears. "For not yelling it out with you last night. I wished I hadn't sent you home."

I smiled sadly. "Yeah. You and me both."

She looked so sweet and guilty as she averted her gaze. "Then today I didn't talk about anything with you."

My smile slipped. "Yeah, but you were busy." I tried to keep the frown off my face as I asked, "How's Nick?"

She shrugged. "Miserable and in pain, but he'll live. He's mom and the kids are with him."

I nodded, trying to not let my true feelings show.

Then Lynn laughed and said, "I get it now."

I furrowed my brows. "Get what?"

"Why you got so mad last night. Why you couldn't stop yourself."

A wave of shame hit me. "That wasn't my proudest moment."

"No, but I get it," she smiled, cute but deviously. "I felt the same way when I saw your ex, too."

I laughed, resting my head on hers. "Well, you have my permission to deck her if you ever get the chance."

"Watch it. I just might. You might need to bail me and my short girl energy out of jail."

"Short girl energy?"

She giggled, then said, "Ask Preston. Apparently I have it."

"Hmm," I smiled, squeezing her tighter to me. "Must mean you're adorable all the time."

She grinned and shook her head against mine. "No... I think he meant the opposite."

"Nah. There isn't a single thing about you that isn't adorable or perfect." I sighed, relishing the moment of having her in my arms. "I missed you."

She softly closed her eyes, basking in me as I was basking in her. Then, when I thought nothing in the world could ruin this moment, she whispered, "You kidnapped my dog."

Both of us laughed, but still wouldn't let the other go.

"I did," I admitted. "I'm keeping him hostage."

"Well," she ran her finger down my chest, "What do I have to do to get him back?"

I stared down into her sweet, playful eyes and said in the softest voice, "Take me home."

Chapter Thirty-Nine

Ransom

Feighlynn

Vin's lips came crashing to mine as he lifted me and carried me up the stairs.

"My dog," I protested.

Vin let out a low, impatient growling noise. "You get him back when my payment is received." Then his lips fervently devoured mine again.

I giggled, pushing against his chest. "How very villainous of you. You just said to bring you home," I mumbled against his mouth. "You never said-"

"It was implied," he cut off all protest as he kicked open the bedroom door.

Oh well. Kevin should be fine with Miss Velma for a bit. Right?

I had a feeling this wouldn't take just a bit, though. Vin seemed desperate and I can't say I wasn't feeling the same. I needed him. After everything that had happened, I needed to put everything to rest for good by drowning in only him.

Vin was holding himself back. I could feel his resistance as he laid me gingerly on my bed, never moving his mouth from mine. He was trying to be gentle; he was trying to be controlled, but controlled was not the Vin I wanted right now. I wanted him to imprint himself on every inch of me, making me feel I was his entirely and he was mine.

I grabbed his collar, pulling his body in as I whispered against his lips, "If you're going to be a villain, do it right."

He chuckled. "Are you threatening me or giving me permission?" He pressed his hard length against my heat, then circled his hips. "I want you to feel cherished, Lynn. I'm not trying to maul you."

"I happen to like being mauled," the corner of my lips lifted as I thought about all the times in the past where he'd been a little rough. I liked it. I liked his mauling tendencies a lot.

He pressed his lips to the sensitive shell of my ear. "Are the kids coming back tonight?"

I arched my needy body into his as I shook my head.

"Tomorrow?"

"No," I gasped as he pressed his weight further into me. "They're gone the rest of the weekend."

A low, guttural moan left him. My eyes went wide as he grabbed my hands and pinned them above me. He was so hard, and the friction felt so good as his hips circled mine.

"You're going to be sore tomorrow," he rasped in my ear, making shivers wreck my body. "I hope you're ready."

"Shut up and do it already," I whined impatiently, making him laugh.

Then, he trailed his hands down my arms, his feather soft touch making my restlessness grow. My nipples perked under his touch as he skimmed over my breasts to the collar of my shirt. He gave me a devious, sexy smile, then ripped my shirt right down the middle.

I gasped. "Wha-... What?"

"Villainous enough for you?" he smirked, pulling his shirt over his head.

Grinning, I shook my head, making him laugh deeper.

He unfastened his belt, slowly sliding it from his waist. "I can tie you up then," he wrapped the belt slowly around his wrist. "Lock you away in this room and never let you out again?"

"Maybe next time," I giggled.

"Hmm," he tossed his belt off to the side, then stood to kick off his jeans and boxers. My eyes wandered his muscled physique. He was yummy. Oh, so yummy. Being locked in a room with him forever didn't sound bad at all.

His eyes roamed my body with a hungry look. Then he grabbed my thighs roughly, yanking me to the edge of the bed and making me yelp. He fisted my pants on either side of the button, then jerked to pop the button right off. My pants and ruined panties were on the ground with his.

I saw the look in his eyes as he stared down at my breast. I covered my bra with my hands. "This is my favorite."

He let out the sexiest laugh, breaking the villain facade to help gently unfasten and remove it. Then he gingerly set it on my nightstand.

"Good?" He lifted a brow.

"Thank you," I smiled in satisfaction.

He laughed again, then bent over my body. "Fuck, you're adorable."

"That's what you keep telling me." I wrapped my arms around his neck.

"Are you getting sick of hearing it?"

I bit my lip and shook my head. "No. I could never tire of that."

"Good," he growled, pretending to bite into my neck. "You'll be hearing it the rest of your life."

My heart quickened at his implication. He was telling me we would be together for the rest of our lives.

My body was on fire with every kiss as his mouth traveled over my skin. Both of my hands were in one of his, pinned above my head. My back bowed, wanting no distance between us.

"Fuck," he hissed as he sank two fingers into my wet, ready opening. "This pussy is so ready for me."

"Then take it," I whimpered, gyrating on his fingers. "It's yours."

"Fuck," he groaned before slowly sinking into me. "Yes-ss," he hissed, his face full of ecstasy. "This pussy is mine." He dragged his length out, then pushed back in, his girth making my walls ache in that delicious way. "All of you is mine."

"Vin," I whimpered in an airy plea, struggling to pull my hands free.

"Yes," he suddenly slammed his full weight into me. My eyes rolled to the back of my head.

He released my hands, but grabbed my throat gently and brought his lips back to mine. This was just the beginning. My villainous action hero would take his ransom well into the morning. I already knew.

***

My eyes fluttered open at hearing the door open. Vin was coming back in, and upon seeing me, he gave me an apologetic smile.

"I'm sorry, baby," he kicked out of his pants while pulling off his shirt. "Did I wake you?"

"A little," I mumbled, hugging my naked body into my pillow. "Where did you go?"

"To check on Kevin and mom," he slipped into bed behind me, then pulled me back against him. "Kevin's sleeping at the foot of her bed. I'll go back and get him in the morning."

I chuckled sleepily. "She likes him now. That's cute."

"It is cute," he laughed. "Maybe I should get her own dog."

"She can just borrow Kevin whenever she wants."

Vin laughed softly. "He seemed happy enough to be there."

I never thought Miss Velma would be the type to like dogs. She never seemed to when I would see her outside while taking Kevin for his walks. I guess things have changed. I know they have for me. She's no longer the forgetful elderly woman living across the street who we occasionally helped. She was the mother of my action hero. My villainous action hero who steals puppies and holds them for ransom.

I rolled over, snuggling against Vin's chest. "I don't think I paid enough ransom yet."

"No?" he snickered, placing his fingers under my chin to pull my gaze to him. "Do you have more to give?"

I giggled, pressing and moving my body against his in all the fun places. "Villains take. I'm not giving you anything that isn't already yours."

He sighed, resting his forehead on mine. "God, I love you."

I stopped squirming against him as those words sank in. It was the first time he had said it, and I think he realized it at the same time that I did.

Vin lifted himself on his elbows, gazing down at me with so much intensity and sincerity. "I love you, Lynn," he said again. "I love you completely."

I bit my lips as tears burned behind my eyes. "I love you too." Reaching up, I rested my hand against his handsome face. "I love you completely, too."

I did. I loved this man completely. Hero or villain, it didn't matter. For the first time in my life, I was deeply and madly in love.

CHAPTER FORTY

Surprise

Vin

Eight months later....

"She's coming!" Jessie giggled, hiding with Kate and her family inside the shop on Main Street.

"Go," Preston pushed me out the door. "She's going to get lost looking for us if you don't hurry."

"You got this, Mr. Anaconda!" Kate whispered loudly.

"Quit calling him that!" Wes groaned at his wife.

Kate's been calling me Mr. Anaconda this entire family Christmas trip to Disney World. She called Lynn Miss Mole Rat, which I found hysterical after Lynn shamelessly explained it to me.

After the Disney trip last summer for Jessie's dance competition, we planned another when Kate's kids heard about how much fun we had. Having Kate here was also perfect, because she was the one that helped me organize this whole thing.

I nervously patted my pocket, feeling for the box I had stashed away for this very moment. Emma and Kate helped me pick it out, but I was still worried the one it was for wouldn't like it.

Lynn was walking through the crowded street, approaching the Walt and Mickey statue, where a cast member was smiling and waiting to record the entire thing. She had two cups filled with Dole Whip, one already with a bunch of tiny bite marks taken from the top. Her personalized Minnie ears were slightly askew, and she was wearing her new Disney shirt after spilling ketchup on the one she wore into the park.

So fucking adorable.

"Where are they?" I heard her mumble, spinning around while taking another nibble of the treat.

"Lynn!" I waved my hands, trying not to laugh when she came to an abrupt stop as she saw me. She almost fell, but caught herself at the last moment, her full hands lifted in the air like she was more scared of losing her snack than falling on her cute little ass.

"There you are!" she said with a mouth full of yellow sugar. "Where are the others?"

I shrugged, trying to seem nonchalant. "I hid them."

"You hid them?" She gave me one of those looks where her nose wrinkled, and her eyes lit up with amusement. "Hid them where? Where's Kate? I got her stinking Dole Whip. It's going to melt."

Placing my hands gently on her waist, I took a breath to steady my nerves, then said, "I kidnapped them."

"Kidnapped them?" She raised an eyebrow at me. "At Magic Kingdom? This is the happiest place on earth!"

"Hmm," I squeezed her hips briefly as I leaned down and whispered in her ear, "I still kidnapped them, so what are you going to do, Lynn? What are you willing to give me to get them back?"

A mischievous smile lifted her face. "They can stay gone. They're with Kate. I'm sure they're fine. They're probably learning how to haggle for pins right now. We should get in line for the Dumbo ride! The kids won't ever ride it with me."

I rolled my eyes. Lynn hadn't caught on yet. She was in her Disney high, as she had been all day.

Straightening her ear, I said again, "You don't want to pay the ransom to get your kids and sister back?"

She thought about it for a second, taking another small bite of Dole Whip. I could almost see the lightbulb in her head click on as she finally got it.

"Oh!" She looked around us, like she was suddenly scandalized by what I said. She leaned in a hissed, "Here?! It's Disney!"

"The happiest place on earth," I repeated her words.

She giggled, then asked, "Okay, Mr. Villain. What do you want as a ransom?"

"Well," I took a step back, pulling the box from my pocket.

Lynn looked confused for a second, then when her eyes landed on the box, they grew wide. She gasped, dropping both Dole Whips as she brought her hands to her gaping mouth. As I dropped on one knee and opened the lid, she began bouncing on her feet.

"Lynn, baby. Take a breath and let me say this before you-"

"Yes!!" she screamed, throwing herself at me, wrapping her arms around my neck in a vice grip.

I held her around the waist, laughing as I kept us both from falling to the ground. People were cheering and clapping all around, but I barely heard them. Suddenly, it was like we were in our own little bubble; her clinging to my neck with a ring box between us.

I kissed her cheek, then said, "Feighlynn, baby. You are the best thing that has ever happened to me. You and your dog came into my life like a whirlwind, clearing out all my loneliness. You fill my every day with so much happiness already. I'd be a starved man without your smile and your endless giggles. You're my home." I reached for her beautiful face, pressing my thumb over her teary cheek. "Marry me, Lynn."

"Yes," she grabbed hold of my face, kissing me deeply. When she came up for air, she was smiling. It was the sweetest, purest smile I had ever seen on her breathtaking face. "So many times, yes."

My smile was so wide it hurt. I was choking on my own tears as I finally slipped that ring on her finger. When she saw it, she threw herself at me again, wailing loudly at how beautiful it was. Thank fuck.

Her sister, Wes, their kids, and Jessie and Preston came through the crowd, clapping louder than anyone else.

Everyone congratulated us, and Lynn went to everyone at least ten times to show them her ring. She was so fucking cute, and now she was more than just my girlfriend. She was my fiance and would soon be my wife.

"Your turn!" Kate shoved a gift shop bag at her sister. "I found what we talked about. It's in there, ready for you."

Jessie and Preston gave their aunt an odd look, then Preston's eyes went big. He looked between Lynn and me, and I wasn't sure what to make of his expression.

Lynn was blushing, staring into the bag with a shy grin. When she pulled out a onesie with "Baby's first trip to Disney" written on it, I was as confused as everyone else. Then Kate mumbled to her husband, "Seems they've been putting that anaconda and naked mole rat to good use."

Lynn placed the onesie on her chest, then brought one of her hands down to her belly.

"I had a surprise of my own. You'll have to pay your ransom over the next seven months."

"You're pregnant?" I whispered, wrapping my head around the fact that I was going to be a dad. I impregnated this amazon woman, and she was going to give birth to *my* child.

"I'm going to have a sister?!" Jessie squealed eagerly.

"Please be a boy," Preston muttered, crossing his fingers.

"I'm going to be a dad?" I placed my hand over hers on her belly. "Really?"

She nodded, her glimmering eyes swimming with fresh tears. "Are you happy?"

"Baby," I pulled her in, burying my face in her hair as my own tears broke free. "So fucking happy. You're having my baby."

"And marrying you," she added in an airy whisper.

Fuck. I couldn't be any happier than I was right at this moment.

"Happiest place in the world," I said once again.

She giggled. "The happiest."

Epilogue

Feighlynn

Three Years and Seven Months Later...

S tanding at the kitchen sink, I took a second to enjoy the peace in
the cool stream of the AC. I could still hear the squealing and
laughter of half a dozen toddlers and other kids out in the backyard.
The pool was in full use and we had a water slide set up with a bounce
house in the back of the yard.

Preston, on a break from college, was acting as lifeguard for Joy's
third birthday party, and Jessie was helping Kate scoop ice cream into
dozens of little cones for everyone to eat with their cake. The cake was
minnie mouse themed, and now I have pink frosting down the front
of my shirt.

I used washing the cake knife and my shirt as an excuse to get out of the heat for a second. I knew how torturous it was being this pregnant during a Texas summer, but my pregnant brain forgot that as I was planning our daughter's party.

"There you are," a deep, inviting voice made me grin as my husband approached me from behind. "I was looking for you."

"I'm hot," I whined, leaning back against the hard chest of this incredible man.

"Yeah, you are," he murmured suggestively, bending over me to rub his hands down my swollen belly. He cradled them under my abdomen and lifted, helping to relieve the strain on my insides.

I sighed in relief. "I love when you do that."

He chuckled in the sexy way he does, kissing the top of my head. "I love doing it for you." Rubbing his thumbs over where little feet started pressing against my womb, he murmured, "This little guy is ready to come out."

"Kevin the third," I giggled.

"That's not his name," Vin grunted.

"It is if I get a hold of that birth certificate first."

"That will not be an issue," he laughed softly against my ear. "I'll slip the nurse a fifty to bring all the paperwork to me."

"Fine," I smiled, leaning into him. "Phillip it is."

"I thought you liked Phillip?"

I shrugged. "I like Kevin a whole lot, though."

"You're sweet, baby," he snuggled my neck. "Do you not like Phillip after all? We could have another Disney movie night with the kids to come up with a name like we did for Joy."

I confessed I got Jessie and Kevin's names from Disney movies after we named our daughter Joy. Joy was also from a Pixar classic. He pointed out that I usually pick characters that act most like me to fixate on, so I stepped back and let him pick this baby's name.

Phillip.

Vin told me about a friend that he deployed with that never made it back home, and when he suggested the name, I knew it was important to him. Al even teared up a bit when he heard the name. Emma knew who Phillip was to our husbands, and we sat and listened as the men reminisced the rest of the night. It was a sweet moment for the guys to tell stories about their fallen friend.

"I was just teasing you, Kevin the first. I think Phillip is the perfect name."

I felt his smile against my skin before he kissed my neck one more time. His soothing hands on my belly were so tender and nurturing, I could never imagine naming our child anything else.

"Daddy! Daddy!" Joy suddenly came hurrying into the kitchen, dragging someone behind her. "Joy gib cake to Ick!"

Vin laughed, slowly releasing my belly to shake Nick's hand. "Hey. Glad you could make it."

"Thanks for the invite," Nick said, then smiled down at Joy. "Maybell has your present, sweet girl."

"Pe-sent!" Joy threw her hands in the air and cheered.

Vin kissed my cheek. "I'll take care of the cake and set up the presents. Take your time cooling off."

"Okay," I grinned, watching as Joy dragged her daddy back outside. Joy was little bitty, even for a three-year-old, and Vin was still huge. It was funny watching a twenty-five pound toddler command a two-hundred and thirty pound giant.

"Do you need help with anything?" Nick asked me, hesitating at the door.

"Nope. Just hiding in the air conditioning for a minute before rejoining all the fun."

Nick snickered, looking at my belly, "You sure pick the worst months to be pregnant."

"Hey," I waved an extra ice cream scoop at him. "You just wait. Maybell will be waddling around your house pretty soon."

He grinned, looking as happy as could be at the thought. "Yeah. I can't wait."

With a wave, he followed Vin and Joy back out to the yard.

Nick quit his job at his firm soon after the incident in the parking garage. I think he finally realized he was surrounding himself with jerks and that lifestyle was rubbing off on him in all the worst ways. He started working for a smaller firm out of the city where he met Maybell, a paralegal who was also a single parent. Her son was actually one of Preston's friends.

They hit it off, and after dating for a year, Nick sold his condo and bought a house for the both of them. I like Maybell, and so did both of my kids. Maybell and her son are actually a big reason Preston and his dad get along today.

Maybell and Nick got married at the courthouse three months ago, and Maybell called to tell me last weekend that they were expecting. I couldn't be happier for my ex. He had to reach rock bottom, but he's sure come a long way, and I can see with him and Maybell what Vin and I have.

First marriages don't always last. Statistically, Nick and I lasted longer than most before the inevitable divorce. That didn't mean either of us was incapable of love. I think we both just had to grow into ourselves and learn how love was supposed to be. It's not always butterflies and chest tingles. It takes work. It has to be with the right person or it will all fall apart.

Nick finally found his right person. I found mine in Vin. Vin and I may go through more storms together, but I know Vin and I can make it through. Together.

It helps that I still get those butterflies and chest tingles even after four years together. My action hero was as swoon-worthy today as he's been since the day we met, the day he saved my dog from a stray cat.

"Mom," Jessie poked her head in the back door. "Vin's having trouble keeping Joy out of the presents now that she's seen them."

I laughed, knowing we didn't have long before Joy had tore into every package like the little whirlwind she was.

"Alright. Let's go."

I waddled my way outside, sticking my tongue out at Kate when she started making fun of my walk. Vin was holding our daughter, who was crying against his shoulder, with an ice cream cone in one of her fists. It was dripping down his shirt, but he didn't care.

"I! Want! Pe-sents!" Joy took a haggard breath and screamed.

"I know, baby girl. Mama just needs a few more-" Vin saw me and he visibly relaxed. "Look," he nudged Joy. "Mama's right there."

Joy lifted her face to make sure I was there. I waved and her tears instantly stopped. A huge smile spread across her ice-cream coated face.

"Pe-sents!"

Everyone around laughed. "Let me get your mama a chair, then we can start," Vin said, kissing her curls.

"Mama!" Joy ran towards me. "Joy gib all duh pe-sents!"

"I see them!" I giggled as she grabbed my hand and hurried me along.

Vin had a chair ready for me before we reached the pile, and I gratefully sat down. There was no stopping Joy once she got the green light. I had to observe and catch the cards and write who each item was from quickly as she tore through every package at record speed. She was adorable, running to each giver after opening their gift and thanking them with a big, sticky hug.

"I fucking love you," Vin whispered in my ear when all the presents were opened, and the chaos was done. "You know that?"

"Hmm," I giggled, pretending to think while turning my face towards his. "Do you know I love you more?"

"Not a chance," he retorted.

Just then, Wes came back into the yard from taking out the present trash, and a stray cat walked by. Kevin saw it, and before the gate could close, he dashed for it.

"No, Kevin!" Velma got up from her chair, looking more concerned than anyone. I wasn't worried. I knew a hero would come save the day.

"Damn it," Vin groaned.

I laughed. "Go save the day again, my action hero. I'll be here feeding your baby another slice of cake."

He kissed me one more time, resting his hand on my belly before taking off before Kevin got too far.

Watching him run to catch my dog, all I could think about was how lucky I was to have succeeded in love with this amazing man.

About the author

C. Hazlewood is an independent author living in the southern part of the United States. For more information about her and her other works visit her website at www.chazlewoodauthor.com